Also by S.W. Clemens
TIME MANAGEMENT, a NOVEL
EVELYN MARSH
THE SEAL COVE THEORETICAL SOCIETY

WITH ARTISTIC LICENSE
S. W. CLEMENS

For Mary Katherine

"The straw that stirs the drink"

This is a work of fiction. Any resemblance it bears to reality is entirely coincidental.

Copyright © Scott W. Clemens

Fezziwig Publishing Co.

ISBN: 978-0-9966123-3-3

Cover by Perry Elisabeth Design | perryelisabethdesign.com Images © robarmstrong2 | pixabay.com; kchungtw, pisu, agphotographer, vnlit | canstockphoto.com

Prologue

Fortune is a moving target. We take aim at the future as though wearing blinders in a shooting gallery, never sure when the next duck or rabbit will cross our path. Sometimes we're intent. Sometimes we're distracted. Sometimes we're so preoccupied by an itch, we don't see the ducks waddling across the path right in front of us. Sometimes we're so focused on the foreground, we fail to see the background. Some of us are quick on the trigger; some are too late. Sometimes one's misfortune is another's fortune.

Politics and religion, war and peace, prosperity and want, invention and tradition, famine and plenty, health and sickness, emotion and logic and luck all exert a gravitational pull on our individual ambitions, providing the context in which our personal tales play out their inevitable scenes. At the intersection of the historical and the personal, the choices we make or avoid making lead to opportunities seized or opportunities missed. These moments of nexus are rarely sought and even more rarely anticipated.

PART ONE
THE GALLERY

Chapter 1

Sunday September 21, 2008

On a Sunday afternoon in late September 2008, with the world's financial infrastructure teetering on the verge of collapse, a silver Honda Accord and a black Volvo sedan pulled to the white curb on Washington Street. Both cars were filled with boxes. Both drivers held a cell phone to his ear.

From the curb, concrete steps led up to a concrete courtyard before a brick apartment building. Three stark concrete benches sat heavily around a large concrete planter box, from which a twenty-foot-tall sycamore spread branches with golden leaves that quivered now in a cool breeze.

On the block of eight to twelve story buildings, four were boarded up, surrounded by wire fences, and rubble-strewn gaps showed where two buildings had been demolished. Nine over-arching, 60-year-old elms lent the street an air of community and history. Building activity could be seen on both sides of the street — yellow dumpsters, trash shoots and scaffolding, one rooftop crane, heaps of broken wood and bricks, the white dust of gypsum, pick-up trucks and vans, and the sounds of pneumatic hammers and electric saws. In a year the whole street would have the hopeful look of gentrification.

The driver of the Honda opened the door and stepped out, phone still to his ear. He looked up at wispy mare's tails that laced the pale blue sky, and saw a pair of tennis shoes dangling from the telephone wire overhead. He glanced back at the Volvo with a pained look on his face. In his early thirties, 5'10", fit, with close-cropped brown hair and long nose, he wore old jeans and an oversized baseball jersey with the number 19 on the back. His name was Curtis Cooke (his mother loved the alliteration).

The driver of the Volvo got out, his phone still to his ear and looked tentatively toward Curtis. He was barrel-chested, with full lips, aquiline nose, wire-rimmed glasses and thick, curly brown hair, a year or two younger and half a head shorter than Curtis. He wore jeans and an unbuttoned, well-worn plaid flannel shirt over a faded blue T-shirt that contrasted with his smart gold wristwatch and wedding ring.

Curtis patted the top of the Honda, thinking how best to phrase his next comment. He sighed and spoke into his phone. "Listen, Elliot, I appreciate your helping, I really do, but I could do without the marital advice."

"It's just I don't get why the husband is the one who always has to move out," said Elliot Fine.

"It's not just about me.

"But..."

"Hang up, Elliot."

"Hang up?"

"Hang up."

They put their phones in their pockets, closed their car doors and resumed the conversation at the back of the Honda. "It's not so easy," Curtis said, opening the trunk. "Sammy's going to be going through enough without uprooting him, too. Six-year-olds need stability."

"Yeah, I understand that. But if she needs her space, why doesn't *she* move out and leave the house to you and Sammy?"

"Nothing's changed at work; I'll still be gone a lot," Curtis said ruefully, thinking with regret that his willingness to accept business trips had played a large roll in his failing marriage. There were a lot of things he'd do differently if given a second chance, but he could not turn back the clock. "Anyway, I can't be home when Sammy gets out of school, and Linda doesn't have anywhere to go," he added, realizing as he said it that he hadn't anywhere to go either, until he'd found this apartment. The extra expense was going to be difficult.

He handed Elliot a cardboard box, put two suitcases on the sidewalk and extended the handles, then pressed the automatic lock button on his key chain, hearing the trunk lock thunk satisfyingly into place. He glanced up and down the street scouting for possible thieves. "I'll have to move it to the garage after we unpack — a car like this wouldn't last two days out here."

After seven more trips to the cars they stood on the bare, hardwood floor in the middle of the eighth-floor artist's garret. An enclosed bedroom and bath occupied the back-left corner. An open kitchen occupied the back-right corner, separated from the rest of the room by a breakfast bar. Above the kitchen an 18-foot ceiling with skylight sloped steeply to eight-foot high, floor-to-ceiling, north-facing windows.

The room was bare except for the boxes and suitcases they'd carried up, a director's chair, a small wooden box filled with half-used tubes of oil paint, and a dozen paint-splotched canvases of various sizes in the corner by the window.

"At least it comes with original art," Elliot quipped.

"I think there's a reason the previous tenant left them," Curtis said with a critical eye.

"It looks kind of empty."

"I'll rent some furniture this week."

"And a TV," Elliot added. "It won't be so bad."

Curtis knew it would be bad and nothing anyone could say could make it any better. "It's just a three-month lease. With any luck I'll be back by Christmas. She just needs some time alone."

"We'll miss you around the 'hood, bro." Elliot stepped over to the window. "You want me to pick you up on the way to work?"

"No, I think I'll drive myself tomorrow — see how long it takes."

"Hey, Curtis, there's some kids by your car."

The five teenagers were all dressed in uniforms of drooping jeans and hooded sweatshirts and baseball caps, but from eight stories high it was too far to see their faces clearly. Three were taking turns jumping their skateboards up onto one of the concrete benches. One was leaning on his car, and another sat on the right front quarter-panel, rhythmically swinging his legs. Curtis louvered open the bottom part of the window and yelled, "Hey, you, get off my car!"

The one leaning against his car looked up and laughed; one of the skateboarders paused long enough to give him the middle finger of both hands. The guy who'd been sitting on his car held up his hand as if to demonstrate what he held (it was too far away to see what it was), then walked the length of the car, grooving the silver paint. Then the five of them skipped a step or two with glee, and jogged and skateboarded away.

"That's why I lease," Curtis said.

In his dream he was giving his usual dog-and-pony show on financial investment. He was looking down the boardroom table crowded with faces turned intently his way, and at the end of the table his wife sat conversing with the man at the left corner. She was oblivious to his presentation and this both annoyed and worried him.

His cell phone started playing Ode to Joy. He awoke in the dark. His hand shot out, expecting the night table at home and knocked over an empty wine bottle instead. He cursed, found the lamp on the floor next to his air mattress and switched it on. Then he grabbed the phone. "Hello, hello?"

"Curtis?" It was Linda — his nominal wife. "Curtis, Sammy won't sleep until he talks to you." Jesus, she had a lovely voice.

"Okay, put him on," Curtis said, coming fully awake now and looking about his surroundings with sudden recognition and disappointment. He lay on his air mattress on the floor of a room with windowless, bare white walls. Strewn about the sky blue carpeting were an empty wine glass and bottle, both on their sides, an alarm clock, the clothes he'd been wearing in a pile by the foot of the bed, and an open red rolling duffle bag. It was the kind of room he would have been happy with in college, but it was such a long step backward that he couldn't help feeling depressed.

"Hi Dad."

"Hey Scooter."

"Mom said I can call."

"Yeah, good, I'm glad you did."

"You said you'd call before I went to bed."

"What time is it?" he asked, more to himself than to his son, while he looked at his watch. It was just 10:30. "Oh, god — I fell asleep; I'm sorry."

"That's okay. I couldn't sleep." There was a long silence. "Daddy?"

"Yes?"

"I miss you."

"I miss you, too."

"Can I come visit?"

"It's all set. Your mom's dropping you off Saturday morning."

"Is that a long time?"

"No, no, it's just a few days. Don't worry about it, buddy, okay? You get some sleep now."

"'Night."

"Love you."

The phone went dead. Curtis flipped his phone shut, turned off the light and stared at the ceiling for a long time before he fell into a fitful sleep.

Chapter 2

Monday September 22 – Thursday September 25, 2008

In the morning he rushed into the office seventeen minutes late, briefcase in hand, suit coat slung over his shoulder. He paused, short of breath, at his secretary's desk. "Barbara!" he moaned theatrically. "I'm sorry; I don't have this new commute down — I thought it would be so quick, but..."

Barbara, a thin black woman with short-cropped hair and an attitude of studied disdain looked up from her magazine and observed, "You were drinking last night."

He arched an eyebrow. "Is it *that* obvious?"

"Mr. Erickson would like to see you," she said flatly, with a look that implied he'd been caught with his pants down. "By the way, the Market's taking a dive."

John Erickson stood behind the enormous desk in his corner office, looking concerned. He was tall and thin, with large wire-rimmed glasses that slightly magnified his pale blue eyes, which matched his pale blue tie. He gave the impression — by his pasty skin (just two shades darker than his white shirt), his colorless hair, his watery eyes — that he was not entirely there, that he was semi-transparent. He spoke slowly, in his mild (rather girlish) voice, as though vaguely troubled. "Sit down, sit down. How are you, Curtis? Are you doing...alright? You don't look well."

"I'm fine; I just didn't sleep much last night," Curtis said, the wheels of his mind churning. This certainly wasn't about his arriving late, nor about his slight hangover (that was an anomaly). He'd always had an uneasy relationship with Erickson. The man was so stiff and restrained it was hard to have a normal conversation; there were often uncomfortable silences, which Curtis felt obliged to fill with foolish prattle. Though the man was only four years his senior, Erickson always threw Curtis off his game and made him feel like a clueless child.

Erickson remained standing and, leaning over his desk, bent toward Curtis like a vulture. Curtis watched as his boss looked left out the window for a long moment, then at his desk, and finally straight across the table. It was almost enough to make him pee in his pants. "I've heard, from certain quarters, that you've had some personal problems..."

"Yes, sir," Curtis said. It had always galled him to say 'sir' to someone he considered his equal in age and education, but Erickson had a way of making him quail, of doubting his own abilities, of making him feel he was only masquerading as an adult.

"These things happen," Erickson said, and turned toward the window as if contemplating something philosophical. "Do you need some time off?"

Curtis was caught off-guard by the question; it wasn't what he expected. "No. Uh, uh. I...I don't think..."

"Good."

"...I don't think it will affect my work," Curtis finished.

Erickson brightened and seemed to shake out his stiffness. "Good, good." There was a long pause as he looked out the window again and then slowly fixed Curtis's eyes. "You're all right with your presentations this week?"

"Yes, fine, perfect."

"No distractions?"

"No, well yes, but work is a...good diversion."

"Okay, that's fine, then. So, you're going to Chicago this week?"

"We leave tomorrow."

"Who's handling your clients while you're gone?"

"Swenton; and I'll be checking in by email."

"And how are your clients doing? Did you have Lehman in any of your portfolios?"

This was a touchy subject. He'd held Lehman Brothers stock in virtually all of the portfolios he handled, and the company had gone belly up. "We took a big hit. We had some AIG, as well."

"Any complaints from clients?"

"A few."

"But you're still ahead for the year?"

"It's a close thing — depends on the portfolio. This has been a rough month."

"I see." Erickson seemed uncomfortable with how to end the conversation. There was another long pause as he gathered his thoughts. "Well, I'm sorry you're having problems. I know it can be difficult. So...let me know if there's anything we can do," he said, making a shooing motion with the back of his hand as he sat down in the chair behind his large desk.

"Barbara, could you ask Elliot to poke his head in?" Curtis asked as he passed into his glass-fronted office.

Barbara turned her head and shouted, "Connie, tell Mr. Fine to get his ass down here!"

"Barbara-a-a!" Curtis admonished. She swung around in her chair and looked at him with upraised eyebrows. He pursed his lips and shook his head reproachfully. She mouthed "sorry," shrugged, and swiveled back to her desk.

Constance McClarity poked her head around the door. "Elliot's had car trouble, but he'll be in soon."

Curtis was presently engrossed in his work. He handled ten corporate clients and four individuals, two of whom were worth more than four of the corporations. He could have handled many more, for they all had the same stocks in their portfolios. From a list of 40 stocks he followed, he was constantly on the lookout to jettison under performing stocks, and to pick up those whose momentum was just on the upswing. He worked in tandem with Elliot (aka the Bond King) to help companies (and individuals with excess cash reserves) to protect and grow their investments through risk management techniques.

He spent his day before an array of four monitors following the markets, monitoring news that could have an impact on his portfolios, and the flow of institutional money in and out of various industry sectors. He studied technical charts, back tested strategies, read analysts' reports, and made the occasional trade. When he made a trade in one portfolio, he generally made the same trade across several portfolios. He'd made some horrendous mistakes early in his career, but he'd learned from his mistakes and he now had a formula that had worked amazingly well until the past month.

Elliot came in more than an hour late looking harried. He burst into Curtis's office, at once disheveled, upset and out-of-sorts. "Sorry. Damned Volvo...I don't know, water pump or.... Triple A towed it to the shop, but they have to order a part."

"Whatever. DOW's falling like a rock," Curtis said. He wasn't in the least interested in Elliot's car troubles. "You have everything in order for Wednesday?"

"Yeah, you know — it's the same ol', same ol'. Can you give me a ride home? You can stay for dinner."

"Yeah, sure," he said off-handedly, before remembering that he no longer lived across the street from Elliot. The apartment was on this side of the river and it would take an extra twenty minutes in each direction to drive Elliot home. But he'd agreed and was reconciled by the promise of one of Vicky's meals. "Barbara!? Who has the tickets?"

"They're e-tickets," she said, passing the paper with the confirmation number to Elliot, who passed it to Curtis. "I couldn't get two seats together; the flight was full."

"These are Economy Class."

"Mr. Carretta wouldn't okay the upgrade."

Curtis and Elliot marched down to Al Carretta's office.

"Why can't we fly Business Class?" Curtis said, feeling put out.

"Those days are over," said Carretta, a beefy middle-aged man with a florid nose. "Arthur has issued a decree."

"What the hell?" said Curtis.

"How does it look to our clients when we fly Business Class?" Carretta explained. "We're all about preserving capital, not spending it frivolously."

"I don't find it frivolous. We need to be fresh when we get there."

"You don't have a presentation until the next day," Carretta said, a hint of sarcasm in his voice.

"Yeah, well..." Curtis could think of nothing to say. It was true. But he was used to flying Business Class and didn't like the idea of flying umpty-ump miles a year in steerage.

That evening as they pulled onto Westlake Drive, Curtis started to turn into his own driveway before he caught his mistake. "Sorry, force of habit." He backed out and turned into Elliot's driveway, catty-corner across the street. It was with a profound sense of displacement that he stepped out of the car and looked wistfully back at his erstwhile home.

"Daddy!" Sophie yelled when Elliot opened the door. Elliot scooped his five-year-old into his arms and she clung to his neck, beaming.

Vicky appeared in the doorway to the kitchen. She was short, with sensuous lips, a long straight nose and curly black hair. "Nathan's down for his nap, so keep it quiet. Thanks for driving him home."

"Victoria," Curtis said, bowing ever so slightly with mock formality.

Elliot put Sophie down. "I want to get out of this suit; be back in a minute," he said, and disappeared down the hallway.

Sophie settled on the floor with her playhouse full of miniature tables and chairs, and plastic Playmobil people. Curtis followed Vicky into the kitchen and sat down at the counter behind the center island, as she cut up vegetables for a salad.

"You're settled into your apartment?"

"Still in boxes. Furniture comes Friday; I'll have to take the day off work."

"Do you think it's permanent?"

"God, I hope not, but she seems..." he began in reply and was arrested by the memory of her cold stare and business-like tone, the sheer effrontery of her saying so matter-of-factly (and so succinctly), 'We've grown apart. I want to be free to pursue my options. I'd like you to move out.' She said it with the same voice, the same sense of surety that she had said in college, 'I think we should move in together.'

"Resolute?" Vicky supplied.

Resolute. There was a word. Determined, unwavering, fixed on a position she was unwilling to discuss. "I don't know; she won't talk about it. She just needs her space. I know it's my fault — all the travel."

"It comes with your job. She knew that when she married you."

"I know, but..."

"I never told you, but I've always felt she was a little too slick for you, a little too calculating. There's a reason we never became fast friends."

"She's a bit reserved."

"No, 'reserved' is what you say about someone who's shy or uncomfortable in social settings. I always got the impression (forgive me for saying so) that she was arrogant, that we were never good enough for her." She filled a bowl with handfuls of lettuce and tomatoes, mushrooms, olives and green onions. "So you think you might reconcile?"

Curtis sighed deeply. "Who knows?"

"She hasn't found someone else?"

"Linda? No, I don't think so," he half laughed, but it wasn't a mirthful laugh. He just couldn't imagine his prim, passionless wife might have a secretly passionate life. It would be too out-of-character. "No, not possible."

"Hmmm."

There was a long moment of uncomfortable silence as Vicky busied herself at the stove. He regarded her silence as evasion. "Why do you ask?"

Vicky turned toward him and, as though to buy time as she ordered her thoughts, wiped her hands on a towel tucked into the waist of her apron. "Well, maybe it's not my place to say, but I never thought she sold all those houses through great instinct. I mean — most of her clients were men who were going through divorces. I always thought she was shopping around."

Elliot came in dressed in sweatshirt, jeans and alpaca slippers. "What's for dinner?"

The goal of Bass Erickson Asset Management was to devise strategies to preserve and grow excess capital for both individuals and companies. There were three teams within the company, each with different areas of expertise. Elliot and Curtis comprised one of the teams, and eight times a year traveled to potential clients to put on their "dog-and-pony show." Those they were able to bring into the firm were divvied up among the Associates (the so-called Cubicle Rats), but Curtis and Elliot got an extra signing bonus for each client they brought in. Every third week, they would split up and travel to current clients to present year-to-year results, and discuss the economy and strategies for the upcoming year. The trips were typically two to three days long, and he was usually home on the weekends.

Getting off the flight in Chicago on Tuesday, Curtis waited for Elliot where the gangway exited into the busy terminal. Towing his carry-on and looking disgruntled, Elliot said, "Remind me to remind Carretta why

Business Class makes sense; the guy in front of me leaned back so far I couldn't open my laptop."

"Mine ran out of juice; there's no plug in steerage. What's the schedule?"

"Lemme see," Elliot said, fishing a crumpled page from his jacket pocket. He shook out the wrinkles and read, "Tomorrow morning, Ontro." A loudspeaker blared out boarding instructions, and Elliot paused, looking at the ceiling as though personally affronted until the speaker went quiet, then continued. "Tomorrow afternoon, Waveform. Late afternoon — Proctor. Then Thursday it's a private guy (guy who owns a company called Advanced Battery Technologies); then we go across town for a brief meeting with the new President at 3 C Group, do a late lunch presentation at a law firm — Rheingold, Jacobs, Zoller & Malkovich, and finish with a dinner presentation for a non-profit family foundation — big money. Some fancy restaurant (they're picking up the bill)."

"You want to go out tonight?"

"I'm too tired," Elliot yawned. "I'm gonna have a beer, order room service, and get to sleep early."

The next morning they set out for their presentation to Ontro Industries, walking the three blocks from the hotel. The street bustled with energy and a frenetic hum of people walking and talking, of cars and buses and delivery trucks accelerating and braking, of metal doors being rolled up for the start of another workday. The morning smelled of diesel exhaust, newsprint, doughnuts and cooking oil, and the faint odor of sewage seeping up from manhole covers.

Curtis felt hopeful. He'd slept better in the hotel than he had in his apartment, and he faced a day in which he would play his circumscribed role, confident that he would give a decent presentation, whether or not it brought in new business.

He'd eaten a light breakfast of coffee, a banana and an unbuttered roll filled with thinly sliced ham. He was cognizant of the downfall of a former colleague, Daryl Tucker, whose short stay with the company was hastened by his reluctance to forswear the all-you-can-eat breakfast buffet. Daryl's preference for greasy sausages, fried potatoes, scrambled eggs and acidic juice had first resulted in a loud fart in the middle of his presentation; the next time his stomach had made such gut-wrenching gurgling and wringing sounds that it seemed as if he would be torn apart; and finally he had run out of a presentation to be sick in the bathroom. Curtis wasn't nearly as nervous, but he wanted to err on the side of caution.

Elliot was animatedly speculating on the up-coming World Series when Curtis's cell phone rang. He stopped to take the call and when he was done his face had clouded over. "Linda."

"Judging from that look on your face, it must be bad news."

They started walking again. "She wants me to transfer money into her account, for Christ's sakes. She makes as much as I do; she's sold six houses this year. What does she need more money for?"

"She has expensive tastes," Elliot observed. "Vicky used to comment on that."

"Every day I tell my clients to be thrifty, to buy quality over glitz; then I come home to a shrine to 'designer' this and 'designer' that — stuff she gets tired of in six months, or throws out because it's no longer 'in.' I could clothe all the homeless people in the park on what she throws out in a year! Perfectly good stuff, but it's no longer trendy. She wouldn't buy toilet paper if it wasn't 'designer.'"

"At least she has a job."

"You know why she became a realtor? Because I wouldn't let her buy a BMW. That's the truth. The Honda was an embarrassment. It's always about the labels —clothes, cars, shoes, food. Doesn't matter. We went to a restaurant she just hated, couldn't stop complaining about it all the way home — the service was slow, the food was mediocre. The next week it's written up in the Times and she's bragging she'd been there!"

The thought of supporting her profligate spending, while he was living in an apartment and she was still living in their house, offended his sense of justice. For the past three weeks he'd been on an emotional rollercoaster of disbelief, confusion, betrayal, anger, sadness, and a terrible sense of futility as he saw that so much of what he'd worked to achieve over the past decade had come to ruin. He had pleaded his case to deaf ears, had willingly taken the blame for their estrangement, had promised to work harder to spend more time at home, and yet she had coldly insisted he move out. "I don't want to hear it," she'd said. "I don't even know who you are anymore. I need some time alone to think this through." Time alone? Isn't that just what she'd been complaining about — that he was gone too much for work, he spent too much time at the neighbors, and he wasn't engaged when he was home? He now understood that his safe world of easy routine and pleasant expectations had been based on erroneous assumptions. He had assumed she still loved him. He had assumed they would grow old, each content in the other's company. He had always assumed he would be a daily part of his son's life (except when at work or traveling on business). He was, he admitted, less attentive than he might have been. He could have been a better husband, a better father, but it wasn't for lack of desire or commitment that he had fallen short. Up until now he had felt confusion, even guilt for his part in the failed marriage. But this call, in its emotionless, cold, business-like tenor, left him feeling belligerent.

"You notice," he added, as they rotated through the revolving door 30 floors beneath Ontro, "she's the only realtor in that office who doesn't wear the official jacket. She refuses. She always goes to work with her Tiffany earrings, Jimmy Choo shoes and Louie Vuitton bag. Says she has to appear on the same level as her clientele."

"She *has* sold a lot of houses," Elliot reminded him.

"Yeah, but..."

"If it helps her make a sale, what the hell?"

"Yeah, but..." He wanted to come up with a clever rejoinder, but he had nothing. The proof was in the pudding; she did make the sales. But she did not understand value.

That day and the next went by in a blur:

Standing at the end of the one boardroom or dining table after another, facing eight to ten seemingly bored or hostile faces, he would launch into his spiel and drone on with no more sense of reality than if he were in a dream. His mind was elsewhere. All he had to do was hit the bullet points:

• "Bass Erickson has many facets to match the profiles of each of our clients, and today we'd like to tell you about two strategies we can offer that we think could fit your needs. In a minute you'll hear about bonds from by colleague, Elliot Fine."

• "In this uncertain economy, preserving capital is paramount to the health of your business. Many companies are foregoing capital expenditure and reducing debt. Others are buying back their own stock at historically low prices. But the questions are: 1. How do you preserve your capital? And, 2. Can you still put your cash reserves to work?"

- "My role is to identify companies with impeccable financials, companies that have momentum and offer high returns..."

- "Let's look at a real-world scenario." *Here he would click on his computer to project a graph onto a screen.* "First, we look for the best companies, not necessarily the best known. Let's take Potash Corporation, for example. What is potash? It's not sexy. It's not a flying car or a cell phone that records TV programs, or anything so exotic — it's fertilizer. You can see from this chart that at the beginning of 2008...."

And so it went, one company to the next. After each presentation he yielded to Elliot, who gave a presentation on bonds. It may have been dry to some people, but he found an element of excitement in trying to assess and control the risk, and a sense of accomplishment when he succeeded.

Chapter 3
Friday September 26, 2008

He answered the door shortly after one o'clock, his mouth full of tuna fish sandwich, and gestured the movers into the room. For the next half hour they bustled in and out, bringing in the furniture: a night stand, bed and chest of drawers, an area rug, a sofa bed, a leather arm chair, coffee table, lamp table, table lamp, floor lamp, two stools, two folding oak chairs, a gate-leg table, a DVD player, a flat screen TV and a table on which to place it.

When they were gone, he kicked off his shoes, poured himself a Scotch and water, and walked around his living room. The apartment no longer seemed so stark, nor as spacious, but it did seem more like a home. Yet something was missing. He fussed here and there, pushing the chair a few inches, angling the coffee table. First, he sat on the sofa, testing its bounce, then the chair. He pulled the coffee table closer and propped his feet on it. It was a nice tableau, but still something was missing. He reached for the remote and turned on the television, surfed through a dozen channels and turned it off, dissatisfied.

Something was definitely missing; he just couldn't put his finger on what it was. It wasn't just that this wasn't his home, that this wasn't really his chair, his table, his *life*. He understood his old life was gone, for the present, and that these things would make up a part of his new life, but even within that context they just didn't feel right. There was something much more basic out of alignment, something more in line with (he had no other word for the concept) *Feng Shui*. It was a mystery.

He walked around the room, cocking his head first to one side, then to the other, trying to puzzle it out. He took off his sweater and threw it haphazardly onto the sofa. That didn't seem to help.

Later that afternoon he walked two blocks in either direction, scoping out the new neighborhood, and eventually stopped at a small market. He ranged the aisles buying groceries and the odds-and-ends of supplies that caught his fancy, and searching for that thing that might tip the balance from unfamiliar to familiar, from his sense of being a visitor to being a resident. He bought some cola and potato chips for Sammy. It wasn't in Sammy's best interest, he knew, and his mother would disapprove, but it might offer a small consolation in his transition to this forlorn and unknown territory. He picked up milk, bread, butter, sugar, salt, pepper, a sandwich for dinner, a bottle of Chilean Merlot, two cans of soup and Cherrios. In the magazine aisle it occurred to him that perhaps the coffee table needed some magazines to lend the room a lived-in look. He tossed *Fortune* and *Men's Health* into the cart, and a *Highlights* for Sammy. More magazines were offered at the checkout counter. He didn't know if he should despair or be amused at the tabloid headlines announcing the latest gossip about Katie and Tom, Brad and Angelina, Jennifer and J-Lo and Brittany, as if in using first names they invited their readers to indulge in the fiction that these celebrities were of one's extended family, and their personal problems and inclinations of concern to the general populace. He passed on these, but did add *People*, *Newsweek*, and *Time* to the cart, and to give his apartment a subtle sense of femininity that it so emphatically lacked, he bought a *Good Housekeeping*.

Perusing other checkout displays, his gaze settled on refrigerator magnets: smiling carrot people, dancing broccoli, a zucchini with arms & feet, a dried old apple face, a winking banana, a jovial cauliflower. He bought one of each.

The sun was setting as he unloaded the groceries. Then he carried the magazines to the living room and threw them, one-at-a-time onto the coffee table, trying to convey a sense of casual abandon, of haphazard nonchalance. The magazines helped. It was better, but it wasn't right.

Next he turned on the lamps and stood back to look. The lamps gave a warm glow to the scene. That was much better, but even so it didn't have the desired effect.

He stood by the windows to take in the whole room. "Sofa, yeah; chair, check; coffee table, yup; lamps...oh!"

That's when he realized the solution. In a minute he had picked out two abstract canvases from the previous tenant and set about hanging them on the walls. When he was done, he nodded to himself. Yes, that would do for now. The once stark room was starting to look like a place he could comfortably inhabit, a place where his son might feel at home.

In the bedroom he rummaged around a couple cardboard boxes and found what he was looking for, a shoebox filled with photos. For the next hour he was lost in reminiscence as he turned over one photo at a time, each a tangible spark that ignited a chain of memories — a time, a place, the stuffed animal Sammy had loved, the silly Halloween costume, Easter, Christmas, the incompetent waitress, the new year's eve party that had resulted in a horrible hangover, the time they'd left Sammy with her mother and driven up to the mountains for a weekend alone, his brother holding an infant Sammy, a two-year-old Sammy in Superman pajamas, Sammy at three, at five, the look in Linda's eyes as she had smiled into the camera: no mistaking the look of love. She was so pretty, so aware of her appearance. She had never let herself go the way some women do after they have kids.

He took the selected photos back to the kitchen and laid them on the counter: Sammy at 14-months taking a bath in the kitchen sink; Sammy on the beach in San Diego; three-year-old Sammy and Linda on their knees in front of the Christmas tree; five-year-old Sammy on his paternal grandfather's shoulders; a naked four-year-old Sammy, with long curly hair, sitting in a stream. And all at once the magnitude of his loss hit him and tears coursed down his cheeks. He took a deep, shaky breath, and quietly stuck the photos to the refrigerator with the vegetable magnets.

Chapter 4

Saturday September 27 – Sunday September 28, 2008

Linda was supposed to deliver Sammy at 9 a.m. and Curtis rose early to get ready. He showered, dressed, ate breakfast, drank a cup of coffee and paced the room, glancing at his wrist watch every few minutes and walking to the wall of windows to see if he could spot them arriving.

He was as nervous at the prospect of seeing Linda again, as he was at wondering what to do with his son in his new apartment. That she was actually leaving him, that there might be no reconciliation, was just beginning to sink in. And if this change of address were permanent, it would inevitably change his relationship with Sammy. Having him visit on weekends was a poor substitute for being a full-time dad, wasn't it? Well, maybe not, if you considered how little time he actually spent with his son when he was home. There had been no conscious effort to exclude his wife and son, but the time he spent at home was quiet time, and it *was* time he mostly spent alone, or with the neighbors. Most of his "free" weekends were spent in his study, going over technical charts and analyzing financial reports on his laptop. An hour or two before sunset, he might wander out to the neighborhood badminton court, play a few games and gossip, while Linda stayed home. At first, she didn't accompany him because she found gossip pointless, and for the past two years she'd spent most weekends between 10:00 and 3:00 p.m. showing houses, while Curtis and Sammy visited with the neighbors.

If this separation were to proceed to divorce and shared custody (god forbid) he would probably only get Sammy on alternating weekends. He would lose track of the myriad changes that go on in a child's life on a day-to-day basis — the cuts and scrapes, the new toys, new skills, new friends, his progress in school, the tidbits of knowledge that Sammy gleaned from teacher and classmates and TV, all of his subtly changing likes and dislikes.

At ten minutes to 9 in the morning Linda was on the phone in the kitchen of their two-story suburban home. She was pretty and purposeful, with curly blonde hair, cut just above her shoulders, a sculptured face and an athlete's trim body. She wore negligible makeup, a smart Ralph Lauren skirt in olive-green plaid, and Jimmy Choo shoes. More subtly, but as noteworthy, she was not wearing a wedding ring. From her pinched brow it would have been obvious to anyone that she was displeased.

The kitchen was spotless. The cherry wood cabinets were polished. The stainless steel appliances (stove, dishwasher and refrigerator) gleamed. The sink was empty and the counters were bare of all but two vases of newly cut flowers. Sammy sat at the kitchen island drawing a picture with crayons on a plain sheet of 8X10 paper. He was a small boy, with his mother's curly blonde hair and blue eyes. Still listening on the phone, Linda whipped the crayon out of Sammy's hand, held up an index finger in warning, spread out a newspaper under the picture and slapped the crayon down on the island. She turned her back, one hand on her hip, the other holding the phone to her ear, seething with annoyance. Sammy drew three figures with oblong bodies and heads, and sausage-like arms and legs — a mother, and a father holding his son's twiggy hand. He could draw better, but he was only doodling.

Linda dropped the phone to her side, rolled her eyes to the ceiling and let out a sigh. Then she dialed Curtis.

"Listen, Curt, I can't drop off Sammy. Jennifer was supposed to show a house this morning but she's sick, so I have to meet her client at the house. I'm supposed to be there in 20 minutes. There's no way I can get to your place and back again in that amount of time. I'm going to take Sammy with me. You can pick him up there. Do you have something you can write on? Good. The address is 5210 Belknap Court. It's in Diamond Heights."

It took him fifteen minutes to get out of the city, and another twenty to make his way to Belknap Court. It was a fancy suburban neighborhood with big houses set far back on landscaped grounds, the kind of houses he had always aspired to own. That wasn't happening any time soon. 5210 was vaguely English in style, two stories with tall mullioned windows, a wide lawn with a big magnolia out front, and a horseshoe shaped drive that curved up to a *porte cochère*, and thence back down to the street. He pulled up under the portico beside a new silver Mercedes SLR roadster and Linda's white BMW three series.

On the drive over he had run through half a dozen scenarios in his head, reminding himself to act polite, imagining various ways a conversation could play out, quelling the impulse to grovel at her feet and beg to be let back into his house, his life. No, he knew he would not advance his case by groveling, yet there must be something he could do to change her mind. She had always put on a vivacious face in public, but at home she'd been more subdued. Subdued, but not unhappy, he thought. Not miserable. Not depressed. He had missed all the signs. He was clueless.

On the covered brick walkway that led up to the front steps he turned over possible conversational entry points and composed his face. There was a moment, just a moment, when he felt the tears start to well up, then suppressed the emotion and continued up to the large double doors. The right door swung wide. Sammy sprinted out and jumped into his arms with a cry of "Daddy!" Linda stood briefly in the doorway looking down at them, brow furrowed in...what? — Impatience? Disapproval? Annoyance? She pointed her keys toward her car and pressed the button to unlock the doors. "Sammy's things are in the back seat. I'm with clients. Sammy, you behave yourself; I'll see you tomorrow night." Then she closed the door. There would be no conversation this day.

Parked in the basement of the building on Washington Street, Curtis took a box of toys out of the back seat and handed Sammy a miniature green and yellow rolling suitcase and his pillow.

"This is a great old building. It just needed someone with vision to see what it could be. They fixed it up real nice. This street is going to be great. It doesn't look like much now, but give it a year."

Upstairs Curtis opened the door and ushered Sammy in. "This is it."

"I like it, Dad."

"There's no yard, like at home, but there's a park I'll take you to in a minute. Let's put your stuff over by the TV."

"When are you coming back home?"

"I don't know." The question about broke his heart. In an effort to spare their son the trauma of a yelling match, they had been restrained, taking the argument into the bedroom and on tense walks around the block. Sammy must have known something wasn't right, but they hadn't actually sat down and discussed the reality of the situation with him, and Linda had obviously not explained anything in the ensuing week since his departure. "Your mother doesn't want me back right now."

"She doesn't like you anymore?"

"No, she doesn't."

"Do you like her?"

"I love your mom. I think she loves me, too, but she's mad at me. She doesn't like me very much, right now."

"I like you."

"I like you, too. You're my favorite."

That afternoon they went to a Burger King and then to the neighborhood park, two blocks east and one block south of the apartment. It was an old municipal park with picnic tables in the shade of large oak and chestnut trees. At the west end there was a baseball field with a backstop, a dirt infield, and a grass outfield. The middle of the park was designed for the little kids, with two slides, three teeter totters, six swings, a jungle gym, a merry-go-round, and a wooden play-park made to look like a fort with ladders leading up to four look-out towers that were variously connected by a rope bridge, a wooden walkway, a monkey ladder, and an acrylic tube big enough to crawl through (if you were a kid). The east end was divided by a tall privet hedge. A pond and gazebo lay on the northeast corner, while teenagers hung out on the southeast corner at the basketball courts. Sammy's energy seemed to know no bounds, and Curtis was thoroughly exhausted by the time they arrived back at the apartment around four.

"I need a nap, Scooter; you wore me out."

"I need a nap, too."

Curtis kicked off his shoes and flopped down on the bed. Sammy curled up beside him and they fell asleep.

Sometime later Sammy woke up and left the bedroom. He took a wooden car from the box of toys and rolled it on his hands and knees to the end of the area rug. At the edge of the hardwood floor he gave it a push. It raced across the floor until it collided with the wall under the windowsill and overturned. He ran to the car and bending to retrieve it he looked out the window. In the late afternoon shadows, he saw three teenagers "tagging" the side of the brick building across the street. The building stood next to a rubbly lot and presented a wall unbroken by windows. Sammy watched with interest as they worked with spray paint, mapping out a mural of odd-shaped letters. He bent for his car again and sent it whizzing across the room, where it came to rest against the stack of canvases next to a box of brushes and half squeezed tubes of paint.

At twilight Curtis came groggily out of the bedroom, into a room aglow in the pink tones of a fading sunset. Sammy stood at the corner where the wall and the windows came together. In his hand he held a paintbrush. Paint was splotched on his hands, on his cheek, in his hair, on his shirt and on the floor. On the wall he had painted a building taller than his head, not unlike the building across the street, a rectangle of burnt sienna with black rectangles for windows. Next to it, about a third as tall, stood a tree in brown and green, and next to the tree stood a figure in black.

"Oh, lord," Curtis exclaimed, striding across room, grogginess replaced with a jolt of adrenalin. "How am I going to get that out of your hair? Your mother is going to kill me. How am I going to get that off the floor? How am I going to get that off the wall? What were you thinking? You know better than that!"

Sammy's lower lip stuck out in a pout and his eyes gleamed with tears. "I drawed a pitcher for you," he said, feeling dejected at his father's reaction.

"But why on the wall? Why not on paper?"

"I like dwawing big. Like those boys," he said sniffing and pointed to the taggers, who were almost finished.

"What they're doing is against the law," Curtis said, and at that moment, an elderly white-haired man dressed in a white short-sleeved shirt that seemed to glow in the near darkness, ran out the front door and around the side of the building to confront the taggers. Even at this distance they could hear the old man scream epithets at the boys who took off at a jog. "See, they're getting in trouble."

"But why?"

"Because not everyone appreciates their art."

"I 'preciate it."

"Yeah, but you don't own the building."

"But you own this house."

"Well, not exactly."

Curtis stood back, arms and legs akimbo, appraising his son's work. "You drew that for me?" Sammy nodded. "Well, it's not bad. But you aren't ever to draw on the walls again. Do you understand? It's not allowed. I really don't own this house." Sammy hung his head. His paint spattered arms hung limply at his sides. "Okay, it's already a mess, so go ahead, paint away. But we have to spread newspapers, so you don't get any more on the floor. How am I supposed to clean that up? I don't have paint thinner."

Chapter 5
Monday, September 29 – Sunday, October 5, 2008

Barbara opened the door and tossed a paper into his inbox. "Itinerary," she said in explanation. "You fly into Boise on Saturday. There's a golf date with Dickson Pauling Associates on Sunday. Then Burditch on Monday morning, Mosaic Chemicals for lunch, and home by 8:45."

"Crap," he said, thinking that this was the first weekend he'd had to travel since moving out, and he wouldn't see Sammy for almost two weeks. That he'd *miss* his son was of secondary importance, as he knew from experience that he'd be too busy to think much about it while he was gone. But he didn't want to let Sammy down. He'd already made a mess of his marriage; he was determined not to alienate his son. "Close the door behind you," he said to Barbara, and picked up the phone.

Linda was just on her way out, Bluetooth earphone in place, when the phone rang. She flipped her blonde hair over her ear and touched the earphone to answer. "*Hel*-lo," she said in a bright voice that Curtis barely recognized.

"Linda? Don't hang up."

"Why would I hang up?"

Curtis noticed the change of tone immediately, from cheerful and friendly to cold and aloof. "Well, you haven't wanted to talk lately."

"Not if we're going to go over the same old territory."

"No, I just had to tell you I'll be out of town this weekend, so I won't be able to take Sammy."

"I wondered how long it would take."

"What's that supposed to mean?"

"Nothing."

"Can I ask you something?"

"Hold on, I'm backing up."

"What? Where are you going?"

"To pick up Sammy. First grade lets out at one o'clock." There was a long pause as Linda backed out of the driveway and started down the tree lined suburban street that had been their neighborhood for the past five years. "Ok, what did you want to ask?"

"Can I take you out to dinner or something, so we can talk?"

"We're talking now."

"It's not the same."

"I don't know how to tell you this, but I can't look at you without feeling angry, and that's not where I want to go with my life."

"But I need to know why this is happening. I don't understand."

"You don't understand," she stated flatly. "That's the problem. You really don't get it."

"No, I don't."

"You just called to tell me you were going on a business trip, and you don't get it."

"What? Am I missing something here?"

"See, it all comes down to understanding, and you're clueless. You're incapable of thinking about anyone but yourself, your own little sphere of needs. I guess I found that part of your boyish charm in college, but you've never really grown up, and I'm ready for a more adult relationship."

"What do you mean by more adult? Give me an example."

"Did you ask if it's all right with me if you went on this trip?"

"No, but it's a *business* trip."

"Did you ask if I had anything to do this weekend?"

"Well, no, but..."

"But I do, as it happens. I have two houses to show. Almost all of my on-premise work is confined to the weekends. But you never thought of that, did you?"

"No, I..."

"You never do. You have this big important job and travel all over the country, while I..."

"They're *business* trips."

"...I always have to stay home and take care of the details of your life, paying the bills, taking care of the house, taking care of Sammy. It's like I'm your friggin' maid and secretary, and I resent the hell out of it."

"What am I supposed to do? — Travel is part of my job."

"Fine, but have you ever asked how it effects me? Have you ever even asked if I might like to go?"

"It's business," he said with dismay. How was he supposed to take her on a business trip? Why would she want to go on a business trip? It was all work: quick, crowded commuter flights, one box of a hotel room after another, airport lines, traffic and tight schedules. It wasn't his idea of fun.

"We never went anywhere together. In all the years since Sammy was born, where did we go? Your parents', Disneyland. Whooppee!" she cried sarcastically.

"Is it just the travel? Is that what this is all about? Because we can take more trips."

"That wouldn't solve anything. That's just a symptom. The problem is you. You weren't even involved when you were at home. We were like furniture to you. You're too self absorbed, too oblivious to my needs. I can't take it anymore. I just want out. Look, I'm here at the school. The bell's about to ring."

"So tell Sammy I'm sorry I can't see him this weekend."

"And that's it?"

"What else should I say?"

The school bell clanged out its raucous signal that First Grade was done for the day. Kids began pouring out the front door.

"You still haven't asked if it's ok with me. After all I've said."

"It doesn't matter if I asked you; I still have to go. I don't have a choice."

"Neither do I; I have two houses to show."

"And?"

"You still don't get it, do you? You announce you're going out of town and you expect everyone else to drop what they're doing and take care of it. But would it ever occur to you that maybe *you* should be the one to arrange for a baby sitter, so *I* can go to *my* work? No, of course not." Sammy ran up to the car, opened the door, threw his backpack on the floor and jumped in. "It always falls to me. I'm expected to drop everything I'm doing to accommodate *your* life. Well, I'm damn tired of it and I'm not going to take it anymore."

"Daddy says 'damn' is a bad word," Sammy said.

"Damn right," Linda replied. "You want to talk to your father?" She handed him the phone. "Put on your seatbelt."

"Hi, Dad."

"Hey, kiddo. How was school?"

"It was ok."

"What did you learn?"

"Nothin.'"

"You should always learn something new every day; that's your job. Listen, I called to say I have to go on a business trip this weekend, so we can't be together."

"Oh," Sammy said. It was a simple exclamation, but the tone of his voice declared his disappointment as eloquently as an essay.

"I'll call on Friday night and we can talk. Ok?"

"Ok." Again the flat tone conveyed disappointment, betrayal and resignation.

"I'll try to make it up to you next week. I promise."

Sammy handed the phone to Linda. She turned it off with her thumb. She'd said all she was going to say.

That morning the sell off started early and accelerated throughout the day. When the final bell sounded, a cheer of relief went up from the offices and cubicles.

A moment later Curtis heard an order shouted: "All Account Managers to the boardroom! Five minutes, people!"

Barbara opened the door and before she could speak he said, "I know, I heard."

She looked at him queerly. He looked dazed. "Are you okay? I take it the Market had a bad day?"

"It was ugly; down 778 points."

They assembled in the boardroom, a group of shell-shocked executives in white or blue dress shirts and plain or diagonally striped ties, and Curtis noticed that everyone stood around the boardroom table; no one took a seat; there was too much tension to sit. Erickson paced at the head of the table like a worried general. "Okay, we got hit today. But this is what we get paid to do. This is where we prove our worth to our clients. So where do we stand? What strategies are working?" He searched the faces, the downcast eyes, the hanging heads. "Anyone?" Three hands went up tentatively. "David?"

After the three volunteers had explained their anomalous successes, Erickson called for attention. "Listen up, the rest of you. I want a report on my desk by Wednesday on where you stand for the year and the past month, and what strategies you're going to employ going forward. And I want to know why. That's all."

The managers dispersed amid a lot of grumbling.

Curtis turned to Elliot. "What a disaster."

"Yup," Elliot agreed. "Atlas didn't just shrug; he had a heart attack and dropped the ball."

Curtis had no sooner sat down than Erickson stepped into his office. It was an uncharacteristic move; Erickson usually summoned his minions to his office. Without his coat, he looked lanky and emaciated. He withdrew a handkerchief, snatched off his glasses and began to clean them. "I have a favor to ask, Curt."

"Shoot."

"I'd like you to take on a special client, my college roommate. He's inherited some money. He's placing four million with us; I'd like you to oversee it."

"Sure. Do you want me to give him a presentation?"

Erickson held his glasses up toward the fluorescent panel in the ceiling, inspecting the lenses for smudges. "A phone call should be sufficient, " he said, putting his glasses on. "He's bright, but he doesn't understand investment vehicles."

"What's his name?"

"Jim Dayton. His father was an inventor — held a number of patents. Jim is an epidemiologist. Smart, but a bit of a flake — not very good with money. I'll give Barbara the contact information."

Curtis still had some post-Market work to catch up on, analyzing charts, reading reports and Market commentary. He checked his emails: questions from subordinates, a query from a client he wished to avoid, and an email from Linda with the terse message, "Your mother called." After a while he found himself staring dumbly out the window, playing his conversation with Linda over and over in his head, thinking of things he should have said, and some things he should have left unsaid.

It wasn't hard to read Curtis's emotions; he was utterly transparent. When he came across the parking lot toward the Volvo, Elliot had only to take one look at him to see he'd had a miserable day.

Elliot wasn't cruel, but he did find other people's emotional outbursts entertaining, as evidenced by the hours he spent watching "Reality" TV. Besides, he was too curious to remain tactfully silent. "Had a rough day?" he prodded.

"I've been a shitty husband."

"What brought you to that brilliant conclusion?"

"I talked with Linda today."

"That's progress."

"Not really. She just made me see things a little differently, and I don't like what I see."

"In what way?"

"I've had my head up my ass."

"How colorful. Would you care to elucidate?"

"Well," he sighed, "where to start? I've never, you know, been able to put myself in her shoes, to see the world from her viewpoint. I'm not sure I'm capable. I never understood why she chose me in the first place, and that's what it was, you know; it wasn't the other way around. This gorgeous girl comes up to me in French class and starts talking, and the next thing you know we're hanging out together, and then we move in together (her idea). There was a sense of inevitability about it. You know, I never even asked her to marry me (I didn't think she'd have me). We'd been living together for a year or so and I kept expecting her to tell me it's over. Then I graduated and got a job, and she was still going to school, and one day she says, 'when do you think we should get married?' Not, 'do you *think* we should get married?' but '*when* do you think we should get married?' I just sort of went with the flow. It seemed like a good idea at the time. Thanks for the ride, by the way," Curtis said.

"It doesn't make sense for both of us to drive. Not with gas and parking so steep these days. It's just seven minutes out of my way."

Emotionally wrung out by the time he arrived at the apartment, he poured himself a tall glass of Oregon Pinot Gris and picked up the phone. A conversation with his son would set everything to rights, put it all in perspective.

"Hi, can I talk to Sammy?"

"Hold on," Linda said. Curtis was thinking about things they might do together the next time Sammy came for the weekend. He would propose a visit to the zoo or the aquarium. Linda came back on the line. "He doesn't want to talk; he's playing with his trucks."

"You told him it was me?"

"Yes. I think he's mad at you."

"Can you ask him again?"

"Sammy?" she called. Sammy scooted on his hands and knees, rolling his truck, and disappeared under the dining room table. "Nope. He doesn't want to talk."

"Tell him I love him," Curtis said, and hung up. He hadn't even gone on the trip yet, and he was already paying the price. He resolved he would have to do something special for Sammy to make it up to him.

On the flight to Boise Curtis said, "I should have seen it coming. I mean, the bedroom is the early warning system. Things haven't been right in the sack since May." Elliot came alert but kept his mouth shut, hoping for more salacious details. "She tried to blame me for her lack of libido. I remember one time I was taking longer than usual, because she wasn't participating; she was laying there, looking bored, and she says to me, 'Just pretend you're making love to' — I don't know, some actress or other (Katherine Heigel, or Heather Graham, or somebody). And I thought, why should I think about some actress?"

"Don't you ever fantasize?"

"Why would I fantasize when I'm in bed with a real woman? I don't need a fantasy; I just need to be in the here and now. It would never occur to me to fantasize. I mean, what does some actress have that Linda doesn't? Jesus, she has a body to die for. But she turned into a fucking ice maiden. She was so passionate in college, but it all went down hill after we married."

"So naturally," he continued in the cab to the hotel, "I asked her if she had to fantasize to have an orgasm, and she admitted it. I asked how long this had been going on, and she said forever. She's been mentally cheating on me since the very beginning. When I'm banging her she's thinking about George Clooney. That's such a turn off."

"I don't know," Elliot remarked. "I've always thought he was kind of sexy."

Tom Fischer watched his ball sail out over the fairway, the trajectory low but rising, slicing slightly to the right. The ball lost momentum, sank to the grass and rolled another 30 yards, coming to rest beside four yellow poplars that fluttered in the breeze.

He turned, smiling. "You're up!"

Curtis was gazing down slope from the Tee to where ducks paddled around a pond fringed with cattails. The color of the water was intriguing, changing from green to blue and reflecting high clouds and the yellowing cattails. And he remembered how, when he was a boy of 10 or 11, his father had shown him how to make fine torches by soaking cattails in kerosene.

"Curt, you're up!" Tom turned to Elliot and noted, *soto voce*, "He's got his head in the clouds."

"Ah, his wife threw him out," Elliot explained.

"Curt!"

Curtis looked up, coming back to the present. He sauntered over to the tee box, teed up his ball and aimed for the left side of the fairway, knowing he always sliced his wood shots. His irons and putting were solid enough, but his tee shots were miserable. That flaw in his game cost him 50 yards a drive. It was a frustrating game, but necessary for business. When his ball had come to a rest and they headed for their carts he asked no one in particular, "Why don't we ever play tennis?"

"I don't like being beat," Scott Rhys offered with a laugh.

"We're happy to gratify your over-bloated sense of manhood," Elliot replied to Scott.

Tom grabbed a 3-iron from his bag. "I'll ride with Curt; we're on the same side of the fairway."

"Not close enough, though," Curtis said; "I can't get the distance."

"You have a wicked slice. Elliot tells me you're getting a divorce."

"No, we're just separated."

"That's just the warm up for the divorce. Do you have a prenup?"

"God no, we're not rich."

"If you have anything left, be smart next time: insist on a prenup; it takes the wrangling out of the divorce. I *know*; I've been married three times." The electric cart whined down the paved path, jostling over bumps that set the clubs to rattling in the back.

"Three times! Have you learned anything?"

"Yeah, women are a mystery. You can never trust what they say; take my first wife. After the kid came, she lost all interest in sex. She said she didn't understand what all the fuss was about. It wasn't important, she said, so I took her at her word. I got a little on the side, and then you can believe it was important. My god, you'd think I'd killed her mother, the way she went on."

Curtis walked out to his ball and hit a decent iron shot that rolled to the lip of the sand trap just off the green. Tom, meanwhile, moved the cart opposite his ball, and Curtis caught up with him just as he swung. There was a click as the club contacted the ball, Tom twisted gracefully like a pro, and the ball soared high into the air, slowed at the apogee and dropped onto the green twenty feet from the pin.

"Beautiful shot."

"Thanks. Best of the day."

They walked back to their cart.

"So you were talking about your marriages," Curtis prodded. "What happened with the second one?"

"Oh, well, I married the mistress. So you'd think she'd forgive a little slip; she knew my appetites, but she was as vindictive as the first one."

"Any kids?"

"One, with the second wife. They live in Tucson — haven't seen them in years. You have kids?"

"One. He's six."

"That's how old I was when my parents divorced."

"Did you get along with your father after that?"

"Dad? Yeah, sure, I didn't blame *him* anyway. My mom was the one who was always yelling at him, and I didn't understand any of it at six. I was just happy they stopped fighting. He had a nice place down in Florida, where I spent my summers. He was a pushover, didn't believe in rules. He didn't believe in prenups, either, and he died broke. Four wives sucked him dry — dumb shit."

Curtis thought Tom's experience was indicative of conflicting attitudes and emotions. The cynicism inherent in a prenuptial agreement was born of repeated failure, yet the fact that Tom and his father had gone through seven marriages between them was a mark of eternal optimism. But how could you be optimistic when you expected the marriage to fail? And why would anyone but the very wealthy need a prenuptial agreement? A prenup precluded trust, without which marriage would be anguish. What a mess! Was Tom right about the separation? Was this what happened to divorced people? Would he be joining that multitude?

As they were having lunch in the airport, waiting for their flight home, Elliot picked up the thread of their earlier conversation. "Come on, you mean you've never played French maid? Or the pillaging pirate?"

"Linda is not that imaginative."

"You just said she fantasizes. That's imagination."

"Do you really do that?"

"Do what?"

"Play a pirate."

"Not since Sophie came along; she likes to sleep with us."

"How romantic."

"I know, I know. But it's not every night."

Back home Sunday night, Elliot told Vicky, "He claims he doesn't fantasize, except to — you know," he cleared his throat, "when he pleasures himself."

"Too much information," she replied, putting her hands over her ears and grimacing.

"Do you have to fantasize to have an orgasm?"

"Of course."

"About who?"

"It's not so much who; it's more a situation."

"What kind of situation turns you on?" he asked, nuzzling his wife's neck.

"You really want to know?"

"Yeah. I really want to know what goes on in that pretty little head of yours."

"I don't know," she replied reluctantly.

"I'll tell you mine, if you tell me yours," Elliot pressed.

"Well...ok. I'm a priestess, and young boys are standing naked at attention all around the lip of a volcano. The orange light is glowing from below, and they're all sweaty, and I'm inspecting them, like a general inspects his troops. They're not allowed to move. I dance around them." Vicky began swaying her hips and waving her arms in an undulating fashion, demonstrating her priestess dance.

"What are you wearing?"

"Priestess garb. Like a belly dancer."

"Sexy."

"I dance up close to one of them," she said, brushing her breasts against his arm. "And I rub my hands over his glistening, sweaty body." She ran a finger up the inside of Elliot's thigh. "And when he's fully aroused, I take a paddle and spank him hard, and shove him into the molten lava." Elliot looked stricken. Vicky smiled smugly, like the cat that ate the canary. "Now tell me yours."

"Mine is not so...imaginative," he said, thinking of his paltry nurse fantasy.

Chapter 6

Monday, October 6 – Sunday, October 12, 2008

O n Monday, October 6th, a buzz and commotion ran through the office. Institutional money was being pulled out of the market at an alarming rate and the mighty DOW was in free-fall. Every eye in the office was glued to a computer monitor, watching in stark terror as the index fell a jaw-dropping 800 points before stabilizing and beginning to edge back up. All around the office trades were sent off with the almost silent click of a keyboard key, along with occasional groans and expletives. Davidson, one of the associates, drew glances when he stood up in his cubicle, yelled "Son-of-a-bitch!" at the top of his lungs, and stormed out, muttering, "I can't take any more of this." No one took a lunch break. Sandwiches were passed out to those who wanted them. Curtis's stomach was too tied in knots to eat. Instead, Barbara supplied him with warm cups of Chai tea.

Passing through the more upscale end of Francis Boulevard on the way home, Curtis spied a glass fronted art store. "Hold up! Take that parking space there."

"What's up?"

"I need to buy something. Wait here a few minutes."

Bolton's Art Supplies was "a miracle of supply" on two levels. On the ground floor, shelves were stocked with paper — loose paper, bound paper, sketchpads, paper of different weights, sizes, colors, textures and composition. Bins of poster board, colored cardboard and stretched canvas stood along one wall. There were shelves of water colors, crayons, pastels, oil paint, acrylic paint, tempera, colored markers and pens, colored pencils, graphite pencils and charcoal. There were models of articulated wooden people, tracing projectors, packages of red and green modeling clay, paint-by-the-numbers sets, painters' palettes, erasers, carving tools, Exacto blades, rulers, paint brushes, scissors, portfolio cases, art books, scrapbooks, bound books of plain paper, pads of plain paper and graph paper. There were instructional books on drawing, painting, portraiture, landscapes, architectural rendering and perspective, books on carving, and woodworking and stained glass. At the end of the aisles stood easels, and drafting desks, lamps and plastic bins for storing art supplies. A stairway led up to the framing and print department on the second level.

Curtis moved up and down the aisles carrying a plastic basket, into which he placed a set of 64 crayons and a ruler. A young woman in a dark blue skirt and white blouse approached. More curvaceous than elegant, she was full-breasted with dark, shoulder length hair, dark eyebrows and brown eyes behind round, wire-rimmed glasses. Her name tag read "Stephanie."

"Can I help you?" she asked, flashing a smile that seemed more real than cant.

"Maybe you can; I'm at a bit of a loss. You see, my son was painting on the wall and I'm looking to channel his artistic impulses in a less destructive direction."

"How old is he?"

"He just turned six."

"Is he gifted? I mean, I know most parents think their children are gifted — what I mean is, has he shown any unusual abilities, had any instruction, or is he just having fun?"

"Just fun. Do six-year-olds get instruction?"

She rolled her eyes. "I know it's hard to believe, but a lot of parents who come in here think they're raising the next Renoir, and they push their children into classes and competitions. I think it takes the fun out of it at that age, but..." She finished the sentence with raised eyebrows, a shrug and a cocked head, as if to say *It's not my place to say, so what can I do?*

Curtis wondered if she was speaking from experience; she was about 27, he estimated, so she might have a son or daughter of her own. He glanced at her left hand and saw no ring, so he thought not. Perhaps she had nieces or nephews.

"So, let me see," she said, peering into his basket, "you have crayons. Does he like coloring books?"

"He used to, but these days I think he likes to make his own pictures."

Stephanie led him around the aisles filling up his basket. "All kids love art; it's natural. But they don't like being judged or pushed into anything. It's like negative association."

"He has enough on his plate without being pressured to perform."

"I agree; kids are way too stressed out these days. But it's good to encourage creative outlets so they can express themselves — and art is a great stress reliever."

She had a nice smile and an easy, comfortable way about her that made her seem less like a sales person than a helpful, interested friend.

"He might like a set of colored pencils." She put a set in the basket. "And you'll need a pencil sharpener, unless you already have one — no?" She added a pencil sharpener to the basket. "And a good eraser. This kind works really well with colored pencils. And I'd recommend a sketchpad (they're cheaper than loose paper and it keeps the mess in check), nothing fancy. What do you think: 8X10 or 11X14?"

"Hmm, well...I don't know. What do you think?"

"If it were me, I'd go with the 11X14. The 75-sheet pad is the same price as 100 sheets of 8X10, but most kids like it better."

Elliot came in, looked around and headed toward them. "You almost through?"

"Just about. You want to pick something up for Sophie?"

Elliot's face brightened. "That's not a bad idea; I'll score some points with Vicky." He turned to Stephanie. "Do you have any coloring books?"

She led them to a table where Elliot picked out a *Finding Nemo* coloring book and a *Cars* connect-the-dots book.

"How old is your daughter?"

"Five."

"Do you know if she can count to fifty?"

"Fifty? I don't know; I doubt it," Elliot said, puzzled.

"Because that connect-the-dots book has some pictures that have up to fifty dots. Here, take this one instead; this one only goes up to 20."

On the way out to the car Elliot said, "I used to love connect-the-dots books. I should have got one for myself."

"Can you count to 50?" Curtis snorted.

They drove several blocks in silence, each separate in his own thoughts. Curtis was thinking about his marriage, wondering if there was any way to save it. He missed his house. He missed living in the same house with Sammy, though if truth be told, he had spent more hours with his son the previous weekend, than he had in the previous month at home. He missed the small talk with Linda. Where had they gone wrong? When did she decide that she no longer loved him? How long had the idea played at the corners of her mind before she gave it credence? How had he been so self-involved that he had missed all the signs?

He had met her in French class. She was so beautiful that he had not even considered approaching her; then she had approached him. She was elegant and sophisticated; she had been to Europe, spent time in Paris. Everything about her was polished. She was better dressed, smarter, more focused than any of the other silly girls he'd met in college. And (inexplicably, he thought) she had been attracted to him.

Idling at a stoplight, Elliot said, "She was nice."

"Who?" Curtis asked. Elliot couldn't be thinking of Linda. He hadn't said anything nice about her for as long as he could remember. Polite, yes; nice, no.

"That girl, back at the store."

"Oh," Curtis replied noncommittally.

"You didn't notice?"

"Not my type," he replied. The mental picture of his "type" — the kind of woman he was attracted to — was Linda, in all respects: lithe and petite, blonde-haired, blue-eyed, smart, witty, competent, a study in femininity both coming and going. "She's more your type; she and Vicky could pass for sisters."

Tuesday and Wednesday the sell off continued. Curtis sat glued to his computer screen watching the debacle with a mixture of dread and fatalism. He could make no sense of this market.

Barbara opened the door to his office.

"Where's the bottom?" Curtis asked rhetorically, staring at his charts.

"Huh?"

"We're down 745 points in two days! Where the hell is the bottom, for gods' sakes?"

"Don't ask me, you're the so-called expert. Humph. I'm glad I don't have no money to invest. I'm goin' to lunch, if you don't have any objections."

Curtis waved her away.

On Thursday the DOW fell 814 points, the worst percentage loss since 9/11 and a four-day loss of more than 18%.

On Saturday morning he sat on the concrete bench under the sycamore in front of his apartment building. The low sun streamed yellow down the quiet street, lighting the pavement and the east side of the trees. He wanted to talk to Linda, and he was worried about work. In the shade the air was a little chilly for his short sleeves. He wished he'd put on a sweater.

Linda's white BMW 320i slid to the curb. He went down the stairs to greet them. Sammy got out and put on his backpack, while Curtis took a boy-sized rolling suitcase and a Teddy bear from the backseat. Linda sat in the driver's seat looking straight ahead. She obviously wasn't getting out. He knocked on the passenger side window. It rolled down and he leaned in.

"Can we talk?" he pleaded.

"I don't have anything new to say."

"Maybe *I do!*" he half screamed in exasperation.

"Not in front of Sammy," she said quietly.

"Not in...fine! Then where? When?"

"You can call my lawyer. I don't want to argue with you."

"Lawyer?!" he exclaimed. It hadn't occurred to him that she might be talking to a lawyer. "You have a lawyer?"

"You can drop Sammy off after dinner tomorrow."

The window rolled up. She waved at Sammy and pulled away from the curb.

Curtis was thoroughly perplexed. Why the acrimony? His stomach churned with bile.

Upstairs as they entered the apartment he asked, "What do you want to do today?" thinking that fatherhood in his apartment was more like being an entertainment director.

But Sammy just shrugged.

"Do you feel like going out?"

Sammy shrugged again.

"Well, just play with your toys, then."

"I wanna paint," Sammy said and ran over to the corner behind the TV where he'd painted the mural. "Where's my pitcher?"

"Pic-ture," Curtis corrected. "I had the wall painted. And I told you — you can't paint on the wall. Here, I got you something."

He brought out the crayons and colored pencils and sketchpad. "That should keep you busy for a while."

For the next hour Sammy tried out all of the colors, making rainbows with the crayons and drawing dinosaurs with the pencils. His Tyrannosaurus was all head and teeth, a tiny body and arms with three grasping fingers (his father stuck it onto the refrigerator with the smiling carrot magnet). Then Sammy scribbled a multi-colored background with green and yellow and orange pencils, and drew over it with crayons.

"What's this?" Curtis asked, when Sammy handed him the page. It was a family all standing in a row, in wild colors of blue, orange, red and purple. There was a man and a woman holding hands, and a man and a child holding hands.

"There's me," Sammy said, poking the smallest figure, "and you, and Mommy."

"And who's this?" Curtis asked, pointing to the extra figure.

"Roger."

"Roger?"

"Mommy's friend."

"Oh," said Curtis, feeling like he'd been sucker-punched.

That evening they ate pepperoni pizza at the kitchen bar. He'd never been much of a cook, though he could grill hamburgers and chicken on the Weber in their backyard.

Later Sammy watched an inane adolescent sit-com on the Disney channel, while Curtis sat in the armchair, sipping a cheap Chardonnay, and flipping through the various charts, searching for a pattern that would unlock the key to profitable trades. Sammy lay on the rug drawing for awhile before pushing the pad away — he looked exhausted and unhappy.

"What's the matter, Scooter?"

"I like to draw big."

"You can't draw on the wall."

"They have big paper at school."

"Okay. What do you say we go to the art store tomorrow and get bigger paper. Will that make you happy?"

Sammy gave his dad a hug, curled up in his lap and fell asleep.

Everything seemed in sharper focus in the fall. The air was cool and clear. Sound seemed to carry farther. There was a mental sigh of relief from the summer's heat, and an atavistic compulsion to pack as much as possible into each day in anticipation of the coming winter. Despite his dissolving marriage, the season still had him in thrall.

Sammy sat beside him on their way to the art store, no longer legally confined to the baby car seat in back, but riding upfront, secure in his entitlement, excited by his anticipation of the discoveries that lay ahead. The world was wide and the pleasures were many.

Sammy chanted:

"Two little monkeys sittin' on the bed
One fell off and bumped his head.
Mama called the doctor and the doctor said,
No more monkeys sittin' on the bed."

Curtis said, "You know, my father used to sing me a song when I was little that went something like that. You want to hear it?" Sammy nodded and Curtis sang:

"Two little babies sittin' on the bed,
one of 'm sick, an' one most dead.
Called the doctor an' the doctor said,
'Feed them babies on shortenin' bread.'
Mammy's little babies love shortenin', shortenin'
Mammy's little babies love shortenin' bread."

He didn't know if he'd gotten it right; it was an old song that he hadn't heard since he was a little child. He suspected it had fallen out of favor because of the word "mammy," which was now politically *verboten*. It had probably been politically incorrect when his father sang it to him, but his father had never cared about such things.

The song brought to mind a memory of riding to the hardware store with his father on a Saturday morning not unlike today, and it made him quietly aware that this was a special moment to be cherished on the spot, here and now, because there would be fewer of these moments ahead even if he and Linda reconciled. This was good and he wished he could make it last, because six was a good age and only eight years separated Sammy from the sullen adolescent he was sure to become. He wished he could stay time and keep his son forever young, carefree and full of wonder.

Sammy was excited when they entered the store. Curtis tried to lead him to the paper and canvas, but Sammy was entranced by the unmitigated abundance. The impossible array of choices left him breathless. "I want this, Daddy!" he said, holding up an articulated wooden figure.

"Do you know what it's for?"

"It's a toy."

"Sort of. It's an artist's model, so when you draw a person you can see what it should look like — the proportions (you know — how long an arm is compared to a leg) and how the body bends. Have you ever noticed when you walk you swing your arms? And the way you swing them is opposite of the way your legs are going. Like this." He demonstrated by walking away and coming back. He knelt down to Sammy's level. "So, if you were to draw somebody walking, you'd bend it like this. See?"

"Very good, Mr. Cooke."

He recognized the voice and wasn't surprised to see Stephanie the saleslady when he looked back over his shoulder. He didn't remember telling her his name. "You have the advantage," he said.

"How's that?"

"I know you're Stephanie — from your name tag — but how did you...?"

"I did run your credit card, and I try never to forget a customer."

"That's a good skill. I can never remember names, myself. I'm great with faces, but terrible with names, unless I have a visual like your name tag."

"Are you going to introduce us?"

"Oh, sure. Stephanie, this is Sammy. Sammy, this is Stephanie-ie...?"

"Walzer."

Stephanie bent at the waist and shook Sammy's hand. "Are you really six?" she asked, again surprising Curtis by her recall.

"I'm in first grade."

"Let me see your teeth." He obediently spread his lips in a half grimace. "You must have just turned six; you haven't lost your front teeth yet." He nodded. "What can I do for you today?"

"I wanna paint big," he said, holding his arms wide.

"I have just what you need," Stephanie said, taking his hand. Curtis followed along behind. She led them to the aisle with shelves of sketchpads and loose paper on one side, and bins of pressboard, poster board, colored cardboard and stretched canvas on the other. "What are you making your picture with? — crayons, or pencils, or...?"

"I wanna paint," Sammy said with assurance.

"Hold on, Sport," said Curtis. "We didn't say anything about paint."

"I like paint," Sammy pouted.

Curtis rolled his eyes to the ceiling and back to Stephanie. "I moved into an apartment, an artist's garret. The previous tenant left some canvases and paints behind, and Sammy got into them and..."

"...drew on the wall," she finished for him.

Curtis was impressed. "You *do* have an amazing memory."

"What kind of paint was it?"

"Oil paint."

"Oh, my god. And he didn't get it on anything else?"

"Oh yes, he did."

"What a disaster!"

"Yes, you could say that."

"So, what did you do?"

"The paint was still wet, so I cleaned it up as best I could with a towel — I didn't have any paint thinner."

"And his clothes?"

"Forget about it."

"I should say so."

They stood and looked at each other for a moment, holding back the laughter.

"Do you have a suggestion?" Curtis asked.

"Yes," Stephanie said with a chuckle. "Don't ever let him get hold of oil paint. Oil paint is very hard to clean. And if you're going to keep oils around, you need paint thinner."

"I know; I had a hard time getting it off the floor. So what do you recommend? Acrylic?"

"It's a complicated question. Acrylic will clean up with water, if it's still wet, but it's probably more a question of pigment. Some pigments — like Prussian blue, or certain reds, for instance — you'll never get out. It's like pomegranates or beets."

"So what do you recommend?"

Sammy had been waiting throughout this exchange to get his two cents in. "I wanna paint," he said.

They had both forgotten Sammy and they now looked to him for guidance, but it was obvious that guidance was just what he was asking *them* for. So Stephanie said, as though she were his mother and upset about the added expense of buying paint, "But you just got crayons and pencils, didn't you?"

"But I wanna paint."

"Dad?" Stephanie asked.

"Oh, well, whatever...whatever he wants, I guess."

"Okay," she sighed theatrically. "Sammy, I hear you're good at making messes. Is that right?"

"I try not to."

"It's hard to paint and not make a mess, isn't it? I suggest you try some watercolors. They're easier to clean up. And Dad?"

Curtis perked up. "Hmmm?"

"Are you going to use watercolors, too, or try something else?"

"Me? Oh, no — this is just for Sammy."

"I want you to paint, too," Sammy said, jumping up and down as though he had springs in his shoes.

"You want me to paint, too?"

"We can paint together."

"Well, I don't know — Painting is pretty hard; I don't think I'd be very good at it."

"You can do it; you can do anything."

"Not quite."

"You could try pastels," Stephanie interjected.

"Isn't that like grown-up crayons?" Curtis asked.

"Precisely."

"Well, okay then, that's right up my alley."

"Very well," Stephanie said. "Now, here's a paper that would be perfect for pastels. A 12-sheet pad, 18 by 24 inches. It's about a dollar a page, but you can draw on both sides. You'll need different paper for watercolors. Watercolor paper is very specific to watercolors. The 140-pound cold press is nice; it has texture. I'd recommend a block."

"What's a block?"

She discoursed on the different papers and the different price levels, which ranged enormously from student to professional.

A heavy-set man in his early 20's asked her about tempera paint. Another customer asked her about framing, and then they were alone again.

Then she led them to the paint aisle, where she explained the difference between professional and student watercolors, the advantages and disadvantages of gift sets, the various types of brushes and instructional books.

"You should stay away from the cadmium watercolors; they're nearly opaque and besides, they're poisonous (not so good for kids who tend to put their fingers in their mouths)."

He selected beginners' books on watercolors and drawing with pastels, a painter's smock for Sammy, and pastels for himself. He was looking at a porcelain artist's palette when she said, "Plastic is cheaper."

"I can see you don't work on commission," he observed dryly.

"Yes, actually, I do."

"Then aren't you supposed to be up-selling me?"

"I don't believe in that nonsense. If I didn't give you good value, you wouldn't come back."

"That's refreshing. What do you recommend for brushes and paints?" He hesitated for a second as a thought occurred, then added, "Let's get *two* sets," and turning to Sammy said, "that way you can practice when you're at your mom's," thinking *at your mom's, that sounds so strange, but that's what it is now, not 'at our house', not just 'at home', but 'at your mom's'*, because he had his own place now, and Sammy would spend the next few weeks (months? years?) shuffling between the two, never really knowing why, or how it happened, but just that he now went to "Dad's" on the weekends, and stayed the weekdays at "Mom's."

"Are you all right?" Stephanie asked, her brow pinched in evident concern.

"Yes, fine, just thinking," he said, thinking *I've got to stop that; I've become transparent.*

"We have plastic palettes with hinges that close up. That way Sammy can travel back and forth without getting paint on anything."

"That would be great."

Stephanie selected a box of paints, a wide flat brush and a Chinese calligraphy brush.

"You'll find a lot of good tips in the books. You should really browse through the book before you start painting; it'll save you a lot of grief. Just remember that the secret to watercolor painting is 'water.' I know that sounds stupid, but watercolor painting is not pigment painting; it's water painting. It's delicate. The colors should always be thin, because it's the paper showing through that makes your colors come alive."

After paying at the checkout counter Curtis asked, "Do you have any other insights for us before we go?"

"Yes, and it's the most important thing — have fun."

They carried their plastic bags full of art supplies back to the car and started for the apartment. In a minute Sammy said, "That was a nice lady."

This time Curtis didn't have to ask 'who?' She *was* nice.

He mindlessly pointed the car for "home" and overshot the turnoff to the apartment by three blocks.

After lunch (peanut butter and jelly sandwiches) Curtis showed Sammy how to mix watercolors with water, how to mix one pigment with another to achieve another color, and why and how to wash your brushes so you didn't end up with a muddy brown blob on the end of your brush.

Then he unfolded the gate-leg table and laid out two sheets of the art paper. "We probably should read the instruction manual first," Curtis said. "Do you want to look at it now, or just paint?"

"I wanna paint," Sammy said.

"Okay, alright. You paint and I'll draw. Let's draw this guy," he said, bending the 6-inch tall, articulated, wooden model into the figure of a man running.

So they started, side-by-side to make pictures of the little wooden man, Curtis drawing faster, marking the model in with a few strokes of his pastels, then adding clothes. It was crude, but recognizably a human being in motion. Sammy was slower and his proportions were not as precise, but the essence was the same. Curtis drew some buildings in the background. Sammy's page was much bigger, and he filled it up with mountains in the background, a sun in the upper right corner and water on the lower left, so his man seemed to be running into a lake.

"That's good," Curtis said.

"This is fun," Sammy said.

Curtis gave Sammy a high five.

"Keep it to one page today. Okay?"

In the kitchen Curtis boiled rice and green beans, and sautéed chicken breasts. By the time he called Sammy to dinner, Sammy's picture included a blue sky, a plane, a boat, a house and birds. The one thing Curtis could say about painting "big": There was plenty of room to add extra elements.

After dinner they packed Sammy's clothes, his brushes and traveling painter's palette into his backpack and drove out to the suburbs and "home." A new Mercedes SLK roadster was parked in the driveway. Curtis eyed its sleek silver lines as they walked up the path to the front door. He tried the door. It was locked. He fished his keys out of his front pocket, unlocked the door, and followed Sammy inside. He closed the door loudly enough to announce their arrival and heard a yelp of surprise from the living room. Linda came in, breathless, looking alarmed.

"You scared the devil out of me!" she said. "Didn't you think to knock?"

"It's my house."

"Not any longer."

"I'm still paying the mortgage on it, so I guess it is, whether you like it or not. Whose car is that?"

"A friend," she said evasively, folding her arms and standing legs apart, effectively barring the way into the living room.

"Sammy," Curtis said, "give me a hug; I gotta go." He picked up his son and kissed him on the cheek. "You know I'm only a phone call away, anytime you want to talk." And to Linda he added, "I should be able to pick him up Friday night."

"Your parents called," Linda said. "I told them you'd call. Why haven't you told them?"

"I didn't want to upset them."

"They have to know; I can't keep pretending you're here. They asked me about Thanksgiving."

"I thought you might want to come. They don't have to know."

"I'm not going to pretend for the sake of your parents."

"Well, but...I bought the tickets back in August."

"Then you'll just have to cancel mine; I'm not going."

"Alright. I have to go, Linda."

He was anxious to get out of the house; he didn't have the nerve to face her new "friend." He wasn't at all sure he could act civilly.

Cleaning up that night he found the picture that Sammy had drawn the day before. He cut "Roger" out of the picture, letting the figure slide ceremoniously into the trashcan, and hung the now happy family of three on the refrigerator door with a smiling broccoli magnet.

Chapter 7

Monday October 13 – Sunday October19, 2008

Curtis usually took some solace from the metronomic regularity of his work. Stocks and commodities, bonds and currencies went round and round the seasons, smoothly surging up and coming down like carousel horses. But somehow in the last month the gears had come unhinged; the horses were jerking and bucking. The Market had become manic-depressive — elated one day, sunk in deep depression the next. For those who actively traded the Market, the carousel had turned into an emotional roller coaster.

"You're in a good mood," observed Barbara Monday morning.

"DOW's up like a rocket today."

By the end of the day, the DOW had posted a gain of 936 points, its biggest point gain in history, and its biggest percentage gain since 1933. Curtis felt like a genius.

Just two days later panic took hold of the Market once again. Barbara could feel the tension, as every few minutes Curtis groaned in disbelief. Throughout the day she fended off the worried clients who called, and as the end of the trading day approached, she got together a tall glass of water and an Alka-Seltzer, and brought them into his office. "Bad day?" she asked rhetorically.

"Bad? No, it wasn't bad; it was a fucking disaster. Second worst day in history, and my clients are now fully exposed. I'm a fucking idiot."

She placed the Alka-Seltzer next to the water. From her purse she took out a pint flask of vodka, unscrewed the top and poured a generous amount into the water. "This, too, shall pass," she said, quoting scripture he had no doubt.

It was already dark on Washington Street when Elliot dropped off Curtis on Wednesday evening. Curtis held up a left hand spread wide in farewell. Discreetly hooded lights lit the edge of the concrete stairs, and a ground-level spotlight shown up through the yellow leaves of the sycamore in the courtyard above. Halfway up the stairs he stopped to help a lady who was struggling with a wire cart and two grocery bags. He'd seen her before. She was about his mother's age, late 50s, and (but for the crepey neck and crow's feet) she was still a good-looking woman.

"Here, let me help," he offered, and took one of the bags.

"Thank you. Thank you so much. The cart helps, until I get to the stairs, and then it's a pain..." she left the last part of the phrase unsaid, leaving it to his imagination as to which part of her anatomy was pained. "You don't have your little boy with you," she observed. "I've seen you in the elevator."

"He lives with his mother," Curtis said, then added as an afterthought, "on weekdays."

"Ah," the woman said knowingly. "You're divorced, then?"

"Separated."

"Is there another woman?" The question came with a raised eyebrow and an edge of disapprobation in her voice and she immediately apologized. "I'm sorry, that's none of my business."

"That's all right; and the answer is no, there is no other woman. It's...more complicated than that. My wife is.... She's...unhappy."

"And you don't know why?" She sounded incredulous.

"Not a clue."

She made a dismissive grunt, smirked and shook her head, as if to say 'men are so witless.'

"Well, maybe I could have been more attentive," he conceded.

They reached the courtyard at the top of the stairs. She parked her rolling cart and put her bag into it. Curtis, chivalrous to a fault, took the cart handle and they walked toward the front door.

"Your boy is how old?"

"He just turned six."

"It's got to be hard on him."

"I think he's more resilient than I am."

"Maybe it's easier when they're younger. I don't know. My husband left me when our kids were 13 and 16, and I don't think they've ever really gotten over it. My daughter blames me. My son blames his father."

Curtis opened the door. They strolled to the elevator. Curtis pushed the plastic button. The numbers above the door lit up successively as the elevator passed each floor on its descent.

"My name's Irene, by the way. Irene Niece." She held out her hand and they shook politely.

"I'm Curtis."

A single bell chimed. The elevator doors opened and they stepped in. Curtis pressed 8. Irene pressed 7.

"You live above me, I believe."

"8C — It's small, but it has high ceilings and a lot of light."

"Victor used to live there. Moody artist living on his father's money. Loud parties. I think he painted as a way of getting girls to take off their clothes. There were a lot of girls."

The elevator came to a halt. The doors opened, Curtis relinquished the cart and Irene stepped out. "Take care, Curtis. What's your son's name?"

"Sammy," he called as the doors closed shut.

It was a small and insignificant exchange, yet having a neighbor whose name he now knew, left Curtis feeling more at home in his apartment. He poured himself a glass of Riesling and raised it as a toast, looking at the floor as though he could see through to Irene's apartment below. "Good night, Irene," he said, and the tune of the same name sprang to mind.

On Thursday Barbara quietly opened the door to his office and dropped a paper in his in-box. "Itinerary," she said. "You fly into Tulsa on Friday night..." Curtis didn't hear the rest of her recitation.

He left the building. FedEx and UPS and office supply trucks, taxis and cars and buses clogged the street. Pedestrians streamed along the dirty grey sidewalks. Despite the travel that came with the job, it was rare to be asked to fly on weekends. He needed time with Sammy. When he was living at home, he justified his absences by convincing himself that it was for the good of the family. Now he had to ask himself what he was working for.

He stopped at a Subway sandwich shop and ate a quick lunch that he barely tasted, as he was lost in thought, weighing consequences.

Exiting the elevator on his return he marched past Barbara to Erickson's corner office. Unlike his own office, Erickson's corner office wasn't glass fronted, so he didn't know if Erickson was even in.

Allison Essman said, "You can't go in there; he's busy."

Curtis ignored her. He rapped twice, entered the office and closed the door. His boss was standing behind his desk with the phone to his ear. He frowned at Curtis and turned his back, sitting on the edge of the desk. Curtis sat down in one of the two visitors' chairs.

In a minute Erickson said, "Hold on a minute, Arthur," and turned to Curtis. "Do you mind?"

"No, go ahead."

Erickson looked annoyed. "Arthur, I'll call you back." He hung up and faced Curtis with a furious stare, but for once Curtis was not intimidated. He truly did not care anymore and it gave him a feeling of serenity.

"This better be good," Erickson warned.

Curtis had thought it out at lunch. If worse came to worst and he was fired, he'd find another job. If he couldn't find a job, he'd insist on selling the house. He could live a long time on his half of the sale, even in this slumping housing market.

"You have me scheduled to fly to Tulsa this weekend. I'm sorry, I can't travel on weekends anymore."

"You have a conflict this week?"

"Not just this week — any week. I just can't travel on weekends anymore. You'll have to reschedule me."

"It's the divorce, isn't it? I knew this would happen — you get caught up in personal crap and your commitment goes out the window."

"Why does everyone keep talking about divorce? We're not getting a divorce; we're just separated. And my commitment hasn't changed. But weekends are the only time I have with my son."

"So? Is that more important than your job? I have a daughter, but I work 12 to 14-hour days, every day, because I also have responsibilities, and so do you — responsibilities to this firm, to your clients, to the thousands of people your clients employ."

"It doesn't extend to weekends. It's not part of my job description."

"Fuck your job description. If you won't go, I'll find someone who will."

"Be my guest."

"Don't expect a bonus."

"I'm still willing to travel weekdays. Weekends are just out of the question right now." He got up to leave.

"There are people counting on you, Cooke. Your clients are counting on you. *We're* counting on you."

"My son is counting on me. I already screwed the marriage."

Curtis walked out of Erickson's office, leaving the door open.

Erickson called angrily after him, "Bonuses are reserved for Team Players, Cooke!"

Curtis walked down the hall to Elliot's office and recounted his meeting with Erickson.

"Jesus," Elliot, the nominal Jew exclaimed. "Where does that leave *me*?"

"I don't know. He may pair you with someone else. He didn't say. I'd give him a day or two to think it over."

"You know you'll never get a promotion after this."

"It's not important," Curtis said, and he meant it. In a way, this separation from Linda was like a death; it brought into focus the things that counted.

Around 3 o'clock Glen Putnam knocked once and came into Curtis's office. Glen was the office anomaly, a man in his mid-sixties who, one supposed, had never aspired to rise up the corporate ladder; he seemed content to methodically turn out quarterly reports for clients and board meetings. Always polite, always cheerful, he called everyone by his or her first name, even Mr. Bass, and somehow he got away with it. He was 6'3" and thin, with short white hair, thick glasses, and deep creases that ran from the corners of his large nose to his chin.

"Hi, Curt. I just came over to offer my congratulations."

"For what?"

"For insisting that your weekends are your own." Curtis had to wonder how the word had gotten around the office. Had Allison been listening at the door? "You know, they have everyone working scared. People work weekends. They don't take sick days. They don't take vacation days. Everyone figures if they don't do it, they won't get ahead, or worse — they'll lose their jobs. But what the hell are we working for? Right?"

"Right," Curtis replied, leaning back in his chair until the springs squeaked. *What the hell* are *we working for? To pay the bills. To pay the taxes. To save for vacations and college for our kids.*

"You know, you never saw an epitaph that read 'He Was a Good Employee,' did you? 'Beloved Husband, Devoted Father' — that's what you see on a tombstone. That's what matters."

"Absolutely," Curtis affirmed. *Beloved Husband, Devoted Father.* That was something to aspire to.

"Keep it in perspective," Glen said on his way out. "Keep it real."

That's one very nice man, Curtis thought.

Back in the office for Friday, Curtis felt energized. The morning sun was dazzling, the colors bright in the rain-scrubbed air. But his optimism disappeared as the trading day progressed. The DOW moved up nicely in the morning. Then, despite no new reports to spark the stampede, the Wall Street lemmings headed for the exits in full-scale panic.

His stomach in knots, his head spinning, he told Barbara, "I'm going for a walk," and left the building. He walked around the Financial District in a daze, looking at all of the people bustling down the streets, bunched at the corners waiting for traffic lights to change, working people, shoppers, bums begging change, the usual grimy homeless guy with his market basket filled to the brim with plastic bags of bottles and cans. He smelled diesel exhaust and sweat, the lovely floral perfume of passing women, the yeasty aroma of the pretzel vendor on the corner, the sweet dark smell wafting from the door of a chocolate shop, the rotten, earthy stench rising from storm drains. He listened to the surge of car and bus engines, the sound of feet on pavement, the general hubbub of conversation, a jet passing high overhead like the rumble of distant thunder, and behind all of the individual sounds the massive chorus of the city, a sighing like wind through a forest, or waves rolling toward a sandy shore.

At one corner he found a small urban park shaded by young trees, with four green metal benches and a small fountain that flowed from between two granite boulders. Two benches were taken up with homeless men sleeping under dirty coats. Curtis sat on a bench under a tree, on the edge of a brick path that cut diagonally across the park. His head was spinning with unformed thoughts, and vague competing emotions that left him feeling anxious and a little nauseous. He sat there for several minutes, trying to relax, to find the calm at the center of the storm. He looked at the pattern of the bricks, the fallen leaves, the trash receptacle with its green metal canister inside a concrete cylinder that was studded with thousands of smooth pebbles. A line of ants snaked out of the receptacle, passed down the side of the concrete, crossed under some ivy and disappeared into a hole at the base of an azalea. It was a two-way street with ants moving in either direction, some carrying food, others just running their ant errands. There was a frantic restlessness all about him, ants and people and thoughts. And yet there was a calming sense of purpose about the ants. They knew what they were about.

On Saturday he made up a picnic lunch and put it in Sammy's backpack, along with a paperback of *Love Over Scotland*, by Alexander McCall Smith, on the off chance he might find time to read. They packed up the watercolors and Sammy's smock, and headed off for the park.

They ate their lunch in the shade of an old chestnut on the fringes of the baseball diamond. The wind picked up, blowing the first leaves of the season from the trees. Low clouds scudded overhead, their shadows gliding over the playground, mounting the sides of the buildings on the far side of the park and disappearing into thin air, pursued by the clouds themselves.

Curtis blew bubbles that sailed away on the breeze. Sammy laughed and chased them, popping as many as he could, his face a picture of bright, unadulterated joy.

When he'd had enough, Sammy came back to paint. Curtis helped him on with his smock and they set up on a picnic table. Curtis used pastels to sketch the outline of the surrounding buildings and passed the paper to Sammy to fill in the lines. Sammy painted dry on dry with thick, undiluted watercolors. He'd been at it about ten minutes when a gust of wind stole under the corner of the paper and sent it sailing out over the lawn, where it landed face down. The paint was smeared with thousands of little "strokes" from the blades of grass. Wary of getting paint on his hands or clothes, Curtis carefully folded the paper in half, with the paint on the inside.

"I think that's it for the day, Scooter."

"It's too windy," Sammy said disconsolately.

"We'll have to check with Miss Walzer to see what we can do about it."

"What can we do?"

"I don't know, but people do paint outdoors. I'm sure she'll have a solution."

And so she did.

"Back again?" she greeted them the next day. "You can't have run out of paint so soon!"

Curtis explained their plight.

"If you'd be content with a smaller size, you could go with a block of paper. It won't blow away in the wind."

Sammy looked distressed. "I like to draw big," Sammy said, shrugging.

"Or you could draw on a clip board. We have clipboards that hold up to 20 by 24-inch paper." She held up a clipboard to demonstrate. "Beyond that we only have easels, but they're far more expensive."

"How much?" Curtis asked.

"Well, we have a wide range. I'm afraid the least expensive is 88 dollars."

"Ok. Let's cover the bases. We'll take one easel, one of the clipboards, six sheets of 20 by 24-inch paper, a block of 18 by 24-inch paper, and another set of brushes and another palette (I'm going to give it a try myself)."

"You're not taking a class?" she asked suspiciously.

"No, we're just having fun."

"We like to paint," Sammy added.

When they turned onto Westlake Drive, it was dim but not yet dark (the streetlights were not yet on). He saw Linda on the walk between the front stoop and the driveway and in a split second decided to pull into the driveway instead of to the curb, so they'd be closer to her when Sammy got out. It was a natural thing to do. But had he been looking in the direction in which she was turned, he might have thought differently. Turning in at the hedge at 10 miles an hour, he had only a second to see a man waving to Linda as he backed a Mercedes roadster down the driveway. Curtis slammed on the brakes and laid on the horn. Linda screamed. The two cars jerked violently like bucking horses with a simultaneous screeching of tires, the bumpers dipped and touched with a tiny bump, and they stopped.

The drivers jumped out of their cars to see if there was any damage.

"Sorry," the Mercedes man said, holding his hands up like he was being arrested.

"Jesus, we're lucky the airbag didn't go off!"

They looked at the bumpers. There was just a little scratch on both.

"Christ!" exclaimed Curtis, who habitually used religious epithets despite his complete lack of religious conviction.

"I wasn't expecting.... I'm Roger, by the way."

The man held out his hand. Halfway to extending his own, Curtis felt a sudden revulsion, shrinking at the hypocrisy of shaking the hand of a man whom he so thoroughly despised, yet it was too late and the motion too ingrained. They shook and Curtis took stock of him in an instant. Roger was at least ten years his senior, with a fair amount of grey peppering his thick hair. He was clean-shaven, five inches taller than Curtis, with a strong grip and piercing blue eyes that reminded him of Linda's. He wore pleated khaki pants, a pale blue argyle cashmere sweater, and new tennis shoes. He fixed Curtis with a wary but benign gaze, then smiled broadly with perfect teeth and waved to Sammy, who waved wanly back.

"Roger...?"

"Anderson."

"Right. I'll get out of your way," Curtis said and sidled back to his car, feeling diminished. He knew it was silly, but in his worn-out jeans and flannel shirt he felt like the poor cousin. He re-parked at the curb as Roger pulled out of the driveway, turned on his lights and, with a wave, drove away down Westlake Drive just as the streetlights winked on.

Linda came down to meet Curtis on the wet sidewalk. "That was awkward."

"I can't believe you're dating."

"We're separated, Curtis."

"What about needing time to be alone?"

"Alone from you."

"I don't get it. What's he got that I haven't got?"

"For one thing, a *lot* more money," she replied flippantly. "No, that was a cheap shot. He's attentive, and he listens to me. He doesn't work 24/7."

"Look, Mom, I drawed a jack-o-lantern," Sammy said, holding out his picture.

"I'm working less, now. I've told Erickson I'm not traveling on weekends anymore."

"That's helpful — a little late, but helpful."

"I've taken up painting."

"I'm happy for you," she answered sarcastically.

"See my jack-o-lantern?" Sammy asked.

Linda took it from him, "That's nice, honey. Good job."

"What are your plans for Halloween?" Curtis asked Linda.

"I guess I'll ask Roger to watch the house, while I take Sammy around the block."

"Don't do that; let me take him out."

She shrugged. "Sure, whatever, if that's what you want."

"That's what I want."

He drove back to the apartment mulling over the change in his status. He had always assumed that the separation was meant as a time for reflection, a time for both of them to look at their priorities and figure out how to save their marriage, not a time for trying out replacement spouses. "Oh, damn," he muttered, as tears blurred his vision. He hated being at the mercy of unbidden emotion, but he couldn't help it; he knew what he was losing, and the future looked bleak and lonely.

Chapter 8

Monday October 20 – Sunday October 26, 2008

Wednesday morning Curtis awoke to his cell phone playing Ode to Joy. Beethoven is either jumping for joy or rolling over in his grave, Curtis thought. The windowless bedroom was dark and he had to switch on the light to find the phone. A glance at the clock told him all he needed to know. "Sorry," he blurted, "I forgot to set my alarm. Come on up and have a cup of coffee while I get ready."

He buzzed the lobby door open for Elliot, unlocked the apartment door and jumped into the shower.

When he emerged from the bedroom a few minutes later, tie and shoes in hand, he saw Elliot standing in front of the easel.

"What the hell is this?" Elliot asked.

"A dream I had."

"Looks like a nightmare. I wouldn't show that to your therapist."

"What's wrong with it?"

"Well...it's...it's..." Elliot shook his head. "It's awfully phallic."

"It's more like a lighthouse."

"Whatever you say, cap'n." While Curtis put on his shoes, Elliot picked up a picture of a dinosaur. "Hey, this is good — Sammy do this?"

"Yeah, he likes dinosaurs."

"What kid doesn't? Still, this is pretty good," he said appraisingly. "There's something about it. I don't know, but I can't see Sophie drawing anything like this."

"She's a year younger."

"Yeah, but still...."

"How'd your trip go?"

"Oh, lord. Our flight on Saturday was canceled, so we were stuck in the airport all day trying to go standby. We finally gave up and flew out Sunday instead. Davidson was in a lousy mood; he bet against the dollar and his clients are pissed."

"Can't be worse than stocks."

"No, I suppose not. What did you do all weekend?"

"Stayed in with Sammy. Painted. Oh, and I met Roger, the guy Linda's been seeing."

"What's he like?"

"I don't get it. I don't get what she sees in him."

"Describe him to me."

As they went down to the car and started off for work, Curtis tried to describe his fleeting impression of the man, spurred on by Elliot's probing questions.

"So," Elliot said when he was finished, "why do you think she's attracted to him?"

"I don't know — money?"

"No, be realistic."

"I am being realistic."

"Okay, maybe there is some of that; women value security. But look at him like a package you're trying to sell. He drives a fancy car. He wears nice clothes."

"So?"

"He comes gift wrapped, while you're in brown paper. He's better at marketing himself. And then he pays her the compliment of being attentive. I'm guessing you didn't continue to court Linda after you were married, and it made her feel unappreciated."

"It's a two-way street," Curtis said defensively. But it was true, he had stopped doing the little things he'd done in the beginning. He couldn't remember the last time he'd bought her flowers, or even cut flowers from their garden. Or bought her a surprise present. And they hadn't been away alone together since Sammy was two. "After a while marriage becomes more like a business relationship and less like a romance," Curtis mused. "It's all about paying bills and saving money."

"And fixing things around the house," Elliot added.

"Running errands."

"Coordinating schedules."

"It kills the romance."

"It's bad marketing," Elliot concluded.

Back at the apartment he shed his suit, poured himself a glass of Alsatian Pinot Gris and set about a project he'd been putting off, a collage of bits and pieces of Sammy's throw away doodles and pictures. He put aside a watercolor on which water had spilled, blurring he paint into a beautiful abstract of barely discernible buildings, and a painting with vermilion clouds streaked with wispy grass blade strokes. Neither was attractive as a whole, but by isolating parts he was able to piece together an interesting design.

It was all Sammy's work, but the way Curtis had cut and mounted them made the whole, better than the parts. Curtis's own paintings were getting better, too. He had never considered himself particularly creative. He hadn't painted anything since grade school. He could draw reasonably well, copying whatever he saw before him, never anything imagined. So he found it fascinating that his paintings took on a life of their own. Through his own lack of expertise, when he added color to a penciled scene it never came out the way he thought it would or should. It was always different, and sometimes better than he'd expected. There was a serendipitous nature to art that he found liberating.

Ode to Joy rang out from his cell phone. He looked at the caller ID and was momentarily startled, stopped in his tracks by a word: HOME.

It was Linda. "Your parents called again." There was a menacing edge to her voice. She was silent for a long moment. "Don't they have your cell phone number?"

"I don't think so. Linda?"

But she'd already hung up.

He finished the Pinot Gris and poured himself another, then walked over to the wall of glass and looked out into the night. There were lights on the walkway and stairs below, and a spotlight that made the green-gold leaves of the sycamore glow. Across the street about a third of the apartments were lit up. Backlit curtains glowed in a few windows, but most were pulled back, revealing living rooms and kitchens where his unknown neighbors lived and moved like actors on multiple stages.

As he stepped back the window became a mirror, reflecting his own small apartment, the lamp and the chair, the kitchen counter, the gate-leg table. It was a lonely-looking room and he made a mental note to buy some plants. A potted fern and a ficus would work wonders.

He thought he'd put off calling his parents. What would he say? How could he admit his wife had thrown him out? That could wait for another day.

On the last weekend of October, the first storm of the season rolled over the city. Dark clouds lowered, the wind came blustering down the streets and the temperature dropped by fifteen degrees.

Elliot and Curtis worked late on Friday. He picked up Sammy at 7:15, and on the way back to the apartment he stopped at Pier One Imports to buy two teakwood screens. Each screen was made of four hinged panels that were six feet high and two and a half feet wide, and could only be fitted into the car by folding down the rear seats, allowing access through the trunk.

When they got back to the apartment Curtis placed them behind the sofa and effectively divided the one room into a living room on one side, and the kitchen/dining room on the other. It had a pleasing effect. By visually compartmentalizing the room, it felt cozier. It was an interesting exercise in manipulating his emotions by rearranging his environment. He wondered what else he might do to make himself feel better.

That night they watched a DVD of The Secret of NIMH. Sammy watched from the sofa bed and Curtis from his easy chair. They'd both seen the video half a dozen times before, but it never failed to delight. The voices of the characters were expressive — menacing or appealing by turns. It was a drama of duplicity, death, danger and fear, pitted against gallantry, sacrifice, integrity and hope. And now for the first time, they both noticed the background painting. The farm was mostly rendered in watercolors. Rich colors with soft edges. It was funny how you never noticed things until you had a personal connection. It was like when you bought a new car and suddenly you saw the same model everywhere.

Saturday morning was dark and chill. Thunder cracked overhead and wind-driven rain lashed the roof in waves. Sheets of rain blew down the length of the street. Sammy stood at the window looking out at the storm, too fascinated to be frightened. He had a bird's eye view from the eighth floor, out across the chasm of the courtyard and street, over the tops of the trees to the facing building, and further out across the rubble-strewn lot beside it to the backyards of the buildings that fronted Francis Boulevard. Water streamed down the window, distorting everything outside.

"Where do birds go when it rains?" Sammy asked.

"Home to their nests, I guess. And under ledges. And lots of birds fly south to warmer climates."

"I dreamed I could fly."

"I have that dream sometimes."

Curtis put on a Stan Getz recording and slouched in his easy chair as he browsed through Beginning Watercolors, by Serge Dvorak. The introduction was encouraging. "Listen to this, Sammy" he said, and read aloud, "'No one paints exactly like you. The way you paint is a combination of your individual vision, temperament and technique. Mastering the techniques presented in this book will not necessarily make you a better artist, but they will give you more tools with which to express your own unique vision. We are familiar with viewing paintings as subjective observers. But just as watching a ballgame is different than playing the game, as an artist you'll find that making a painting is different from passively observing a painting. For the artist the final product is often less important (and less satisfying) than the process. Don't get discouraged if you have trouble duplicating the exercises in this book; you may master some techniques in a day; others may take years. The important thing is to have fun along the way. Enjoy the process.'" Have fun. That's what Miss Walzer had said.

There were a lot of tips on each page. There was more to learn than he'd anticipated. What he liked best were the step-by-step examples. On one four-page spread he could see a penciled line drawing of a shack, followed by the addition of the sky and meadow, then pink blooming flowers that climbed up the side and onto the roof of the shack, along with lavender flowers out in the meadow, and on the final panel the grey weathered boards of the shack. Each panel described one of the four different techniques: wet on wet, wet on dry, dry on wet and dry on dry.

While the rain poured down Curtis and Sammy painted with watercolors on the gate-leg table. Curtis was discouraged. The colors were either too thin or too thick. Paint ran toward the bottom of the paper where it pooled along the edge. His hand was unsteady, and one stroke appeared brighter than another. What he lacked in technique was matched only by his lack of imagination.

"This watercoloring is hard."

"I like it like that, Dad. The colors are pretty."

"It's not as good as yours, though."

"You'll get better," Sammy said encouragingly. The colors in his own painting were unfettered by reality; his buildings were dark blue, red and purple. His windows were pale blue and yellow; the trees were orange.

That evening Curtis browsed his CDs in search of something soothing. He selected a compilation of Eric Satie piano pieces. Satie's music could be ethereal or jarring, so listening to an entire compilation was out of the question. He programmed Trois Gymnopedie, Les Gnossiennes 1 – 6 and Je Te Veux to repeat. The cover of the album was a line portrait of the composer by Henri Matisse. Curtis sat in his easy chair and took up his pencil and sketchpad. He made a line drawing of Sammy on the floor playing with old-fashioned wooden blocks.

"What're you drawing?" Sammy asked.

"You."

"Let me see."

"Hold still."

When he finished, he called Sammy over to see the results. "See this portrait?" Curtis asked, showing him the Matisse. Sammy shook his head. "This is a picture that Henri Matisse drew of his friend, Eric Satie (the guy who composed the piano music we're listening to). They were both Frenchman who lived at the beginning of the last century. Matisse was a painter, but he also did these line drawings. I tried to do this whole portrait without lifting the pencil from the paper. You want to try that? You do one of me. Try to keep it to no more than four lines."

Curtis sat still, staring at their reflection in the window, musing on the changes a year had wrought. In a minute Sammy jumped up and brought him the portrait. Curtis laughed with delight at the squiggles. "Now, let me do you again."

Sunday a soft rain sifted down the sky, adding to yesterday's puddles. In the morning, they had baths and played horsey until Curtis's knees were sore. In the afternoon they painted while watching a DVD of The Black Stallion. Sammy spent half an hour carefully drawing a blue, long-necked dinosaur in pastel on his biggest sheet of watercolor paper.

"That's a really nice dinosaur," Curtis commented. "Why the long face?"

"You didn't hanged any of my pitchers on the wall."

"Pictures," Curtis corrected. "You're right, we should hang some of these paintings, but let's get them framed first." Sammy brightened at that prospect. "Hey, it's Halloween next Friday. Draw me a jack-o-lantern."

The rain abated toward sunset. When he dropped off Sammy that evening there were no lights on in the house. In the orange glow from the streetlamp on the corner, they could make out the edge of the paved path that split the front lawn on its way up to the front stoop. The door was locked, and when he tried his key he found the lock had been changed. He rang the doorbell. A light came on in the bedroom window overhead. Another light from the stairway illuminated the pebbled glass by the side of the door. Then the porch light came on and the door opened. Linda was wrapped in a satin robe, her hair disheveled and her forehead scrunched with pain.

"Hey," she said in a tired voice.

"Hi Mom," Sammy said and scooted past his mother.

"See you next week," Curtis called after him.

As she started to close the door Curtis said quickly, "Can we talk?"

She leaned against the door jam and her words came slowly, thickly, as though drawn from a cesspool. "Not now, Curtis; I have a migraine. I can't talk to anybody right now."

The door closed quietly. The porch light blinked out.

Chapter 9

Wednesday October 29 – Sunday
November 2, 2008

Passing the art store on the way home each day that week, he would have to restrain himself from asking Elliot to stop. He didn't really need anything; like a kid in a toy store, he just wanted to look.

On Friday, October 31st, they left work early. Elliot dropped off Curtis and hurried off to help Sophie carve her pumpkin. Curtis changed and followed twenty minutes later. He arrived just before 6:00 pm., as the sun disappeared over the horizon.

Linda answered the door in a witch's costume. "Don't even say a word," she commanded.

"I wasn't even thinking it," Curtis said. It would have been only too easy to make a snide remark, but the truth was that she made a beautiful witch — blond, blue-eyed with translucent skin. And no warts.

But what struck him was that she was wearing a costume that had been put in a box that he'd stashed in the rafters in the garage, and she would never have climbed a ladder herself to get the box down. That was *his* job, *had* been his job, and the only explanation was that she'd asked Roger to do it. He felt violated. Roger had been going through his things. And they weren't only *his* things; they were his *family's* things. The costumes and Halloween decorations belonged to all of them and communally to the house. Separation, it seemed, was so much more than the separation of just two people. It was also the separation of all of the things that carried within them all of the memories of their life as a family. To cut it away required a skillful surgeon with a very sharp scalpel, but they'd forgone the surgeon for a do-it-yourself operation that was far more brutal.

Sammy came wheeling into the room in his pterodactyl costume. It was made of felt in various shades of orange — a long beak, wide eyes, and wings that fitted onto his arms.

"Hey, Scooter," Curtis said. "Are you ready to carve a pumpkin?"

Linda answered, "We did that yesterday."

Another prerogative preempted.

"You can put them out on the stoop and light them," she offered as consolation.

He did, while Linda set a bowl of candy, light sticks and skull rings on the floor by the plastic cauldron at the front door.

"I forgot the dry ice," Curtis admitted.

"That's ok; Roger brought some. It's in the kitchen."

"He's here?"

"Yes. I asked him. He's in the living room."

Curtis felt a terrible hurt and jealousy sweep over him. This was all going way too fast. He didn't have time to readjust.

"I can't believe you let him get into our stuff."

"You better get used to it."

The words stung. Sometimes she could make him feel so small and insignificant. "You know you're killing me. Right now I feel so...god, I feel so *angry!*" These last words came at a volume he instantly knew would draw a negative response.

"Outside," she said evenly, and gently pushed him out onto the stoop. "No arguing in front of Sammy."

Barely restraining the impulse to strangle her, he shook with anger. "You can tell Roger to keep his fucking hands off my stuff." He liked to think he was smart enough to articulate the nuances of his emotions. But he was unable to suppress the hostility that had been bubbling under the surface since she'd banished him from his house.

"Maybe you should leave," she warned.

He pushed her away dismissively, instantly disappointed by his inexpressible fury. Roger came through the front door with a box of dry ice to dump in the plastic cauldron. Then he saw what he'd walked in on. "Oh," he said.

Curtis thought that simple word was becoming the refrain of his life. "Oh" stood for so many things. "Oh, shit!" "Oh, god!" "Oh, my!" "Oh, no." Oh, oh, oh.

"Bitch," Curtis said quietly.

"If you can't control yourself, I'll call the cops and have you removed," she said.

Roger put the box of dry ice on the stoop and turned back into the house.

Almost as quickly as the anger had flared up, it was gone, replaced by regret. *Oh, shit*, Curtis thought, *I handled that really badly.* About as badly as he could have imagined.

He filled the cauldron with water and dumped the dry ice in. Creamy white vapor bubbled up over the rim and spilled over the side.

Sammy came flying through the room with outstretched arms. Curtis wondered if he'd heard any of the altercation, but Sammy seemed unperturbed. He was fascinated by the dry ice vapor and spent several minutes listening to the cold water boil, and sticking his hands into the dense cold billows.

"Can we go out now?" Sammy asked.

Curtis left Linda to man the front door and took Sammy by the hand, feeling like a criminal in his old neighborhood.

It was damp and chill, just three days past the new moon. They wandered the streets following dark forms and giggling ghouls. Sammy was excited just to be allowed out in the cold night, but Curtis's heart wasn't in it.

His thoughts kept looping back to the fight. He'd reacted badly, but how did she expect him to act, given the circumstances? He fantasized how their next conversation might play out:

"*There is no excuse," she would say.*

"*What did you expect? Last time I checked, we were still married. Do you expect me to welcome another man into our bed?*"

"*First of all, we are married in name only. Second, I'll date whomever I choose, and I'll share my bed with whomever I choose. You are going to be civil or I'll get a Restraining Order.*"

In this he was prescient, for that was the first thing she actually did say to him when he and Sammy returned to find her at the house alone.

"...or I'll get a Restraining Order."

"Don't invite him to family affairs."

"We don't have a family anymore. And I don't care if it's Roger or somebody else, I'll invite whomever I choose, whenever I choose. Are we clear?"

The supercilious sarcasm made him want to strangle her, but he kept his tongue and his anger in check.

"Get Sammy ready. I'll wait in the car."

In the cold, dark quiet of the car he watched the last of the witches and hobgoblins, pirates and princesses, cartoon characters and super heroes make the rounds of the neighborhood. He recognized a few of them, mostly older kids at this hour, unaccompanied by their parents.

He enjoyed the little kids, kids Sammy's age and younger, for whom Halloween was still an adventure, but he distrusted the older kids, owing to his own memories. He and his friends had done a lot of stupid things, goading each other on in a contest for adolescent supremacy, succumbing to peer pressure to perform mindless petty vandalism, scare little kids, toilet paper a girl's house. And one time lighting a bag of dog shit on fire on Mr. Doliva's front porch, so they could laugh as he came out and stomped on the warm, gooey shit. That, in retrospect, actually had been funny.

As an adult, he'd put in an effort to get in the spirit. One year he went in drag, wearing a dress, wig and female mask. He'd walked into his neighbor's houses, flirting and causing a sensation as they tried to guess who it was (he'd thoroughly embarrassed Pablo "Paul" Poblador by dancing with him). Another Halloween he enlarged a digital photo to make a mask of Elliot's face. This year, however, he wished for anonymity.

Earlier, when he was walking the neighborhood with Sammy, he'd recognized Elliot and Sophie's voices in the dark and had slunk away, not wanting conversation in the mood he was in. He'd skipped all of the houses of their closest friends — the Fines, the Veeder's, the Samuelsons, the Pobladors and the Pearles. He wasn't sure whose friends they were now (how did you divide up friends?). And he didn't want to see them living their same undisturbed lives, while his own had been turned upside down.

He was sorry now he had agreed to move out. In moving, he'd lost not only his wife, but his friends and neighbors, his place in the community. It was too much. Far too much.

He knew his anger was counter-productive, but how did you control something you didn't even know was there? It had flared up so suddenly, like a spark in tinder. For a few seconds his conscious, rational self had been completely out of control. He'd had a glimpse of how easily things could go wrong, how the easy-going man next door might end up on the news the next morning, and his neighbors would say, 'He seemed so normal. Just like the rest of us.' Just like the rest of us, because we all have a streak of violence buried under the surface. It scared the hell out of him. This night had so not gone according to plan.

The lit windows of the houses were warm and inviting. Jack-o-lanterns glowed on stoops and porches. Linda handed out candy at the door (the light sticks and skull rings were long gone by this time), and generally took her time getting Sammy ready. It gave Curtis a lot of time to think. She knew how to push his buttons, but he knew on a cerebral level that he should never allow himself to be provoked. It didn't serve him. It wasn't productive; it wouldn't change anything, and it might harm his relationship with Sammy.

He'd calmed down by the time Linda brought Sammy out to the car. He got out and put Sammy in the car. "Stay here; I need to talk to your mama for a minute."

Then he turned to Linda. "Walk with me a minute."

Her natural hesitancy was overcome by his contrite tone and they walked slowly down the damp sidewalk in the pale glow of the streetlamp. The trees were still dripping. "Look, I know I lost it tonight and I'm sorry. I didn't know I would, but I just couldn't stand the thought of somebody, anybody, going through our stuff. Then I was thinking about Christmas, and what it would be like for someone else to be hanging our ornaments, and it's like I've died. Like someone else is living my life. Can you understand that?"

"It doesn't excuse your anger, Curtis; you really scared me. You should've seen the look in your eyes."

"I know, I'm sorry. I think the only thing to do is sit down and make a list of things that are off-limits. It's not that any of it's valuable; it just has..."

"...associations?"

"Exactly."

"Ok, fine; you set the date."

He sighed and felt a weight lift from his shoulders — just one brick, but a weight nonetheless.

As though by that telepathy peculiar to intertwined lives, they reached the boundary of their course and turned in unison back towards the car.

Curtis cleared his throat. "Can I ask you something?"

"You can ask, but I won't guarantee I'll answer."

"Did you know Roger before I moved out?"

"Yes, but that's not the real question, is it? What you really want to know is if I slept with him before you moved out, and the answer is no. I never cheated on you, ever."

He knew that was as much as he would ever get from her, and he knew he'd have to resign himself to never truly knowing the moment their marriage had ended in her mind. Was it something he'd said, or left unsaid? Was it a look? A tone of voice? A personal habit or idiosyncrasy she'd overlooked for years, that now drove her crazy? He might never know.

At the bookstore Saturday they made a beeline for the children's section, Sammy pulling his father by the hand.

"Come on; you'll see, I can read."

Sammy sat cross-legged in front of the Little Golden Books kiosk. He opened *The Little Red Caboose*, by Marian Potter, with pictures by Tibor Gergely. He read aloud, haltingly but steadily, "The little red caboose always came last."

Curtis sat on a stool and looked over Sammy's shoulder, helping on the hard-to-sound-out words (words like "tight" and "through"), but Sammy didn't need much help. The words were simple and there was a lot of repetition.

The pictures were wonderful evocations of a by-gone era. The style was American Primitive and seemed to be rendered in watercolors, Curtis thought. At least the ponds and rivers and ocean were rendered in watercolors. He was less sure of other elements, which were bright and crisply edged and seemed so uniform in color as to hide any brushstrokes. The old-fashioned steam train sped through the landscape on each page, passing adults and children engaged in work and recreation. On one page the middle part of the train passed a circus complete with a lion and elephants and clowns. In the background, people frolicked in the lake, swimming, diving, and rowing boats. It was an idealized world. The people and the animals were all happy — happy in work, happy in play, happy in their camaraderie and united in their love for, and admiration of, the train.

Perspective was somewhat capricious. For example, a forested mountain might have upon its summit a big horned sheep that was taller than the tallest tree, a car might appear as big as a bus, and portions of the scene were flattened, all of which added to the charm. What Curtis liked best was the perception of depth. Roads and rivers wound around hills that diminished in size from foreground to background, and always on a distant hill there was a little town with houses and factories and steeples, and on one a castle, and on another an onion-domed church that must have come from Gergely's memories of his native Hungary, rather than any scene he'd encountered in the New World.

When he was finished, Sammy twisted around and looked up at his father with pride.

"That was terrific, Sammy. I'm so proud of you. I'll tell you what — I may not always buy you candy or a toy, but from now on, until you're all grown up, every time we go out you can have any book you want."

It was the same pact his mother had made with each of her children, and they'd all ended up inveterate and voracious readers. Even his brother, who had been an indifferent student, was never without a book.

Sammy picked out two books for himself to read. Curtis chose Arnold Lobel's *Frog and Toad are Friends* to read to Sammy, and the latest Philip Roth novel for himself.

The woman behind the counter was about Linda's age, short, dark and pudgy, with black hair that had been hacked short, as though by miniature machete-wielding explorers blazing a trail across her scalp. No doubt she had paid good money to a stylist for this abuse. Her ears were each studded with six silver hoops. Her left eyebrow was likewise pierced. Her eyelashes were thick with mascara, and he noticed as they passed the books and credit card back and forth, that the inside of her wrists were tattooed in script: *Ignorance* on the left wrist, *Want* on the right.

In his mind, he heard the Ghost of Christmas Present intoning to Scrooge, "This boy is Ignorance. This girl is Want. Beware of them both, and all of their degree, but most of all beware this boy, for on his brow I see that written which is Doom...." A bigger contrast to Linda could scarcely be imagined. If he let her get away, if they never reconciled, how would he ever find anyone even remotely as smart and pretty and desirable?

That evening they lay on the sofa bed and watched *The Secret of Roan Inish*, a fanciful tale set on the remote coast of Donegal, Ireland.

"That was a good story," Sammy declared when it was over.

"What did you like about it?"

"The little boy came home again."

"That was sweet," Curtis agreed. It was a reassuring tale of loss, faith and redemption.

"Are you ever going to come home?"

"I don't know. I want to come home, but I don't think your mother wants me to right now. Maybe later."

Sammy was silent for half a minute, then said, "Can I have a dog?"

"We don't have room for a dog. Besides, I'm gone all day."

"Zack has a rabbit."

"You can't potty train a rabbit."

The phone played *Ode to Joy*. It was Linda, asking if she could take Sammy to visit her mother the following weekend. Wanting to keep it civil, Curtis agreed.

"You know I'm planning to take Sammy with me on Thanksgiving," he said.

"I assumed so."

Linda negotiated for Christmas, Curtis for the day after Christmas, New Year's Eve, and New Year's Day. He liked talking to her; she had a beautiful voice when she wasn't upset with him, and having a reasonable conversation gave him a glimmer of hope that they might salvage their relationship.

"You *have* told your parents?"

"Of course," he said, making a mental reminder to make the call.

"Have you made a list of your things that are off-limits?" she said.

"No, I need to look through things. Maybe when I bring Sammy back tomorrow."

"I have a house to show until 3:30."

"We can be there at 3:45."

He hung up the phone, and Sammy picked up where he'd left off. "Danny has a hamster."

"You don't want a hamster. When I was your age my best friend had a hamster. The mother ate her babies. Yuk! No hamsters. Now it's time for you to sleep."

"Read me a story."

"Okay, but just one; it's late."

He read *Mr. Wishing Went Fishing*, by Irma Wilde, with pictures by George Wilde. The prose was worthy of Hemingway with its short, declarative sentences. It began, "Mr. Wishing was a funny little man who lived in a house by the sea. It was a tiny house with just one room," (almost like this apartment, Curtis thought). Mr. Wishing looked for a friend for his pet fish, Skipper. He caught a starfish and a crab for Skipper, but Skipper didn't like either of them. Then he found another little fish he named Flipper, and Skipper was happy to have a new friend to play with. "'I'm a lucky, lucky man,' said Mr. Wishing, 'to have two pets like Skipper and Flipper, and my ship-shape little room.'" The illustrations were marvelous, the story beautifully and simply told, and when it was over Sammy was asleep.

No one was home when they arrived back on Westlake Drive, late on Sunday afternoon. "I don't have a key, champ; your mom changed the locks."

"I have one," Sammy said. He fished it out of the outside pocket of his backpack. Curtis unlocked the door and, as Sammy bounded inside, he discreetly pocketed the key. It might come in handy, and his name was still on the mortgage.

"Your mom's taking you to see your grandma Louise next weekend, so I won't see you for two weeks."

"Can you come?"

"No, your mother doesn't want me to come. But you can have fun with Sadie." Sadie was Louise's Golden Retriever. "Draw a picture of her for me."

The kitchen was as immaculate as ever. It stood in contrast to his own kitchen with its photos and drawings stuck to the refrigerator, the counter strewn with a loaf of bread, salt and pepper shakers, spices and olive oil, and the sink filled with an assortment of dishes, cups and flatware waiting to be rinsed and transferred to the dishwasher. Since she'd learned how to stage a house for sale, Linda kept nothing extraneous on the countertops, walls or refrigerator, unless one counted an artistically arranged bowl of fruit, or a teapot calendar with her schedule penciled-in three weeks in advance. She was a little obsessive, he thought, in a way that made her more effective.

After Linda came home with a load of groceries, Curtis wandered through the rooms taking note of the things he wanted kept off-limits. He wasn't excessively territorial, he thought, but he didn't want Roger, or any other man who might come around, sitting at his desk in the study. His books were off-limits. The clothes he'd left behind. His ski equipment and bicycle. "We'll get the Christmas tree *together* with Sammy, and *I'll* put it up. I don't want anyone else touching the Christmas ornaments. I'd like a few for a tree in the apartment." Anything else she was free to share with whomever she wished.

"You could come over to the apartment for Christmas," he offered hopefully.

"No, I don't think so."

"Or Christmas eve?"

"No."

When Curtis was leaving, Sammy ran up with a silhouette of a pumpkin cut out of orange construction paper. "This is for you."

"Thanks, I'll hang it on the refrigerator. Give me a hug." Curtis carried him on his shoulders out to the car. The sun had already set. The highest clouds had turned pink, and a contrail cut like a white scar across the cheek of the sky. Their breaths made steam in the cold air.

"I don't want you to go," Sammy said, resting his head on his father's shoulder.

"I know. I wish you could stay with me, but I have to go to work everyday, and you have to go to school. And don't forget, you can call me anytime." He put Sammy down on the sidewalk. He reached into the backseat of his car and brought out a sketchbook and a set of colored pencils. "Here, take your sketchbook to your grandma's; it'll fit in your backpack. And here are some pencils (your mom doesn't like paint). Draw me a picture a day, and next time you come over we'll pick out the best one and hang it on the wall. Now go back inside; it's cold out here. Love you."

Chapter 10

Tuesday November 4 – Friday November 7, 2008

There was a lot of nervous tension ahead of the election, though most of the office staff conceded that it would have little, if any, effect on the stock market, as the economic problems would take a long time to unravel, and the new president could do nothing until February at the earliest.

Curtis was still registered to vote at his home address. After Elliot dropped him off at the apartment, he changed and followed on to Elliot's house. Turning onto Westlake Drive, he passed his house. Lights were on in the kitchen. He slowed, peering through the windows, trying to get a glimpse of his old life, and pulled into Elliot's driveway.

Vicky had voted in the morning. Elliot and Curtis walked the four blocks to the middle school, where they stood in a line of over 50 to vote. Afterwards, they went to the Samuelsons, where a good number of his former neighbors gathered around a big flat-screen television watching election returns, drinking wine, and eating junk food. Fred Van Gleason poured a glass for Curtis and said, "We missed you at badminton last week."

Overhearing the comment, Doug Veeder added, "Just because you moved, doesn't mean you can't come back and hang in the 'hood. Elliot says you're just 15 minutes away."

"More like 20," Curtis replied. "I've been busy with Sammy on the weekends."

"Bring him along," Fred said.

"Call me, next time."

They both said they would call, and Curtis felt sure they meant it.

Elliot had been eavesdropping. "It's like I said, 'I don't know why it's the husband who always has to move out.' You notice nobody invited Linda."

It might have been the wine, or the way his neighbors inquired with interest about his new apartment, or watching history unfold together, but whatever the reason, for the rest of the evening Curtis felt a warm glow of acceptance and camaraderie. There would be no need to divide up their friends; they were all his friends.

Chapter 11
Saturday November 8 – Monday November 10, 2008

Linda was having a cup of coffee with her mother in the kitchen of her mother's house, when Sammy came in with Sadie, a Golden Retriever.

"Can I have a dog?"

"No, I'm not ready for that kind of commitment. You can play with Sadie while we're here, but I'm not getting any dog. A dog is a lot of work and expense. Take her out in the backyard." Sammy and Sadie banged out the screen door into the warm morning. The scent of grass wafted back through the screen.

"Curtis is a nice enough young man," Louise said. "You could do worse. Ask yourself why you married him in the first place."

"He was smart. He was grounded. He knew what he wanted and how to get it."

"So, what's changed? Why now?"

"I don't know. Nothing's changed. He's just so into work, even when he's home, he's not home — you know what I mean? Not mentally. It's been going on for a long time. I would have dumped him three years ago, but I couldn't afford it; he was making all the money. Now I have my own career; I don't need him anymore."

"Just remember, there are always two sides to every argument."

"Exactly, that's what I'm saying. There's no discussing it with him, because he never sees my side. He never listens. God, I've tried. It's like he sees my lips moving and doesn't hear my voice; he just keeps on doing what he's doing. He never changes."

"Far be it for me to stand in the way of true love, but it's been my experience that men never do change. You either take them as they are, or you leave them."

The phone rang while Curtis was reading the latest Time magazine. It was Elliot, saying that the neighbors were getting together for a barbecue at the badminton court that afternoon, and asking if he'd like to come.

The badminton and bocce ball courts were two doors down in the adjoining backyards of the Van Gleasons and Veeders. It was a bright, clear, late autumn day, warm in the sun, cool in the shadows, with light swirling winds. Badminton season was all but over. Cold weather would be setting in soon. This would likely be their last barbecue until spring.

His neighbors formed a fairly homogeneous group of between 27 and 37 years of age, all living in single-family dwellings with children (except for the Van Gleasons, who were childless), who favored a similar range of favorite entertainments and consumer products, as befitted their ages, education and income bracket.

As Curtis skirted the back of the Pobladors' and approached the Veeders', he surveyed before him a scene of such domestic conviviality that he felt a pang of loss, as though far from being a part of the group he was now an outsider, an unwanted interloper. He slackened his pace and checked his watch (a quarter past one), and was considering turning back, when Fred Van Gleason, a tall, thin man in sandals, shorts, polo shirt, micro-fleece vest and baseball cap, spied him and raised a beer in salute. Nothing to be done now but make his appearance, and if the awkward feeling persisted, to make a hasty departure.

The infants were sprawled asleep in a portable playpen. Other children were scattered across the lawn and in the sand of the bocce ball court, paired up by sex and age. The older children were missing, perhaps preferring to avoid the excruciating embarrassment of seeing their old parents interact with other old parents, continually and inexplicably making fools of themselves.

Among the husbands gathered around Doug Veeder's picnic table, were two financial advisors, a banker, contractor, demographer, attorney, recording engineer, importer and tile shop owner.

The wives lounged around a round glass table in a circle of lawn chairs under an umbrella. There were several bottles of wine on the table, and a platter of Vienna sausages with hot sauce. A mutt puppy was tethered to one of the table legs. Two older Labradors wandered aimlessly around the table, hoping for a scrap of food. Among the women were a nurse, an artist, an attorney, a high school teacher, a V.P. of Marketing, an accountant, and two stay-at-home moms who had previously been in public relations.

As Curtis approached, Roddy Flynn turned, grinned and, feigning an upper-crust English accent, cried, "Captain, oh, my captain!"

"Mister Flynn," Curtis responded, snapping a military salute.

"Here he is," said Doug Veeder.

"There's beer," Samuelson offered.

Curtis bent to the cooler, listening to pick up the thread of the conversation he'd interrupted. It revolved around the economy, a subject he was hoping to avoid on the weekend. "It's a house-of-cards," Elliot observed. "The really shocking thing is how everything is so tied together globally."

"Time for male bonding," Mary Veeder called after them half facetiously, as they made off for the courts.

Beverly Flynn grunted and hooted, mimicking a chimpanzee dominance display.

The husbands smiled good-naturedly, graciously admitting the basic tenet: Badminton, like most sports, was a bonding ritual of sorts. But the women couldn't appreciate the subtleties, Curtis thought. While women found their place in the social hierarchy determined by beauty, ornamentation and conversation, men found theirs through sport. It wasn't so much about winning, as it was learning your strengths and weaknesses, and working to maximize the effectiveness of your set of talents, while minimizing the effectiveness of your opponent. It was a kind of dance. After you'd played against someone for awhile, you knew something of the way he approached life; you knew who took charge, who was calculating, who could adjust to new circumstances, who understood strategy, who made excuses, who was hot-headed, who choked in the clutch, who you could trust to protect your back.

Curtis's strengths included his serve and his reflexes, but he had a weak backhand and was only marginally successful at returning slams aimed at his face. Paired with Flynn, Curtis got into the rhythm of the game quickly. They were good at anticipating each other's moves, and Flynn had a devastating backhand. They played against Veeder, who had a lightning slam, but let emotions get the better of him when he was behind late in the game, and Poblador, who played a mostly defensive game and had a good dink that changed the tempo. After winning handily, Curtis chose to sit out, so that others could play.

He went in search of a glass of wine.

"Oh, here he comes, poor dear," Roberta Pearle cooed. "Come here and give me a hug." She held out open arms, but didn't get up. He bent down to receive his hug and a peck on the lips.

"Pull up a chair, Mr. Cooke," Annette Jancee said. She was originally from South Carolina, and invariably addressed her friends by Mr. and Mrs.

"Is there a glass?"

"On the table, dear," Roberta pointed.

He poured a glass of Pinot Noir and pulled up a chair, tuning into the conversation as Ellen Samuelson was saying, "Our cat is having a conniption fit since we got the puppy."

"Sounds like Dennis and Stevie," Mary Veeder said, referring to her 2-year-old and 1-year-old respectively.

"Really?" Vicky Fine piped in, offering by way of contrast that "Sophie just adores her little brother."

"It's because they're so close in age," Annette suggested, referring to the Veeders.

"And they're boys," Donna Van Gleason said. "My brothers used to fight like cats and dogs, but they always took care of me." She lit a cigarette. "Of course, my father would have whipped them good, if they'd hurt his little girl."

Roberta turned to Curtis and patted his hand. "You doin' all right?"

"As good as can be expected."

"Yeah?"

"Yeah; it's not so bad. My personal life is in harmony with the general chaos of the universe. I miss the neighborhood."

"Well, we miss you too, Mr. Cooke," Annette Jancee said sympathetically.

"Someone said she's at her mother's this week?"

"Yup."

"She's not sick, your mother-in-law?"

"Not that I know of."

"I wish my mother-in-law would get sick," Annette said, "something short and fatal."

"Ouch!" Donna laughed, blowing a stream of smoke above her head. "I see you really like the old biddy."

"I know I shouldn't be so harsh, but it's hard to like someone who disapproves of you; she never misses a chance to make a snide remark."

Comments about mothers-in-law, both approving and disapproving, ran around the table and petered out. The Vienna sausages were passed around. Vicky picked Nathan out of the playpen and began feeding him Cheerios. Curtis poured another glass of Pinot Noir. The puppy whimpered and strained at his leash until Anita (accidentally on purpose) dropped a sausage in front of him. The older dogs rested their heads on their owners' laps, looking pitiful and hopeful.

"My grandmother's worried about her investments," Ellen said. "It's tough being on a fixed income."

"Does she have health insurance?" Mary asked.

"She better; I don't know; I better ask. God forbid she should get sick and move in with me. We do not get along. She's so-o-o ...friggin' ...petty."

Curtis finished his glass and removed himself from the table. He looked toward the badminton court, listened as Flynn announced the score, and lay down on the grass, pulling his cap over his eyes. It was only then that he noticed the breeze. It swept over him in intermittent waves, caressing his bare arms and cheeks. He opened his eyes under the dome of his cap, and listened to the ebb and flow of the conversation, and to the shouts of self-reproach and victorious glee from the badminton and bocce ball courts, and eventually his eyes grew heavy and he dozed.

He awoke and found the conversation had strayed to a recent trip the Pearles had taken to New Orleans.

He played two more games, pairing up first with Jancee, with whom he played reasonably well, then with Poblador, with whom he was never in sync.

Doug Veeder fired up the gas barbecue and began cooking. Curtis poured a glass of cheap Chardonnay and sat down once again, as the men joined in the mix of conversation. It was a convivial group. The food was good, and the conversation lively.

Glancing around the table, he was reminded of Renoir's "Luncheon of the Boating Party," and wondered how difficult it would be to paint them. It was one of his favorite Impressionist paintings, as it caught one of those informal but exquisite moments in time. It was 1881, and the party sat and stood around tables, talking and drinking wine and enjoying their camaraderie, reveling in their leisure time together. The clothing was different, but this scene before him was not so unlike that boating party, 127 years and an ocean apart. It was something to savor. Their conversations were not profound (though they could be on occasion); it was enough to share the ordinary pleasures and trials of everyday life, to go through it with company instead of alone.

By the time the party began to break up around four-thirty, Curtis was satiated.

Elliot invited him over for coffee. Curtis helped gather up the trash, and then he followed the Fines across the street.

Curtis and Elliot drank coffee and played chess, but Curtis was too tired to concentrate and made foolish errors.

Elliot eyed his friend's glazed eyes. "You don't look up to driving back to the city tonight. Why don't you stay here?"

"I don't want to be a bother."

"You don't want to get into an accident either."

"Linda's not home. I'll just sleep in my own bed for a change," he said, thinking that she'd probably be pissed, though in the mood he was in, he didn't much care. What could it hurt? He was still paying the mortgage, after all. It was as much his house as hers, and though he knew she would begrudge him a night in his own house, he felt she was just being spiteful these days.

It was after 9 o'clock as he crossed the street. Lights glowed warmly in all of the houses on the street, save the windows of his own house, which were veiled in darkness. The house seemed to lurk forlornly in the shadows, a cold, empty and unwelcoming presence. At the curb, he stopped to extract the mail from the mailbox and marched up to the front door. The orange sodium-vapor streetlamp cast just enough light through sparse leaves that he could see the keyhole if he didn't look directly at it. He flipped on the entry light, leaned his racket against the wall in the entry, and by habit pried off his shoes. He'd performed this same action on numerous occasions, coming home late from the neighbors and trying his best not to wake Linda or Sammy. If the house had been quiet then, it was now as silent as the grave. He wandered the lower floor, feeling an emotional bond with his house, his first house, the walls that encompassed his life, his ersatz skin. Flipping on lights, he came to the kitchen, where the hum of the refrigerator gave a welcome semblance of animation to the stillness.

He sorted the mail, making piles of catalogues, bills and junk mail to be recycled. He slid a finger under the flap of the VISA bill and scanned the pages. $4,234.89: Safeway, Chevron, some minor miscellaneous charges. The major purchases were Nordstrom ($379), QVC ($266), Saks ($613), Orvis ($343), Victoria Secret ($525), and Willowbrook Farm ($811). He would have to go into their savings account to pay his rent. Victoria Secret? She hadn't worn a negligee since Sammy was born. Willowbrook Farm? The name was on the tip of his tongue.

He filled a tall glass with water and had carried it up to the bedroom when the phone rang. He hesitated at the door, listening as the answering machine in the kitchen told the caller, in his own voice, to leave a message. His mother's flustered voice began, "Linda? Are you there? Well, I suppose you're at the movies, or something. I just called to find out what flight you're coming in on."

Curtis picked up the extension by the bed.

"Hi, Mom, I'm here."

"Hi sweetheart, I just called to get your flight number. Are you staying through the weekend? You've been so hard to get hold of. You've been working too hard."

"I've been busy."

"Your dad wanted to know what flight you're coming in on."

"I don't know; my secretary made the reservations. It's on my computer at work. I'll give you a call on Monday."

"Because your father wants to know when to pick you up."

"I'll call on Monday."

"Is anyone allergic to anything? Is there anything Sammy won't eat? Your brother and sister are coming, but Patrick's had a cold; I hope he's not contagious."

"Don't worry; nobody's allergic to anything, and Sammy doesn't eat much. A little turkey and mashed potatoes will be plenty for him."

"But I'm making a pumpkin pie, and your sister is making a pecan pie."

"It's more than we can eat, I'm sure. Listen, Mom, I have to go; I'm dead tired. I'll give you a call on Monday."

"OK, sweetheart. We're so looking forward to seeing all of you."

He hung up, feeling guilty for not telling her that Linda wasn't coming, but he didn't have the mental energy to have that conversation tonight. It would have to wait until Monday. Two days to think about how to tell his parents.

In the bathroom, he turned on the shower. As he waited for the warm water, he undressed and closed the bathroom door. Two new, white, terrycloth bathrobes hung on the back of the door, one large, one small, each emblazoned with a gold embroidered tree and the words "Willowbrook Farm."

She didn't need time alone, as she'd said; she just wanted him out of the way. He'd been gone only two months and he'd already been replaced. As much as he loathed Roger, his real venom was reserved for Linda. "I always thought she was shopping around," Vicky had said. Was he disposable? Something to be cast off when the new model came out? Oh, he understood being attracted — he'd been attracted to several women since he'd married, even flirted with a couple, but he had never seriously thought of cheating on Linda, let alone leaving her. There were few women he found more physically attractive than Linda, but there were many who were easier to be with. She was sleek as a thoroughbred, and just as skittish. He mulled the thought over as hot water poured over his knotted shoulders.

In the beginning, she had made him feel smart, sexy, worthy, and surely what he saw was merely a reflection of what she actually felt. But time had dulled her appreciation for the familiar. The daily business of making money, marketing, cooking, doing laundry, scheduling appointments, taking care of Sammy, running errands, paying bills, and adjusting for one another's preferences, deficiencies and moods, had taken the luster off of their love and her opinion of him. In her eyes, he now felt ordinary, unattractive and unworthy: In a word — small. He had neither been as attentive, nor as communicative as she would have liked. But he had been loyal, he'd worked hard, and he had never stopped loving her, though that love was now tainted by anger, jealousy and resentment.

He dried off with his towel (the towel Roger, no doubt, used on weekends), his thoughts a swirl of negative emotions. In bed he lay in the dark, trying unsuccessfully to push away thoughts of Linda and Roger in that very bed. Willowbrook Farm. Willowbrook Farm. The name reverberated in his consciousness. Then it came to him — a luxury resort and spa, two hours north.

Curtis threw back the covers and went in search of his sleeping pills — still in the medicine cabinet, to his relief; he'd never get to sleep until he could shut off his mind. He took two pills, and when he awoke ten hours later after a dreamless night, he felt rested but woozy.

HE WAS FOCUSING ON a real-time candlestick chart of Southern Copper, down 10% from the open, when Barbara opened the door and said, "Call on one."

"Take a message."

"It's your wife."

"Tell her not now; I'll call after the Market closes."

Barbara withdrew. He studied a report on Dry Ships, a Greek container ship company, trying to understand how shares could have fallen from 111 to 9 dollars in just five months. It didn't make any sense.

His cell phone vibrated on the desk. A text message from Linda read, 'call me now.' He ignored it.

A minute later Barbara came in again. "I think you want to take this call," she said with raised eyebrows.

Exasperated, Curtis hit the button on his speaker-phone and barked, "Can this wait? I'm busy."

"Were you in my house?"

"*Our* house."

"Where did you get a key?"

"Does it matter?"

"It matters to me. And you were snooping through my mail."

"I opened *our* VISA bill. The VISA bill *I* pay, I might add. What the hell do think you're doing, spending my money at Victoria Secret and Willowbrook Farm?"

"That's none of your damn business. And your mother left a message. You said you'd talked to her, which was obviously a lie; she wanted to know when we're arriving for Thanksgiving."

"I know, I talked to her. Listen, Linda, I don't have time for this right now. I'm in the middle of things. Why don't we talk tonight. You're obviously out-of-sorts, and I have work to do. Call me around 7." At that, he hung up. No 'bye,' no 'see ya,' no 'talk to you later,' and definitely no 'I love you.' He couldn't remember when he'd cut her off so peremptorily, but he had enough problems at work without listening to Linda's diatribe.

He turned back to his computer screen and was soon lost in concentration studying chart patterns, trying to find a correlation between the movement of the underlying stock, volume, moving averages, Stochastics, Bollinger Bands, money flow, and historical volatility.

"You're unusually silent," Elliot prodded as the evening commute crawled along Francis Boulevard — three lanes of 'beep and creep.' A fender bender a mile ahead had backed up traffic from the river to the park. They would be awhile getting home.

"She wants a divorce," Curtis said incredulously.

"She said so?"

"Her lawyer said so. He called this afternoon. I tried calling her; she wouldn't pick up the phone."

"Do you have a lawyer?"

"No. I haven't even thought about it yet. I want to talk to her first."

"Sounds like she doesn't want to talk to you."

Curtis pushed the button to lower the window on the Volvo, letting in the sound of revving engines and creaking brakes, and a momentary gust of cool air that carried with it the pungent reek of diesel exhaust from a bus in the next lane. The three lanes of cars and trucks and buses moved in a herky-jerky fashion along the boulevard, slowing, accelerating, jerking to a stop, starting again. It was maddening. The streetlights had already come on in the gloom. Curtis closed the window, reclined the seat as far as it would go and closed his eyes. The radio delivered rapid sound bites of bad news. The DOW (he didn't need to be reminded) had fallen another 224 points on the day. The reports of the day were ominous: Housing starts fell to the slowest pace on record, going back to 1959, indicating that the housing sector remained in a severe slump.

He called Linda as soon as he got back to the apartment. This time she picked up.

"I don't suppose you'd consider a marriage counselor."

"If I could turn back the clock...I don't know, that might have worked four years ago; it's a little late now. Anyway, I'm tired of talking about it. Things are never going to be the way they were, so it's time to stop hoping and get on with our lives."

"Whatever happened to 'for better or for worse, in good times and in bad?'" He almost added 'forsaking all others' but thought he'd better not push his luck.

"Give it a rest, Curtis; it's over. I mean — you would not believe how annoyed I was with you. There wasn't a day went by when I didn't feel taken advantage of. When you moved out it was like a great weight lifting off my shoulders. I like you a whole lot better now that we're separated; I'm not so angry."

"I can change. I *have* changed."

"You think spending a few weekends with our son makes up for years of neglect?"

What planet was she living on, he wondered. Neglect? That was a loaded term. "That's a bit harsh," he said. "Anyway, I can't see the world exactly through your eyes, but whatever you think I did or didn't do, that's the past. I'm making changes. I'm spending more time with Sammy. I've given up traveling on weekends. What more do you want me to do? Just tell me and I'll do it. I *can* change."

"No, Curtis, you can't, and even if you could, it wouldn't matter. When love is gone, it's time to move on."

His parents had to know. There was no point in putting it off, and yet he shrank from making the call. Living a thousand miles away from his hometown allowed him to mentally compartmentalize his life: one physical locale was associated with his childhood, the other with his adult life, and the only time they mixed was when his parents came to visit in the space between Christmas and New Year's, and when he took Linda and Sammy to his parents' for Thanksgiving. His old room was like a museum to his childhood. Old books and trophies, pictures on the wall, a signed baseball, his glove and bat. It was silly, he knew, but when he thought of home, he always had two places in mind, the home of his childhood and his home in the suburbs. They were the physical manifestations of life's journey; they connected the narrative of his life. That he was about to sever one of those connections was tantamount to watching the first three acts of a five-act play, then being told to leave the theatre; the actors had gone on strike; the author had died before completing his work. And where did that leave him?

Feeling slightly nauseous he dialed his parents' number and began pacing as the phone rang. How could he admit to the failure of his marriage after just eight years, to parents who had been married for 35?

Curtis was the eldest. His younger brother, Patrick, and sister, Eloise, were both married now, though neither had kids. This divorce was going to change the family dynamic. Being the eldest, he had always been held out as a role model to his siblings, particularly to his brother. He couldn't help it; birth order dictated that he would be the first to do everything: the first to play sports in high school; the first to go to college; the first to land a good job, to get married, to have a child, to buy a house. And now he had the dubious distinction of being the first to get a divorce (the first ever in his family, as far back as anyone knew). If truth be told, his brother was a little sick of coming off second best, and now that Golden Boy had been knocked off his high horse, Curtis thought Patrick would secretly gloat while offering his condolences. Curtis dreaded returning for Thanksgiving.

His mother answered.

"Hi Mom, I have…"

"Hi sweetheart, do you have the flight number for me? Are you staying through the weekend? What time do you have to go back?"

"Well, actually, I have some news for you."

"Good news, I hope."

"Not exactly."

"Uh, oh. You *are* coming? You didn't lose your job? You're not sick?"

"No, Mom. Linda and I have split up." There was a long, long silence on the other end of the phone. "Mom?"

"You can't just split up. You went to a marriage counselor? What are you saying? You haven't taken up with another woman?" She was trying to wrap her mind around it, but it was more than she could comprehend. She needed more time to process the information and make sense of it — which was exactly what Curtis had been trying to do all afternoon and evening, with little success.

"No, there's no other woman. And no, we didn't go to a counselor. Linda's already made up her mind."

"Well you just get her to unmake it."

"I've tried. She's not interested."

"Not interested? This is your *life*. What do you mean, not interested?"

"It's not a life she wants to lead anymore. She's.... Look, she'd made up her mind before she ever mentioned it to me, and you know her — once her mind's made up, it's made up." He didn't know when the tipping point had been reached, because he never realized that the scale was being loaded. She must have been weighing everything that was good about their marriage against everything that was not so good, his merits against his shortcomings, for a long time. And all the while he'd been obliviously content — maybe not ecstatic or joyous, but content. He could give himself that much. "There's nothing I can say or do to change her mind. I've already done as much as I can. I'm not happy about it, but it takes two to tango, and my partner has decided to sit this dance out."

"Oh, my god," Silvia Cooke said. "Oh, my god. William!? William! You have to pick up the phone. Your son. Linda's left him. But Curtis, what's going to happen to Sammy? She's not taking Sammy?"

"Sammy's fine. He's still living at home with Linda. I moved out."

"But you were just there," she said, sounding confused.

"I moved out in September, Mom. I was just there for Saturday night when you called, because Linda and Sammy were at her parents."

"Wh-why should you move out? She's the one who wants the divorce!?"

"But Sammy needs some stability."

"Are you on the phone, William?"

"I'm here. How are you, son?"

"I've been better."

"That's tough. Women. What can you do? I don't know why your mother's put up with *me* for so long, but still...sometimes there's no understanding them, why they keep you, why they let you go. I don't know."

"I don't know, Pop," Curtis said, smiling at the thought that his cluelessness might be an inherited trait.

"But you're ok?"

"I'm ok. I wasn't so good at first, but it's getting a little easier."

"'Cause I know what that's like. Well not exactly, but before your mother, I had two girlfriends who dumped me. Well, I guess you should be happy about that — you wouldn't have been born if I'd married one of *them*. I thought everything was fine, then boom, end of relationship! So...it's not exactly the same, but I understand getting dumped."

"Thanks, Dad."

"But you know, maybe it's all for the best; who knows? Maybe there's another girl out there for you, and sometime 30 or 40 years from now, you'll be tellin' another son that you understand what it's like being dumped, and that he wouldn't exist if your first wife hadn't thrown you out. You know? Nobody knows what's for the best."

"Thanks, Dad, that's..." (he paused, searching for a word) "...a comfort. That's a good way to look at it."

"But what about Sammy?" Sylvia asked.

"He's taking it very well. Linda has him during the week, and I have him weekends."

"That's great," his father said.

"Yeah, we're actually doing more now than we did when I was at home."

"That's good," both of his parents said at once.

And it *was* good. It was very good. It was an improvement.

"We're even learning to paint together."

"Paint?" his mother said. "Your father used to paint."

"No, Sylvia, I *drew*."

"Pastel portraits," Sylvia said. "I still have the one you did of me when I was twenty."

"You don't."

"I do."

"I haven't drawn anything for longer than I can remember. Where are you staying now? How do we get in touch with you?"

Curtis gave them his address and his cell phone number. "Call Patrick and Eloise and give them the news for me. It's not the kind of thing I want to keep repeating. I'm actually ok, if I don't talk it to death."

"I told you it was risky, marrying a girl whose parents were divorced," his mother reminded him.

It was a tactless thing to say, even if it was the truth. The fact was that in the 21st century it was almost impossible to find a girl of marriageable age who did not come from a broken family, or who wasn't, herself, divorced. He decided to let the comment pass and told them he'd see them on Thanksgiving.

That had been way easier than he could have imagined, and having gotten past it he felt a burden lift almost palpably from his shoulders. It hadn't been so bad. His parents hadn't berated him or scolded him for his inadequacies. They'd shown real concern. And maybe his father was right. Maybe there was *another girl out there* for him, another child or two in his future. The future was yet to be revealed, and who knew? — It might be better than his past. Anything was possible.

He poured another glass of wine and closing the refrigerator he noticed the pictures stuck to the door — a photo of Sammy in the stream, another of Linda and Sammy by the Christmas tree, and Sammy's pictures of the Tyrannosaurus, and of the family (sans Roger), and the turkey silhouette. He sipped his wine and took stock of each. Then he twisted off his wedding ring and carried it to the bedroom, and put it in the drawer of his nightstand, remembering the day they had bought it, and pondering how it had all gone to hell in a handbasket.

PART TWO
DISTRACTIONS

Chapter 12

Tuesday November 11 - Sunday November 16, 2008

On Wednesday, November 12th, Secretary of the Treasury Paulsen pushed stocks over a proverbial cliff with the announced restructuring of the banking bailout.

After the Market closed, Curtis called a meeting of his Associates in the conference room. One after another of them recounted the same tale of woe. Their collective opinion was best expressed by Clayton Gantz who said, "We should all go home and wait for spring. It's ridiculous. Come on, there was a nine-hundred-and-eleven point swing on the day! No one can trade this Market. You get screwed coming and going."

Driving away from Westlake Drive on Friday night, a light mist pelted the windshield. *If I was religious, I'd think God was spitting on me*, Curtis thought darkly. "Tell me about your trip. How was grandma Louise? Did you draw a picture of Sadie?"

"I drawed lots of pitchers."

Sammy told him about grandma Louise and Sadie and uncle Joe, as they drove to Mezza Luna, a little Italian restaurant in their old neighborhood. It was dimly lit with candles. He and Linda had eaten here the first week they'd moved into their house, and then again on Sammy's second birthday. An eclectic collection of Italian music played in the background — arias from famous operas, bouncy tunes Curtis associated with old Hollywood movies set in Rome, the 1950's kitsch of Dean Martin singing 'That's Amore,' and Rosemary Clooney singing, 'Come ona My House, My House' (a strange tune written by the Armenian-American writer William Saroyan, and about as Italian as sushi). He wondered what Italians really listened to these days. Probably hip-hop.

He helped Sammy order. Then he asked, "What did you do at school this week?"

"We did computer games with numbers, and another one with words. And then we finger painted, and played on the swings and slides. And Danny Barger got in trouble for pulling down Debby Brown's underpants on the jungle gym."

"I imagine he did."

"He had to go to the principal's office," Sammy said in a lowered voice, as though he didn't want anyone to hear of Danny's shame. "And we learned about Pilgrims, and we made turkeys out of colored paper for Thanksgiving."

"You had a big week."

Sammy nodded with satisfaction.

"How's your mom?"

"Not so good."

"Why is that?"

"She can't sell her houses."

Curtis nodded at that. The housing market was in turmoil: record foreclosures, falling prices and extremely tight credit. It was the kind of market that would make some people very rich over the next five years, and he thought Linda was shrewd enough to be one of them. "Does that worry her?"

"Uh huh. Roger can't sell his houses either."

"He sells houses, too?"

"He builds houses."

"Ah," Curtis said knowingly. Judging by his car and his clothes, he was no carpenter, which must mean he was a developer, and that was a very bad position to be in at the moment. He'd be lucky not to go bankrupt.

"Show me some of your pictures," Curtis said. They were mostly colored pencil line drawings, of the kind they had practiced before, utilizing no more than five lines. There were several of the dog, Sadie, of which two were exceptionally good. There was one of uncle Joe, two or three of Linda, and another couple that could have been Linda or her mother. There was a drawing of a car, a room, a water tower, a flower garden, and a single heart-shaped flower. The latter caught Curtis's eye, as it was done in one continuous line with a red pencil, beginning at the point of the heart, looping up to the left lobe, the right lobe, and down to the point again, continuing in an S curve to create a stem, then another sinuous climb to the right and back to the base (creating a tulip-like leaf), with another to the left, followed by an ellipse at the base to form the top of a pot, a line down, across the bottom and back up to form the body of the pot, and ending in a zig-zag pattern down the front of the pot. "I like this."

"That's a love flower."

"It's very nice. What're you going to call it?" Curtis asked.

"Make Love Grow," Sammy said.

Curtis took up the pastels and printed 'MAKE LOVE GROW' in an arch over the top of the paper, each letter in a different color. They stood back and admired it. "If only it were so easy," Curtis sighed.

Saturday Curtis and Sammy drove to the city's tallest building, where they took the express elevator up to the observation platform. Sammy was fascinated by the broad sweep of the city, the rooftops, the ant-like people, the tiny cars. Curtis saw it all anew through his son's eyes.

Curtis picked Sammy up and pointing into the distance he said, "You see there past the river, where the trees start? Now look past that. You see that second line of trees? That's where our house is." He inwardly winced at the reference, but it was still true for Sammy.

He scanned the landscape from horizon to horizon as they made a circuit of the platform. There was his house, there his office, there his apartment. Like scenes from *The Little Red Caboose*, this world sprawled out into the hazy distance, diminishing in size, revealing neighborhoods and towns and the promise of a future where anything could happen, where people were busy about their tasks, each living a story whose ending had yet to be written. His future lay somewhere out there, and for the first time he looked toward its discovery with more excitement than trepidation. He needn't lose all he had been. He hadn't lost Sammy. He hadn't even lost Linda. Their relationship had changed, but no matter what happened, even if they never reconciled, as long as they had Sammy they would always be part of each other's lives. It was up to him to make it as cordial as possible, even if he had no clear idea of how it had all unraveled. Life would go on. The next chapter would be written. Anything was possible.

On entering Bolton's Art Supplies, Curtis looked expectantly for Stephanie Walzer and saw her with a customer at the cash register. Roy asked if he could help and Curtis told him they'd wait. He liked the personal service he got from Miss Walzer. He caught her eye and she smiled back at him as she rang up her other customer's purchases.

While they were waiting, they went down the paint aisle (Sammy had gone through most of the blue and red watercolors). Curtis examined the brushes. He thought it would be good to have a wider brush to spread water and the blue of the sky. Almost all paintings included sky, and it was hard to make a uniform blue with a small brush (the brush strokes were always apparent).

"Can I help you, gentlemen?"

Stephanie was dressed differently today, Curtis noticed. She wore a burgundy skirt to mid-calf, brown boots and a ruffled blouse. Something else was different, but he couldn't place, however the one thing he'd learned in his adult life was that when someone went to the trouble to make a change, they wanted people to notice So he asked, "Did you cut your hair?"

"No."

"Something's different."

"Contacts," she explained. "I don't wear them often; they irritate my eyes. But they cost so much, I can't abide leaving them in the drawer."

"You look nice," Curtis said reflexively, and instantly wished he could take it back. She *did* look nice, but he didn't want to give the wrong impression because, when all was said and done, she wasn't his "type."

"Thank you," she acknowledged simply and without self-consciousness.

Curtis explained that they wanted to get their pictures framed.

"Let me see," she said, first taking Curtis's tower. She looked at it silently, with raised eyebrows.

Curtis could feel the horror. "It was just a dream I had."

"Ah. Strange dream," she said, echoing Elliot's impression. "It's just..."

Curtis remembered Elliot saying it was phallic and added, "It's a lighthouse."

"A lighthouse," she said, grasping for something positive to say. "It's...uhm.... You've done a nice job with the background."

Curtis thrust Sammy's blue dinosaur into her hands.

"Oh, this is very good," Stephanie said with obvious relief. "You've done a much better job with this one."

"It's not mine; it's Sammy's."

Miss Walzer looked astonished. "Sammy, is this yours? This is wonderful." Sammy beamed with pride. She studied it more closely and looked back and forth between the painting and Sammy. "This is really remarkable."

Curtis was thankful for her indulgence. "Sammy thought we should have some of our own art on the walls, so I said we'd get them framed."

"Yes, of course," she said, looking oddly at Sammy. "You should, by all means. Our framing department is upstairs. Sarah Wilson is in charge. Sammy, you see that clearance table over there? See if you'd like anything over there and I'll meet you in a minute." Then to Curtis she said, "Mr. Cooke?"

"Curtis, please."

"Let me show you upstairs."

Sammy scurried off and Stephanie led Curtis to the stairway up to the loft.

"Did you help Sammy with this dinosaur?"

"Me? No. I know dinosaurs weren't blue, but that's the way he wanted to do it, so...." He let his explanation hang in mid-air. He didn't see the objection.

"Do you remember when I said that most parents think their children were gifted?"

"Yes."

"Well, your son really is."

"What? Because of this dinosaur?"

"Do you know how a six-year old is supposed to draw?"

"No, Sammy is my first and only."

"This is not normal. It's remarkable. But it's not normal. Six-year olds don't draw like this. A normal six-year old would draw a profile. Look what you have here: A dinosaur from the back, looking over its shoulder. Do you know how...?" and then she stopped. "No, obviously you don't know. Wow. Let's just say this is unusual. He has enormous potential, but you could screw it up so easily."

"That's the story of my life," Curtis quipped.

"Just..." She seemed at a loss for words. "Encourage him."

They'd reached the top of the stairs. The loft was filled with frames of different colors, styles and sizes. She pointed toward the counter. "That's Sarah. I'll look after Sammy until you're done."

Stephanie found Sammy at the clearance table. He was looking at an art book.

"My dad says I can have any book I want. I can read."

"I have no doubt." She reached out her hand and he took it. "You like to paint?"

"Uh huh."

"I do, too. It's fun, isn't it?"

"Uh huh."

"What else do you like to do?"

"I like to go places with my dad."

"Where have you gone?"

"Today we goed to the bookstore and the top of a building. And tomorrow we're going to the pitchers."

"The movies?"

"No, where they have pitchers."

"Oh, the museum, where they have pictures?" she corrected.

"Uh huh."

"That will be fun," Miss Walzer said.

Sarah Wilson reminded Curtis of Linda's roommate in college — blonde and well proportioned, though short, with a cute nose and the lovely, translucent skin of a 20-year-old. Then she spoke and his fantasies dissolved. She had a nasal, whiney voice that would drive him nuts in five minutes. Linda's voice was musical, by comparison.

He followed her around to the mats and the frames, voyeuristically admiring her firm posterior, momentarily glad to be a man and a fool. But that voice! What a pity.

When he was done he found Sammy and Stephanie among the books. Sammy held up a beginner's book on how to draw. "Stephanie gave me a present."

"How much is it?"

"It's a present; it's nothing," Stephanie said in a voice that was so much more soothing than Sarah Wilson's.

Early Sunday morning, just as the new-risen sun sent shafts of light glancing off the buildings on Washington Street, Curtis wandered around his apartment in robe and slippers, listening to the soulful sax of Ben Webster and the rapid arpeggios of Art Tatum's piano. He stood by the wall of windows looking down on the street, sipping strong black coffee. Sammy was still asleep. They'd had a big day on Saturday, and planned to go to the museum today. At home, he'd slept in, but now his weekends with Sammy were filled with activity. He wondered which he liked better. It was nice to sleep in, but he'd had more new experiences with Sammy in the past month than he'd had in the previous two years. It had been paradoxically easier to be alone at home; there were more rooms, and Linda could take care of Sammy's needs.

In his memory, his own father had always been away at work. He was held out as punishment — "Wait until your father comes home!" No matter the infraction, the real punishment had been the waiting for hours in anticipation of the unknown. If his father was in a good mood, he might be instantly forgiven. If his father had had a bad day at work, he might be spanked, or sent to his room without dinner. At the very least, he would be scolded.

His father was somewhat remote in his childhood recollections. He'd always presided over the holiday meals, and on the weekends he could always be found futzing around in the yard. He'd stand hose-in-hand staring into space for 20 minutes at a time. As an adult, he'd come to view his father as a man with a lot on his mind who did the best he could to raise two sons and a daughter, pay the bills and keep his marriage together. It was an admirable, if minor, accomplishment.

Curtis and Sammy determined to leave for the museum when the Sunday morning cartoons had concluded. Curtis stood in front of his closet trying to make up his mind what to wear. He'd been thinking of what Elliot had said about Roger being better at marketing himself. It was fascinating how many preconceived ideas you had about people, based solely on their clothing. It was natural.

Prejudice is a survival skill, he mused. If you were on a city street and saw young men in business suits approaching you, you would judge them no threat. But if the young men wore baggy pants and bandanas (with tattoos and piercings), you might feel inclined to cross the street, because that demographic could pose a threat. It was, as Elliot so succinctly put it — marketing.

Ever since Elliot had called attention to his clothes, Curtis had been observing the clothing of the people he passed every day. A great many wore drab exercise gear — grey, black or blue formless sweatshirts (often with the manufacturer's logo), sweat pants and running shoes. They had a uniformity of style that belied their professions — doctors, lawyers, students and clerks all might look the same when they were off work.

He considered that he might want to put some thought into what he wore on his days off, but he'd have to go shopping for new clothes first. For today he elected to wear a newer pair of jeans, a green polo shirt and a brown cardigan. He dressed Sammy in a similar outfit (Linda had bought the matching cardigans the previous Christmas), merely substituting a T-shirt for the polo shirt. Curtis opted for loafers, and Sammy had tennis shoes with red lights that flashed when he put his weight on the heels.

They parked downtown in the McKinley Street parking garage, where Sammy enjoyed driving up the spiral ramp to the sixth floor. They took the elevator (another treat for Sammy) to the ground floor, and started off for the museum.

As they waited on one street corner for the light to change, a small band played. It was a jazz band consisting of a saxophone, a stand-up bass, an acoustic guitar, and a fiddle. Sammy was only six years old and had no experience with musical instruments. Neither of his parents were musical, and this the very first time he'd heard a live band. He was fascinated. Other pedestrians passed the band without a second glance. Some gave them a wide berth, as though playing music in public was somehow unseemly. Undoubtedly a few viewed the band as little better than beggars. Fewer still tossed a coin or a bill into the open guitar case. When the light changed Sammy pulled back.

"Come on, buddy, we'll lose the light."

"I want to listen."

"Alright then, just for a minute." Curtis had been so focused on his thoughts and their path that he'd shut the band out. Now he began to listen more intently and the blinders came off.

The bass and the guitar were the rhythm section, while the saxophone carried the tune and the fiddle filled in the parts usually reserved for piano, ranging between solid accompaniment, to percussive riffs and lively solos. They played jazz standards and ballads, and even Curtis (who was a jazz enthusiast) had to admit that they were a remarkably tight and professional band. Many street musicians were amateurs and wannabes. These guys were obviously professional and had probably decided to pick up a few dollars while practicing. They'd been playing *Gone With the Wind* when Curtis and Sammy arrived. Now they played a version of *Stormy Weather* that began with a bluesy saxophone in place of a vocal, giving way to a duet between the bass and the guitar, and progressing to a fugue-like, almost Classical variation by the fiddle (or more properly a violin, the way it was being played), only to end in a beautifully structured restatement by all of the pieces together. When they finished, Sammy clapped with delight and appreciation. Curtis dropped four dollars into the open guitar case.

"Thanks man," the guitar player said, and turning to Sammy said, "Nice shoes,."

"Can I have a CD?" Sammy asked.

The sax player smiled at Sammy. "Nope. No CDs. Just live music."

"You sound great," Curtis said. "What do you call yourselves? Do you have an upcoming concert?"

"We're not really a group. We're just studio musicians between gigs."

The light changed (they'd missed three lights during *Stormy Weather*). The band launched into *Skylark*. Curtis took Sammy by the hand and they crossed the street.

"I want a CD," Sammy said, looking back over his shoulder.

"They don't have one."

"But I like them."

"I did, too, but they don't have a CD."

"Why?"

"I don't know — luck, maybe. The best musicians aren't always the most successful."

"Why?"

"Because you don't have to be the best to be the most successful; you just have to know how to market yourself. And there's a certain amount of luck involved. That's true of everything, not just music." That, no doubt, was true. Even a research scientist working alone in a lab had to know how to market himself. Otherwise, he'd never get the grants needed to keep his research projects afloat. He remembered what Elliot had said about Roger: "It's all about marketing."

The city was indolent on the weekend. Downtown was depopulated. The people who remained moved at a slower pace, and the general hum of the city had been turned down a notch or two in both volume and cadence.

"I work down there." Curtis pointed as they crossed a street.

"Let's go there."

"Not today; it's not open. Anyway, they don't allow children."

"Why?"

"I suppose they think it would be distracting."

"Why?"

"Because kids have a hard time staying still and being quiet. Kids are full of energy, which is a good thing, but it can be distracting at work."

"Why?"

"Because you keep asking 'why,' and then I have to take time to answer, so I couldn't get anything done."

The museum was housed in a grand old building built in the 1890's, with high vaulted ceilings in wide galleries that radiated out from a central glass dome. Diffused light cascaded into the lobby and reflected from the marble floors, making the marble statuary seem to glow. There were anonymous sculptures from ancient Greece and Rome, three busts by Rodin, and six superb busts by Jean-Antoine Houdon from the late 18th and early 19th centuries.

They walked around a pedestal topped with the bust of a young French aristocrat. His face was composed and handsome with wide-set eyes, a sensitive mouth and soft chin. His hair curled over his forehead, and his neck was sheathed in the sort of cravat prevalent in the Romantic Era. Curtis looked at the brass plaque on the pedestal: "bust of Jean-Baptiste Girard, Comte de Versilly, 1789." In 1789 Jean-Baptiste posed for his bust with a confident vision of his future as an elite member of society. But history had other plans for him. That fine head, Curtis realized, had likely fallen under the guillotine less than five years after the sculpture was completed. No one knew how to prepare for the strange twists of history, the unforeseen events that moved through people like a threshing machine through a wheat field: Politics, plagues, wars, discoveries, scientific advancements, inventions, chance encounters, natural catastrophes all lay unseen just over the horizon. History was, he imagined, like a treadmill with an ever-changing picture coming up on the tread and never enough time to get out of its way.

They turned into a gallery of portraits of the 17th through 19th centuries. They admired Johannes Vermeer's *A girl Asleep*, and Nicolas de Largilliere's *A Young Man and His Tutor*.

"Before photography was invented in the 1830s," Curtis explained, "the only way to know what a place or a person really looked like was to paint them, so it was important to paint as realistically as possible."

Curtis told Sammy about the styles of dress in the different eras, not knowing if he understood. At what age were children capable of comprehending historical time? He wasn't sure. He didn't remember exactly when the concept became clear to him, though at the age of 10 he'd been fascinated by the Civil War photographs of Matthew Brady. Surely, by that time, he'd had a grasp of time and the passing of eras. But that past was black-and-white and lacked the reality of the present day. And he remembered a moment in his early 20's, not 10 years ago, when he'd discovered the photographs of Sergei Mikhailovich Prokudin-Gorskii. Some of the earliest examples of color photos, they depicted pre-revolutionary Russia, and they'd brought into his Present an era he had always relegated to the black-and-white Past.

They stepped to the right and stood before Pierre Paul Prud'hon's *David Johnston, 1808*, which revealed a youth of 19 with expensive clothes and windblown hair — the epitome of a vulnerable Romantic poet. Curtis could imagine him succumbing to consumption or dying of a broken heart. However, the plaque informed the reader that Johnston had been elected mayor of Bordeaux in 1838, and had founded a ceramics business in 1843.

They moved on to the next painting: Jacques-Samuel Bernard's *Still Life with Violin, Ewer and Bouquet.* Curtis picked up Sammy so he could see the painting at eye level.

"This kind of painting is called a Still Life, because nothing in it is moving. This one was painted in 1657, almost 200 years before photography, so it's representational art (that means it's realistic; it represents what the painter saw).

"Didn't he know what grapes look like?" Sammy asked without the slightest trace of sarcasm.

"Well yes, he did know, but sometimes the artist just paints something he likes, something that's pretty. Or maybe what he likes isn't any one thing; maybe it's the way the things are arranged together that makes it interesting, or makes a statement."

He craned his neck to scan the room and crossed to William Michael Harnett's *After the Hunt.* "Now, see this one? This was actually painted in 1885, 50 years *after* photography was invented. Even then, some painters painted realistic scenes, because photography was still black-and-white and not as pretty as a picture. Why do you think he painted this one?"

"Dunno," Sammy shrugged. "He liked rabbits?"

"This kind of picture tells a story by grouping related things together." It was a life-size Still Life of items hung on the back of a door: a pistol, a rifle, a pike, a knife, a hunting horn, a hat, a canteen, two dead birds and a rabbit. "You know just by looking at the items that the hunter is back from a successful hunt. There's a beautiful use of shadow, don't you think?" The life-size objects and the shadows gave a *trompe l'oeil,* three-dimensional feel to the painting.

"He's a good painter," Sammy agreed. "I can't paint that good."

Curtis chuckled. "Neither can I. It takes lots of practice to get that good."

The next painting, William Keane's *The Old Banjo,* was in the same vein. They paused briefly before it, then strolled past some lesser works, and coming to the end of the hall, turned through the door to the next gallery, which housed Impressionist and Post-Impressionist collections.

They stood behind an elderly woman with thin grey hair, a young woman with shoulder-length, wavy black hair, and a little girl with long straight brown hair that hung to the middle of her back, but from his perch atop his father's shoulders, Sammy could see over them just fine. "Now this painting was done by August Renoir. It was painted the same year as *After the Hunt*," Curtis said quietly, assuming a muted, museum voice. He had no idea why he was compelled to talk softly in a museum, but for some reason that escaped him, it seemed as inappropriate to speak loudly in a museum, as it would have been in a church or a library, where it made at least a modicum of sense. The older woman walked away and they moved into her spot. "See, after photography came along, artists didn't feel the need to be realistic anymore."

"But he borrowed something from photography," the woman next to them said.

Curtis glanced sidelong at her. "Hello," he said in surprise.

"Mr. Cooke. Hi, Sammy."

"Curtis, if you please," Curtis said. Stephanie bowed slightly in mock-formal acknowledgment, the hint of a smile at the corner of her mouth. "I thought you worked Sundays."

"I usually do; I traded days with a co-worker, so I could have some time with Gwyn." She stepped back, revealing the 10-year-old girl by her side. She appeared shy, peering around her mother at the two strangers. "Gwyn, this is Mr. Cooke and Sammy. This is my daughter, Gwyneth."

Gwyn raised a hesitant hand in greeting.

"Pleased to meet you," Curtis said, bowing ever so slightly with Sammy on his shoulders.

Sammy asked Gwyn, "Do you have a dog?"

"Uh, uh; we had a cat, but she died."

"I want a dog."

Curtis asked, "What were you saying about Renoir borrowing from photography?"

"The way he blurs out the background, like a photo with just the foreground in focus."

"I like the colors," Sammy said.

"They *are* nice. You can see all the little brushstrokes, and the way all the different colors blend together — especially as you step away." She wheeled around and pointed across the room. "Like that one, Monet's *Cliffs at Etretat*. See how the colors look from a distance? See the sailboat? Now come over here." They all followed Stephanie across the room. "Now see all the different points of color, and what we took to be a sailboat is nothing but a single stroke of white against the blue. It's a trick of the eye."

Sammy bounced in silent excitement, hurting Curtis's shoulders. "Down you go," Curtis said and swung him to the floor.

Stephanie held out her hand and Sammy took it without hesitation. Curtis followed along behind as she led Sammy and Gwyn to the next painting, a Monet water lily study, then to a self-portrait by Van Gogh. "Most of us would never think to paint a face using green and yellow and purple, but Van Gogh saw things in a new way. People didn't appreciate his work when he was alive. He sold only one painting before he died, and that was to his brother."

"He didn't know about marketing," Sammy said.

Stephanie's head snapped around in astonishment. Curtis laughed to himself, pleased and surprised that Sammy had actually been listening.

"Exactly," she replied, glancing at Curtis as if to ask silently 'what have you been teaching this child?'

They strolled on to Cezanne's *Basket of Apples, 1890-1894*, and *Chateau Noir 1900-1904*. "There is no right way to paint. Everyone paints in his or her own way. Everyone's vision is unique. That's the beauty of art."

Curtis hung back, watching the three move from painting to painting. Sammy seemed really interested. And it was fascinating to observe Stephanie outside of her work environment. For one thing, she looked different in jeans and boots, and a loose, natural wool, crew-necked sweater. Asking Gwyn and Sammy what they liked and didn't like, she pointed out the differences between one painting and another in a way that made art entirely unintimidating.

As they passed line drawings by Henri Matisse, cubist paintings by Paul Klee, the bright surrealism of Marc Chagall, and geometric compositions by Mark Rothko and Frank Stella, she expounded on the way art had evolved over the past century. Curtis listened attentively and held his tongue, content to be the observer. At one point she dropped the children's hands as she pointed out various aspects of a painting, her hands seeming to pull shapes out of the air, describing the painting in terms of geometric forms, and then, hands on hips, she stared with a smile of satisfaction on her face, as though she had painted it herself. When they moved on he noticed that Gwyn had taken Sammy's hand. Sammy skipped, the red lights in the heels of his shoes blinking like the brake lights of a car.

The gallery ended in the gift shop, where Gwyn and Sammy went off in search of treasure.

"You have a nice daughter."

"She's a joy. Sometimes I feel like she's raising me, instead of the other way around."

Curtis was torn between his natural curiosity and a fear of impropriety; he had a reputation for tactlessness (at least according to his mother and to Linda, who had complained on numerous occasions). "I don't see a ring," he plowed ahead, "so I assume you're a single parent?"

"Yes."

"How long?"

"Since she was born. Her father was hit by a bus when I was pregnant."

"Jesus," he exclaimed. "That's awful."

She shrugged. "It was bad at first. I never could have made it through that time if it wasn't for Gwyn. Newborns have to be cared for; you don't have a choice; you have to get on with your life because they depend on you. But it was rough. I've always regretted her father missed seeing her; he would have been so proud."

"It must be difficult."

"Being a single parent sure makes scheduling your life more complicated. But there's a lady in our apartment building who helps out, and my brother sometimes. The worst part is I don't get enough time with her — I'm working, or taking classes."

"It's new territory for me, but I only have him on the weekends."

"He's a nice little boy."

"We never did much together, when I was at home. He had his playmates; I had my work. The painting has been something we can both do," he said, returning to a subject they had in common. "He likes it, and it keeps him busy."

"And do you like it?"

"I'm no artist, but it's fun."

"You *are* an artist. You may not be a *good* artist," she laughed melodiously, "but you do make art."

"Are dabblers artists? I don't think so. Real artists have to have a singular vision."

"What about commercial artists? Or take medical textbook artists? They draw perfect representations of anatomy. Aren't they real artists?"

Curtis considered a moment. "Uh oh — You've got me in a corner. I could probably argue my point, just to be contrary, but maybe I should think it through first. Could we hold that discussion for another time?"

"By all means. What do you do for a living?"

"I'm a boring Asset Manager."

"Why do you say that? — Boring."

"Well, most people think it's boring."

"And what do you think?"

"Actually, I find it kind of stimulating. You know, it's all about risk assessment and managing your resources. It's not something that provokes witty conversation, but it's intellectually interesting."

"Are you good at it?"

Curtis thought about that for a moment. It was a difficult question to answer, given the current economic turmoil. "I used to think so; I'm not so sure now."

"The Market's been a mess, lately," she observed.

In prior years he would have been surprised by the comment. It was a subject that was usually far from the public's mind, but this year the economic downturn was affecting everyone. The sub-prime meltdown, the instability of global financial institutions, the enormous public debt, the rising price of gas and groceries, record foreclosures, devalued stocks and shrinking retirement accounts had everyone on edge.

"It's been challenging," he said.

"I wonder what it would be like to live in another country. It seems like we're always in the middle of a crisis."

"Where would you live?"

"I've always thought New Zealand would be nice."

Sammy came running up. "I found a book," he said with excitement.

"Why New Zealand?" Curtis asked Stephanie, and "Let me see," he said to Sammy, taking the book, a paperback catalogue of the museum's collections. He checked the price and handed it back without comment.

"Because it seems like you could live there and not worry about what the rest of the world was thinking about you. Nobody cares about their politics. No terrorist is going to attack them; they don't count. If one of their banks went under, it wouldn't affect half the world." Stephanie asked Sammy, "Can I see?" She held the book at arm's length, studying the cover. "They never quite get the color right in reproductions, but it's a nice way to remember what you've seen."

She handed it back as Gwyn walked up, holding out a small box. "Can I get this?"

Stephanie took it and looked at the picture on the side of the box: a mug decorated with a Van Gogh self-portrait. Then she read the print, read it again, and finally read it aloud. "Disappearing ear mug. Simply pour in your favorite hot beverage, and watch Van Gogh's ear disappear." Her jaw dropped.

"That's so appalling, it's almost funny," Curtis said.

"My god, who thinks of these things?" Then addressing Gwyn she said sternly, "Absolutely not," and handed the cup back.

Without complaint, Gwyn left and returned a minute later with a Monet water lily mug.

"How much is it?" Stephanie asked.

"Seven dollars."

"I don't know, honey."

"Please."

Sensing Stephanie's discomfort, Curtis said, "I'll get it — my treat."

"No, I couldn't let you..."

"You gave Sammy a book. Let me give Gwyn a cup."

After a moment's hesitation, she agreed. He paid and they headed out of the museum. It was close to one o'clock.

Addressing Sammy, Curtis said, "I'm hungry. Do you want to get something to eat?"

"Can we go to Burger King?"

"I don't know; I don't know what's around here but we'll find something." He asked Stephanie if she and Gwyn would like to accompany them.

"Oh, we couldn't," Stephanie demurred.

"I'll pay."

"No, no, we really should be going. It was nice to see you again."

"Likewise."

Gwyn thanked him for the cup.

"My pleasure."

They walked down the stairs and parted ways at the sidewalk.

"She's a nice lady," Sammy said.

"Yes, she is," Curtis said. "Very nice." He wished Linda could be more like Stephanie. Stephanie was so easy to talk to, so non-judgmental. With Linda it was like walking on eggshells, wondering when he would inadvertently offend her.

At Macy's Curtis admired himself in the mirror. "What do you think?"

Sammy scrunched up his nose and said appraisingly, "You look like Roger."

"That's good, isn't it?"

Sammy just shrugged. Curtis took another look in the mirror. He did look somewhat like a younger version of Roger, though maybe the pale blue argyle vest was going a bit overboard in mimicry. In the end, he bought pants; three sweater vests, an Irish fisherman's knit sweater; a grey wool cardigan with smoking patches on the elbows; three pairs of socks, and a pair of Florsheim loafers.

In the Boys Department he bought Sammy a matching fisherman's knit sweater, a blue sweater vest, and a pair of brown corduroy pants.

Sweeping out of the store laden with bags of new clothes, Curtis was in an ebullient mood. "We're going to look spiffy!" he declared to Sammy, who marched along beside him, wary of the swinging bag.

Chapter 13

Monday November 17 – Sunday November 23, 2008

On Tuesday the Market stabilized, so Curtis put business aside to focus on his personal problems. He conferred with three associates. Audrey Rice's attorney was an aggressive woman who had raked her cheating husband over the coals. Daniel Rosso's attorney had helped him avoid a costly divorce. Randy Krepsbock was dissatisfied with his attorney, "a wimpy bastard who gave away the store." Rosso's attorney, one Bruce Niederer, agreed to meet on Friday afternoon.

Curtis stared at the headlines on his computer. CNBC declared, "Washington Paralyzed. Wall Street Gets the Shakes: With the lame-duck Congress and Bush officials unable to agree on any action to ease the financial crisis, the DOW has plunged 2,000 points since election day." His heart was racing. He felt sick and scared. Two of his clients had called repeatedly. He knew that Erickson would now be examining his portfolios in detail, and that could not end in Curtis's favor.

The call came late in the afternoon, and while expected, it made his stomach turn somersaults. Barbara didn't look him in the eye, as she delivered the summons to his boss's office. He went, feeling like a grade school kid being called before the principal.

Allison Essman looked up with an expression comprised of equal parts reprobation, disgust and pity, and buzzed the intercom to announce his arrival. Erickson sat at his desk looking gravely at the computer screen before him. He gestured to Curtis to sit down. The gesture reminded Curtis of a trainer telling a dog to sit. He was the dog.

"I got calls from Symington of the Symington Harvard Endowment, and Marquette...you know: Marquette, Bradley, yada, yada. I managed to put off Marquette for the moment, but Symington is threatening a lawsuit.

I agreed to a meeting tomorrow, where you can explain why the stocks you bought in June are worth 60% less today. Consider yourself on probation."

At the end of the meeting the next day, Curtis knew he was in trouble.

"I've never been more humiliated in my professional life," Erickson said when Symington had left. "It's indefensible. You made us look like rank amateurs! What the fuck have you been doing? Are you teaching your Associates this same recipe for disaster?"

Curtis stood silently while his boss delivered himself of a string of oaths and invectives, unable to voice any defense or, for that matter, apology. The strategies he'd relied on, that he'd learned from a former manager, had worked well for five years. But it was not a model that worked in such a volatile market.

"I want a report on my table on Tuesday. And Cooke? — Turn things around or I'll have no choice but to cut you loose. Do we understand each other? Now get out of my office."

Curtis left work at three o'clock and drove north out of town under a lowering sky. His route took him through the warehouse district, over the river and into the edge of suburbia, where Rosso's attorney kept his office over a Walgreens drugstore, in a strip mall, in a neighborhood of used car lots and discount electronics. It wasn't a setting that inspired confidence. Curtis took the linoleum stairs to the second-floor office with a mixture of trepidation and foreboding. At the top of the steps, a dimly lit hallway was fronted by a series of beveled glass doors. The second door bore the stenciled title, Bruce Niederer, Attorney at Law. Curtis wondered what else you could be an attorney at: Attorney at Rest? Attorney at Work? Attorney at Play? The possibilities seemed endless. Attorney at Vacation? Attorney at Fraud. Attorney at Accounting. Attorney at Law seemed pompous and redundant.

The door opened onto a small waiting room and a counter, behind which sat a matronly woman with white hair and thick glasses, who took his card and asked him to have a seat. The chairs were of worn blue fabric with blond wood armrests. On the walls hung framed caricatures of English barristers in wigs. A dirty window overlooked the parking lot. From his seat, Curtis could see only the grey sky, the high branches of the barren trees that lined the street, and the tops of the parking lot lights, upon the nearest of which perched a grey-blue pigeon.

Magazines were spread across the lamp table: *Epicurean, Road & Track, Newsweek, Time*, and *Cosmopolitan*. The Cosmo girl wore pink this month, displaying amazing cleavage and arched eyebrows. The cover headlines promised "Ten Sex Tips to Make His Toes Curl!", "How to Make Him Last Longer", "How to Tell if He's Two-Timing", and "Red Carpet Fashion: Who Has It, Who Doesn't". He picked up the Cosmo, hoping to learn how to last longer, when the receptionist handed him a clipboard.

"We'll need this information first. Let me know when you're done."

It was a long questionnaire with the usual places for names and addresses, when married, when separated, number of children, spouse's attorney etc., followed by a series of questions next to two columns of boxes to be checked under YOU and SPOUSE. The instructions directed the client to "indicate by checking the boxes, whether the following statements apply to you or your spouse (leave blank if you're unsure)," such as:

"I have been physically abusive:

Never

Occasionally

Often"

and

"I am vindictive"

Bruce Niederer leaned back in his chair until it creaked and read the questionnaire. He wore a white dress shirt rolled up his hairy forearms, and a striped tie loosened at the neck. He smiled occasionally as he scanned the answers. "Under your spouse, you checked 'I have committed adultery,' but then you crossed it out. Why's that?"

"She didn't do it until we were separated, so I guess it doesn't technically count as adultery."

"Does she have many men?"

"No, just one, I think."

"Is he reputable?"

"He drives a Mercedes."

"Could he be in any way considered a bad influence on your son?"

"Is this necessary?"

"To get a divorce, no; this is a no-fault state. But it could be useful if there's a custody battle."

"There won't be a custody battle."

"They all say that. You want the usual arrangement? You get the kid every other weekend?"

"Every *other* weekend? No, I get him *every* weekend. Unless he goes somewhere with his mother, or like this week, when he goes with me for Thanksgiving."

"You're keeping it civilized, so far," Niederer snorted, then turning back to the questionnaire he muttered asides to himself: "Hm. Ah! Oh, great. Um hm," before looking up and asking, "You indicated here that she has a job. How much does she contribute to your joint income?"

"I suppose it was about half of our income last year. She had a good year."

"What does she do?"

"She's a realtor."

"Her income this year?"

"I'm not really sure. Down a little, but not much, I think."

"That's good, that's good. That saves you from alimony. You'll still have to pay child support, of course."

"Of course."

"Do you want to keep the house?"

"I think it would be best for Sammy."

"This is a community property state. If you were to split your assets in half, do your other net assets equal the value of the house?"

And so it went, a long, dry recitation of what his marriage was worth in the eyes of the State. The meeting wasn't as bad as he had anticipated it might be. In the end, it wasn't much more unpleasant than a trip to the dentist.

Saturday morning revealed a blue sky with broken clouds. Curtis asked Sammy what he wanted to do. Sammy suggested they go out for breakfast.

"I know a place by the park," Curtis said. "We could eat, and then you can play in the park. And we can paint."

"I wanna fly a kite."

Curtis folded up one of the easels. Sammy carried a plastic tube containing his kite and string.

The park was two blocks east and one block south. They walked east along the northern edge of the park, past the baseball diamond, past the playground, to a small pond separated from the basketball courts by a tall privet hedge. A willow-shaded path followed the irregular grassy verge around the pond. A green gazebo stood guard at the western end. Ducks paddled around cattails, frogs croaked, and statuesque turtles sunned themselves on rocks.

Overnight the expected storm had pushed north, leaving a mackerel sky. As clouds moved slowly overhead, the park was cast in intermittent sun and shadow, warm one moment, cool the next.

Curtis and Sammy stopped at Jack's, a century-old restaurant famous, according to the sign in the window, for its dollar-sized Swedish pancakes. They took a sidewalk table to enjoy the fresh air and a view of the pond. Curtis had a cappuccino, toast, ham and hash browns. Sammy ate scrambled eggs and pancakes.

Curtis was in a contemplative mood, thinking of Linda as she was in college. Despite the current state of their relationship, he could not change his feelings for that Linda, the 19-year-old Linda. She'd been lovely, smart, and vibrant with youth and ambition. As for the present, the sadness and regret he felt at his own failures were tempered by his anger at Linda's betrayal, and yet at the same time his anger was mitigated by the love he felt for her younger self. Love and attraction were fluid, and when they were on the wane it took a leap of imagination to bring back the old magic, the reason why you fell in love in the first place. Both he and Linda were guilty of a failure of imagination, of submitting to the mundane and so forgetting what made both of them, in each other's eyes, so special that they had bound their lives together. Without Sammy, they might go their separate ways with little regard for one another in the future. With Sammy, they were inextricably bound together for life.

"She's painting," Sammy observed.

Curtis looked up and followed his son's gaze toward the park. On the western edge of the pond by the gazebo, an artist had set up her easel. Curtis was vaguely annoyed; he'd planned on painting in private, but now that a real artist had claimed the territory, he was too intimidated to set up his own easel. Perhaps (he held up a finger to gauge the wind) they could fly the kite instead.

"I wanna feed the ducks," Sammy said.

Curtis paid the bill, then tore up his toast into tiny pieces, which they carried across the street to the pond. When Sammy threw a morsel into the water all of the ducks converged, quacking and jostling for position. Curtis picked out a female mallard that looked deserving and tossed her a piece. She was closest to where it landed, but was overtaken by three aggressive males. Curtis then threw behind her, but the males again swarmed the spot before she could get to it. Finally, when Sammy tossed a handful to the left, drawing all of the aggressive ducks in that direction, Curtis managed to land a piece right in front of the timid female, who snatched it up in an instant. When they'd exhausted their supply of toast, Curtis brushed the crumbs off his hands and they proceeded down the path toward the gazebo, where they would pass the painter.

They approached quietly from behind, not wanting to disturb her concentration. It was the polite thing to do, Curtis thought, knowing that he himself would never be able to paint with an audience. The artist, a young woman he judged by the shape of her ample ass (a little big for his taste), wore jeans, a man's plaid flannel shirt, and an adjustable khaki baseball cap, through the back of which projected a black ponytail. They looked over her shoulder at the painting. It was of mixed media. Watercolors had been used to color the sky, as well as the pond (in various shades of blue, not its actual green). Instead of buildings across the park, she had painted a distant countryside from her imagination. The watercolors had obviously been painted earlier, for the paint was thoroughly dry. On the left side of the painting, she'd drawn cattails and a willow in oil pastel. The middle had been left intentionally blank. She was in the process of penciling in a quarter of the gazebo and a young girl who sat at the railing with her chin on her hands, gazing at the ducks with a melancholy air.

"Hey Gwyn!" Sammy waved at the girl in the gazebo. Stephanie twisted on her folding stool to eye them.

Curtis raised a hand in surprised salute. "I had no idea you were an artist. You're really good."

"You've brought your easel."

"Oh, I...," he stammered. "We were just going to have some fun."

"That's the spirit. I'm glad you've kept at it. Most of my customers quit after a week."

"We've been having fun with it, but I'm no artist. Not like you."

"You might consider taking one of my classes."

"You teach?" he asked rhetorically, feeling stupid the moment he let loose the words. Of course she taught; hadn't she just said as much?

"At the store on Wednesday nights. It's two hours."

"Ah, but didn't you say that taking a class was a bad idea?"

"When you're just starting, yes, I believe that, particularly for children. You should just try to have fun and let your creative juices flow. You don't want your creativity to be inhibited by a lack of technique. But if you've stuck with it awhile, as you have, then you might want some pointers on technique."

"I don't have any technique to speak of," Curtis said.

She asked for his email address and phone number and painted the information on the bottom left corner of her painting. "I'll email you the details. Now, set up your easel."

"Oh no, I couldn't."

"Why not?"

"I'm not a real artist."

"Everyone is an artist. You don't have to be a professional to be an artist."

"I'm not any good. I'd look like a fool"

"Everybody has to start *some*where. You just need practice."

"How long have *you* been at it?"

"Ten years...a little more."

"See."

Sammy ran to the gazebo to visit with Gwyn.

Curtis asked if they lived in the vicinity.

Stephanie gestured with a nod of the head to Blake Street along the eastern edge of the park. "Four blocks down that street. Now, set up your easel. I'll give you a free lesson."

"I'd be embarrassed."

"Why would you be embarrassed?"

"Anyone can paint better; I'll look like a *poseur*."

Stephanie sighed with exasperation. "You need to work on your self-esteem."

"It's taken a beating lately."

"Never mind; just set up."

"I really will look stupid next to you."

"Painting is not a competitive sport."

Curtis hesitated, trying to think of an excuse and feeling a bit manipulated.

"Come on," she coaxed. "I'll make it simple. Let me guide you."

Curtis reluctantly set up his easel. Stephanie picked up four oil pastels. "May I?" she asked and drew a rather abstract representation of the corner of the gazebo in four quick strokes, each line in a different color. "Ok, now wet the paper and color three bands corresponding to the sky, the park and the pond. Here, use my broad brush."

As Curtis followed her instructions, Stephanie finished her pencil sketch and started filling in the lines of the gazebo in white oil (though the real gazebo was dark green).

Gwyn looked up from her pose. "Are we done yet?" she whined.

"Oh, sorry. Yes, that's good. Thanks, hon."

"We're going to fly a kite," Gwyn yelled back as the two kids skipped off toward the grassy expanse between the playground and the baseball diamond.

Stephanie glanced at Curtis's picture. "Let that dry a few minutes," she instructed.

As she drew paint across the canvas she spoke. "Is Sammy still painting?"

"Yes, and drawing. This past couple of weeks we've been trying to do a picture a day. He went to his grandmother's last weekend..." And so the conversation turned from art to grandmothers and mothers-in-law, very briefly to Linda and the divorce, to business, and business travel, and hence to travel in general, and the fact that Curtis and Sammy would be flying to San Diego for Thanksgiving.

"I was a beach bum as a kid."

"I've always wanted to visit California. Why on earth did you leave?"

"I went to school out here; I was recruited out of college by a brokerage; the job was here."

"Have you ever thought about moving back?"

"I couldn't afford it. Besides, Sammy's here." After a moment he asked, "What about you? Where are you from?"

"Right here. Well, Lewiston, actually, but close enough. I always thought I'd live in Paris."

"Do you speak French?"

"Just high school French. Have you ever been?"

"We went to Paris on our honeymoon."

"What's it like?"

"Well, you've seen the pictures; it's a beautiful city. Huge parks and boulevards. Great food."

"What was your favorite part?"

"I suppose climbing to the top of the cathedral of Notre Dame. Then the stained glass in Sainte-Chapelle."

"There's a religious theme there. Is religion one of your interests?"

"God no!" he blurted out almost reflexively. Then they both burst into laughter at the ironic exclamation. Gaining control of himself again, he added, "But I do find religious architecture inspiring."

"And religious art?"

"Oh no, I don't care for it. We went to the Prado in Madrid. They should call that..."

"The Prado? You're so lucky. I've always wanted to go to the Prado."

"I was going to say, they should call it the Museum of Christian Suffering. It's nothing but Christ going up on the cross and Christ coming down from the cross. Gruesome images."

For a couple of minutes, Stephanie was lost in concentration as she worked on the portrait of Gwyn.

"Do you sell your paintings?" he asked.

"Now and then. I don't make a living at it, if that's what you mean."

"But you're an art teacher."

"And a clerk, and a student."

"Art History?"

"No, I'm taking business courses. Right now, I'm taking a class on Marketing and Public Relations."

"Seems a long way from your passion."

"Even an artist has to pay the bills, and to pay bills as an artist you have to know how to promote yourself. There are tens of thousands of talented artists you'll never hear about, because they don't know how to promote themselves. I know; I've been one."

"That's funny; that's just what I was telling Sammy about musicians."

"Is your background dry?" she asked, indicating his watercolor. She scooted her stool over to Curtis's easel and demonstrated how to make the semblance of cattails with a combination of oil pastels and watercolor. "There, try that."

After a few minutes she said, "That's not bad, but you're being too meticulous; it'll take you all day if you do it like that. Here, look at this."

She made a number of quick strokes on her own canvas. "Now, for these three or four in the foreground, I put more effort into it, more focus. I load the brush with two shades of green and twist the brush as I make the stroke. See? This way your eye is drawn to these few blades, the rest are just background."

Curtis followed suit. He was a quick study, and was soon absorbed in the work.

Stephanie leaned over to look at his progress. "Very good; you've got it."

They had worked silently side-by-side for quite a while, when Gwyn and Sammy came back, *sans* kite.

"The stwing bwoke," Sammy said, slipping into baby talk and looking dejected.

"The kite's on top of that building," Gwyn added, pointing.

"*C'est la vie*," Curtis said.

Sammy sidled over to Stephanie's easel and cocked his head to the side, taking measure of her work. "That's good," Sammy pronounced.

"Thank you, Samuel. I hear you've been drawing, too."

"I drawed Sadie," he said.

"His grandmother's dog," Curtis supplied.

"Ah. Do you like Sadie?"

"She's a big dog. She likes balls. You wanna see my pitcher?"

"I'd love to."

"You can come home with us."

"Oh, well thank you, Sammy, but I can't today," she said smiling, silently communicating to Curtis that she knew the invitation of a child was not to be taken seriously.

"We would be happy to have you," Curtis said, extending an adult invitation that she could accept or decline.

"Can we, Mom?" Gwyn pleaded.

Curtis hoped she'd come. He liked Stephanie, though he had to admit there was no chemistry there. In fact, it was the lack of chemistry that made her so easy to be with. She was so *not* his type that he felt no need to posture or flirt. She was like a sister, he decided, a nice young lady to be admired but not pursued. Some women were like that. Others elicited a visceral response that nearly made him growl (or purr) with sexual excitement. However, he could use another friend, particularly a female with a kind word to say.

"I really can't," Stephanie said. "I have to be careful getting this painting back to our apartment without smearing the oils. And I'm working this afternoon. As a matter of fact, I'll be late if we don't hurry. But we'll take a rain check, if you don't mind."

"Why not come over after Thanksgiving?" Curtis offered. Then, as they began to break down their easels, he mumbled, "I'll finish this at home."

"It's done, isn't it? At least, to my eye, it is," Stephanie said. "It's important to know when to stop. I think you've conveyed the essence of the scene."

"No, there's no life in it. No ducks, no turtles, no people. I wish I could paint people."

"That's where technique comes in. It's simply a tool to help you achieve your vision. If you had the technique, what would you include to make the painting complete in your eyes?"

"I'd add a few ducks at the edge of the pond, a little girl feeding them, and Sammy in the background flying a kite."

"Would you like me to show you how?"

"Sure."

"This won't be realistic. That would take more time. This will be impressionistic."

With oil paint she added a few brown ducks and a little girl with pigtails crouched at the edge of the pond, one hand outstretched. In the background, she painted a red kite with a bowed string reaching down to a little boy in a red shirt and blue jeans. The strokes were spare — the boy was nothing more than a combination of two strokes of blue for the legs, a red rectangle for his body, an ochre streak for an arm, and a brown splotch of hair. Yet viewed from five feet, it was undeniably a little boy flying a kite. It was just right.

"I could do that," Sammy said with confidence.

"I have no doubt," laughed Stephanie.

Chapter 14

Monday, November 24 – Sunday, November 30 2008

Wednesday morning Curtis monitored the Market from his apartment while he packed his bags. He picked up Sammy on the way to the airport. He had expected Linda to somehow duck a confrontation by shoving Sammy out the door, but she surprised him by carrying Sammy's suitcase out to the car. She gave her son a big hug and a kiss on the cheek and saw him into his booster seat. Then she turned and pecked Curtis on the cheek. Her eyes were sad and her mouth twisted as though unsure whether to smile or cry. Her demeanor confused him; she had shown so little emotion during their break-up, and now, at last, she seemed to grasp the enormity of her decision. "Say hi to your parents for me." Tears pooled in her eyes. She turned up the walk, hanging her head and holding her cardigan sweater closed against the blustering wind.

Thanksgiving was an orgy of gluttony. They served the meal at mid-day. Curtis's brother Patrick and his wife Denise, showed up at 11:30, bearing pumpkin pie and asparagus wrapped in prosciutto. William had baked the turkey. Silvia had made macaroni salad, stuffing, cranberry relish, and green beans with bacon bits. Curtis went out to the liquor store and brought back a Gewürztraminer and Pinot Noir. Eloise and her husband Jeff arrived just as William was carving the turkey, bringing with them fruit and a pecan pie.

It was a festive and happy gathering. The subject of Linda was studiously avoided throughout the meal in deference to Sammy, and Curtis was grateful for the respite from the subject that he'd been obsessing about every spare moment, awake and asleep.

The conversation was lively, flowing from shared reminiscence to plans, from business to family, from books to movies. His mother engaged

Sammy in conversation about the flight, his school, his likes and dislikes at six-years-old. She commended his accomplishments, and told him how much he reminded her of his father at the same age. "He was very proud of reading, too. I remember he had three favorite books: *Bobby and His Airplanes; Mr. Wishing Went Fishing;* and... oh, what's the third?"

"*Fuzzy Dan,*" William supplied.

"We have those!" Sammy exclaimed.

"They must be the very same books; your father never throws anything away."

The mood didn't even sour when Patrick turned the focus to politics, pointedly demanding an opinion of Curtis. "How is the financial community taking the election of a Socialist?"

"Socialist? Obama?"

"You don't think he has a Socialist agenda?"

"If you understood the least little thing about our economic system, you'd know it's a hybrid system; it's not purely Capitalistic. Have you ever noticed that the same people who fear Socialism are the first to complain if anything threatens Social Security or Medicare? You can't have it both ways."

"You voted for him, didn't you? I can't believe it, my own brother turning liberal."

"Let's not get into name-calling," their mother remonstrated.

"I refuse to be sucked into labeling," Curtis retorted. "The problems in Washington can't be solved by following rigid ideologies. It takes cooperation, and who knows? — Maybe Obama will be able to get a dialogue going between the parties. That would be a welcome change."

"I wouldn't hold my breath."

"We can hope, can't we?"

"Here's to hope," their father said, raising a glass.

Between the meal and dessert, the table was cleared and Eloise whipped fresh cream. Curtis made a pot of Earl Grey tea. Jeff cut the pecan and pumpkin pies into wedges and put the berries into bowls.

While they ate pie they tried to catch up on personal news. Then, as they sat satiated during a lull between subjects Eloise said, "Sammy, I have a big present for you, but you can't have it until May."

"What is it?" he asked, bouncing in his seat.

"A cousin."

There was stunned silence, followed by a sudden eruption of congratulations all around the table.

After dinner, Eloise left for a second meal with her parents-in-law. Curtis sipped a flowery Gewürztraminer with his brother at the fence in the backyard of their childhood home, watching the sun drop slowly toward the Pacific.

"That's great news about Wheezie," Curtis said (Wheezie was their nickname for Eloise). "We'll be uncles. It's times like this I wished I lived closer."

"Yeah, that's great," Patrick said in a preoccupied tone. "Denise wants to start a family."

"I'm glad to hear it."

"I'm not so sure. Can I ask a personal question?"

"Go ahead."

"Did you cheat on her?"

"On Linda? God, no! Why would you think that?"

"Weren't you ever tempted?"

"I never met anyone I thought was more attractive."

"No, but looks aren't everything. What about compatibility?"

Curtis sensed the focus shift. "Are we talking about me here, or you?"

"I'm just saying — sometimes people just aren't meant...sometimes they don't fit."

"Are you and Denise having trouble?"

"It's nothing big; it's just, we've never been super compatible in the bedroom, and it's frustrating."

"Are you having an affair?"

"No, no, nothing like that. But there's this girl at work; we have lunch together, and we really hit it off. And sometimes I think, what if I found my soul mate and I'm already married? Do you follow your heart, or stick to your obligations? Do what makes you happy, or do what's expected of you?"

"I'm maybe not the best person to ask, considering my wife just dumped me for another man."

"Ooooh, sorry big brother. I didn't know. I mean, I knew about the divorce, of course, but I didn't know about...Damn, that sucks."

"It can be a messy business, following your heart."

"Is there any chance you might reconcile?" Patrick asked.

"Not likely."

"Then I gotta tell you, and I hope you don't take this the wrong way, but she wasn't my favorite person."

"Have you seen this?" their father called, waving a piece of paper at them as he crossed the lawn. It was a picture Sammy had drawn of a house and a tree by the ocean.

"We've been painting," Curtis said. "He's pretty good for a six-year-old."

"It's terrific." His father squeezed his arm. "I'm glad you came out."

"I thought it would be good for Sammy."

"What about you? Isn't it good for you?"

"I really didn't want to come. Don't get me wrong; you've all been great, but I'd just like to be alone. I feel like I let everybody down. I mean, you've been married 35 years, and I couldn't make it last eight."

"Marriage isn't a contest, son. Some marriages are sprints; some are marathons, and it's not always easy. Some don't go the distance, but at least you got a few good years, and you got Sammy. That's something to be proud of."

"You and Mom make it look easy."

"We've had some shaky moments. We almost didn't get married at all. I was going with a girl who happened to live next door to your mother when we were in college. Isabelle. I was crazy about her, but she didn't feel the same way about me. Then she went home on Spring Break and got knocked up by the boy next door. Your mother was going through a breakup of her own. So we spent time commiserating with each other, and one thing led to another. You know, I admire your mother enormously, but she wasn't Isabelle, and for a long time I knew your mother was thinking what life would've been like with Ralph. But we managed. We built a life. I don't know what makes a marriage work. Sometimes it's just a matter of putting up with one another; nobody's perfect."

The sun began its slide over the edge. Curtis finished his wine and propped the glass on a fence post. From what his father had said, it was obvious that Curtis's own existence was in many ways a fluke, a chance occurrence, a matter of Isabelle Somebody preferring someone else over his dad, and Ralph Somebody leaving his mother. But for that, he may never have been, and others who may have been, never were. One's very existence turned on the most ephemeral threads of needs and attractions.

"Look for someone who wants to make you happy," Bill Cooke said. "You still have a lot of life in front of you. And don't think about how the rest of us feel about it. Trust your heart."

"That's what I was telling him," Patrick said.

Curtis and Sammy woke early, as they had yet to adjust to the time zone. They let themselves quietly out of the house and walked down to the beach. Sammy took off his shoes and ran along the hard wet sand at the water's edge.

"I've got to get you here in the summer when the water's warm enough to swim in."

"Are there sharks?"

"Just little ones, and banjo sharks."

"They play banjos?"

"No, no. I don't know why they're called banjo sharks. They're shaped more like a shovel. Anyway, they're about as long as I am tall, grey and kind of flat, with itty-bitty mouths. They rest on the bottom and cover themselves with sand. We used to sneak up and grab their tails, and they'd go tearing off, and if we could hold on we'd get a pretty wild ride."

"I wish Mom was here."

"I know, buddy; me too." They walked in silence for a while, stopping at a heap of amber kelp to examine its roots for tiny crustaceans and brittle stars. "Has your mom talked to you about what's going on?"

"Uh huh."

"What did she say?"

"You aren't coming back home."

Curtis thought about that for a moment. He didn't want to convey that the choice was his; Sammy might interpret it as an act of abandonment.

Nor did he want to lay the blame solely on Linda, because Sammy had to live with her, and it wouldn't be healthy to promote resentment.

"As much as I'd like to come home, your mother doesn't want to live with me anymore. I don't expect you to understand; I hardly understand, myself. Adult relationships are difficult. Just know that your mother and I may live apart, but that doesn't change how we feel about you. You want to know a funny thing?"

"What?"

"I'm not related to your mother, but I'm related to you; you're part of me. And you're part of your mother. So you'll always be a part of both of our lives. You'll come to my place on the weekends, when you want, and I'm always just a phone call away."

"Why doesn't she want you to live with us?"

"It's complicated. I guess I got so wrapped up in my work I forgot what was important. I didn't pay her enough attention. I didn't know what she was feeling, and she didn't say anything until things had gone too far."

"She likes Uncle Roger," Sammy said disconsolately.

So Roger had been promoted to uncle. Curtis could live with that; they could call Roger anything they wanted, as long as it wasn't 'dad.' "I guess she does. He seems nice enough. Do you like him?" Curtis carefully modulated his voice to make sure the question was not leading. As much as he despised Roger, it wouldn't help to turn Sammy against him.

"He's okay," Sammy answered, taking his father's hand. "Do you like someone else, too?"

"You mean a girl? No, I haven't been looking. But I don't like living alone. I might meet someone I like in the future. Of course, you'd have to like her, too, or I wouldn't have anything to do with her." Curtis hoisted Sammy onto his shoulders and held him steady by the ankles. "Because you're the most important person in my life."

At this time of year, the beach was nearly deserted. To their left the waves rolled into shore. Three hundred yards ahead, a couple walked hand-in-hand. Farther down the beach a jogger and his dog steadily approached.

"I'm sorry, Sammy. I'm sorry things turned out like this."

"It's okay, Dad," Sammy said, pretending that the locks of hair he held were the reins of a bridle and his father was a tall horse.

"Did you have a good time?" Linda asked Sammy with enthusiasm when she opened the door.

Curtis almost mistook her bright warmth for genuine interest, had he not noticed Roger's car parked across the street, and recognized her animation for what it was — covering. He guessed that Roger was keeping out of sight to avoid a confrontation. He needn't have bothered; Curtis had his emotions in check. "We had a wonderful time, didn't we Sammy?"

"We flied on top o' the clouds," Sammy boasted. "And Daddy grabbed sharks by the tail."

Linda looked askance.

"An old story," Curtis explained without explaining.

"Ah," was all Linda said, meaning that she was not really interested.

Sammy went into the house dragging his little suitcase. Linda stood squarely in the doorway, her physical posture eloquently forbidding Curtis to enter.

"Next week is the week we usually cut our Christmas tree," Curtis said, blowing steam like a whale in the cold air. "So, I was wondering..."

"I bought an artificial tree."

"Oh," Curtis barked, taken by surprise. She had never even wanted to buy a pre-cut tree, had always insisted that they cut their own. "Do you want me to come over and decorate it?"

"No, I think we can manage."

"Okay," he nodded. "I was going to get a tree for the apartment, too, but I'll need some ornaments."

"Yeah, sure, take anything you want. I'll have the boxes down when you pick up Sammy on Friday."

"Okay, okay. And I'd like a few of the Christmas CDs."

"We'll divide them up when you pick up Sammy."

"That's okay, then."

"Good night, Curtis." With that she turned and closed the door behind her.

As he opened the car door he looked back at the house. The living room glowed dimly, as though by a single lamp. The kitchen window was brightly lit, as was Sammy's bedroom above it. He had a relationship with this house. This was the physical manifestation of the last five years of his life, with all of its hopes, its successes and failures, its sacrifices and expectations. It represented everything he had aspired to. On other nights, returning from the Fines, the lights had been a beacon, a haven, his safe harbor. Tonight the sodium vapor streetlamp threw a tattoo of leafless elm branches across the front of the house, and the glowing windows seemed distant and unwelcoming.

On his way back to the apartment (he still couldn't bring himself to think of it as "home") he detoured to Bed Bath & Beyond. He needed a wall clock for the bathroom, and some pillows to lean against while watching movies from the sofa bed. In the clock department he was assisted by a young lady of no more than 19 or 20, he supposed, a thin brunette with a pinched nose, too much make-up and a nasally accent. He remembered his father saying, *"Maybe there's another girl out there for you."* But, he concluded instantly that this girl was not his type, and besides, she was too young. Another young lady in the pillows and bedding department was another matter entirely. She was striking, 22 to 24-years-old, he surmised, with bright, engaging green eyes, light brown hair and a winning smile that made him glad to be young and alive. Then he noticed her wedding ring and discreetly turned off his libido. But there was a certain excitement in the freedom he now felt in just looking. The store was full of women. He felt like a shopper in a clothing store where some of the clothes were new, some old, some attractive, some worn out, some already sold, some not to his liking, and others that he might like to try on for size. Like Goldilocks, he thought, one was too hard, one was too soft, but one was bound to be just right. *Maybe there's another girl out there for you.*

He felt buoyed by the freedom to feel desire. Since the previous spring, as Linda had responded to his sexual overtures as though put-upon, he had felt guilty, as though his desire was somehow unwholesome or contemptuous. *It's a wonder the species has survived,* he thought. Then considering the way humans had overpopulated the planet, he thought there must either be a lot of unhappy, put-upon women in the world, or other women were not so dispassionate.

Away from Linda's glare, Curtis felt free to open the cage of repressed desire. He loved women. Unabashed appreciation of feminine charms was one of the most basic emotions that made his life seem worthwhile. And though he sometimes found their minds dark, labyrinthine traps, their physicality was breathtaking: the softness of their skin, the entrancing timbre of their voices, their gentle curves, their elegance of line, they way their breasts jiggled, the way their hips swung, the way they laughed with such unfeigned joy. Like sweets in a candy store, the world was full of women — wonderful, beautiful, beguiling women.

PART THREE
DUCKS and RABBITS

Chapter 15

Monday December 1 – Sunday December 7, 2008

Barbara stood at her desk, buttoned her coat, wrapped a muffler around her neck, and bent to fish her purse out from under the desk, presenting her skinny posterior to the window/wall that separated her workstation from Curtis's office. But Curtis was far too engrossed in staring at his computer monitor to notice. Angie Osterfeld and Kendra McDonald, the two secretaries shared by his cubicle crew, arrived then, dressed warmly, with purses slung over their shoulders. Kendra looked ready to party. Barbara rapped on the door and opened it to say, "It's after five. You want anything before I go?"

"A crystal ball," Curtis answered facetiously, then glanced up and answered in earnest, "No, you go ahead." His eyes slid off Barbara's shoulder and caught Angie's forlorn gaze. He smiled what he hoped was a kindly smile, having been privy to the "secret" shared by Barbara, that Angie's boyfriend of two years had dumped her. *Welcome to the club*, Curtis thought. They might all be part of the *Looking for Work Club* if the Market didn't stabilize soon.

The previous holiday-shortened week had seen broad-based gains across all sectors as panic abated. However, a weekend's reflection had brought on another panic attack on Monday. The DOW had plummeted 680 points, a loss of 7.7%, and yet the mood in the office had been quiet. There were no groans, no sudden expletives shouted, just unrelenting tension and silent resignation. These huge swings now elicited a yawn, as everyone knew that tomorrow could bring a similarly monstrous move to the upside. The problem was that the underlying structure, upon which valuation was based, had broken.

Earlier that afternoon Erickson had sent out an email notification canceling most business travel. "In light of the Credit Crisis and the resulting instability of the stock market, all travel for marketing purposes is hereby canceled, with the exception of those of you in the ETF and currency markets, which continue to offer attractive hedge positions." Curtis read the memo, ruefully reflecting that the travel ban came too late to save his marriage.

"Listen to this," Elliot said, directing the music with his right hand as they sped down the boulevard toward home. "This is where Sinbad's ship goes to pieces on the rocks. You hear the way the music surges? This piece has become such a cliché, but Beecham's rendition breathed life into it!" Classical music was Elliot's particular passion. Listening to a piece on the radio he could usually tell the name the composer, and often could identify the orchestra, the soloist, and conductor. As they drove home along the boulevard on Thursday the radio played the fourth movement of Scheherazade, and Elliot was telling Curtis about the conductor, Sir Thomas Beecham, when Curtis's cell phone began playing Ode to Joy. Elliot turned off the radio. Curtis answered.

Linda screamed into the phone, "What were you thinking — buying Sammy paints?!"

"He wanted...."

"He's got it all over the bedspread!"

"Sorry, but..."

"You confer with me before you buy anything again!"

The phone went dead. Curtis stared at it as though he'd been slapped. "Linda," he said to Elliot, who turned the radio back on. Suddenly, and for the first time, Curtis was not unhappy to be going to his apartment instead of his home. It was a refuge from his wife's inexplicable fury.

"What did she want?"

"She just wanted to yell at me. Sammy made a mess with the paints I bought him, and she's pissed. They were only watercolors." Still thinking about paint a minute later, the sign for Bolton's Art Supplies came into sight ahead. "Pull over at the art store; I want to grab something. I'll only be a minute."

"They turned out nicely," Stephanie said, as Curtis paid for the two framed paintings.

"They really do look a lot better framed."

"You know, I was thinking: you ought to try watercolor pencils and pens. I should have suggested it before, but I honestly didn't expect you to stick with it (so few do)."

So he bought a set of watercolor pens and pencils, and Stephanie gave him another book on technique. "The cover got ripped on this one, so we can't sell it," she explained, "but it's still a good book. It has a section on how to use the pencils." Curtis politely asked to be remembered to Gwyn, and left.

When he arrived at the apartment Curtis flipped on the lights, turned up the thermostat, shucked off his suit coat, tie and shoes, and spent half an hour deciding on finding just the right place to hang the two framed paintings. They weren't great paintings, but the framing made them seem more legitimately "art" somehow. He hung both of them on the dining room side of the screen, where they lent the room an air of permanent habitation that was previously lacking.

That task accomplished, he poured himself a glass of King Estate Pinot Gris, and emptied his pockets onto the counter — money clip, credit cards, receipts, change and keys — and turned on his cell phone (he hadn't bothered to install a landline). The cell phone chimed, indicating that he had voicemail. He didn't receive many calls on the cell; not many had his number; it might be Linda or Elliot, his parents or siblings, or perhaps his lawyer.

"Hi, Mr. Cooke," came Stephanie Walzer's voice, "I forgot to mention our upcoming watercolor class on Wednesday, from 6:30 to 8:30 at the store. I hope you can make it, but no pressure if you don't have the time. If you have any questions you can call me at the store, or on my cell...." She left a number and hung up.

He sat down to watch Monday night football, and in the back of his mind he debated whether or not to take a class. It would require a commitment of time. On the other hand, it was mid-week, he had nothing better to do, and there might be single women. It had been so long since he'd been "on the market," so to speak, that he hardly knew how to proceed, and he wondered if he was rushing things in even thinking about it. Did he really need a woman in his life? The answer was a tentative "yes." He felt incomplete — unfulfilled both sexually and emotionally, and a new relationship would be his affirmation that he was ready to move on and embrace his future in a positive way, instead of wallowing in self-pity for what he'd lost. Linda had moved on; that was clear.

Nevertheless, how did one begin dating again at an age when the most desirable women were all taken? Was he, himself desirable to women? The thought occurred to him that younger women might view him as admirably mature. But would they distrust a divorced man? Would Sammy prove a deterrent? And where did you meet them? There were a couple of attractive, unmarried women at work, but inter-office romances were discouraged. He didn't know which way to turn. As Elliot had so sagely observed, it was all about the marketing. He had to learn how to market himself.

He muted the television and called his sister. "Don't pick up women in bars," she advised. "Do you really want to settle down with the kind of woman who picks up men in bars? Join a club, or take classes at the community college."

"There's a painting class I was thinking of taking."

"That's just the thing," she said, making up his mind for him.

He was happy to relinquish control. He didn't want the internal debate. *Just tell me what to do*, he thought. *Instruct me.*

Having lost interest in the game, he set up his easel in front of the television and began doodling with paint.

Where once he had begun his workday full of confidence, in this current climate of whipsawing markets he approached the day with fatalism, secretly convinced he would soon lose his job, and for good reason. His assumptions were no longer valid; his strategic model no longer worked.

He discussed alternative strategies with Elliot as they drove to work on Tuesday.

"You've been trading on fundamentals," Elliot said, "which might have worked in a sane market, but this is not a sane market. This is nuts. The only way to really survive this market is to take short term positions, really short term, and play them both up and down."

Elliot was going through a Russian phase and they were listening to Dimitri Shostakovich's Symphony Number 2. "Listen to this part. I often wonder what his work would have been like if he'd composed in the West," Elliot mused. "He was a loyal revolutionary, but his work was periodically banned by the Soviet government. He always had to please some committee."

Curtis thought about this awhile. "There's always a struggle between art and commerce."

"They wanted epic music, music to glorify the workers. He couldn't write love songs. Art should be democratic. It should be left up to the public whether it's good or bad, not some government committee."

"The public's not always the best arbiter of taste."

The left lane came to a halt and the middle lane rolled slowly forward. Under the sound of the symphony, a low frequency thumping shook the Volvo like the concussion of distant artillery. "What the hell is that?" Elliot asked rhetorically. The thumping grew louder until it rattled their windows and made the rearview mirror buzz rhythmically. A royal blue Toyota Corolla came abreast of them, its chrome hubcaps spinning crazily even as the car slowed nearly to a stop, its subwoofer doling out a punishing bass line to every ear within a block. The vibration passed through their bodies like cosmic rays.

"There ought to be a law!" Elliot roared. He aimed a finger at the Toyota and pulled an imaginary trigger.

The Toyota pulled ahead, but the subwoofer still pounded out its hip-hop beat over the symphony. Then the center lane stalled and the left lane began moving slowly forward. The volume increased with every foot gained. When they came abreast of the Toyota the left lane stopped. Elliot slid the passenger side windows down, opened the moon roof and cranked up the Shostakovich to maximum volume. Elliot bellowed, "Take that, you fucking Philistine!" Curtis doubted the Toyota driver would know a Philistine from an Armenian. The lanes now moved together, cellos and horns blaring, electric bass and subwoofer pounding. Curtis felt the noise like a physical assault. The Shostakovich boomed, the hip-hop music thumped his sternum with each beat. Suddenly he sat bolt upright, yelled "Enough!" and punched the button to turn off the CD player.

Elliot looked offended. "I'm just trying to spread a little culture."

"Just drive."

"I had a good day today," Elliot said as they exited the building in the twilight. The sky was a rich twilight blue. The neon signs of the bottom floor retail shops and restaurants gave a festive air to the downtown. "If I could do that every week I'd be sitting on a beach in (I don't know) Aruba or someplace."

"That would be sweet." Curtis hoped his friend was on to something. What a wonderful relief it would be to become financially independent. It opened the door to dreams. "What would you do if you won the lottery?"

"That depends — how big?"

"I don't know — 40 million."

"You mean after I quit my job in the first millisecond? I'd buy a second home in the Caribbean, or maybe Hawaii, and learn to surf."

Curtis looked skeptical; he couldn't imagine Elliot as an athlete. "That'll be the day."

"What would *you* do?"

Curtis had daydreamed about that on a few occasions. "I'd be a philanthropist. It's the one job in the world where you could really do some good and feel good about yourself."

On his way to the restroom Wednesday afternoon, Curtis could sense a furtive tension in the air. People were avoiding eye contact and it was unusually quiet. Standing at the urinal next to Nick Pacelli he said, "People are acting a little strange today. Is there something I'm missing?"

"You heard about Olmsted?"

"What about him?"

"He was fired this morning. They escorted him out of the building and had Debby pack up his personal stuff in a box. Rumor has it he was moving funds around to make it look like his biggest client wasn't getting burned."

Curtis flushed and zipped up. "Who's taking on his clients?"

"I don't know; I just know I don't want anything to do with it."

The Introduction to Watercolors class was held in a basement room of Bolton's Art Supplies. Stephanie had proposed the formation of the class to

Mr. Bolton himself, explaining how the store would receive $35 per student for supplies, as well as another $35 from those who decided to go on to the intermediate class. "And of course there are bound to be repeat customers."

"Give me a day to think about it," he'd said, because he never made a business decision without reflection. But in the end he acknowledged that he'd "be a fool to say no." For her part, she charged $48 per student for four two-hour-long classes spread over a month and a half (accounting for a break during the holidays).

Elliot dropped Curtis off at 6:20. The class was to start at 6:30. The classroom was a windowless room with three rows of long tables and three demonstration easels at the front. There were 14 students varying in age from 20 to over 50. Being one of the last to arrive, Curtis sat at an available seat at the back of the room. He was immediately struck with the fact that he was the only one in a suit. To make himself less conspicuous he hung his coat on the back of his chair, took off his tie and rolled up his sleeves.

Curtis tried to be attentive to Stephanie's directions as he checked out the women. He had hoped to find a date among them, but of the eleven women, eight were either wearing rings, or were too old. Of the four without rings, and therefore presumably single, he found two unattractive. The other two sat in the front row on either side of a man in his late 50's with thinning grey hair.

Stephanie took roll, remembering the several students who were also clients of the store and with whom she was already acquainted. When she had passed out kits of paints and brushes to those who needed them, taken payment from those who hadn't paid, and made sure that everyone had the proper tools and had paper cups filled with water, the instruction got underway. She proved to be a competent teacher, beginning with a few comments on artistic pursuits, doing her best to make the subject as unintimidating as possible, then passed on to the properties of watercolor and its uses. She provided examples on the easels as the class followed along. Curtis was lost in the process of creation, each stroke beginning as an idea and ending in a line on paper that either did or did not conform to his expectations. At this point it hardly mattered: He was not skilled enough to produce what his mind conceived, so he had to content himself with enjoying the process and the occasionally serendipitous end product.

He paid only half attention. He didn't deceive himself; he knew he'd come here more to scope out the women than to become a better painter. Men could be almost predatory at times, he admitted to himself, and as one of that class, he was subject to the same drives and desires as most men. Certainly, that was natural. The problem was that he didn't know what women wanted. If women were driven by the same desires as men, they would be easy to figure out. But their motives were hidden from his view. Why would any of *them* be interested in *him*? What did he have to offer? And if women were merely mercenary, trading affection for security, looking for the highest bidder as some anthropologists suggested, did he really want to subject himself to such humiliation and debasement?

Stephanie demonstrated how to load the brush with paint, and how to use the brush as a sponge to sop up excess water. Then she guided them through the process of preparing a background using the wet-on-wet technique. "Now let's take a 15-minute break to let the paper dry."

As his fellow students filed out Curtis stood, hoping to catch the eye of the blonde in the front row. She did look at him, he smiled, and she smiled back as she filed out of the room. Most were headed to the restrooms, a few went outside to smoke, and a few killed time by wandering the store upstairs. Curtis waited for the blonde to return.

"Did you have a good trip?" Stephanie asked.

Lost in his thoughts, Curtis took a moment to respond. "It was better than I thought it would be."

"And Sammy?"

"He had a wonderful time. He loves to fly. And we took him to the zoo, my parents and I."

"Sounds like fun." There ensued an awkward silence as Curtis searched for a response. Then Stephanie broke the silence. "If your invitation is still open, I'd like to bring Gwyn by and see some of Sammy's paintings on Saturday. I don't get off work until three."

"We're going to cut our Christmas tree on Saturday. But we should be back by three."

"Oh," she said a little wistfully, "that sounds lovely."

"You could come with us, if you'd like," Curtis said without thinking, though in retrospect he didn't really regret the offer; it might be nice to have company.

"I'm sorry, we can't."

"We could reschedule."

"No, really, I don't know why I said that. Honestly, I can't afford it. Anyway, I have to work. I've just always thought it would be nice." Then she added, almost apologetically, "We wait until after the 20th, when they drop the prices at the tree lot in the park. Thanks, though. Thanks for asking. Where do you go?"

"A Christmas tree farm up near Willhamsette."

"I've heard it's nice; I've never been; I don't have a car, so we don't get out of the city much."

"We should be back by three," he reiterated. "You'll need the address." He tore off a corner of watercolor paper and wrote his address on it, then excused himself to pay a visit to the restroom and search for the blonde.

He found her looking at a bulletin board in the hallway. She wore tight-fitting jeans and a coral-colored loose-fitting sweater with the sleeves pushed up her forearms. She was about 25, he thought. She was pretty, though she wore more makeup than he preferred — mascara, smoky eyeliner and pale pink lipstick that made her lips glossy.

"Where'd you get your coffee?" he asked. It was a stupid question; the cup was emblazoned with the Starbucks logo.

"At Starbucks. Across the street."

"Thanks." He started to leave and turned back. "Do you have the time?" he asked, though he could have looked at his own watch.

She glanced at hers. "7:35."

"Oh, I guess I don't have time, then. To get to Starbucks and back," he added.

"Probably not. You want a sip of mine?"

"That would be great."

"It's a Latte."

"Great. It's been a long day; I need a jolt." He sipped the nearly scalding coffee and handed it back. "I'm Curtis," he said, extending his hand.

"Gretchen," she said, smiling, and shook his hand in the way women did — rather soft and weak, as if not quite sure to trust the hand proffered.

"Have you been painting long?" he asked.

"Me? No, never. You?"

"I started a couple months ago. I'm not very good yet."

"That's why we're here."

Other students were filing back into the room. "We better get back to it. Thanks for the coffee."

For the next 45 minutes, Stephanie guided them through the steps of adding foreground elements by applying wet-on-dry and dry-on-dry techniques. In the end, everyone had the semblance of a waterfall, wooded mountaintop and sky at sunset.

At the conclusion of class, as everyone made ready to leave, Curtis addressed a general question to the class, asking if anyone wanted to share a cab. He received a few negative answers and shaken heads in reply. He checked his cell phone. There was no reception in the basement. He was on the stairs when Gretchen asked, "Which way are you headed?"

"The Western Addition, just past the small park there."

"It's not too far out of my way; I'll drive you."

She drove a Honda Civic with a moon roof. On the way to the apartment, he learned she was an unemployed sous chef, working on a cookbook while she searched for a job. When they pulled to the curb Curtis asked, "Do you want to come up for a drink?" It was a stock question requiring a stock answer, a way of judging interest.

She looked at him with an amused smile. "As long as it's more than one," she said playfully.

Gretchen drank her first glass of wine as she stalked around the room like a cat taking measure of its surroundings. She paused at the window to look down, then moved from painting to painting. "I thought you said you just started painting."

"That's right. Just a couple of months."

"These are really...different."

"Some of them are my son's; he's six."

"But they're really good. I like this one," she said, pausing in front of the white tower. "It's big."

"It's a lighthouse."

"Sure it is," she laughed. He poured her another glass of Chardonnay. "What kind of music do you have?"

He had brought a few CDs away from Westlake Drive. As he'd always assumed he'd be returning, he'd left the majority of his collection at home. Here he had just five jazz CDs, three classical CDs, and two rock-and-roll CDs. She looked at them with a smirk. "No hip hop? I gotta turn you on to hip hop. This stuff is ancient."

"You might like this," he said, slipping a Paul Desmond CD into the player.

In the short time she'd been looking at the music, she had finished her second glass of wine and now poured another to the brim. Curtis had not seen anyone make a concerted effort to get smashed since college, and he watched with fascination and a bit of apprehension, hoping she wouldn't end up passed out on his floor, or worse — throwing up on the floor.

"You got anything with a beat?" She was looking at his music again. "Ok, here," she said, slipping a Dire Straits CD into the machine. She began dancing to the music, moving to the beat. She possessed that peculiarly feminine trick of being able to move her hips in the opposite direction from her torso, a sensual, undulating movement that extended out her arms to her fingertips. And through it all, swaying and bobbing in a most serpentine fashion, she managed not to spill a drop. "Come on and dance."

"I'm not much of a dancer."

"It's easy. Come 'ere." She set the half-drunk glass on the counter and pulled her sweater off over her head, mussing her hair. She wore a white tank top, revealing a tattoo on either bicep. The right arm sported crossed chef's knives, the left a whisk. She pulled him close as she danced. He had his hands on her waist, feeling the pulse of her hips. "See, it's easy." She rubbed against him, eliciting the usual male response. She kissed him then, a long, slow, sensuous kiss, and for the first time in his life he discovered a woman who compared favorably to Linda, if only in this one regard. This woman was a superior kisser.

He found himself staring at her tattoos. Though it was becoming commonplace among his generation, he still had an aversion to tattoos, as his early impressions had been of low-life types, rough characters in gangs, biker chicks, ex-cons. And there was the memory of an old lady at the beach, whose tattooed mermaid had sagged into a grotesque caricature on her leathery skin. Then there were the tattoos that people would come to regret in time, those that spoke of youthful passions and fancies that would seem remote and ridiculous with the passing of years. When she caught him looking, he said, "Those are clever tattoos."

"You wanna see my pig?"

What could he say to such a rhetorical question? She turned around, pulled up her tank top and bent over. A blue outline of a pig with the diagram of various cuts of pork was tattooed on the small of her back.

"Oh lord!" Curtis exclaimed, not at the tattoo, but at her exquisitely shaped ass so provocatively presented. He had the urge to mount her right there, and that thought reminded him of Linda, who did not encourage sexual athleticism. In college, in all of their years of marriage, she had allowed him to test half a dozen positions, none of which were to her taste. So, to please her they had settled on a life of low impact missionary-position sex, except on his birthday when she consented to be on top for part of the time. He reached out his hand and stroked Gretchen's pig.

"Ooo, that tickles!" she squealed, jumping up and turning around with eyes wide open and a crooked smile. "You wanna see my snakes?"

"Sure," he said, finding the beat of the music now, and just a bit entranced by the show she was putting on.

Gretchen unbuttoned the front of her jeans and pulled the zipper down, revealing two snake tattoos, one red and one blue, rising from the cleft of her pudenda, as he could clearly see through the semi-transparent pink thong that barely concealed her shaved crotch. "I'd like to introduce your snake to mine," she said, running her hand up the inside of his leg and licking her lips. "You really need better music. I like to fuck to music. Do you like to fuck to music?"

Common sense left his head as blood began rushing to his groin. *Why turn down a gift?* he thought. He said not a word, but cupped her ass and pulled her close as he kissed her. He knew he ought to feel guilty, but who was taking advantage of whom? And it had been a long dry spell.

"I...I don't know," he stammered. "I never really...I've never done it to music."

"You can get a good rhythm goin'," she said, grinding her hips against his.

Through the next forty minutes he entered a world of which he had no knowledge, except in fantasy. Even in college, in her most ardent moments, Linda had never approached him with such insatiable lust. Gretchen rode him on top while listening to hip hop music on her iPod and singing raunchy lyrics. She bade him take her from behind, she reawakened his flagging desire with oral stimulation, she wrapped her legs around his and left him feeling thoroughly used and satisfied. He fell asleep with her curled around him, arm and leg flung over his chest and genitals, her mouth breathing softly against his neck.

He dreamt that he was shopping in the supermarket, naked except for his socks. He tried to hide his nudity with the shopping cart, then a cereal box, but no one took notice, save an old lady who glared at him, clucked her tongue reproachfully, and shook her head. Then he began to float above the aisles like a helium balloon that has lost its moorings. A redhead and a blonde peered up at him in surprise and jumped up and down, trying to grab his wagging cock, but it was just out of reach. In his dream, he was aware that he'd drifted over the produce aisle because he smelled rotting vegetables, mushrooms perhaps, or pumpkins.

His eyes snapped wide open as he came awake. Something was wrong. The air was filled with the palpable stench of rotten eggs. His first thought was that the pilot light must have gone out on the stove and they were in danger of being asphyxiated or blown to smithereens. Then he remembered the stove and water heater were both electric. What's more, a candle guttering by the bed had not set off an explosion. Gretchen flung back the covers, releasing a bouquet that would have wilted the flowers on the nightstand, had there been any, and padded silently to the bathroom. A moment later she let rip with such a prodigious blast that he wondered it didn't shake the door. The toilet flushed. She reentered the room, closing the door quietly behind her, and stole back to the bed trailing a noisome vapor that clung to her like a shroud. *At least,* he thought, *she left the bulk of it in the bathroom.* It was but a fleeting hope, however, as the cloud began to seep under the closed door. With his full concentration on the bathroom, the sound of water filling the toilet bowl awoke in him a sudden and insistent urge to pee. This was trouble; he really had to go, but he couldn't bring himself to willingly march into that fog.

A soft pop issued from Gretchen's side of the bed and it was as though the door had been flung wide on a crypt. Curtis fought the urge to retch, scooted discretely to the edge of the bed, pulled the sheet to his nose to filter the air, and feigned sleep.

He waited a full five minutes as his bladder expanded, before slipping from the bedroom. Her breathing was shallow and even, an indication that she was asleep (he didn't want to embarrass her by acknowledging that he knew who had dealt it). The front room/kitchen was dimly lit by moonlight. He navigated his way to the kitchen, felt through the cabinet for a tall glass, and for the second time that night thanked the holy darkness that he was a man. He relieved himself, poured it down the drain, and gave the glass a cursory rinse.

Now what? He really did not want to walk back into that room. The barrage might be over but then again.... His feet were cold. There was only one alternative and he took it, unfolding the sofa bed and crawling under the covers.

He fell asleep almost immediately and was awakened shortly after sunrise when Gretchen emerged from the bedroom. The fresh young woman of the night before had been replaced by a frowzy, haggard crone with a hangover and bags under her mascara streaked eyes. She was already dressed and holding her shoes in one hand. "What are you doing out here?" she asked in a tone that was part inquisitive, part accusatory.

"You were..." he stammered, "...you were...snoring."

"Oh, yeah, I've been told that before. I've got to get home; I have to get ready for a job interview." She stumbled over to the kitchen and before he realized what was happening, she had taken the glass he'd peed in and filled it with water. *Why wouldn't she use a clean glass?* he wondered and hoping to stay her hand offered, "Can I make you a cup of coffee?"

She stared into space for a moment, contemplating the question. "Yeah, I could use a jump start." Then she took a large mouthful of water, gargled and spat into the sink.

God! he thought, *I hope she doesn't ask for a kiss!*

He made her coffee, told her to keep the commuter cup (he had several), saw her off, and headed for the shower, wondering if he would ever see her again, and he thought he might, as the sex had been good, really good — the best ever. But he didn't have her number (hell, he didn't even know her last name) and then there was the matter of...well, that could happen to anyone, poor girl. As long as it wasn't a chronic condition, he could forget about it.

He had never had a one-night-stand before, and it left him feeling a bit sleazy regardless of the momentary satisfaction. Yet throughout the following week he was haunted by the image of those snakes moving rhythmically on top of him, and of that pig as he banged her from behind.

Curtis spent Thursday evening doing laundry in the basement, and shopping for Christmas and Hanukah presents on the Internet. He bought Sammy a Fisher-Price digital camera, a sweater for his brother, a novel and calendar for his sister, a biography and a cookbook for his mother, and a National Geographic travel book for his father. He was stumped on what to get his secretary. For Elliot, he bought a CD of the obscure 19th -century pianist/composer Gottschalk. They had always exchanged Christmas cookies and bottles of wine with the other neighbors, and last year he'd given the Pobladors *The Finer Points of Sausage Dogs,* by Alexander McCall Smith, because they owned a Dachsund. He doubted Linda would continue the tradition.

"By the way, the neighborhood Christmas party is the 13th," Elliot said as they inched forward in the morning traffic listening to Corelli's Christmas Concerto.

"Whose turn is it?"

"It's at our house."

"Didn't you do it year before last?"

"Uh huh, but it was your turn this year, and since we didn't hear anything from Linda, Vicky volunteered."

"Okay, well thanks," Curtis said, wondering what other changes were occurring at his house, and in his imagination he could hear Linda saying, *It's not your house anymore.* And she was right; if it was his house, he would be hosting the Christmas party and he wouldn't have an aluminum tree. "What day is Hanukah?"

"Why"

"I have a present for you."

"Bring it to the Christmas party."

"Do you ever find it strange?"

"What?"

"Being Jewish and throwing a Christmas Party."

"I'm as much a Jew as you're a Christian."

There was that. Your antecedents determined your genes, but they didn't necessarily determine your beliefs. "I'm only a Dickensian Christian," Curtis declared upon reflection.

"What's that mean?"

"I believe in *A Christmas Carol* and its message of charity and generosity and living the Golden Rule, and always keeping in mind the past, the present and the future."

"I can get behind that. Besides, I like Christmas trees. I was always pissed as a kid, because even though my parents weren't practicing Jews, we were the only family on the block without a Christmas tree. I like Christmas trees."

"They're pagan."

"That's my point. And Santa is an elf. Besides, Christians have good music. Jews and Muslims will never win converts with their music."

Shadows of leafless trees ran over the Honda as it sped down the flat, two-lane road to Wilhamsette. They passed farms with stubble fields thinly veiled in snow. Mist drifted above the fields in the late morning sun. They drove in silence, Sammy sitting high in his booster chair, looking out the window at the passing scenery, Curtis keeping a lid on a stew of emotions that bubbled under the surface. He kept replaying the scenes of the morning. The Christmas boxes were piled on the living room floor. He'd transferred all of the ornaments he wanted into one of the boxes, fully expecting to have to negotiate over his selection, but Linda had gone into the kitchen to make coffee and seemed disinterested.

She showed little more interest when he announced his desire to take some of the CDs. About his jazz collection she cared nothing, but she did insist on having a say in the division of the Christmas albums. She took Bing and the Carpenters, James Galway, Dean Martin, and "It's Christmas, Charley Brown." He took Sinatra (the second album), Tuck Andress, Leon Redbone, and Dylan Thomas reading *A Child's Christmas in Wales*. They flipped for Nat King Cole and Curtis won. He was almost disappointed that no fight had ensued. There seemed no emotion in her, no anger or resentment, nor even annoyance. He might have expected *something* in those eyes — if not tenderness and love, perhaps contempt, impatience or pity. It was disconcerting to look into eyes that had once brightened when he walked into a room and find utter indifference, as though he were a ghost and simply irrelevant.

He'd also retrieved some Christmas DVDs, a heavy coat, a raincoat, after-ski boots and ski gloves — there was still so much that he'd left behind and now had no room to store in the apartment. Soon he'd have to pack all of the clothes and books and tools and memorabilia into boxes, and move them to a storage unit where they would molder until he could afford a bigger place.

The scenery passed by unremarked by Curtis, as in his mind's eye the morning's scenes kept intertwining with writhing snakes and cuts of pork. What was he going to do about Gretchen? Did he want a repeat performance? Could she possibly figure into his future? Could this sexual acrobat really provide a stable home for him and Sammy? She was, he remembered, a chef, so they would undoubtedly eat well. That was a plus. But chefs had horrendous hours, working from afternoon to late night, including weekends. When would they see each other? Did they have anything in common? They had started out all wrong. You were supposed to work up to sex, get to know each other first, flirt, pet, talk, dream, anticipate. She had most likely played her strongest card first. Or was it just that she was in the mood and he was available? If that was the case, if she was the kind of woman who embraced spontaneity and opportunity, could she be trusted to commit to a monogamous relationship? He didn't think he could handle an open marriage.

"A cow!" yelled Sammy.

There was, in fact, a herd of cows blowing steam at a feeding trough in a muddy field beside a white, weather-worn barn. A quarter-mile beyond the cows the road curved through leafless woods and began the climb into the mountains, hardly more than foothills really, but the highest ground in three counties — the nearest ski resort was a further 45-minute drive to the north. The road rose in long switchbacks, winding into the evergreen forest past dark fir and cedar and pine. Rhododendrons and ferns grew in the shade of the forest floor, and patches of snow lay in their shadows. At the ridge they came to a crossroads. Curtis turned right and took the ridge road that wound and undulated across the backbone of the mountains. Occasionally, as they came out of the trees, a splendid view would open before them of dark trees falling away to a patchwork of farms before the river and the city beyond. Everything was dusted with snow, lit by a thin sun veiled by a layer of wispy alto cirrus. Then they would be running between the trees again like a needle running through the grooves of a record. As the image came to mind, Curtis smiled in amusement as he realized that by the time Sammy was his age that analogy would probably be met with puzzled looks.

They passed through another crossroads and the hamlet of Willhamsette, a diner, gas station and gift shop, population 142. The Christmas tree farm spread up-slope away from the road. They stopped at a little wooden kiosk to pick up the saw and instructions — all trees were $51 with tax; the bottom two branches were to be left on the stump, as a new tree could then grow out of the old. The air was crisp, the ground muddy, as they walked hand-in-hand between the rows inspecting the trees. Curtis was thinking about the last time they had cut a tree. Just a year. Such a year. Someone had told him that getting a divorce was like a death in the family; there was a grieving process to go through. But there was nothing to be done now. Roll with the punches. Another layer of his mind was assessing the trees. He now lived in an apartment with very high ceilings and on that account he could buy a very tall tree. The problem would be getting it up to the apartment. He guessed the freight elevator, designed to move furniture, would accommodate a 10-foot tree. It would be a bigger tree than Linda's fake tree, and it would smell like a Christmas tree should. It was easier without Linda. She always directed the choices by exercising her veto. His first choice would be too tall, the next too short, the next too sparse on one side. And she would have wanted to eat in a restaurant on the way home.

It took a mere forty minutes to find the right tree, cut it, drag it back to the car and lash it to the roof with ropes passed through the open doors. It would have taken twice as long with Linda's input. Then they were speeding down the mountain toward home. They stopped for gas and a bathroom break, and picked up sandwiches at the deli in the general store in the tiny town of Brannock.

Getting the ornaments and CDs and clothing upstairs was easy enough, but the tree was another matter. Linda had always played the part of the weak female when it suited her; she would rather delegate than perform a physical task, so he'd always counted on his friends and neighbors to help him move the tree from the car to the house. Here in the apartment he didn't know any of his neighbors, and Sammy was too small. The only thing to do was to drag it, which he did, leaving a trail of needles from the elevator to his door.

The tree was lying on the floor next to the gate-legged table, and he was contemplating how to get it into the stand and upright when the intercom buzzed. He pushed the answer button. "Hello?"

"We're here," came Stephanie's voice.

He had totally forgotten about their visit, and it must have shown in his voice as he stammered, "Oh! Yeah. Oh, good," prompting her to ask if it was all right.

"Absolutely. I could use your help."

When he opened the door Gwyn strode past him and presented a bucket of sidewalk chalk to Sammy. He, in turn, led her to his toy box.

Each time Curtis had seen Stephanie she had looked different than the time before; today her dark hair was pulled back over her ears. She was wearing a vee-necked, dark blue flannel dress that reached mid-calf, flat-soled shoes, and a long, grey, hooded wool coat that she shucked off the moment she entered the apartment.

Curtis stood arms akimbo, staring at the supine tree. "I've been trying to figure out how to get this tree up." After a short discussion of the logistics, Stephanie guided the base into the stand, while Curtis pushed the trunk into an upright position. "Thanks, I couldn't have done it without you."

"My pleasure." She saw a wry smile as he gazed up at the tree, which was over 10 feet tall in the stand. "Problem?"

"No, it's just...I just realized I'll need a ladder. There's always something like that. I'm so used to having everything I need close at hand in my garage. I'll have to pick it up when I drop off Sammy."

"Do you have aspirin?"

"You have a headache?"

"They say a tree lasts longer if you put aspirin and sugar in the water."

While Curtis got an aspirin from the medicine cabinet in the bathroom, Stephanie found a pitcher in the kitchen and dissolved sugar in water. He found her on her knees under the tree, adding water to the reservoir. Her ass looked better in a dress than in jeans, he thought. "We make a good team," he said, handing her the aspirin.

"Is it coated?" she asked. He shrugged. She took it from him and went to the kitchen. She placed the aspirin between two spoons on the counter and leaned her weight on them until the aspirin was pulverized. Then she bent under the tree and poured the grains into the water reservoir. Curtis felt a momentary surge of interest as he contemplated her bottom. "It smells so good!" she declared as she straightened up. It was true: the tree gave off a fragrant sappy scent that reminded him of Christmases past. Linda's synthetic tree might be perfect, Curtis thought, but it could never be real.

"Hold still," Curtis said and plucked a few fir needles from her hair.

He admired the way she saw a problem and attacked it without asking. Linda was more likely to tell him what to do than to do it herself. But Stephanie was used to taking charge; she had no one else to rely on, at least no one he knew about.

"Can we go outside and play?" Gwyn asked.

"First I'd like to see Sammy's drawings."

Sammy was only too happy to oblige. They sat at the gate-legged table, Stephanie studiously, Sammy fidgeting with excess energy. "They're just dwawings," Sammy said. "My mom wouldn't let me take paint to Grammy's."

"Who showed you how to draw like this?"

"My dad."

"We were playing with line drawings," Curtis explained, "like Matisse. Not more than five lines."

"Um hmm," Stephanie acknowledged noncommittally. "*This* is nice."

"That's Sadie," Sammy supplied, "Grammy's dog. And that one's Grammy, and that's Mommy, and that one is a house, and Uncle Joe, and a car. That's my dad."

"And this one has a title: Make Love Grow. I like that."

"My dad wrote that. I just dwawed the pitcher."

"Pic-ture."

"Picture," he corrected himself.

"It was Sammy's title," Curtis said. "I just printed it."

"In a rainbow of colors," Stephanie noted, suppressing a smile. "Very nice."

"It's a love flower," Sammy said. "And that one's Sadie again. She sleeps a lot. I want a dog like Sadie."

As the statement had been added for his father's benefit, Curtis answered, "That's up to your mother. I can't have a dog in the apartment."

"This one of the beach house is nice."

"Dad let me take pastels to San Diego."

"Very good. Would you like a tip?" Sammy nodded. "Next time you're doing a landscape like this, just remember to do it in stages. Here, look out the window. What's the farthest thing you can see?"

"The buildings?"

"Farther than that."

"I don' know."

"The sky. See, the sky behind everything? Then those buildings across there. Then what?"

"The lot," Sammy said confidently.

"Right. That's the middle ground. And what's in the foreground?"

"Those buildings across the street?"

"That's right, very good. Start with the background. Then draw the middle ground. Then the foreground. One lays over the other," she explained, holding one splayed hand in front of the other. Background. Middle ground. Foreground."

"Can we play outside now?" Gwyn asked.

Stephanie looked to Curtis for affirmation.

"Sure, but stay in the courtyard down there, where we can see you." He indicated the area between the front door and the steps that led down to the street. "And come in when it gets dark." It was four o'clock already. The thin sunlight streamed low from the west.

The kids left with the chalk. "Thanks for the present, by the way," Curtis said.

"It's nothing. I thought it would keep them occupied."

"Would you like something to drink? I have wine, beer, Scotch, tea."

"White wine would be nice."

As he went to the kitchen she wandered slowly about the room looking at the art on the walls, and pausing to look at the meager collection of books (The Encyclopedia of Chart Patterns, No Fear Investing, and a few novels — Maeve Binchy, Alexander McCall Smith, Stephen King, C.S. Forester).

"This is the perfect artist's garret," she observed, "big windows, north light."

"The previous tenant was an artist."

She browsed his short stack of CDs (J.S. Bach, Mozart, Satie, Dave Brubeck, Ben Webster, Lester Young, Chet Baker, and the Christmas albums). "Can I put on some music?" she called over her shoulder.

"Be my guest," Curtis said, thinking it was a funny expression, as she really *was* his guest. The sight of her bent over his CD collection reminded him of Gretchen, who had no use for anything that was not hip-hop. Stephanie did not present quite as pleasing a posterior, but she had better taste in music, for in a moment he heard the melodious sax of Lester Young.

Curtis handed her a glass. "It's a Sauvignon Blanc from Alto Adige."

"Northern Italy?"

"Exactly, you have a good grasp of geography."

"I do a lot of armchair traveling. It's my dream."

"To many happy travels, then" he said, clinking his glass to hers.

"Someday maybe. In the meantime, here's to happy kids," and she clinked her glass against his.

At the window looking down on the courtyard she said, "I suppose you know you have a genius on your hands."

"Sammy?" Curtis chuckled. "I don't think so."

"I don't know about academically, but look here."

Curtis peered down at the courtyard. Sammy had drawn a big version of Make Love Grow. It was a simple picture; it didn't look like much to Curtis — a heart shaped flower in a pot. "What?" he asked, wondering what was so special about that.

"It's 20 feet tall and the proportions are just the same as the line drawing there on the table. He can't even see it all from his perspective, but he's got the proportions right."

"And?"

"That's what my daughter would call 'freaky weird.' It's highly unusual."

"Then I hope he can make a living with it."

"Making a living isn't everything."

"Maybe not, but it helps if your natural talents help pay the bills." As they watched, Gwyn added two dots and a crescent, making a Smiley Face of the heart-shaped flower. "That's a nice touch," added Curtis.

"How are *your* natural talents fairing? Aren't you a captain of industry?"

"Me? No, I'm a minion of industry."

"Financial Analyst, isn't it?"

"Asset Manager is the official title."

"Should I be hiding my money under the mattress?"

"I wish I had the answer."

"I thought you had your fingers on the pulse of the economy."

"I wish!" Curtis laughed. "I don't wag the dog; the dog wags me! Nothing I learned in the last nine years has prepared me for this Market. There hasn't been anything like it in three generations, and I..." He paused, wondering why he found it so easy to talk to this woman. "...frankly, I don't know what I'm doing," he admitted. "I've made some serious missteps; nothing seems to be working the way it's supposed to work. It scares me, if you want to know the truth."

"You're not inspiring confidence."

"I'm not a cheerleader."

"How much worse can it get?"

"This could turn into a full-blown worldwide depression."

"My mattress is looking better and better."

They looked down on the kids. One or both of them had drawn the outlines of an airplane on the courtyard, and they were sitting in the cockpit.

"My dad's worried about losing his job," Curtis said. "He's 60, and employers don't look for 60-year-olds. Hell, I'm worried about losing *my* job. I can barely keep my head above water as it is, with a mortgage and this apartment, and two car payments." He was halfway through this utterance when he realized how ridiculous it must sound to a single, working mother without a house or a car. "I'm sorry, I wasn't thinking."

"About what?"

"About *your* situation. I mean, who am I to complain?"

"No worries; it's all relative. My sister lost her job in August and had to move back in with my mother. I'm glad I'm not *her*."

"It's nice to have parents close enough to take you in," Curtis said, thinking that it would be easier if his parents lived closer.

Stephanie seemed on the verge of saying something but looked away, and a subtle tightening of her lips and the hardness that passed over her eyes made Curtis aware that's he'd broached a sensitive subject. Maybe she didn't get along with her parents. To steer the subject in another direction he asked, "Is she older or younger, your sister?"

"Stacy is four years older. Stephen is 6 years younger. I'm the middle child, so if I'm screwed up, that's my excuse."

"You don't seem screwed up."

"Thanks for the vote of confidence," she laughed, the light coming back into her eyes.

"Another glass?"

While he poured them both another glass of Sauvignon from Cantina San Michele Appiano, Stephanie studied the photos and drawings on the refrigerator.

"And you?" she asked. "Do you have siblings?"

"A sister and a brother, both younger."

"Ah, the eldest. You must be the over-achiever."

Curtis was about to demur, but smiled instead. Why should he pretend to be humble? He'd been humbled enough lately; it felt good to be dubbed an over-achiever, and as she said, it was all relative. "They're in San Diego, so they couldn't take me in if they wanted to, or rather, they would, but I can't leave Sammy, so this is where I'll stay."

Stephanie strolled back to the window to look down on the children in the courtyard. Curtis joined her.

"I don't know how you do it, without your husband," Curtis said and immediately regretted bringing up a subject that must be difficult. What was he thinking? That was the problem: He wasn't thinking; he was just saying the first thing that popped into his head. It came from feeling comfortable around her; he wasn't playing the usual games, wasn't flirting or trying to be witty. The upshot of it was a boorish insensitivity and he reminded himself to censor his thoughts before he opened his mouth. "You have a wonderful daughter," he said, hoping she had not heard his previous remark. "It's nice of her to entertain Sammy."

"She *is* wonderful. And it's a pleasure for her; she doesn't have any siblings."

"Cousins?"

"No cousins. She doesn't even have any kids her own age in our neighborhood."

"Girlfriends?"

"One classmate who lives seven blocks away, but her mother is a pill." They stood silently looking down at the children for a long moment, watching them play hopscotch, before she added, "I should clear up a misconception, though; he wasn't my husband; he was the father of my child. We were living together. We intended to get married, someday, but we hadn't yet. We were crossing Stuart Street. I looked left and stopped. He looked right and stepped out, and that was that. It was a long time ago. I'm not looking for sympathy; I just wanted to be clear — he wasn't my husband."

Curtis didn't know what to say to that and stayed silent. His hand hovered tentatively over her back to give a little pat of sympathy, but it was

sympathy she didn't ask for and perhaps didn't want, so his hand dropped
to his side. Some people were sensitive about being touched, about having
their "personal space" invaded. He felt that way himself when jostled by a
perfect stranger on a crowded bus, though with people he knew, he had
very little sense of maintaining his own space.

He'd left his easel in the corner, straddling the remaining canvases
of the former tenant. Stephanie moved over to it and cocked her head,
considering. Clipped to the easel was another of his attempts to capture
the buildings across the street. Across the upper part of the 16 X 20 paper
he had laid down an angry sky in wet on wet, and in the lower portion,
slightly off-center and to the right, a trapezoid of green (the empty lot).
The buildings were outlined in pencil. His previous attempts had all been
failures, as he was entirely baffled at how to depict the color and texture of
brick, and of windows (some of which reflected and some of which glowed
with the warmth of electric lights from within). "I can't figure out how to
paint this," he admitted. He flipped up the paper to reveal previous versions
that had turned out badly. "I'm no artist."

"Are we going to go over that again? How do you define 'artist'?"

There was an edge to her voice that he hadn't heard before, and rather
than being annoyed, he rather liked it; you did not show anger in front
of strangers, or people you were trying to impress, or casual acquaintances.
It was evidence of a certain degree of intimacy, an expression of real
friendship. "Okay, let me think." And in a minute he said, "An artist is
someone with a unique vision and some mastery of technique."

"Some mastery of technique helps, but why does everyone think you
have to have a unique vision? What about medical illustrators? Or people
like Audubon, for God's sakes? — If your purpose is to paint a realistic
wren, can you have a truly unique vision? Can you take artistic license? You
can't paint it purple. Does that make Audubon any less of an artist?"

"Okay, I get it. I guess I stepped in that one."

"No, I'm sorry; this is a sore point with me. I'll shut up."

"No, please, go ahead — say what you mean."

She stared out the window trying to marshal her thoughts. "It seems
that craftsmanship is never given as much respect as artistic vision, and I've
always thought they should be given equal weight." A flood of memories

came back to her, the slights, the derisive comments as she displayed her latest work. "I've had this same argument with professors and other artists, and idiots like my sister, and I'm really sick of it." She put a hand on his forearm. "The best musicians are studio musicians, but do they get any respect? Some of the best art, art that really communicates, is commercial art. It shouldn't be dismissed as worthless." She stared deeply into his eyes and he saw a passion there he hadn't known existed. "I'm so sorry, I really shouldn't be dumping on you. Forget it."

But he didn't want to forget it. This was intellectually and emotionally interesting. "No, tell me what you think. Really."

She pursed her lips and looked out the window with fierce eyes. "I'm not an artistic elitist. That's not to say I think that the lowest common denominator is the best art. I may draw the line at flamenco dancers on black velvet, but I'm not an elitist. I believe that art, any art, is at its most basic a form of communication. So many critics believe that if something is accessible to the public it must be inferior. It's true of all art, not just painting, but music and literature too. So you'll have critics praising James Joyce and dismissing Raymond Chandler, for instance. Have you ever read *Ulysees*?" Curtis shook his head. "It's a piece of crap (excuse the language). It's bombastic blather. Chandler could write circles around Joyce. Maybe he was too accessible; critics are quick to dump on popular art. Not because it doesn't have artistic merit, but because it's accessible to the masses. But why shouldn't art be accessible? What's wrong with being accessible? Art is just another medium of communication. If it doesn't communicate, it isn't doing its job."

Lord, thought Curtis, *get her on a roll and you can't shut her up!* "So you're defending hacks?"

"Why not? Why should you have to break new ground to be considered an artist? I admire people who take risks, but risk-taking isn't a prerequisite to being an artist. When artists do break new ground they're usually laughed at. Take Renoir, Klee, Miró, Picasso, Dali. The critics laughed. Then public perception changed, they became popular and everyone loved them until the next new thing came along. Were they less valid as artists when the critics laughed, than when they were popular? I don't think so. Were they less valid when they were passé? No. They were just lucky enough to be appreciated for a few years during their lifetimes. Not all artists are so lucky." There was a long moment of awkward silence and then she said, "Oh god, I'm so sorry; I didn't mean to rant."

"It's okay."

"No, I was rude."

"You were honest. I appreciate that."

She bit her lip, took a big breath, and sighed. "Most people don't realize we're surrounded by art everyday. Architecture is art. Advertising is art. You may not recognize it, or even like it, but it's all art. Oh god, there I go again — talk about bombastic!" She blushed.

He couldn't help but smile. "It's something you're obviously passionate about." Sensing that he needed to clear the air, as well as to check on the children he asked, "What are the Munchkins up to?" They both went to the window and peered down. The kids appeared to be playing tic-tac-toe. Musing on what she'd said about popularity he added, "I think people always want to feel superior, and if you like what everyone else likes, then you can't be superior; you're just one of the crowd. So there's a tendency to dismiss anything that's too popular. Take Starbucks, for instance — when Starbucks first showed up people thought 'this is the greatest thing since sliced bread: a coffee house with good coffee, some pastries, a place where I can hang out in an arm chair and read a book. This is the life!' But now that you find one on every corner, you hear disparaging remarks. When the good becomes commonplace, it's not good enough."

"That's what I mean; people like success up to a point, but they're suspicious of too much success. How did we get on this subject?"

"I said I wasn't an artist, and you said you weren't an artistic elitist, and that got you onto a rant. I don't remember the sequence."

"You do draw well," she said encouragingly, indicating his unfinished painting. "The perspective is fine."

"I don't know; I've given up on it. I don't have the technique. I think the pencil drawing works, but when I color it in it looks amateurish. What would *you* do with it?"

"Do you mind?" she asked, picking up a brush.

"Please do; you can only improve it."

The light waned as she painted. Curtis turned on the lights, checked on the kids, poured a third glass of Sauvignon Blanc and stole glances at the painting as it evolved. They picked up the thread of conversation, moving effortlessly from painting and art, to parents and children and education. "Sammy seems to like first grade; he's learning to read."

"That's a good age," Stephanie said, adding a few strokes of lighter green to a tree she had placed at the end of the empty lot. Curtis looked out over the lot, now in shadow. There was no tree there in reality; she was taking artistic license. "Gwyn is excited about going to middle school next year — different teachers for different subjects; it's an adventure. But they've cut back on the music program; they won't have band next year, and she was really looking forward to learning a musical instrument."

"Do you play anything?"

"Me? I played flute in junior high and high school, but I didn't keep up with it."

"I always enjoyed school, myself," Curtis offered. "My brother hated the discipline. I think my father was too indulgent; he always sided with my brother, so he felt he could get away with anything. He was a terror to his teachers — made poor Mrs. Everett cry."

"What does he do, your brother?"

"He's a middle manager for an import company. He got a job as a filing clerk right out of high school and worked his way up to a decent position. Seems to like it. The funny part is his wife is a second-grade teacher."

"My parents distrust educated people. They're thoroughly blue-collar. I'm the only one in our family to go beyond high school. But I always had to work, so I didn't finish my degree until I was 25."

"Where did you go?"

"Community college and then University Extension. My degree is in Art History. The problem is there's no money in it unless you teach, and you need a PhD to teach, which I have neither the time nor the money to pursue."

"But you said you were taking a class."

"On Wednesdays and Fridays. I'm just finishing up a class in Public Relations/Marketing. Next semester I'm taking a class on how to bring a product from conception to sales. It's a very demanding course, but the professor is supposed to be great, and the University has arranged mentorships with the private sector, for those who really want to run with it, who really want to do it instead of just talk about it."

"What do you have in mind?"

"I'm not sure, maybe commercial art of some sort. That would play into my strengths."

Curtis cracked open the louvered windows and whistled to get Sammy and Gwyn's attention.

"We should get something to eat," Curtis said. "There's a good Chinese place around the corner, or I could cook up some chicken breasts. I'm not a gourmet cook, but I make a decent chicken."

"Don't go to any trouble on our account. We should be going; we have a long walk. Would you mind if I took this painting with me? I'd like to work on it; I think it has possibilities."

"Sure. Let's give it a few minutes to dry. I'll pour you another glass of wine."

"It's getting dark."

"I'll drive you home. It's easier."

"You don't mind?"

"No problem at all."

She hesitated a moment, glancing at the floor. "Are these your canvases?" she asked, gesturing toward the stack beneath the easel.

"The previous tenant's."

"Would you like to sell any of them? I get a discount at the store, but I can't always afford...."

"You can have them. I've been painting on paper — seems easier with watercolors and pastels."

Then she noticed the box of half used tubes of oil paint. "Are you using these oils? Because if you're not...." When he hesitated she retracted, saying, "I'm sorry; that was so rude."

"Not at all. You're welcome to them."

"It's just they're expensive," she explained, "and they dry out once they've been opened, and I hate to see good paint go to waste. I'll paint you something on these canvases that you can hang on the walls here."

"Not necessary. Anyway, Sammy's not allowed to use oil paints, and I don't know what I'm doing."

"Oh, yes you do. You've made a lot of progress. You're better than you think."

Curtis smiled at the compliment. The children came back inside and he made them hot chocolate. The desultory conversation meandered from personal preferences in beverages and food, to food allergies, visits to the doctor, the cost of health care, the cost of food, to the environmental impact of beef production and the morality of eating meat.

"I always feel guilty eating pork (pigs are so smart), but I still eat it," Curtis said. "Speaking of which, I'm getting hungry. Who would like Chinese food?" He raised his hand and looked expectantly at the kids, who raised their hands. "Majority rules; we're going for Chinese."

Curtis awoke early in the morning when the sun had yet to clear the horizon. Sammy was sound asleep beside him. Curtis slipped quietly from the bed, put on a robe and slippers, and went out to the kitchen to make coffee. The sky was a uniform texture but had yet to take color, so he could not tell if it would be a sunny day, or a grey day.

While he waited for the coffee to brew he wandered about the apartment looking for something to do. If he were at home he would have made a fire and sat by it reading the paper. He had no fireplace, but the thought did send him to the thermostat to turn the dial up to 72 degrees.

He contemplated the tree, taking a full turn around it. It smelled wonderful. He wanted Sammy to help with the decorating — that was part of the Christmas tradition — but you couldn't hang ornaments until the lights were strung.

The coffee maker made a guttural sound as it regurgitated the last of the water in the reservoir. He filled a cup with the bitter brew and added a packet of Equal and a dollop of low-fat milk (not exactly a latte, but it would do in a pinch).

He put Tuck Andress's *Hymns, Carols and Songs About Snow* on the stereo and set to work stringing the lights. He'd finished winding the lights up from the bottom until they reached six feet off the floor (as far as he could reach without a ladder), when Sammy came sleepily out of the bedroom.

Curtis made breakfast. Then they showered, and dressed in their new clothes. Sammy hung ornaments on the bottom of the tree as high as he could reach. Curtis took the higher branches. The sun was hidden behind a high cloud cover, leaving the world outside a dreary grey, but the colorful lights, and Nat King Cole singing Christmas carols, brightened the mood in the apartment. Curtis found a glow of contentment in the continuity of the ritual. There was nothing even vaguely religious in his observances. He loved Christmas for its magic, its music, its fanciful stories of flying reindeer and talking snowmen and magical elves, its sense of community, family and tradition, its spirit of anonymous generosity, the belief that this time of year anything was possible, and though he did not believe in the divinity of Jesus, the story of his birth was an affirmation of the potential that all children brought into the world, the hope that one person might make the world a better place.

Around eleven o'clock they left the apartment for Lowe's, where Curtis hoped to buy a poinsettia and a few more decorations. On the way to the garage, the elevator stopped on the 7th floor to admit Irene Niece. She wore pants embroidered with Christmas trees on both legs, and a black sweater embroidered with colorful Christmas ornaments and ribbons.

"You must be Sammy," Irene said. "I'm Irene. I live below your dad. Are you looking forward to Christmas?" She had a friendly, grandmotherly way about her.

Sammy nodded. "We got a big tree yesterday."

Curtis nodded as well, and explained his dilemma. "I need a ladder to reach the highest branches, but I can't get a ladder in my car."

"Ask the Super. He has ladders and tools. I'm sure you can borrow his."

Irene got out on the ground floor. They continued to the basement garage.

Curtis pushed an empty cart around the nursery department at Lowes, eyeing the plants and the women. He maneuvered his cart to get a better look at one woman who reminded him of a more casual version of Linda — no makeup, jeans and a tight turtleneck that showed off her curves to good effect.

"What're you lookin' at?" Sammy inquired.

"She's kind of pretty, don't you think?"

"She's too skinny."

"What about that one over there?" With a flick of his head, Curtis indicated an Asian girl.

"Too young," Sammy proclaimed.

A sales lady came up to them. "Can I help you find something?"

"We're looking for house plants."

She was a young Latina with a ponytail and a red Lowe's smock over jeans and a white knit shirt. Her name tag read "Elena." He noticed the wedding ring right away, though of course, women often wore a ring to discourage the odd pick-up.

She helped them select a pot of cyclamen, a pot of holly and a palm. Then she led them to the wreaths.

"That one's pretty," Sammy said, pointing.

"Which one?" Elena asked.

"Her," Sammy pointed to a woman of about 30 in a green pantsuit, silver necklace and light brown hair.

"She's a little old for you," Elena said with raised eyebrows.

"She's not for me. She's for my dad."

"I thought you were shopping for plants."

"That, too," Curtis replied with a smile.

They picked out a fern, two poinsettias and a wreath.

On the way to the checkout counter, they passed the pretty lady. Sammy stopped and asked, "Do you have kids?"

"Sammy!" Curtis took his hand. "Sorry," he told the woman, who only looked amused. As he led Sammy away he said *sotto voce,* "That's not the way it's done."

Chapter 16
Sunday December 7 – Sunday December 14, 2008

The top half of the Dutch door was open as they approached Pretty Pets. From inside they heard the sound of a woman's laughter, clear and musical, innocent and so obviously filled with joy that it made Curtis smile. An old-fashioned bell tinkled above the door as they came inside. A young woman of perhaps 25 years came out from behind a row of shelves. She cradled a Border Collie puppy in her arms, and when the dog licked her face she laughed again, showing a bright smile. Her rosy cheeks were dimpled, faint freckles saddled her cute nose, and a profusion of strawberry-blonde curls fell just to her shoulders.

He'd been entranced by her laughter, but the sight of her left him breathless. No matter the over-wrought adjective or metaphor, all of the clichés applied, for Curtis was thoroughly and instantly smitten. It was a visceral reaction and his world brightened as though a grey fog had suddenly lifted to reveal a world of color.

A few minutes before entering the store he'd said to Sammy, "Before we even go in there, just get it in your head — we're just going in to look; we aren't buying a pet. No dogs, no cats, no hamsters, and no rabbits, unless your mother wants to take care of them. Is that understood?"

"Yeah, yeah, yeah," Sammy said with more sarcasm than Curtis had ever heard from his son. He must have learned it from his mother, or his grandmother, Curtis surmised, as sarcasm wasn't in his repertoire.

Curtis had approached the store in a negative state of mind, ready to do battle with his son. He'd steeled himself to reject any begging, the usual "*Please*, Daddy! *Please*! I'll do anything..." blah, blah, blah. He'd heard it all before and he wasn't giving in this time, because taking care of a pet was serious business, and to a degree, Curtis found it distasteful. As much as he'd enjoyed his dog when growing up, he now felt that owning a dog was a little like owning a slave. But all of that flew out of his mind at the sight and sound of this enchanting woman.

"We wan' a pet," Sammy said.

Rhiannon (for that was the name engraved on her plastic name tag) bent down, showing ample cleavage, and held the puppy out. It squirmed and wiggled its tail, and its little tongue snaked out in a nervous effort to please. Sammy held out a tentative hand, let the dog lick it, then petted the soft, furry head.

"We have this beautiful Border Collie. Are you looking for a dog?"

"No, actually," Curtis said, wishing she'd take the puppy away, because who can resist a puppy? Certainly not Sammy.

"A cat?"

"No, I'm afraid the pet's really for my son, here, but it'll be staying with me. I'm gone too much for a dog or a cat."

"My mom won't let me have a pet at our house," Sammy interjected. "She's allergic." Curtis didn't disabuse him of this lame excuse. "But I can have a pet at my dad's."

"It has to be low maintenance," Curtis added. "Something I can leave for three or four days at a time."

"Reptiles would work. Lizards, snakes, chameleons."

"No, not reptiles."

"Birds? We have parakeets."

"I like birds," Sammy said.

"So do I," Curtis said, "but I can't stand the thought of caging birds. The whole point of being a bird is to fly. No offense intended."

Rhiannon laughed again, pure and clear. "I couldn't agree with you more. I've always hated keeping birds in cages. We do, of course," she shrugged in apology, "but I don't own the shop." Curtis looked at her with such unabashed appreciation that she blushed. "Maybe you'd like a fish tank?"

"How about that, Sammy? Would you like fish?"

Sammy clapped his hands and bounced on his toes. "Like Mr. Wishing."

"They're easy to take care of," Rhiannon added.

She took the puppy to a back room (she looked awfully good going away, Curtis thought) and returned to show them the wall of fish tanks. There were three tiers of ten tanks each.

"We have some nice kits available," Rhiannon said. "It's a lot cheaper than buying the individual components." She showed them a 10-gallon tank that came with a light, filter, fishnet, and pebbles. To this, they added live water plants, a couple of snails, a sunken ship with a gaping hole in the side, an algaecide, and fish flakes. The most colorful fish were all saltwater reef fish. "I wouldn't recommend a saltwater tank for a first-timer; it's tricky to keep the right balance of salinity, and they're a lot more expensive." Steered to the freshwater tanks, Sammy chose four neon tetras and a bottom feeder that looked something like a tiny catfish, and Curtis selected three "feeder" goldfish, not because they were the cheapest (which they were), but because they were already doomed to be eaten — he felt the warm satisfaction of a savior; if they lived just one extra hour, he wouldn't feel guilty if they died from his neglect (what the lord giveth, the lord may taketh away).

After they had loaded the tank and equipment and fish into the car, Curtis strapped Sammy into his car seat. Curtis sat behind the steering wheel without starting the car. He was having a mental debate, knowing the outcome and steeling his nerves to accept the rejection he anticipated. "Stay here a minute, Sammy; I forgot something." He marched into the store with a resolve that crumbled at the sight of Rhiannon at the counter with another customer. He wasn't prepared to wait around to ask a silly question, and he couldn't leave Sammy sitting in the car.

He'd already turned to go when Rhiannon called out, "Did you forget something?" The customer, a colorless middle-aged man, glared at him.

Curtis extemporized. "Do you have a card? I'll call."

She directed the customer to a far corner, looked in the cash register for a card and handed it to Curtis.

Curtis stared at it. Rhiannon O'Reilly was her full name. "I really just wanted to ask if you'd like to go out for coffee sometime," Curtis said.

Seeing him blush, she laughed merrily, her eyes a twinkle. "Don't worry; I don't bite. I work Friday through Tuesday, 10 to 6, with a half-day on Sunday from 1 to 6. So any time after 6 works for me." She took back her card and wrote a number on the back of it. "That's my cell."

She's awfully confident, Curtis thought. He left beaming, and could barely restrain himself from skipping back to the car.

On the way home, they listened to the mellifluous voice of Leon Redbone singing Christmas Island, and Curtis mused on Rhiannon O'Reilly. Did he appear desperate? He wondered. He asked himself, did he really need a woman in his life? As much as he liked to think of himself as capable and independent, he had to admit he didn't like being alone. The years ahead would be lonely years if he had no one to share them with. He'd always have Sammy, of course, but that was different.

Curtis spent the afternoon finding appropriate places for the plants, and setting up the fish tank on the counter that divided the kitchen from the dining area. Sammy sat at the table painting a forest of Christmas trees. Assessing the effect of the tank, the cyclamen, fern, palm, holly and poinsettias, and the Christmas tree with its bottom half glowing gaily like a colorful skirt, the apartment was beginning to feel a little like a home.

Monday was one of those blissful days when the Market trended straight up from the opening bell. The Market seemed to be moving back into alignment after the irrational panic that had driven it to generational lows. So, too, was Curtis's mind reclaiming its equanimity, and the pervading anxiety of the past months began to subside.

On the way home Curtis was preoccupied with thoughts of Rhiannon and Gretchen. Did he really want to see Gretchen again? Every time he thought not, those snakes began writhing and that pig jerked with the force of his thrusts. To him, love and lust were intertwined, two sides to the same coin. He'd certainly loved Linda with more tenderness when he desired her. But this thing with Gretchen was different. There was no love in it, just simple animal gratification. That wasn't to denigrate the amazing peace that had come over him when he'd satisfied his carnal desires, but it was incomplete. Though it left him physically sated, it left him feeling emotionally hollow. How was he going to react when he saw her Wednesday? How would she react to *him*? Did he want her again? On one level he wanted to pretend that it had never happened. On another level he couldn't wait to bang that pig again, and to watch those snakes swaying back and forth, up and down.

And then there was Rhiannon to think of. She possessed that freshness of spirit, that guileless demeanor that made him want to take care of her, to shelter her, to be her protector as well as her lover. On the strength of a laugh and a smile he had invested her with a character of good and kind intentions, though he had to admit he knew nothing of her real character. Love at first sight may be real, but it was surely irrational. Emotion rarely *was* rational, and he didn't want emotion to get the better of him. It was all so complicated!

"This is a really lousy recording," Elliot said. "Why would they play this on the radio? The harmonics are excruciating! Henry Cowell should be ethereal, not fingernails on a chalkboard! Forget it!" He switched off the radio, fumbled about in the CD compartment, and inserted Brahms' *Hungarian Dances*. "Cartoons ruined this music for most people. If you can ignore your first impulse and imagine folk dancers instead of Bugs Bunny, you might be able to appreciate it. This is a good recording." Less than a minute later he pressed the eject button in mid-phrase. "Nope. Not in the mood. Let's try something else." Keeping half an eye on the road and steering with his knees, he opened a jewel case and extracted a CD, which he inserted into the player. Boisterous French horns and exuberant strings announced Resphigi's *Pini di Roma*.

"When was this composed?" Curtis asked, only vaguely interested as his thoughts wove a pattern of work and women and turning points toward different futures.

"Sometime in the 1920s, I should think. This recording is Eugene Ormandy and the Philadelphia Philharmonic, early '70s."

"By the way, I'm driving myself the next two days," Curtis said.

"What's up?"

"Just some errands," Curtis replied evasively (he had made up his mind to stop by the pet shop), "and my watercolor class."

"Are you getting any better?" Elliot asked, jocularly dismissive.

Curtis looked askance at this friend. "I should be insulted!" he declared, though he was really more hurt than insulted.

"No more phallic lighthouses?"

"You.... Ah, just screw it," Curtis replied gruffly, finding no amusement in Elliot's ribbing.

"Sorry! I didn't know you were sensitive about it."

"I'm *not* sensitive."

"So, you're enjoying the class? Are you learning anything?"

"It's ok," Curtis replied curtly. "And yes, I'm getting better."

He was, too. His concepts weren't much better, but his technique was improving exponentially. His latest doodles at least bore some resemblance to the pictures in the instruction books.

"We're doing a poker night at Poblador's on Friday. You interested?"

"I'm taking Sammy to a movie."

"But you're coming to the Christmas party Saturday night?"

"Of course."

Tuesday after work Curtis stood beside his Honda Accord in the twilight of Stone Pine Center, a horseshoe-shaped shopping center anchored on the two ends by a Lowe's and a Safeway. In the arc connecting the two were China King Restaurant, River Books, Paul Borden's Karate Academy, Pretty Pets, Blue Note Dry Cleaners, CVS pharmacy, a Bank of the North and a Starbucks. He exhaled a plume of steam in the bracing cold of the evening and crossed the parking lot toward the glowing green sign of Pretty Pets. In his college days he'd made the first step of approaching a girl, getting her phone number and address, but in his shyness, he'd fail to follow through. "What if she thinks I'm a dweeb?" He was older and wiser now, and he knew if he put it off he'd only end up obsessing about it, playing endless scenarios in his mind, inventing dialogue that was as fictional as any movie script. The only real dialogue he could have was with the real girl, and he wanted to get it over with as soon as possible. Maybe he'd find her superficial, or smug, or arrogant. Maybe she was a lesbian — well, probably not; she had given him her number, after all. She surely must have some faults to balance the unreasonable attraction he felt towards her. He hoped she did; infatuation was often a one-sided affair that ended badly.

The light in the store window spilled onto the sidewalk. In the window display a sleeping cat curled comfortably on a plush cat bed. The bell tinkled as he opened the door and stepped inside. Rhiannon was at the cash register and when she turned, her face lit up in a way that he hadn't seen since Sammy was an infant. She was obviously pleased to see him.

All of a sudden he was tongue-tied. He couldn't come up with an opening line, and simply smiled sheepishly.

"Have you come to take me to coffee?"

"If you'd like."

"I just have to put the receipts in the safe. You're not a robber, are you?"

"Not yet."

"I'll just be a minute." She counted the money, noted the amount in a ledger, and sealed the bills in an envelope, which she deposited in a safe under the counter. Then she grabbed a blue cardigan, pulled on a knit hat, and headed for the door.

"What about the cat?" he asked, nodding his head toward the comatose feline.

"She's got the run of the place. Her box is in the back room." Rhiannon switched off the lights, they stepped outside, and she locked the door. Inside, the shelves of fish tanks glowed with fluorescent lights. "The fish never sleep. My boss says the light discourages burglars, but I wonder if fish suffer from sleep deprivation. It's hard to know, since they don't have any facial expression. We read so much into facial expressions." Curtis couldn't help but smile; her banter came as easily as if they were old friends.

She stopped. "Why are you looking at me like that?"

"Like what?"

"That look."

"Oh, *that* look," he said. "That's the look of love."

"Oh my god, what a line!"

They both burst into laughter.

"Maybe it's only the look of infatuation," Curtis said honestly. "Has anyone told you, you have a musical voice?"

"No, but I'm flattered. Who would you sound like if you could choose?"

"Me? Oh, Gregory Peck, I suppose, or Cary Grant, or Richard Burton."

"I see you're a fan of old movies."

"I like all movies, but they have to have a good story. I'm not a fan of pyrotechnics and wild car chases. Movies should be all about the story and the characters."

"I couldn't agree more."

"So tell me about yourself. Where did you grow up?" What he really wanted to know was why such an attractive woman was single.

They stopped at Starbucks and for the next forty minutes they sat and talked over their coffees. She did most of the talking, so Curtis learned that she'd grown up in London, moved to New York with her parents when she was thirteen, spent two years at Columbia before dropping out and moving west. She played the violin (poorly, she admitted), and she liked Medieval music. "I have to get going," she said, checking her watch. "I have to do my marketing for the week." She reached over the small table and squeezed his hand. "I'm glad you came. I knew you would."

"You did? Then you knew more than me."

"I was certain. I was between relationships, but I knew someone would come along. When one door closes, God opens another. I was just waiting for you."

Curtis smiled wanly, thinking, *There's always some fly in the ointment*, and hearing the echo of his father's words, "Maybe there's another girl out there for you." *Well, nobody's perfect*, he thought.

A reliance on divine intervention was not necessarily a deal-breaker. Linda was religious and they'd managed to coexist for nearly a decade. In the early days, when the attraction had been strong and mutual, it had been easy to overlook the big picture. She was religious and he was not. He hadn't held that against her; he was no stranger to living with religious contradictions. His own mother was a Roman Catholic who married a self-proclaimed Protestant (though as far as Curtis could tell his father was Protestant only in the sense that he protested going to church). Both of his parents, nevertheless, believed that morality grew out of a belief in God. Curtis had never bought the argument. But his mother was Catholic (with a big C), as well as catholic in her interests. She was a voracious reader (in fact, she'd read all of his textbooks when he was in college). She read biographies and histories, historical novels, philosophy and books on religion, and by the time he was in high school her beliefs had evolved into Christianity with karma and reincarnation. Not only that, but she believed in karma without believing in the corresponding Christian notion of predestination. How she could live with such contradictions was beyond him, but then religion was beyond logic. Religion was contralogical.

So, when he'd met Linda, a committed Episcopalian, he was used to living with people whose religious beliefs precluded his understanding. For her part, Linda was tolerant of his disbelief, feeling that he'd come around, if given a little instruction. After they'd moved in together, she got him to attend services with her. He'd never been to an Episcopal church. In fact, he'd only been to Easter services with his father until the spring of his twelfth year, when his father said he was old enough to decide for himself if he wanted to accompany him to the Protestant church, or go with his mother to the Catholic church. Since the decision was left up to him, he decided to stay home. So, he'd been to church before, but he'd never been to an Episcopal church, and he only agreed to go to get Linda to shut up about it. They sat in the front pew and he watched her for cues. Ignorant of the rituals he stood when she stood, knelt when she knelt, sat when she sat. The sermon was long and boring. The pew was hard. He was hungry; his stomach growled. The priest's words were delivered in such a drone that he had a hard time staying awake, let alone following the argument. When it came time to take communion she stepped forward and knelt before the railing. He followed suit, kneeling next to her. She smiled beatifically. Curtis watched out of the corner of his eye as the priest made his way down the line dispensing wafers and wine. Curtis's stomach rumbled. At least there was *some* compensation to attending such a boring service.

Coming out of the church she was glowing with joy. She looked at him as though seeing him for the first time. It was a look of deep love and appreciation. "I knew you'd come around," she said. "Wasn't it wonderful?"

"It was a bunch of nonsense."

She stopped dead and dropped his hand. "But you took communion."

"Communion?"

"The wafer and wine?"

So that was communion. "I was hungry. There was a wafer. There was free wine." She stared at him with such disbelief that he was impelled to ask again, "What?"

"That was the body and blood of Christ!"

"Oh, lord!" he blasphemed, rolling his eyes skyward — a beautifully clear sky with no god in it.

"You sacrilegious pig!" she'd screamed.

She didn't speak to him for three days, and was cool for a good two weeks. Then the sex resumed and she kept her religion to herself.

The religious question had not come up again until he said he wouldn't be married in a church.

"You think you're so big," she'd railed. "You think you're always right and millions of other people are wrong."

"Yes," he agreed. "I can't help it if they're ignorant."

"Millions of people are wrong," she repeated as a statement, not a question, as though to state it as fact was to expose him to ridicule (do you know how stupid this sounds?).

"Of course they are. The Christians can't be right if the Hindus are right, or the Buddhists, or the Animists. Hell, there were millions of Greeks who believed in Zeus. That didn't make them right."

"At least they believed in something bigger than themselves."

But Curtis did believe in something bigger than himself. He believed almost everything was bigger than himself. All you had to do is look into the night sky to know where you ranked in the big scheme of things (next to zero). All you had to do was look at a photo of deep space from the Hubble telescope to see that all of humanity, and the earth itself, was just a minute speck of cosmic dust. Why did she think belief in a higher power was necessary to living a decent life?

They'd been married in a civil ceremony, much to her mother's distress, held in a county park ("in the church of nature," he'd chided her). She had not brought up the subject again until Sammy was four, when she'd insisted on taking him to Mass once a month. However, thought Curtis with satisfaction, now that Sammy was spending weekends at the apartment, that was not an option, and that (in his view) was a blessing.

That Rhiannon was religious was obvious from her comment: God had opened the door through which Curtis had stepped. From his viewpoint, this was negative. From her viewpoint, his disbelief was negative. Relationships were always complicated. There were no perfect relationships because there were no perfect people. That thought brought him around to Gretchen. How would he explain Gretchen to Rhiannon, or vice versa? How did either of these women figure into his long-term plans? He sat there staring into space, thinking and yet not thinking — his subconscious weighing the possibilities — when it struck him that he didn't have to commit to anything. Now that he had Sammy's welfare to think about, not just his own, he'd have to be careful and take his time. He didn't have to hook up with someone now, or ever. He didn't have to compete with Linda. If there were another girl for him, she would also have to be good for Sammy.

"I'm taking my son to the movies Friday night. Would you like to come?"

"I'd love to. What time?"

"I pick him up about 6:15. We should be able to make the 7:30 show."

She gave him her address — she lived just over the river, in Wicklow, about halfway to his old house — and walked out of the Starbucks with a wave and a smile. She was almost perfect. She was a pleasure to look at; she had a lovely voice; she played the violin; she liked animals; she was obviously compassionate. But she wasn't perfect, and that was actually a good thing. It would be enough, he thought, to temper his tendency to put her on a pedestal.

On the way back to his car he stopped at an ATM to replenish his cash, and winced as he punched in the pin number, 0617, Linda's birthday. He made a mental note to change it to Sammy's birthday. He didn't need to be reminded of his failures every time he made a withdrawal.

On the way to the apartment he stopped at Target to pick up an ornament for the neighborhood ornament exchange, and he thought about Rhiannon and Gretchen. Memories of writhing snakes and jerking pigs aroused him. He had to wait in his parking space in the garage for his ardor to deflate, before riding the elevator to his apartment. It must be easier to be a woman, he mused; they could fantasize to their hearts' content without advertising it to the world.

Wednesday evening, he showed up ten minutes early at the watercolor class and looked for Gretchen. He'd been thinking about her all day with a sense of breathless anticipation, hoping she might like a replay of last week's entertainment, but she was nowhere to be seen. Stephanie caught his eye, smiled and twiddled her fingers in greeting. He raised a hand in acknowledgment and sat down in the back row, looking over his shoulder now and then to get a glimpse into the hallway. The class began, and still no Gretchen. At the break, he approached Stephanie. "It's a smaller class this week," he said, hoping she would elaborate.

"Someone always drops out," was all she said.

"There was a Gretchen here last week. I don't know her last name, but she gave me a ride home and I left something in her car. Do you know if she'll be back?" It was a little white lie, but what could he say? — 'She was great in the sack and I was hoping for a repeat performance'? No, it was better to lie.

"That's Gretchen Titley. She got a job at a restaurant, so she works nights now. Do you want her number?"

All the way home he wondered if he should bother to call. Restaurant Hours weren't compatible with Banker's Hours. It would be difficult to have any kind of relationship with someone who went to work just as he was getting off. By the time he reached the apartment he was relieved to be free of the distraction, and sorry he had spent so much emotional energy thinking about her.

"Jim Dayton called," Erickson said, one bun propped on the edge of his desk. "He's very pleased with the way things are going. What have you done differently?"

"Nothing, it's just a matter of timing."

"He's recommended you to a friend of his. This guy has a shit load of money. It would be a huge coup to land an account like that. Even if it's only a small piece of his action. If we can win his trust, it could lead to more. It's the kind of account that could carry this firm through the rough times. I just want you to understand how important this is."

"Who is he?"

"His name is Edgar Smith," Erickson said, frowning. "He's on the fucking Forbes List! We're talking obscene amounts of money here, and I have to tell you I'd rather have Davidson handling this, or Arnold. But Dayton recommended you, so it's all on your shoulders. Don't screw up."

Curtis returned to his glass-walled office wishing he could keep a lower profile, and wondering what Davidson had that he didn't. He had never felt less competent, less adult than he did at that moment. His former successes were not really his own; they were the result of luck. Like a fisherman who casts his line into the stream, he'd landed some fat ones over the last five years. How could he fail to do so? — He'd cast his line just as the Market began to recover from the Dot Com crash and 9/11. The Market had trended upward for five years. Anyone could have made money in that environment. The only question was 'how much?' It was only now that the Market was slipping that he understood how little he really knew about economics. There was very little difference, he now realized, between an Asset Manager and a riverboat gambler. Each assessed the risks and probabilities and placed his bets. You tried to bend the odds in your favor, but sometimes the odds played out unpredictably. The odds of red or black coming up on a roulette wheel were roughly 50/50, with the occasional double zero to bend the odds in favor of the house. Your chances might be 50%, but there was a world of difference in how that 50% was distributed. If black and red came up every other spin, that was one thing. If black came up 50 times in a row, followed by 50 times for red, it spelled disaster. He could look the fool or the sage. He could be lucky or unlucky. And now there was this Edgar Smith, who was richer than God, and he would be tested once again, just when he was hoping to disappear into the woodwork.

In the afternoon he called Linda to find out what she planned to buy for Sammy and what, if anything, he had asked for. He spent the evening in his easy chair, searching online toy stores on his laptop, buying a remote-controlled car, a video game and two DVDs. The *piece de resistance*, the gift from Santa, would be Sammy's first bicycle, which Curtis would pick up fully assembled at Cost Co.

Rhiannon lived in the Collingwood Park apartments, a complex of three-story boxes that was, judging by the landscaping, about ten-years-old. The four starkly plain, stucco buildings were surrounded by well-tended evergreen trees and hedges, and were grouped around a pool that was covered for the winter.

Her second-floor apartment, which looked out on the pool, was filled with IKEA furniture. It was a tidy, one-bedroom apartment that had an odd, sepulchral air. The lighting, controlled by a rheostat, was subdued. The low tones of a Gregorian chant vibrated from speakers set on decorative pillars on either side of the front door, and the faint odor of urine emanated from the cat box in the kitchen. The ochre-colored walls in the living room and dining nook were hung with prints of American Primitive art depicting idyllic scenes of an imagined era circa 1900, a world of horse-drawn carriages and sailboats, frolicking dogs and children at play, men fishing and women in long dresses.

A toy merry-go-round rested on the coffee table in front of the sofa, next to a book of Norman Rockwell covers of *The Saturday Evening Post*.

There were, as yet, no Christmas decorations in sight.

Curtis perused a small bookcase while she was getting ready. He often found that a person's books were the best indicator of his or her personality. These shelves were filled with books of the self-help variety, inspirational and motivational books, books on religion, and a whole shelf devoted to puppies and kittens, each arranged by topic.

"What movie are we going to see again?" she called from the bedroom.

The door was open and he peeked in. It was a fastidiously neat little room, with apple-green walls and a devotional depiction of Jesus over the headboard. Two cats, a calico and a tabby, lay curled up in the middle of the white chintz bedspread.

Rhiannon was putting on earrings before the mirror of the chest of drawers. She wore beige polyester slacks with crisp creases, a long-sleeved white blouse scooped both front and back, and three-inch heels. Her hair was pulled back, revealing delicate ears and translucent skin. He wished he could pull her to the bed and feast on all of her soft, graceful, feminine parts, one at a time, starting with those lovely little earlobes.

"The Tale of Desperaux," he said.

"And what's your son's name again? — I'm just terrible with names."

"Sammy."

Curtis studied her face in the mirror and found it hard to stop staring. Her eyes twinkled when she spoke. It didn't much matter what she said; her eyes laughed as though the world and the people in it were both amusing and delightful. He felt he could watch her with pleasure all night.

"And he's how old?"

"Six."

"My sister has a little boy who's seven or eight. He's a monster."

"You didn't mention any siblings before."

"Oh, yes, I have an older sister. She lives in Sussex. Her husband is a professor of something or other. Something classic — Greek or...?"

He put his hands gently on her shoulders, drinking in the heady aroma of flowers and citrus that rose from her skin. Then he impulsively dipped his head and kissed the nape of her neck.

"Don't get any ideas," she said firmly. "We don't want to be late."

He felt immediately abashed. He'd overstepped the bounds. She smiled a small, confident smile to herself, and then her eyes crinkled into a smile for him.

"You look beautiful," he said.

She laughed, her eyes twinkling merrily, and kissed him on the cheek, all forgiven. "We should go," she said, and led the way out of the room.

Curtis glanced back longingly at the bed, where the two cats lay soundly sleeping.

It was only another ten minutes to Westlake drive, and while they spoke of cars and the price of gas, and that she was glad he didn't smoke tobacco like her last boyfriend, Curtis happily fantasized about showing off the new girl to Linda, like a boy with a new trophy. He knew it was shameful, but it would be so satisfying to prove to Linda that he, too, could attract another lover. He wasn't the defective merchandise she had discarded. He was in demand. *Take that, you bitch!*

Westlake Drive was ablaze with Christmas lights, with the exception of his own home. Apparently, Roger wasn't handy with small chores, or maybe Linda just didn't care anymore. Curtis certainly wasn't going to volunteer after being unceremoniously exiled, but it seemed a shame that Sammy had to endure an aluminum tree and a house without lights or decorations.

He went around the car and opened the passenger door, leaving nothing to chance. "Come on, we'll get Sammy together," he said cheerily, giving her no choice but to comply.

They were turning up the front walk when Elliot pulled to a stop in his Volvo. "Hey bro, are you going to introduce me?" Curtis steered Rhiannon to the open window of the Volvo and made the introductions. "I'm making a beer run for the poker game. You might bring some wine to the party tomorrow. Don't be late," Elliot said. "You're coming, too, I hope," he added to Rhiannon.

She looked to Curtis. "I haven't been invited."

"I wish you would," Curtis said.

"If it's not too much trouble," she said, addressing Elliot.

"No trouble at all. It's a neighborhood thing. Bring something for the ornament exchange. Curtis will explain."

The Volvo sped away in the night, its twin red taillights narrowing with distance until it turned the corner.

"I was thinking of asking you," Curtis said lamely, "but I didn't know if you'd feel comfortable."

"You don't have to; I won't be offended."

"But I do want you to come."

"Tell me about the ornament exchange."

Curtis explained as they strolled up the walk to the front door.

The look on Linda's face, the tongue-tied shock with which she gaped at Rhiannon, was a tonic to Curtis's spirit. He smiled diabolically. "Rhiannon, this is Linda, Sammy's mother," he said by way of introduction. "Is Sammy ready? We have a show to catch."

They stood in the foyer until Sammy came running downstairs. "This is for you." He thrust a kiln-fired piece of pottery into his father's hands. It was an imprint of his own little hand. "It's a ornament."

"It's wonderful," Curtis said, and he meant it. Twenty-six years ago he'd given a similar keepsake to his mother. She brought it out like a treasured memory every Christmas.

"How are your fish?" Rhiannon asked Sammy.

"I dunno. Dad keeps'm."

"They haven't gone belly up yet," Curtis supplied.

With that, they made their adieus. All went reasonably well until Curtis let go of Sammy's hand and stepped forward to pay for the movie tickets. The clerk was sliding the tickets under the glass when Curtis heard

Rhiannon's loud and commanding voice — "Get back here, young man! This instant!" She stamped her foot and pointed to the ground at her feet. But Sammy paid her no heed. He was sticking his hand in the fountain at the front of the theatre. Rhiannon clapped her hands, stamped her foot again and looked cross. Handing her a ticket, Curtis said, "He's not a dog," and called, "Come on Sammy, we have just enough time to grab some popcorn before the movie." He bent to one knee and Sammy came running, jumping into his father's arms. Curtis picked him up, glad that he was still small enough and light enough to carry, and not yet self-conscious enough to spurn his father's public displays of affection. Curtis knew these days were numbered, and he cherished every one.

"You shouldn't coddle him," Rhiannon said. "He has to know who is in charge. Children need guidance, not choices."

Curtis said nothing. He was continually surprised how people who had no children of their own, seemed always to know how best to raise them. They didn't understand that children weren't little robots that could be programmed for good behavior. Children were curious, energetic, sometimes fatigued, sometimes willful, often distracted, with wants and needs all their own, just like any other human being. It was often frustrating trying to steer them in a direction that coincided with your own agenda. But raising children wasn't just about making them compliant to your wishes. It was also about your ongoing relationship with them. As a parent you weren't just an instructor, or disciplinarian, or protector, or friend. Until they reached adulthood, you were also an extension of their sense of self, the bedrock of their self-esteem, there to offer support and acceptance in a world that was too quick to criticize and belittle. The wildest kids he'd known in high school came from the strictest parents. Acting like a drill instructor at an obedience school was the surest means of inspiring rebellion, he thought. Children were not dogs.

While they bought their popcorn and drinks Curtis was polite but cool towards Rhiannon. He resented her criticism immensely. For her part, she said nothing more, but her disapproval was duly noted. The smile had left her eyes.

Curtis toyed with the idea of sitting Sammy between them, but thought the better of it. He was glad when the lights went out and he could concentrate on the movie, glad to lose himself in another world, and though he did not reach for her hand during the show, he slowly let his anger dissipate, like gas leaking from a taut balloon, until finally he could take a deep breath and let it all out. Anger didn't serve him. It wasn't as though he was perfect himself, he reminded himself.

Afterwards, they walked to a Cold Stone Creamery for an ice cream. It was a two-block walk, Rhiannon had not brought a coat, and she shivered with the cold. In a chivalrous gesture that would have made his mother proud, Curtis offered her his jacket. She seemed to warm almost immediately. He, on the other hand, felt the sting of the night breeze.

Ahead, a homeless man sat on the sidewalk, as grey as the sidewalk itself, and looking as cold and dirty. Curtis thought again how incomprehensible it was that thousands of people would be risking death from hypothermia that night. Something had to be done. Why did they keep electing officials who ignored the problem? Rhiannon switched sides. He thought to reach for her hand, but she was gripping her purse to her chest. Sammy took his other hand. Curtis saw his son staring at the man who was propped against the side of a building, his face lost in the shadow of a hooded coat. That young man was someone's son. He had probably thought that this could never happen to him, but if we were honest, we all knew that it could happen to anyone, given the right circumstances. No one was invulnerable to misfortune. He considered stopping to give the man a dollar, but there were Rhiannon and Sammy to think about. There were, among the homeless population, drug addicts and paranoid schizophrenics who might present a danger if approached. Yet he felt guilty giving the man a wide berth and averting his gaze. "There, but for the grace of God, or providence, or luck" was the sentiment that came to mind every time he came upon the homeless.

When he thought about the homeless in winter, he was always reminded of a story his grandfather had told him of his days working for Western Union in 1938. His grandfather's job had been to take telegrams from passengers on the train between Cleveland and New York, and run them in to the local telegrapher at each stop. On a February morning in New York City, waiting for the return trip back to Cleveland, he'd stood on the platform watching the early train pull in from Chicago. There had been a terrible blizzard the night before, and he remembered the snow-laden cars filing past, the passengers standing up in preparation for the end of their journey, getting down their baggage from the overhead racks, their collective breath steaming the windows. Then came the flat car at the end of the train, just before the caboose, with its three hobos frozen solid, white as marble statues. The image had stuck with him through the years. Curtis picked up Sammy and held him close like a small heater. Sammy laid his head on his father's shoulder.

"So tell me about this party we're going to," Rhiannon said.

"It's just the neighborhood Christmas party. Six couples, their kids, a few extra friends, a few of my neighbors' parents. Twenty, twenty-five people, and the kids."

"Yes, but what sort of people are they? Do I have to dress up?"

"They're just your usual middle-class mix of liberal and conservative, corporate types, entrepreneurs, nurses, stay-at-home moms. And no, you don't have to dress up. Some do. Some don't. There's no dress code."

"Age?"

"Late 20's, early 30's mostly, but there are kids, of course, and the grandparents."

"Should I bring anything?"

"I'm sure there'll be plenty of food; it's a pot-luck sort of thing; there's always more than we can eat. Linda used to make English Trifle, but I don't think she's coming this year." He asked Sammy, "Has your mother said anything about going to the Christmas party?" Sammy shook his head. "I didn't think so."

"Did you like the movie, Sammy?" Rhiannon asked.

"I liked the mouse and the rat, but I didn't liked the king. He was sad."

At the ice cream shop they voiced their preferences for ice cream, and then the conversation dried up. The silence was natural enough at first, as their mouths were full of ice cream, but on the walk back to the car the silence became uncomfortable. He made a couple of feeble attempts to get the ball rolling. She only answered in monosyllables. Not, it seemed, with any sullen intent, but with an air of preoccupation and weariness. He was embarrassed by his inability to natter on insipidly, to at least paint the illusion of dialogue by non-stop chatter, something at which Linda had excelled. His awkwardness now resulted not from infatuation, he realized, but from a real lack of common ground. He didn't yet know enough about this woman to feel entirely comfortable.

In the Honda, he pushed a CD into the slot (Tuck Andress) in hopes the music would fill the silence that hung between them like a wet blanket.

Back at the Collingwood Park apartments, he pulled to the curb, still unsure of what to say. Rhiannon saved him the trouble by saying, "I'm sorry. This didn't go very well, did it?"

"It wasn't bad, really," he stammered. "It could have been better."

"I'm not used to dating two men," she said with a nod of her head toward the sleeping Sammy. "I was hoping we could get to know each other a bit better."

"I know; I was too. But I'll see you tomorrow, I hope?"

"I don't..." She seemed at a loss for words. "I don't know any of them."

"They're easy enough, and I promise to spend the whole night with you. Sammy will be busy with the other kids."

"All right, then," she said, the smile returning to her eyes.

"I'll pick you up around 6:00," Curtis said. "I'd walk you up to your door, but..." A jerk of his thumb toward the back seat filled in the rest of the sentence.

Driving back over the bridge under the orange glow of sodium vapor lights, he reflected on his disappointment with this first date, if it could even be considered a date. He had not so much as held her hand, nor even attempted a stolen kiss.

It was only then that he realized they had not had dinner. There was no time before the movie. He and Sammy had filled up on popcorn. Rhiannon had noted the high level of sodium in popcorn, of nitrates in the hotdogs, and of corn syrup in the candy. She had eaten nothing but the ice cream. She had probably expected to go to dinner after the show. Why did these things only occur to him after the fact? He could only conclude that he was as incompetent a boyfriend as he'd been a husband.

A light snow sifted slowly down the heavens on Saturday morning. It clung to tree branches and windowsills, and drew a clean white blanket over the rubble-strewn lot across the street. Curtis turned up the thermostat and wished he had a real home with a real fireplace. This was the kind of day he liked to sit with a book and toast the soles of feet in front of a crackling fire.

As he stirred oatmeal with raisins on the stove, he could hear his grandmother saying, "Rolled oats stick to your ribs," just as she had always contended that eating the heel of a loaf of bread would make his hair curly. Strange, the odd bits of memory that defined the players in his life.

Sammy ate and watched the Saturday morning cartoons, while he absently drew fish with colored pencils. When the cartoons were over, he sat down at the gate-leg table and began coloring the fish with pastels. Curtis had noticed Sammy display a degree of independence since he'd started first grade, so he said nothing. Instead, he set the easel in front of the TV and watched the Vikings take on the Lions while he painted a picture of his house as seen from Elliot's front yard. The subject offered plenty of opportunity to practice technique. It was a winter scene. The chestnut tree threw deep shadows across the snowy ground and up the side of the house — in this he took artistic license, for those shadows never fell as far as the house, unless thrown by the streetlamp at night. A half-melted snowman stood by the front walk, its head on the ground.

At halftime, he checked on Sammy. He'd executed two fish pastels, and one of a beach at sunset, a beach that looked curiously like Del Mar. He was just finishing a watercolor of helium balloons tethered to a boat, with five passengers and a dog. From ten feet away the strokes of color actually looked like people.

"Where'd you learn to do that?"

"Stephanie showed you."

"Huh."

"This one is a Christmas present for Gwyn," he said, holding up the balloon-boat, only it came out sounding something like 'Chwistmas prwesent'. "And this one," he said, pushing forward one of his fish paintings, "is for Sophie. And this one is for Mommy. And this one," he put a finger on the beach scene, "is for you."

"You're not supposed to tell me! Christmas presents are supposed to be secret."

"That one isn't a Christmas present. It's just a pwesent pwesent."

"Thanks. It'll make a nice addition to our walls. But how are we supposed to wrap these others?"

"You need frames," Sammy said sensibly, as though explaining a simple concept to a child.

"Yes, but frames are expensive. I'd go broke if I framed all of your pictures."

Sammy looked skeptical. "Just give them to Stephanie. She'll do it." He shrugged.

"It still costs money."

Sammy just shrugged again and slipped away to play with his Lincoln Logs and action figures.

Curtis looked carefully at the paintings. The fish and balloon-boat reminded him of illustrations in children's books. The beachscape, on the other hand, could have been drawn by an adult. The edge of clouds had turned orange and pink in the sunset. It was drawn from the perspective of a person walking down the beach, with the waves on the left, and the houses and kelp-strewn beach on the right, converging at the rise of a sandstone cliff in the far distance. It was really quite remarkable, especially when viewed from across the room. The fish pictures were less realistic, but no less pleasing to the eye. The fish were outlined in colored pencils and filled in with oil pastels. Each fish was different. Sammy had shown a surprising mastery of technique. Striped fish and blue fish, orange fish and red fish, plain fish and multi-colored fish hovered over a reef, and hid in caves. At least the one for Linda solved a big problem — he'd been stymied by what Sammy could give his mother for Christmas. He had considered a lump of coal, but had decided that was uncharitable. This was an elegant solution. It was personal, and he knew it would look particularly nice with the right mat and frame.

Determined to make a better impression, Curtis spent longer than usual choosing his clothes and primping in front of the mirror. It wasn't that he was narcissistic, he told himself; he just wanted to be presentable. He added a blue blazer. This was not the relaxed, careless attire he was used to. He looked smartly casual, comfortable and yet stylish. In Elliot's words, "the packaging" was improved. He dressed Sammy in khaki pants and a blue sweater.

Rhiannon let them in at 6:35. The party had started at 6:00, but she'd had to work until 6:00. "I just need a minute," she said disappearing into the bedroom.

The apartment was just as before, except for the music. A Scarlatti harpsichord sonata played from the speakers. Sammy gravitated to the coffee table. He spun the toy merry-go-round, and seeing the books, he opened *Norman Rockwell, Illustrator.* The calico cat then rubbed against his leg and meowed. Sinking to his knees, he stroked her soft, orange fur. "I loves kitties," Sammy said.

"I know," Curtis said, "but you know the drill."

Rhiannon came into the room, dressed in an elegant, silver pleated skirt and grey knit top with silver piping, and black boots. She crossed the room, closed the book with a frown and lined up the edge of its spine precisely with the edge of the table. "You mustn't touch other people's things without permission," she told Sammy. "Are we ready to go?"

Sammy jumped to his feet and took her hand. Curtis wondered at the guileless ease of children.

On Westlake Drive Curtis parked at the curb in front of his own house by habit. He peered at the dark windows — Linda was obviously out. The moment Curtis opened Elliot's front door Sammy ran past them to find Sophie. In the entry they were assaulted by enticing odors, and a rumble of voices punctuated by sporadic exclamations and laughter. Far in the background, largely obscured by the general hubbub James Galway's flute played Greensleeves. Clusters of people were grouped according to sex, relationship and age. Their clothes displayed an anarchy of style, from flamboyantly colored shirts to black blouses, sequins to turtlenecks, sport jackets to leather jackets, woolen mufflers to diaphanous scarves. Doug Veeder wore a tuxedo, and as if in mockery, Chris Samuelson wore a black T-shirt imprinted with a tuxedo and bow tie. Michael Pearle was dressed in green cords with a white shirt accented by red plaid suspenders and a matching bow tie. Vicky Fine wore an ankle-length, flowing, black pleated skirt and black velvet top that set off a string of white pearls, while Annette Jancee wore jeans, a brown turtleneck, and a red, Gortex anorak. They were free to dress up or dress down as the mood struck. It was just that kind of neighborhood.

Curtis was anxious that Rhiannon should be well received. It was his first time in public without Linda, and it felt strange and oddly liberating. Catching sight of the pair, Roddy Flynn broke away from a knot of people to get a closer look. "Mister Cooke," he said in greeting with a lilting inflection that made the formal address both informal and welcoming. "Are you going to introduce me?"

"Rhiannon, this is Roddy Flynn. He's a demographer."

"So happy you could come," Flynn continued, acting the host, a role that passed from guest to guest throughout the evening according to his or her whim. "Are those for the ornament exchange? You can put them on the coffee table." They did. "Can I get you something to drink?"

"I don't drink," Rhiannon said, which meant, as everyone knew, that she didn't drink alcohol.

This was news to Curtis, who had brought a bottle of Navarro Gewürztraminer. "Not even white wine?"

"No, but I'll take fruit juice or tea."

"In the fridge," Flynn said.

Curtis led Rhiannon to the kitchen, stopping twice for introductions. He put the Gewürz in a tub of ice with a dozen other bottles, and got Rhiannon a glass of orange juice. *Everyone will assume it's a screwdriver,* Curtis thought.

"Tell me about all these people," she said, making a sweeping gesture with her glass. There were close to 30 adults and 15 children. "Do you know all of them?"

"Most of them. They're just friends and erstwhile neighbors and their extended families." Curtis gave her nutshell biographies as they circulated around the room. "Watch out for Van Gleason there. He's fine when he's sober, but he's a skirt chaser when he's had a few."

The kids were watching *Mr. Magoo's Christmas Carol* in Sophie's room. The adults crowded the kitchen and spilled into the living room and dining room around a table spread with hors d'oeuvres — lumpia from the Pobladors; the Samuelsons' *chile con queso* with tortilla chips; Mary Veeder's artichoke dip; Roberta Pearle's stuffed grape leaves; jalapeño poppers from Roddy Flynn; coleslaw from the Jancees; and Swedish meatballs from the Van Gleasons. There were, besides, rice pudding, homemade eggnog, and an array of Christmas cookies cut in festive shapes and studded here and there with red and green sprinkles. It was an abundant feast.

Curtis sampled a popper. "Want a taste?"

"Too spicy," Rhiannon said, shaking her head.

"Meatball?"

"Oh no, I don't eat red meat; you know cattle are full of hormones."

"The artichoke dip is always good."

"It's full of mayonnaise," she said dismissively. "Mostly fat."

"That rules out the coleslaw, then. How about the chile con...oh, right, spicy." Scanning the table, he saw the desserts. They were neither meaty nor spicy. "You could have a dessert," he offered hopefully.

"I try to avoid processed flour and sugar. Don't worry about me."

"Is there anything you *can* eat?"

"What are the grape leaves stuffed with?"

Curtis tried one. "Rice and goat cheese."

"Perfect. I'll have some of those."

Curtis handed her a plate, relieved she'd found something to her taste. This was going to be more difficult than he'd imagined. "I'm going to have a glass of wine."

"Must you?" she asked with such condescension that it immediately got his hackles up.

He was quite taken aback by the tone. It was so like Linda when she was in one of her bad moods, that he had to fight the urge to issue a stinging retort. That wouldn't do at all. To begin a relationship on a note of confrontation would snuff out the romance before it had a chance to kindle. *She's not your enemy*, he reminded himself. "Is there a problem?"

"You're driving."

She was right; he was the designated driver. "I'll keep it to two," he promised, remembering that in the past five years he had been wont to have four or five, as he had only to walk across the street and fall into bed. He had his passengers to think about, and he certainly did not want to be tagged with a DUI.

He went off to the kitchen to pour himself a glass of the Gewürz, committing to memory '*no alcohol, no red meat, no processed flour or sugar, nothing overtly spicy.'* There was so much to learn. He hadn't out and out asked how old she was; that would be rude. She appeared to be in her mid to late-twenties, an age by which most beautiful women were married. He wondered why she was single. Had her previous boyfriends left, or had they been dismissed? She had not volunteered the information. When he returned to her side the question was still niggling away at the back of his mind. Being curious and tactless (he might have said 'being honest and forthright,')he asked, "Are you divorced?"

"Divorced? Me?" She laughed. It was that same delightful, unselfconscious laugh he'd first heard upon entering Pretty Pets. "I've never been married. I've been waiting for the right man."

"You couldn't do better than this one," Elliot said, stepping to her side. He'd been eavesdropping.

"You remember Elliot? From the Volvo yesterday?"

"Of course."

"We work together. This is his house."

"You're Curtis's best friend," she said to Elliot, as though Curtis had said as much. He had not, and Curtis wondered why she would make that assumption, though she was obviously perceptive.

"Yes, I suppose I am," Elliot said brightly.

"Pleased to meet you," she said, shaking Elliot's hand and giving him a 'pleased as punch' smile that made Curtis's heart skip with pleasure. She had a beautiful smile.

"I was going to open up a Vintage Port after the ornament exchange, for those of us who might appreciate it. I bought some Stilton," Elliot said, looking from Curtis to Rhiannon and back again.

"That would be wonderful," Curtis said. "What year?"

"He's driving," Rhiannon said, putting her hand lightly on Curtis's arm.

"I am, but I'll just have the one glass. That will make two, and I'll have plenty to eat, so don't worry."

Rhiannon's brow furrowed and her lips tightened, but she said nothing more. Her disapproval was all too evident. Elliot raised his eyebrows at Curtis, said "Later," and faded into the crowd. Curtis could already hear Elliot saying *'you really know how to pick them.'*

"It can't be so bad," Curtis said with sudden inspiration — remembering she believed that God had opened the door through which he had so opportunely stepped; "Jesus turned water into wine."

"Jesus was surely never drunk, and besides, there were no cars in biblical days."

"Who's your friend?" came a voice over his shoulder.

Curtis knew at once it was Fred Van Gleason and from his slurred speech it was obvious that he'd already had a few too many. As a general rule, everyone was on friendly terms with Fred. He was an innocuous enough character when sober, and even witty when he'd had a drink or two. But he could be an obnoxious drunk. Nonetheless, there was nothing to do but make the introductions. "Rhiannon, this is Fred Van Gleason. He lives across the street."

"Rhiannon," Fred puzzled. "What kind of name is that?"

"It's a proper Irish name," Rhiannon said.

"So, you're Irish?"

"My father is Irish. My mother is English."

"I thought the Micks and the Brits hated each other."

"It's complicated; there's a long history," she answered, and from the tone of her voice it was obvious that she did not appreciate the tenor of the question, nor the apparent prejudices and ignorance of the speaker.

"Where's Donna?" Curtis asked, trying to steer the conversation in a more neutral direction.

"She's around here somewhere. Or else she's gone back home. She's pissed at me. You know what I think?"

"No, what?"

Van Gleason's eyes seemed to glaze over as he looked away. He smiled inanely. After an embarrassingly long silence, he answered, "You don't care what I think. I'm full of shit. Carry on. I need another drink. Or maybe I don't. I don't know." With his parting words he headed for the kitchen.

"Sorry, he gets that way sometimes."

"No doubt he'll blame it on the alcohol tomorrow morning. I have no patience for drunks."

This was going badly. She was in a contrarian mood and the evening had barely begun.

"We really haven't had much time to talk, I'm afraid," began Curtis. "At Starbucks you mentioned you went to Columbia, but you didn't say what you majored in."

"Nothing. That was the problem. I took all the required courses, and then I couldn't decide on a major. I liked History, but I couldn't see myself teaching. Same with English. I liked Psychology, but I didn't want to be Psychologist — who wants to hear people complain all day?"

As though on cue, Chris Samuelson's voice rose testily above the rumble. "I don't care if they bugger each other; I'm just as tolerant as the next guy, but I don't think I should be forced to approve of it!"

"You're just a homophobe," Michael Pearle growled in reply.

"I hope your kids are gay."

"I take it back; you're a bigot."

"You think liberals aren't bigoted? You're inflexibly accepting of everyone. Do you have any standards at all?"

With that, their conversation subsided into the general tumult.

"I think this was a mistake," Rhiannon said. "All these people — it's like meeting your family, but we don't even know each other yet. Can we just start over? Take me home and we'll go on a real date tomorrow."

"We can't go now; Santa hasn't come yet. There's the ornament exchange."

"Santa?" She waited for the punch line that wasn't forthcoming.

Curtis looked around to make sure no young ears were listening. "Every year a friend of Beverly Flynn's dresses up in a Santa suit and shows up with a bag of presents." Curtis had bought a windup airplane for Sammy on a lunch break earlier in the week, had given it to Elliot, who gave it to Vicky, who gave it to Beverly, who gave it to Rex, who would soon be arriving in the guise of Santa to give it to Sammy. "Sammy always looks forward to it."

"Isn't he a little old to believe in Santa?"

"He's only six."

"Oh, I think he knows. Even six-year-olds know what's real and what's not."

"That's more than I can say for most adults," he muttered, uncharacteristically refraining from adding, '*The churches are full of them every Sunday.'* He patted himself on the back for his forbearance and said instead, "It's a pleasant fiction," privately enjoying the double entendre.

"But I don't think he really believes," Rhiannon persisted; "his playmates would have told him."

It was true, there was peer pressure, pressure to believe and pressure to disbelieve. "Last year some of the older kids tried to spoil the fun, and they were sent home without presents, so I don't expect a repeat performance this year."

"That was harsh."

"Isn't that the way heretics are always treated?"

Last year when Tommy Flynn and Paul Samuelson had questioned the veracity of Santa Claus, Sammy had been upset. Curtis told him, "Some people don't believe in Santa Claus. Some people think Santa is an elf. But I think Santa is a spirit." And he really did — he believed that Santa was that spirit of anonymous generosity in all of us. So it wasn't really a lie; it was just a deception.

A year ago, Curtis had hidden a set of jingle bells in the gutter and attached a piano wire that ran over the top of the house. On Christmas eve he sat next to Sammy's bed reading *The Night Before Christmas*, before excusing himself to go to the bathroom across the hall. Reaching the piano wire from the open window, he drew it slowly inside, careful not to pull too fast. The bells jingled merrily across the roof. In half a minute Sammy was whispering loudly at the door. "Dad! Dad! I hear bells!"

"Don't yell, Sammy," Curtis whispered back. "You'll scare him away!"

At that moment, the bells caught on the peak of the roof. Curtis tugged. The thin wire snapped and the bells tumbled in a jangling cacophony back down the roof and into the gutter.

"Dad!"

"I'm coming," he yelled back. He threw the wire into the backyard, closed the window, flushed the toilet and stepped into the hall.

Sammy was bouncing with excitement. "I heard him. I heard him!"

Linda came into the hall from their bedroom where she'd been wrapping last-minute gifts. "Did you hear that?" she asked, dumbfounded.

"It's Santa!" Sammy hissed, jumping up and down. "Let's go see!"

"We might frighten him away," cautioned Curtis. "He won't leave presents until everyone is asleep. Come on, I'll tuck you in and read another story."

Sometimes imagination needed a little boost.

"I don't think he'll even notice, if we leave now," Rhiannon said. "Can't we just go before Santa shows up?"

"I'm really sorry you're not having a good time," Curtis said, "but I don't want to disappoint Sammy. Let's just hang out in the corner and talk. We were talking about Columbia, and what you want to do with your life."

"It's not a very exciting story."

About that she was not kidding. Her story was like so many others, of aimless searching for the right fit, of taking this job or that just to pay the bills. She had passed on to the much more interesting topic (to Curtis) of boyfriends, when the doorbell rang and a squat, portly man with a fake beard and a Santa suit strode in with a "Ho! Ho! Ho!" and a sack of toys slung over his shoulder. He was made for the part.

For the next half-hour, the younger kids sat on Santa's lap one by one as he doled out the presents, and the older kids stepped sheepishly out of the crowd to accept their presents with a smirk and a shake of the head.

When it was over and Santa "ho-ho-hoed!" out the door, Vicky Fine stood up on the hearth and clapped her hands. "Now for the ornament exchange! For those of you who are new, here are the rules: The exchange is only open to those who have brought a wrapped present to exchange (sounds elemental, but it has happened before, so if you haven't brought an ornament, or if it's not wrapped, you must sit out). We'll draw numbers from a hat. The person with number one has the pick of any present on the table. Then number two goes, and so on. You may take any present here on the table, or take a present from someone who has already chosen. If your present is taken away, you may not immediately take back the same present; you are obliged to either pick another from the table, or from someone else. The exchange is over when the last present is taken from the table. And remember, sometimes the best ornaments come in the plainest boxes, and vice versa."

"Like women!" Van Gleason shouted from the back of the crowd.

The coffee table was piled high with colorful boxes and bags and bows. Certain boxes, either by their size or the beauty of their wrappings, were obviously favored. No sooner did a participant pick one of these boxes, than another would take it away. By the time half the boxes were gone, most of the action centered on four boxes already in hand. Mary Veeder had her eyes set on a box with bright green and gold stripes. But, so did Anita Poblador, Vicky Fine and Annette Jancee. Mary took it from Anita who (obligated to take another present) took Annette's, so Annette took back the green and gold box from Mary, who took Anita's, and so on with much frivolity and boisterous hurrahs, until finally one of them broke the cycle and selected another present from the table. But it was a contest that would be revisited later. Other such rivalries broke out in competition for other boxes, so that it was a full forty minutes before the last present was taken from the table. And as Vicky Fine had predicted, the best ornaments did not always come in the prettiest packages. The green and gold box held a wooden star painted with silver glitter, not an ornament Curtis would have treasured. His own prize was a beautiful blue and green, blown-glass parrot.

Curtis excused himself to pay a visit to the bathroom. When he came back Rhiannon was telling Roddy Flynn, "You know how it is: Someone you know knows someone who's hiring, and you need a job. I'm trying to save up so I can buy into the business. Mrs. Singh wants to open another store." This was something she had not yet confided to Curtis, and which he tucked away in his memory for future conversation.

"I'm going to pop that Port in my den," Elliot said confidentially to Curtis, and because he was within hearing distance, he extended the invitation to Flynn.

"No thanks, not my cup of tea," Flynn declined.

"You didn't say what vintage," Curtis said expectantly.

"It's a 1977 Dow."

"Dow — how appropriate. The '77 should be great." Turning to Rhiannon he said, "I'll just be another fifteen minutes and then we can go."

When he'd had his allotted one glass, with a bite of Stilton cheese, Curtis sauntered back into the living room, but Rhiannon was nowhere to be seen. The party was breaking up; half the neighbors had dispersed. He looked in the dining room and the kitchen. He looked into the front yard to see if she had stepped out for some fresh air. Then he went looking for Sammy, whom he found playing with Sophie in her bedroom. "Have you seen Rhiannon?" he asked, but Sammy just looked up from his Playmobil tableau and shook his head. Coming back into the living room, he noticed the sliding glass door to the backyard was ajar, and stepped outside. The cold night was pitch black, but for a quarter moon hidden behind scudding clouds. He was about to go back inside when he heard a woman's laughter. It was maniacally manic, followed by a coughing fit. Then he smelled a whiff of marijuana. He found Annette Jancee and Roddy Flynn behind the leafless tangle of wisteria vines that covered the arbor at the edge of the patio. When she saw him, Annette burst into hysterical giggles, snorting with an effort to control herself.

"You want a toke?" Roddy Flynn asked, holding out a roach. "It's a 2007." It wasn't a bad witticism Curtis had to admit to himself, even if it was at his expense, as the two inebriates guffawed uncontrollably.

"No thanks, I have to drive," Curtis said. "Have you seen Rhiannon?"

"She was here a minute ago," Roddy croaked, trying his best to hold in the smoke and speak at the same time. "She doesn't smoke."

"I'll look out front."

"Tootaloo," Flynn said amiably and took another toke.

Curtis shook his head at their foolishness, though he knew he should keep his opinions to himself. He'd had this debate before about one's choice of intoxicants. As a wine enthusiast, he had no cause to be sanctimonious (other than the obvious argument that alcohol was legal). Wine had its various flavors and complexities, and each bottle contained a history of place and time, but it was an alcoholic beverage, after all, and it could be argued that alcohol was a far greater scourge on society than marijuana, even if the medical debate was still unsettled.

He finally found Rhiannon sitting in his car. "Are you all right?"

"Fine. Can we go now?"

"Let me get Sammy," he said, annoyed at her curt disapproval. She'd apparently been sitting here the whole time. He knew he had no claim on her, no right to demand she behave in any way whatsoever, and yet it did bother him. And he couldn't help being annoyed at himself for expecting her to live up to the fantasy he'd constructed in his head. If who she was in all of her complexity differed from his fantasies, he would have to decide if he was simply being unrealistic, or if there were issues that made them unsuited to one another.

It was only half-past ten when they arrived back at Rhiannon's apartment. This time he walked her to her door, leaving Sammy asleep in the locked car (it was only for a minute, he thought, excusing himself). At her door, he kissed her. She was a compliant, if not particularly skillful kisser.

"I was wondering when you'd get around to that," she said.

He realized how unsatisfactory a kiss could be when one of the participants' heart wasn't into it. "Can we go out to dinner tomorrow, just you and me? I can pick you up after I drop off Sammy; then we can go on to a little Italian place I know in the old neighborhood."

"That would be wonderful, just you and me," she said with a relieved smile.

"Say around six?"

"Would you like to come to church with me tomorrow?"

It was a simple question, but the answer was so much more complicated, and it had ramifications that could seriously affect their relationship. "I don't think so," Curtis said cautiously. "I'm afraid I'm not the religious type."

"That's all right," she said, a note of disappointment in her voice. "I'm not forcing you. But I do go every week, just so you know."

"Okay, then, well, I'll see you tomorrow evening. 6:30, 6:45?"

The next morning, Sammy and Curtis walked in a blustering, cold wind to the end of the park, where they had breakfast at Jack's. The outside seating was closed for the season (chairs were stacked on top of tables and umbrellas were folded and tied tight). They ordered dollar pancakes in the noisy back of the room, near the open kitchen.

In the afternoon they watched *The Muppets Christmas Carol.* Then they painted. Curtis painted the foreground of a scene he'd been working on, off and on, for a week, a depiction of Madison Street Bridge.

That evening Curtis dressed in his new finery, and after dropping Sammy with Linda, he took Rhiannon to Pernicano's, a moderately priced Italian restaurant, whose owner was famous for spinning pizza dough overhead into large flat disks, while singing Dean Martin standards and arias from Rigoletto and Pagliacci. Rhiannon plied him with questions about his childhood, his job and his marriage, but she was not forthcoming herself. Whether from a lack of experience, or from a fear of offending, she offered no personal stories and few opinions. She deflected questions about previous boyfriends, and by the end of the evening he knew little more about her than he had already discovered. This was the first time he'd been out to dinner with a woman since he'd left home, except for Chinese food with Steph and Gwyn, and that didn't count; that wasn't a date. But he was reminded how easy the conversation had flowed then, talking about the kids, and art, and so much more. Why did this have to be so hard? Rhiannon was still lovely to look at. Her voice was still musical. But the glow of infatuation was losing its luster.

Arriving back at her apartment, she unlocked the door and reached inside to turn on the inside lights and the porch light, then closed the door. She turned and said, "Don't want to let the kitties out," with a perky smile. Curtis had been hoping to get lucky, but her body language was telling him to forget it. Was she as attracted to him as he was to her? This constant dancing around, trying to gauge another's feelings and desires was like walking on eggshells. He pulled her close and kissed her, rubbing the small of her back. They were better coordinated this time, and it triggered the usual male response. He drew her closer so she could feel his growing desire, hoping she was of like mind and this would be the key to an invitation inside. "Just so you don't get any funny ideas," she said, pushing away gently, "I'm saving myself for my husband."

"Saving...?" This was not a response he was expecting.

"Just because other girls are easy, doesn't mean I have to be. I'm just not built that way."

"You've never...?"

She looked down and shook her head, then looked searchingly into his eyes. "Is that a problem?" she asked in the sweetest voice he'd ever heard.

"No, no," he heard himself say, while thinking, *yes, yes, this is a huge problem!*

Chapter 17

Monday December 15 – Sunday December 21, 2008

Monday was a mess. Curtis awoke late from troubled dreams; it had rained overnight, the skies were still dark and threatening, with lightning to the northeast; the commute was slow, and Elliot's insistence on playing Corelli's Christmas Concerto didn't improve his mood (he found the piece depressing). "How about some Bach instead?" Curtis asked. "*Jesu, Joy of Man's Desiring*?"

Elliot just glared at him. "After the Corelli," he grumbled. But Curtis knew they'd be at work before it was over.

"Well, what did you think?" he asked Elliot.

"About what?"

"Rhiannon."

"Oh," Elliot said, pausing longer than was polite before adding, "Well, she *is* pretty."

"And?"

"What? I barely met the girl. Although I have to say, I don't trust anyone who doesn't drink — unless they're an alcoholic (that I can forgive)."

Throughout the day, as thunder rumbled and the DOW fell, Curtis was preoccupied with thoughts of Rhiannon. Now he understood why such a lovely woman was still available. There were few men who could endure a chaste courtship. It wasn't just about satisfying sexual desire; it was about intimacy and compatibility. He certainly didn't want to pressure her; if she'd gone this long, he wasn't likely to change her mind. But her decision begged the question: Did she have no sexual desire herself? Could he be happy with a woman who did not desire him the way he desired her? And what if they weren't compatible?

At 5:45 p.m. on Monday, CostCo was jam packed with holiday shoppers. In addition to taking care of his wine supply and dinners for the next week, Curtis bought wrapping paper and ribbons, a silver rope bracelet for Rhiannon, a bike helmet, and a shining, royal-blue bike with training wheels for Sammy.

Packages from his parents and siblings had been left for him in the Superintendent's office. He distributed them under the tree and took the elevator down to Irene's. She looked like she was just going out or had just returned from an outing, as she wore a smart green turtleneck with beige slacks, and sheer stockings on her feet. "Hi, Irene. You wouldn't, by any chance, be spending the holidays here, would you?"

"I'm afraid I am. My son is committed to flying to his parents-in-laws' (he married an out-of-Stater), so we're holding off Christmas for a week. And my daughter is busy. It won't seem much like Christmas, but what can you do?"

"I know what you mean; I get Sammy the day after Christmas. I need a place to hide his bike until then, and I was wondering..."

"Of course, I'd be happy to. A sled might be more appropriate for this time of year, though."

"Too late, I already bought it. I'll just go upstairs and bring it down."

Curtis thought how lucky he was to have made the acquaintance of at least one neighbor, and he reminded himself to give her his extra key in case of emergencies.

That night he painted a leafless oak in a snowy field. Far in the background a red barn stood out against distant hills of grey, deciduous trees. For much of the foreground he applied the paint with a sponge — a technique he'd picked up from the book Stephanie Walzer had given him. He was barely aware of what he was doing, for as he painted, he brooded over Rhiannon's disclosure. There were, if common sentiment were to be believed, plenty of women out there who faked orgasms to please their husbands, women who had very little sexual desire themselves. He believed there must be millions of such couples, bound together not by romantic attraction, but by a shared history, or a common world-view, the bond between them more akin to friends than lovers. But in that case, why get married? Why not simply remain friends? He felt deeply that the mutual longing inherent in a romantic relationship, even when unsatisfied, was something special, as were the tender displays of affection that were the outward manifestation of desire. Desire was that spark that set a romantic relationship apart from simple friendship. Could it be wise to commit to an endless future with someone who was looking for a friend and not a lover, someone with whom he might not be sexually compatible? Ages past were littered with such unhappy marriages. Affairs and mistresses were the result.

Barbara buzzed him. "You'll want to take this," is all she said.

He picked up the phone.

"Cooke?"

"Yes?"

"Dayton here."

"Yes, Mr. Dayton."

There was silence for a moment. Then he said, "I'd appreciate it if you'd drop the 'mister.' Mr. Dayton is my father. I'm far too young to be a mister. You can just call me Dayton, or Jim, whatever makes you happy. Can we have lunch?"

Curtis quickly tried to call to mind his calendar. "What day?"

"Today. Fifty minutes, give or take. You available?"

"I usually just grab a sandwich."

"No, no. I have a couple of people I'd like to introduce you to. I was hoping you could join us for lunch at Corton."

He wondered if Erickson knew about the meeting and decided not to mention it. He didn't need the added pressure of his boss looking over his shoulder. He remembered Erickson saying that Dayton was an anthropologist or something innocuous and academic. Academic types were unintimidating, and as long as the conversation was kept to finance, he could hold his own

Dayton, as Curtis discovered at their meeting, was considerably younger than Erickson, perhaps 30 or 31, leaving Curtis to conclude that he must have entered college at an early age and was a class or two behind his roommate. He had shoulder length, curly brown hair, a drooping mustache, and myopic eyes behind wire rimmed glasses. He wore new blue jeans and an expensive burgundy cashmere sweater with the sleeves pushed halfway up his muscular forearms. His demeanor was disarmingly friendly.

"This is the guy I was telling you about," he said as he introduced his friends (colleagues? Curtis wondered; the relationship was unclear). Jay Purvis was a nervous, clean-cut young man in khakis and a long-sleeved shirt of pale blue gingham. John Bettencourt was a stiff mannered suit in his mid-thirties, with a five o'clock shadow and dark hair combed straight back. "I was telling them the last broker I had lost me a ton of money. You've really turned things around, thank you very much. So, I thought I'd return the favor by spreading the good word."

"Timing is everything," Curtis said. He'd been lucky with Dayton's portfolio. Most of the increase was due to First Solar, a company that speculators had seized upon as likely to benefit from an Obama presidency.

"My broker has cost me 37% this year," Purvis said.

"If it's good, it must be risky," Bettencourt said. "What's your angle?"

He needn't have worried about the meeting; it was the same old dog-and-pony show.

Stephanie announced, "We will have no class the next two weeks, as Wednesday falls on both Christmas Eve and New Year's Eve. Class will resume on January 7th."

This class was spent on complimentary colors, when and how to load a brush with two colors, and a brief exercise in painting rudimentary figures, with techniques she had previously shown Curtis in the park, and which Sammy had already mastered.

Curtis waited patiently at the front of the class until Stephanie had said the last of her goodbyes. Then he brought out several of Sammy's paintings, and one of his own. "I was wondering if you could have these framed. Sammy painted this one for Gwyn. Make that a nice frame, and this other for his mother. The rest I'd like to do a bit cheaper, if we can. Do you have any seconds? Frames with small blemishes? They're just for the apartment."

"Wow, you're getting so much better," she said, admiring the beach scene. "Your perspective is very different, very arresting."

"That's Sammy's, actually. This one is mine."

"Oh, my, he really is.... This is his? It's hard to believe. Yours is nice, too," she added encouragingly. "But this is amazing. He's made such progress. I know Gwyn will be pleased with hers; it was so nice of Sammy to think of her."

"Don't forget your backpack," Linda called to Sammy; it's in the kitchen."

Left alone with Linda, Curtis filled in the awkward space by saying, "We should get together one of these days to divide things up." It was a chore they had been putting off, and one they had to do together.

"No time like the present, if you're not busy tonight. Roger's not here."

"I haven't had dinner," was his only excuse.

"I made macaroni and cheese and broccoli. There's plenty leftover."

So he sat in his kitchen, eating another meal in his house, perhaps his last meal there. They had been so proud when they moved in. He had felt launched into adulthood.

When he finished, they took in each room as she made notes on a clipboard: things she would keep, things he would take, things they would sell. There were books, music CDs, DVDs, tools, furniture, a couple of lithographs, his ski equipment and bicycle, Halloween outfits, Christmas decorations, wedding presents, silverware, china, kitchen appliances, and photos and videos of Sammy that would have to be duplicated. It was obvious he'd need to rent a storage unit: there were more things than he could possibly fit into the apartment, things that he might need, or want, later on. It would have been more convenient to let her have it all, but it stuck in his craw to give her more than her fair share.

Before they left, she said, "You realize that this was Sammy's last day of school until the New Year?"

"Is it?"

"Yes, and I'll need help. I can't work mornings if Sammy's home."

"Why didn't you say something sooner?"

"I was waiting to see if you'd paid attention."

"Oh for Christ sakes, you can't expect me to be on top of these things. Besides, I can't very well take off work. Ask Vicky: She's home all day, and Sammy would love to play with Sophie."

"Maybe you could ask Elliot."

Curtis stared at her in disgust. She was just trying to be contrary, to get under his skin, and there was no need. This little inconvenience was easily taken care of without his intervention. On the verge of an argument, he took a mental step back. What was the use? Without a word, he turned on his heel, walked across the street, asked Vicky for the favor, and reported back to Linda. "Done," he said. "Vicky will be happy to help."

Linda smiled smugly. "Well fine, then," she said.

On Saturday they slept late, arising with the intention of flying Sammy's new windup plane at the park. But the idea was quickly abandoned at the sight of a low sky of broken clouds scudding eastward, borne by a cold wind. Not to be discouraged, they took the change of plans with equanimity, and passed the morning in a leisurely manner watching cartoons, reading, playing with toys, doodling with pastels and watercolor pens, and listening to Sinatra's Christmas album, content in their various occupations.

The music, the tree, the colorful lights, the ornaments — Curtis found comfort in the continuity of these traditions. No matter where he'd been, or what time of his life, December in his memory was always filled with the same music, the same bright colored lights, the same scent of evergreen trees and cinnamon, of mulled drinks and warm cookies.

They had made plans to pick up Rhiannon at her apartment after she got off work. After that, they would go to a casual dinner, and maybe to a movie. It was an appointment that they might have missed, as they had both fallen asleep in the afternoon, had the buzzer on the intercom not awakened them at 5:35. Curtis shuffled sleepily to the intercom and asked who it was. Stephanie was downstairs. He buzzed her up, opened the door, and went to the kitchen to get a cup of coffee.

A minute later she came in carrying several flat packages wrapped in brown paper. She glanced at the cup in Curtis's hand and said, "I'll have a cup of hot chocolate, if you have it." As he prepared the hot chocolate, she left the parcels on the gate-leg table and peeled off her gloves, knit hat, muffler and coat. "It's freezing out there," she said, patting her red cheeks.

"I'm glad you woke us," Curtis yawned; "we have to leave in half an hour."

"That works out then, because I have to get back home to Gwyn. I just got off work, and I thought I would deliver your pictures."

"You didn't have to do that."

"I know, but I wanted to. I think you'll be pleased."

Together they unwrapped the paintings. "This is just your order," she explained. "I have a couple of presents to drop off tomorrow morning before I go to work, if you don't mind — just a little something to pay you back for the canvases and the paint."

"There's no need."

"No, I want to. But they're at home, and I couldn't carry those and these, too (one of the drawbacks of not having a car). First I wanted to show Sammy the picture he made for Gwyn, because I'm taking that with me. Can we wake him?"

Stephanie knelt by the sofa and spoke soothingly. "Sammy? Sammy, it's time to wake up." She rubbed his back and ruffled his hair. He rolled over and his eyes blinked open. She smoothed the hair out of his eyes. "I have a surprise for you. Come on, I'll help you." She had an easy way with children. She picked him up and carried him to the table. "I forgot how light six-year-olds are. I wanted to show you your framed paintings."

First they looked at the picture of the balloon boat (Sammy's present to Gwyn), then the fish pictures for his mother and for Sophie, and lastly the beachscape. "I think you did a marvelous job with this one. It has depth. And it shows you have patience, because this must have taken you some time."

"I did like you said; I did the background first."

"Such a good listener. I wish I had more students like you." Then she put Sammy down and turned to Curtis. "Yours came out nicely." His scene of the gazebo at the pond, the one on which Stephanie had painted Sammy with a kite, had been framed in a simple but elegant maple wood frame with a double mat.

It was a painting that he had been tempted to keep working on, and now he was happy she had talked him out of it. There were no extraneous elements. With her additions — of Sammy with a kite, of a little girl feeding ducks, and of some of the foreground cattails — it looked almost professional.

"That's a beautiful frame," he commented. He checked his watch. "Sammy, go put your shoes on; we have to be going." Sammy got down on all fours and peered under the sofa for his shoes as Curtis continued, "I love the way these look when they're framed. It makes a huge difference." He asked how much he owed for the frames. It was much less expensive than he'd expected. If these frames were seconds, he couldn't find the blemishes. And she'd added mats.

She had done her best to keep the price down, had even used her own employee discount, but even so it had cost her more than a day's wages to pay the bill, so she could hardly help but notice how easily he reimbursed her, nonchalantly peeling off the bills from a money clip, as though it were a trifle. How nice life would be, she thought, if money were of so little importance. How much weight would be lifted from her shoulders.

"Is tomorrow morning okay? To bring the other paintings, I mean," she asked, wrapping brown paper around Gwyn's present. "I have to be at the store at 9:00, so it would have to be early, around 8:15, if that's okay."

"I'll make a point of being up by then." In his mind he was figuring the time necessary for Stephanie to get from her place to Washington Street. Presumably she'd come on a bus, then take another bus to work. It must take 15 or 20 minutes to get here, and another 20 to get to the store, plus the waiting for the buses, which he knew could add another 15 to 20 minutes to each leg. It was only a 10-minute drive in the car. "We're about to leave. Can I give you a lift home?"

"If it's not out of your way."

"No problem," Curtis said, neglecting to add that it was exactly in the opposite direction. Even so, it would only take him 10 to 12 minutes out of his way. She'd gone to the trouble of bringing the paintings. It was the least he could do.

Bailey Place was a street of slightly shabby, mixed residential and commercial two-story brick buildings built before the 1920s, with old elm trees growing in the space between the sidewalk and the street. The Walzers lived in a building that had been converted into four apartments, plus a large basement that might have housed another tenant, had it not been used instead for storage.

Pulling to the curb, Curtis noticed a bum pushing a market basket on the sidewalk approaching her residence. He was dressed in two or three layers of dirty brown clothing, and a stocking cap. The basket was filled with large plastic trash bags that bulged with empty cans. This down-and-out vagrant might be harmless, but many on the streets were addicts or mentally unstable, and others who might not have started out that way became unstable after living on the streets. In either case, Curtis immediately saw the situation as potentially unsafe, and he felt it prudent, as well as his obligation, to walk Stephanie to her front door. He told Sammy to wait in the car, tucked Gwyn's present under one arm and offered Stephanie his other. As they reached the man, Curtis avoided eye contact and steered wide, determined to give him plenty of room. "Spare change?" Curtis heard and gave a curt shake of the head. As they passed, the man pleaded, "Come on, man, I'm hungry," then grumbled sarcastically, "Merry Christmas to you, too."

Stephanie stopped. "Just a minute," she said to Curtis, and addressed the mendicant. "Are you really hungry?"

"I'm starving. I haven't had anything to eat since yesterday morning."

Stephanie reached into her purse, brought out what looked like a credit card and handed it to the man. "The nearest one is three blocks in that direction." She pointed.

"Bless you, God bless you," the man mumbled, turning away. "Merry Christmas."

As they walked up the steps Curtis asked, "What did you give him?"

"A gift card to the Subway sandwich shop. I always buy a few this time of year. Gwyn and I'll use them, and if I happen to meet a beggar, I'd rather hand him a meal than a dollar. I used to feel guilty — you know, 'there but for the grace of god' and all that — but I didn't want to give them money that they might spend on drugs or alcohol. It eases my conscience. Thanks for the ride."

Curtis handed her Gwyn's present and she went inside.

They arrived at Collingwood Park apartments at the same time as Rhiannon pulled into her parking spot, and all went in together, their hair blowing wildly in the wind. "Just let me run to the bathroom and change my clothes. I smell like a dog!" she said cheerfully.

Sammy sat down next to the cat and began stroking it. Curtis walked aimlessly around the room taking in the same books and decorations he'd seen previously. Nothing had changed, save for the absence of music. He went to the kitchen in search of a glass of water. The kitchen was neat and tidy, the way Linda kept things. His own kitchen looked messy by comparison, with its pictures stuck to the refrigerator and the usual assortment of fish food, loaf of bread, coffee mug, wine glass, and partially drunk bottle of wine on the counter. He opened a cabinet. There were four rows of glasses in graduated sizes, each size lined up with military precision. He took a tall glass, filled it with tap water, and drank it off. He was just putting the glass in the dishwasher when he heard a smack and a shriek, and Sammy began to cry. A surge of adrenalin hit his system as he ran for the living room.

Rhiannon was scolding, "You don't touch other people's things without permission! I told you last time."

"What happened?" Curtis asked, looking to Sammy for the answer.

Sammy was on his knees before the coffee table. "She hit me!" he screamed, tears streaming from his eyes, his lower lip quivering with fright.

"Don't exaggerate; I just slapped your hand," Rhiannon said derisively.

Whimpering, Sammy held his hand out to his father as proof.

"Why?" Curtis demanded of Rhiannon.

"He was playing with my merry-go-round."

Curtis was dismayed. "What did you expect? It's a toy, for heaven sakes!"

"It's breakable," Rhiannon said, as though that was excuse enough for her behavior. "And it's not a toy; it's an art object."

Curtis tried to suppress his anger. "Let's get this straight. *If* I think Sammy has done something wrong, *I'll* be the one to discipline him. You're not to touch him."

Rhiannon stood with arms crossed on her chest and a belligerent countenance. "There are rules. You can't raise children without rules. He has to learn to keep his hands off other people's things. He has to learn to do as he's told."

"He's not a frigging dog!" he yelled, as he thought, *'what's more important, your relationship with Sammy, or your stupid merry-go-round?'* Rhiannon tapped her toe on the ground. Then anger got the better of him. He seized the merry-go-round, lifted it above his head and was about to dash it to the floor, when he saw Sammy's wide eyes and stopped. One over-reaction did not justify another, he thought as he checked himself; it set a bad example. He thrust the toy into Rhiannon's chest. She grabbed hold of it. Curtis took Sammy by the hand. "Come on, Sammy, we're going." Looking back before he slammed the door, he said, "I'll call when I'm less upset."

Sitting in the car, he was too agitated to turn on the engine. His hopes for the night had evaporated. His nascent relationship with Rhiannon was in jeopardy. He took a deep breath and looked in the rearview mirror. Sammy sat in his booster seat in the back, where it had been moved to make room for Rhiannon. His eyes glistened with tears and his lower lip stuck out in a pout. "I'm sorry she slapped your hand," Curtis said. "She's not a bad person; she just has...." And then he realized he didn't know how to finish the sentence. She just has...what? She just has issues? She just has a hard time controlling herself? She just has to learn to keep her hands to herself? She just has to learn that people are more important than things? Curtis pressed the palms of his hands to his eyes, remembering how angry he'd been at Roger for going through the Halloween outfits. "How would you like to go to a movie?" he asked. "I need to sit a dark room for a couple of hours."

The movie, *Yes Man*, hadn't been half bad, even if a lot of the humor was lost on Sammy. Sammy had laughed, and that had lightened Curtis's mood for a while, but troubling thoughts of Rhiannon came back to him on the ride home. She was undoubtedly lovely to look at, and her voice could cheer the soul, but there were so many problems. Could he really find happiness with a religious, tee-totaling, vegetarian, virgin who thought more of her toy merry-go-round than about Sammy's feelings? And there were other disturbing signs: the precise way in which she lined up her glasses and arranged the knicktnacks in her apartment hinted at an obsessive-compulsive personality. Curtis resolved to sleep on it, but he couldn't turn off his mind. The same thoughts kept looping through the edge of consciousness and eventually he resorted to a sleeping pill to get some rest.

He was just having his first cup of coffee in his robe and slippers, when the intercom buzzed. It was only then that he remembered Stephanie and buzzed her in. She came in carrying several unwrapped paintings, a wrapped painting, and one long wrapped box. She wore a grey wool overcoat over her store attire — a blue skirt, long sleeved white blouse, and sensible flat-soled shoes.

"Where do you want them?"

"Put them here," he said, pushing paper and pastels aside to make room on the gate-leg table. "I should have picked them up when we dropped you off yesterday; I wasn't thinking. Would you like a cup of coffee?"

She placed the paintings face down on the table. "I don't think I have the time," she said, checking her watch.

Curtis checked his, remembered she had to be at the shop at 9:00, and said, "You'll have plenty of time if I drive you."

"That's not necessary."

"I know, but it's really no trouble; there's no traffic on Sunday. I'll get you a cup."

He poured the mug full. "Sugar and milk?"

"One cube, and just a dollop of milk." She was standing next to the sofa bed gazing down at the comatose Sammy. "He's a tired little guy."

"A fire alarm could go off and he wouldn't budge."

Stephanie put the long present under the tree. "This is from Gwyn to Sammy." Then she picked up one painting and held it to her chest. "I hope you like this. It may not be what you expected." She turned the painting around so he could see it. It was his painting of the buildings across the street, the one he'd given up on. She had added to the scene a shaft of light that fell upon a verdant tree at the far end of the empty lot. The top third of the closest building took on color and texture. Only one window glowed with light, where a man stood looking out, hands stuck in his jeans' pockets. The bottom part of that building, as well as the entirety of the other buildings, were still in penciled outline, giving the impression of a world only half imagined, where reality was tenuous. "You might think it's unfinished," she explained, "but it's intended."

"I do like it. Very much. It reminds me of those full-body x-ray machines you see in old movies, where you see the person's head, but the torso is all bones. It's like seeing under the surface of things."

"You're sure you like it?"

"Absolutely. Where should we hang it?"

"You might want to see the others first. I thought you could use some color on your walls, and I have so many I can't hang them all, so I brought you three others."

"You're so sweet," he said, touched at her generosity. "I'm afraid we didn't get *you* anything. I should have thought...."

"These are just some old paintings I did when I was in school," she said, turning them over on the table. There was an 18 X 20 acrylic painting of a woman from the back, looking out an open window to a lake, a breeze fluttering the lace curtains. "It's kind of clichéd, but it was an assignment." Another was an 8 X 10 oil of a peach and a knife on a kitchen table. The last was an 18 X 24 watercolor of nasturtiums spilling over a weathered board fence.

"They're wonderful. I really like the nasturtiums — something about the way the flowers flow down the paper, almost haphazard, but so...I don't know the word. Perfectly placed. Artful, perhaps? Just right."

"This last one is wrapped. It's for Sammy," she said, and put it under the tree next to the long box from Gwyn.

"We should wake Sammy, and I'll need to get dressed if we're going to get you to work on time."

Curtis went into the bedroom. Stephanie checked her watch, then sat on the edge of the sofa bed and sang softly,

"Good morning, good morning, how do you do my dear?

Good morning, good morning, I bring you lot's of cheer.

The weather doesn't matter; if sun the clouds should hide,

with a happy 'good morning,' we'll make our sun inside!"

She smoothed back the hair from Sammy's forehead. "Time to wake up, sleepyhead." Sammy rolled onto his back. "Your dad's taking me to work, so you have to get up. Sorry."

He opened his eyes and groggily took in his surroundings. "I'm thirsty," he said.

Stephanie went to the kitchen and brought back a glass of water. "Careful not to spill." Sammy sat up, drank two gulps and handed the glass back. He blinked several times, licked his lips, and stared dully into space. "Are you waking up?" Sammy nodded. He looked about to fall back onto his pillow. "Have you had a good weekend?" she asked to keep his attention.

"We seed a movie," he said. "Rannon hit me."

Stephanie wasn't sure she'd heard correctly. "Who?"

"Rannon. Daddy was mad. Then we went to a movie."

"Oh," Stephanie said, taking a blasé tone. She wanted to know more, but didn't want Sammy to suspect she was prying. "Who's Rannon?"

"A girl."

"Ah."

"Dad likes her. I don't like her; she hit me."

"I should say! I wouldn't like anyone who hit me, either." Thoughts of child abuse raced through her mind. Who was this Rannon, and what had actually happened?

On the way to Bolton's she casually dropped the subject into conversation. "Sammy tells me you had a difficult time yesterday."

"I've had better days."

"And who," she inquired, "is Rannon?"

"You mean Rhiannon? Just a friend."

Stephanie knew it was none of her business, and yet she couldn't in all good conscience ignore child abuse, if that's what it was, when it was brought to her attention. "She hit Sammy?"

"She slapped his hand. I wouldn't make too much of it."

"Oh," Stephanie said, thinking that children (even many adults) blew events out of proportion. Their perception was, nonetheless, their reality. "Not good, but not as bad as I imagined."

"I wasn't too happy about it."

"May I ask why? I mean why she slapped him, not why you were unhappy."

"He touched her toy," Curtis said, holding back a laugh, for that was what it was when boiled down to its essence.

"Her toy?"

"A merry-go-round."

The thought, when given voice in the plainest terms, was ludicrous. He had touched her toy. It was beyond ridiculous.

Dropping Stephanie at Bolton's she said, "Thank you, Curtis; I appreciate it." It struck him that his was the first time she'd called him by his first name. He'd been Mr. Cooke, the customer, and Mr. Cooke, the art student. Now he was just plain Curtis, the friend. He smiled — one could never have too many friends.

Back at the apartment, he thought of calling Rhiannon. He didn't like the way he'd left it. Their last words had been sharp, and he was sure she must be full of contrition in the light of day. He called and got her voicemail. She was likely at church, he remembered. He would call later.

When he did call again, he was again directed to her voicemail. "Call me," was the cryptic message he left. They needed to talk, and not just a few words on the phone. He called Pretty Pets in the afternoon, but got no answer — the phone must have caller ID, he surmised, and she wasn't picking up, which meant that she was still upset, whether with him, or with herself, he couldn't be sure. He had not been happy with her the day before, but he wasn't one to carry a grudge. He could put aside yesterday and move forward. The question was, could she?

He resolved to drop Sammy off early and meet her as she got off work at 6:00. His intentions notwithstanding, he couldn't foresee the accident on Franklin that tied up traffic. When he pulled into the rain slick parking lot at Stone Pine Center, the Pretty Pets sign was dark. The alternative was to drive to her apartment, and as he contemplated making the drive, he realized that his appearance at her door might be construed as desperate. If she were truly contrite, she would call and apologize. If not, she might call to express righteous indignation. In either case he had left a message to call him. The ball was in her court.

It did not occur to him until many months afterwards that he may never have given her his phone number, and she didn't know his address, but by that time the moment had passed. Life is full of moments that never were, and might have been, but for a lapse of memory, a slip of the tongue, a word unsaid.

Chapter 18

Monday December 22 – Sunday December 28, 2008

Trading was light in the two and a half days leading up to the Christmas break. The Market closed early on Christmas Eve and the ride back to the apartment was quicker than usual. Elliot handed him a present as he got out of the Volvo, and wished him a happy Christmas, more to keep the semblance of normality than with any real hope that his friend could enjoy himself. Curtis let himself into his empty apartment, keenly aware of what he was missing. He turned on all of the lights, put on the Nat King Cole Christmas album, and fixed himself a rum-spiked eggnog.

He called home ostensibly to wish Sammy a merry Christmas, but really just to hear the excitement in his son's voice in anticipation of the arrival of Santa Claus. Then he called Del Mar and spoke with his parents, a comforting conversation that made him feel less alone. He called his sister and chatted for a minute, but he had nothing to say, really. He called his brother but got only his voicemail. He considered calling Rhiannon and thought better of it.

When Nat had finished singing and the lush strings of Gordan Jenkins' orchestration had faded to silence, the CD changer whirred and the deep, rich voice of Dylan Thomas filled the apartment with the scenes of *A Child's Christmas in Wales*. With his mind on the story of Mrs. Prothero and the firemen, Curtis set about the task of hanging his new paintings. He had been averse to putting nails in the wall when he'd first moved in and had still held the hope of returning home by Christmas. Now he carefully tapped nails into the unadorned west wall above the gate-leg table. The paintings gave life to the room. It was such a nice gesture on Stephanie's part, and he thought he should like to do something nice in return.

Christmas day dawned bright and sunny. Curtis had the next four days off. It was a Thursday, and he was taking Friday to spend a second Christmas with Sammy, as there was little chance of any significant movement in the Market that day.

He took a long shower and pleasured himself out of boredom, writhing snakes providing a pleasant fantasy. He liked his penis; it had given him a lot of pleasure throughout the years. It was a friendly penis. It wasn't much to look at, but it was all he had to offer in that arena, and he hoped some female might enjoy its several charms. He knew he would enjoy bestowing them.

Sitting on the edge of the bed, pulling on his socks, he glanced at the clock: 9:38. Next to the clock was the velvet box containing the silver rope bracelet he'd bought for Rhiannon. He wondered what to do with it. Would he see her again? Did he really want to give her a present after all? He could take it back to the store. It hadn't been terribly expensive, but it was a nice gift that any woman would be happy to receive. Undecided, he swept it into the drawer next to his wedding ring and slid the drawer shut.

After a simple breakfast of eggs, toast and coffee, he opened presents from his parents and siblings. His parents had sent a sweater and a book called "*Life Is So Good*," by George Dawson. Eloise had scanned old photos from their childhood and had them reproduced and printed in book form. Patrick had sent him a $50 gift card to Macy's.

At 10:00 a.m. Curtis called home to get Sammy's report on the morning's proceedings. His present from Santa had been a Playmobil pirate ship. "Santa left something here, too," Curtis said to whet his son's appetite. "You'll see tomorrow morning. You have a fun time with your mom. Can I talk to her?" He arranged to pick up Sammy at 9:00 a.m. the next day. Curtis had spent the morning determined to put on a cheerful face, the conversation had been cordial, but the sound of her voice depressed him.

He opened his present from Elliot — a CD of Django Rheinhardt and Stephan Grapelli, a particularly thoughtful gift, as Elliot wasn't fond of Jazz.

Afterwards, he played Leon Redbone and tried to read, but his mind wandered and he went out for a walk. Kids were out on the sidewalks and in the street playing with new skates, bikes, skateboards and footballs. The sky was blue, the sun warm, the shadows cool. The world turned, and slowly he let go of his cares. He returned to the apartment in the late afternoon, having walked three or four miles exploring the nearby neighborhoods. Exercise was a great stress reducer.

He knocked on Irene's door. She answered in a moment, dressed in red pants and a black sweater embroidered with red, green and gold Christmas ornaments and ribbons. "Hi Irene, I've come for the bike."

"Is he coming tonight?"

"Tomorrow morning."

"It's a beautiful bike; I'm sure he'll love it."

"Would you like to come up for a drink?"

"Why not? I don't have anything better to do."

So they went upstairs, where Curtis poured them both a glass of sparkling wine. They tinkled glasses. "You've done a nice job with the apartment. Lovely paintings."

"They were a gift — well, those there. Some of them are Sammy's. A couple are mine."

"What is it about this place that attracts painters?"

"Must be some magic in the air."

Irene's gaze rested on the tree. "I wish I had a tree. That's one thing I miss. It does get easier, you know, being alone on Christmas. I used to brood about it, but what can you do? The kids have their own lives. At least my son called, which was nice, although he didn't have much to say. He's lost his job. But my daughter is spending the holidays with her father and his bimbo, so I don't expect to hear from her. I shouldn't complain; I have a lot of pleasant memories to look back on. What did you do with your day?"

"Read a little, took a walk."

"What are you reading?"

"*The World According to Bertie,* by Alexander McCall Smith. The protagonist is a six-year-old boy, so I can relate; Sammy turned six in August. How about yourself?"

"Oh, this time of year I always reread *A Christmas Carol.* And I just finished *Skipping Christmas,* by John Grisham. It was really rather touching; it had a lot of heart. They made a movie of it called *Christmas With the Kranks.* The past few years I've gone to the movies on Christmas.

Movie houses stay open. It's the one place I can go and have some company, even if they *are* total strangers. But this year there wasn't anything I wanted to see."

"Would you like to go to dinner? There must be someplace around here that's open on Christmas."

"You must not be dating, yet."

"You can be my date," he said facetiously.

"People will think I'm your mother."

"What are you talking about? — You're a good-looking woman," he said, partly (it was true) to be polite, though she had kept in reasonable shape for her age.

"Oh, puh-leeeease! No, let's be honest, there comes a time when you realize you're no longer attractive to the opposite sex. I have to tell you it comes as quite a shock. I spent half my life fending off advances, only to find myself wishing I could excite someone's interest, anyone's interest. No, it's time to face reality. But I do miss the companionship. Do you know that Indian restaurant on Garfield on the park?"

"No, is it any good?"

"If you like Indian food."

"Shall we?" he said, offering his arm.

Ganesh restaurant was set in an old, three-story home on a small park in the once affluent neighborhood of Dupont Heights. The décor was rich in atmosphere, with carved elephant gods in the entry and above the dining room door, bronze and copper service dishes, potted palms, and colorful patterned fabric that festooned from a center post in the ceiling. Classical Indian music played softly in the background. It was one of the most enjoyable nights Curtis had spent in months. They ate nan, mushroom curry, and tandoori chicken, and talked of Christmas and children, marriage and divorce, and the more abstract notions of success and failure. She was studying Eastern philosophy (dabbling was the way she put it), but hadn't yet decided if serenity was a positive goal. "If we're all content, then no progress can be made. We'd just sit around and smile at each other. It's the discontented individuals who get things done. Then there are times I think I'd like nothing better than to sit in the sun and glory in just being alive. I can't decide if the goal of life is to find happiness, or contentment, or to always be striving to achieve something better. Or maybe it's something else entirely. For that matter, I'm not sure how to define happiness. I know kids these days seem to have it all figured out by the time they're twenty, but I'm at sixes and sevens." She told him of her upbringing on a farm in Kansas, of her marriage to Barry Niece, a car salesman who now owned his own Porsche agency, and of the humbling transition from their four-bedroom house in Chilton to her on- bedroom apartment on Washington Street. Curtis wished his own mother were half as interesting.

"You haven't said anything about your wife. Is there any chance you might reconcile?"

"Not a snowball's chance in hell. She's seeing someone."

"Would you have her back, if she asked?"

Curtis puzzled over the question. A few weeks ago, he wouldn't have hesitated to emphatically answer, "Yes." Now things had changed. "I don't think I could trust her again."

"Well, I'm sure there are plenty of nice girls out there who would be happy to take her place. If I were twenty-five years younger, I'd be interested; you're an engaging young man."

"Thank you, I'm flattered, but I never had any luck with the ladies, except my wife, and I never understood what she saw in me."

"Well, *I* see. You're easy to be with, interesting, and not all that bad looking. You shouldn't have any trouble finding a date."

"I have been seeing someone, but I don't think it'll work out. I don't think she's right for Sammy."

"That's important, of course. Is there no one else?"

"There is another girl I like very much, but she's not my type."

"What do you mean by 'type?'" Irene asked with an edge of reproach in her voice. "What are you looking for in a woman?"

He went on to describe Linda — blonde, blue-eyed, fit, with a nice smile and a pleasant voice.

Irene frowned. "I know you can't be that shallow, Curtis. What if she met all of those criteria and she slept with every delivery man who came to the door? What if she was dumb as a post? Come on, what are you really looking for? What kind of woman would you like to spend the rest of your life with?"

"Well, she has to be smart; she should have self-confidence...." Here he took a moment to consider before continuing. "I'd like someone with a positive attitude, some enthusiasm for life, someone who's good for Sammy. She has to be honest, loyal, someone I can respect. Funny would be nice, but not essential. I suppose we should value the same things — that was always a bone of contention between Linda and me. Oh, and I wish she wasn't as reserved as Linda."

"So, measuring up to those criteria, what's wrong with this girl who isn't your type?"

"Nothing. Nothing at all. Except maybe I'm not as physically attracted as I'd like."

"Well, nobody's perfect."

Curtis felt like a complete idiot. He'd been looking for a prospective mate like he'd shop for a car, attracted to the superficial glitz, the sleek lines and the shiny paint, when he should have been looking under the hood.

By the time they arrived at the apartments, their conversation had turned to the upcoming change of leadership in Washington, a discussion that would not have been permitted at home. Linda simply did not allow for subjects that might spark controversy, which were the only subjects that Curtis found intellectually stimulating. It was one of the compromises he had made in his marriage, and he had forgotten how pleasant it was to argue a point, or to be the devil's advocate. There was no rancor in the arguments, just the exercise of judgment, speculation, supposition and rhetorical prowess. It was in these subjects that Linda so scrupulously avoided — religion, politics, sex, economics, foreign affairs — that he could indulge his intellectual curiosity, and now he could indulge in them without censure. Curtis invited Irene upstairs to finish the conversation over a nightcap. After a glass of brandy (which would have drawn the reproach of both Linda and Rhiannon), he walked Irene down to her apartment. It was a relief to feel so unrestrained in female company. And she had given him a lot to think about.

"Irene, if anyone had told me I would've enjoyed this day, I'd have said they were crazy. But I have to say I had a wonderful time tonight."

"I did, too. It was so nice to spend time with someone younger than myself. My old friends, the few I still keep in touch with, are always complaining about their health problems. You have such energy it made me feel younger, too. Let's do this again sometime."

It was with a feeling of contentment and even a little self-satisfaction that he went back upstairs. Why should he feel blue on Christmas? Linda had probably imagined him moping all day in the apartment. He took a certain pride in refusing to live down to her expectations.

"A bike! Santa got me a bike!" For a long moment Sammy stood before the bike too overwhelmed to move. Then he rolled it out from behind the tree and admired its gleaming, royal blue frame, its silver spokes, its new tires. He'd had a tricycle, but that was for babies. This was his entry into the big world of wheels that he'd envied from afar. He mounted and peddled tentatively around Curtis's easy chair, down to the windows, and back up the other side of the room divider, stopping at the gate-leg table. "Can we go outside?" he asked breathlessly.

"Don't you want to open your other presents?"

"I wanna ride my bike."

"You'll need something else Santa brought," Curtis said, pointing to the bright red bike helmet under the tree.

It was a cool day with hazy sun, more like fall than winter. Curtis walked up and down in front of the apartment building trying to keep warm, as Sammy rode first down the sidewalk to Colfax, then past the apartment to the next intersection at Jackson, and back again. Watching Sammy's back retreat up the street, Curtis assessed the hazards. There were fewer dumpsters and less scaffolding on the street since he'd moved in. Two of the buildings had been fully renovated, and the construction crews had moved on to the buildings further down the block. Like the shoemaker who wakes to find the elves have done all the work during the night, the gentrification of Washington Street seemed to be occurring entirely out of his sight, presumably while he was at work. Sammy rode joyously back and forth until lunchtime.

"Wait'll Mom sees," Sammy said proudly as they rode back up on the elevator.

"I'm afraid the bike stays here, Sammy," Curtis said. He'd thought about the tears and groveling this edict might elicit, but he was determined to be the one who taught Sammy to ride a two-wheeler. It was a father's duty and prerogative. He didn't want Roger to be the one who took off the training wheels. "I'll bring my bike here, and then we can go on bike rides together. We can bike every weekend, as long as weather permits. And by spring we'll have those training wheels off," he promised. That seemed to appease Sammy for the moment.

Sammy unwrapped a robe from his grandmother, two Doctor Seuss books from his grandfather, a Nerf dart gun from his uncle Patrick, and a foot-long wooden sailboat from his aunt Eloise.

After lunch, Sammy unwrapped the DVDs of *Finding Nemo*, and *Toy Story*, a combo pack of vintage video games, and a remote-controlled car. The car kept his attention for a long while as he ran it around the apartment crashing into walls and furniture in the elusive pursuit of hand-eye coordination.

It wasn't until after two-o'clock that Curtis reminded Sammy that there were two more presents under the tree. "They're both for you; one from Gwyn and one from Stephanie. Speaking of which, you haven't commented on the new paintings; did you notice? There's the one you painted for me. It's a nice frame, don't you think? The other ones are by Stephanie." Sammy glanced cursorily at the wall and set to the task of ripping the paper from Gwyn's present. It was a new kite with high-test filament. The body was painted with the head of a Chinese lion. The tail was a rainbow of silk ribbons. "That's very thoughtful," Curtis said. "That'll replace the one that got away. Now open the last one." It was obviously a painting and it came with a note, which read, "Dear Sammy, I hope you don't mind — I used your design for this painting. Hugs, Stephanie." The painting was a pastel version of Make Love Grow, but instead of one "love flower," there were two, their tulip-like leaves entwined as though they were holding hands. Like Sammy's original, the love flowers and pots appeared to be made of one continuous line, but the line subtly changed color from red to green in the transition from the hearts to the stem and leaves, and changed again from green to terra cotta for the pot. Between and above them was a beaming yellow sun. The sun and both of the heart-shaped flowers sported

"Smiley Faces," like the one that Gwyn had drawn when Sammy had used sidewalk chalk to recreate his line drawing in the courtyard. And above it all, a rainbow spelled Make Love Grow.

"How sweet," Curtis said. "Do you like it?"

"It's perfect."

"We should do something nice for Stephanie. That reminds me, how did your mother like your fish painting?"

Sammy shrugged, said, "Okay, I guess," and shrugged again. Curtis could imagine her feigned pleasure, as she wondered where she could hang it unobtrusively without hurting Sammy's feelings.

When Make Love Grow had been put in its place, they both stood back and admired the new paintings. "It's turning into a regular gallery," Curtis said. Then he was hit with a sudden inspiration. "We should give Stephanie a present, and I have just the thing."

Curtis called ahead, and they arrived just before three o'clock. When Stephanie opened the front door, Sammy ran up and hugged her legs. "I'm glad to see you, too, Sammy. I want to thank you for the nice painting you made for Gwyn; she really likes it."

"I like mine, too," Sammy said.

She looked comfortable in jeans and a brown cardigan sweater. She led them up the stairs, Curtis appreciating the swing of her hips in the tight jeans. "I'm afraid it's not what you'd call roomy," Stephanie said, opening the door. The front parlor was an old-fashioned room with a fireplace, bric-a-brac and photos on the mantle, a worn Persian rug over the hardwood floor, a cloth-covered wingback chair faded from red to a shade just this side of pink, and thigh-high bookcases. Above the bookcases to the 10-foot high ceiling, the red walls were entirely covered with paintings in various sizes and frames, perhaps thirty in all. A scrawny Christmas tree partially obscured a tall, narrow, north-facing window of wavy glass that looked out onto an elm. The Christmas tree was decorated with tiny multi-colored lights, silver tinsel, a string of popcorn, and a few old ornaments the worse for wear. An easel with a half-finished painting stood to the left of the window. The room had a comfortable lived-in look, and that dry, dusty smell common to old buildings.

She led the way through a short hallway to a combination kitchen-dining room. It was clean, but cluttered with old appliances, a small wooden table and high, glass-fronted cabinets. She knocked on a door and opened it a few inches. "Gwyn, you have a visitor."

A moment later Gwyn opened the door wide. Behind her they could see a double bed with a white chenille bedspread. Unframed canvases were stacked along the baseboards, and more paintings hung on the white walls. Just above the right side of the bed, so obviously different in style from the rest, hung Sammy's balloon boat. Gwyn pulled Sammy into the room to show him.

Stephanie said, "Would you like a glass of wine? I only have white. It's not the expensive kind, but it's all I have."

"That would be nice." While she got the bottle out of the refrigerator, Curtis looked about the flat for another door. "Where do *you* sleep?"

She nodded her head toward the bedroom, pushed the refrigerator door shut with her foot, handed Curtis a glass and said, "In there with Gwyn. It was easy enough when she was a baby, but it's a bit crowded now, as you can see. I have first dibs on the Burkowicz's, if they ever move (they've been talking about it for years). They have two bedrooms." They clinked glasses.

"Maybe they'll trade with you."

"That's an idea."

"We really like the painting, by the way. All of the paintings. They look really great on the wall."

"As you can see, I have more than I can hang."

"You should sell some of them. Get a booth at one of the street fairs."

"I've thought of that, but it costs money. You have to have a marquee, and a portable wall to hang the pictures, and some tables, and you have to pay an entry fee and a percentage to the organizers. As they say, 'it takes money to make money,' and I don't have the money."

"Here's to your future success, then; may it come swift and abundant." They clinked glasses. Curtis stood before a painting that was unlike any of the others. It was a vertical, perhaps 16 by 20 inches, with an outer border of symmetrical Greek design and a center of Celtic knots, shading from green to gold. "I love this one. This would make a great T-shirt design."

Stephanie choked on her wine and sprayed Curtis as she let loose with a loud guffaw. "I'm sorry!" Her eyes were streaming tears of laughter. "It was just so unexpected. Most of the time my friends are trying to be polite, and they end up saying something pompous."

"I didn't mean to be insulting."

"No, no, you're right, it's probably best suited to some kind of fabric design. It was a school assignment. I'm glad you like it."

They sipped their wine. From his coat pocket, Curtis pulled a black velvet box adorned with a small red bow. "Happy Christmas a day late."

"For me? You didn't have to."

"I know, but you've been so nice to Sammy and me...."

He helped her put on the silver rope bracelet that he'd intended for Rhiannon. "It's beautiful," she said, the last word coming with a hitch, and then she started to cry.

"I'm sorry," Curtis said, concerned. Was it a reminder of another gift and another time? — Perhaps a memory of Gwyn's father?

She went to the kitchen, grabbed a paper towel, dried her eyes and blew her nose. When she turned back she was back in control. "I'm sorry to be so stupid, it's just so beautiful, and it was such a surprise. A very nice surprise."

Curtis felt compelled to hug her, to give her comfort, but he wasn't sure she would welcome physical intimacy; some people were uncomfortable about being touched and he didn't want to offend her. He only knew he wanted to do something nice for this woman.

She excused herself to go into the bathroom, which was through the bedroom. Gwyn came out and whispered, "Don't mind Mom. It's just she didn't get any presents this year, except from Mrs. Bossert, and that was just embroidered placemats. I made some things for her at school, but that's not the same."

"Your move!" Sammy called. He was sitting on the bed in front of a checkered board, upon which were placed wooden pieces both round and square, short and tall, brown and white, solid and indented.

"What's that?" Curtis asked.

"Quarto. Mom got it for me for Christmas."

"It's easy," Sammy said.

She eased up on the bed, sat cross-legged, and made her move.

Stephanie came back to the kitchen looking refreshed, if a little red around the eyes. "I'm such an idiot sometimes," she said. "Sometimes I'm just a bit overwhelmed. I'm going to have another glass. Do you want one?"

They stood in her kitchen talking about Christmas. He told her about his dinner with Irene. She told him that they'd spent the day at home, and together she and Gwyn had made a special turkey dinner. He related Sammy's enthusiasm at the sight of his first bike. She had given Gwyn a coat and a dress, a digital etch-a-sketch, a pogo stick and Quarto. Gwyn had made her a ceramic bowl and a set of beeswax candles.

As they were leaving Stephanie said, "I don't know if you have any plans for New Year's, but the building is doing a round-robin party. We start at Mrs. Bossert's for hors d'oeuvres, then we'll move to the Burkowicz's for soup, the Valsecchi's for cold cuts, and end up here for cake and Champagne. It's BYOB."

Curtis didn't want to make an overt commitment, but he had to admit that he liked this woman's company. "We usually go to the neighbor's (you met him at the store — he bought a follow the dots book?) — But I don't know what the plans are this year." The real question was whether he wanted this platonic friendship to develop into something more, and he wasn't yet sure.

"No worries. The door is open, if you feel like it. Thanks again for the bracelet."

Before Sammy had awakened on the sofa bed, Curtis turned on the local morning news, unaware that he was watching his future in the making. A sinkhole had swallowed an apartment house in Florida. A navy jet had crashed in practice for an air show. A little boy had been kidnapped from a playground in Santa Fe, New Mexico. Hugo Chavez was slinging more vitriol at The United States. There was a retrospective of the December 26th Indonesian tsunami of 2004. And Israelis launched air attacks on Gaza in retaliation for rocket attacks on Israeli cities. He wondered who decided which news stories were worth airing. Few people, save those actually involved, would be affected by these mostly tragic stories. He picked up the remote and switched off the TV.

Waiting for Sammy to wake, he stood by the window sipping a cup of strong black coffee. Yesterday's scenes kept playing in his head. He needed a truck to transport his bike to the apartment. Then he thought about their visit to Stephanie and Gwyn, whose apartment was old and worn and cramped, but full of life. He admired Stephanie's gumption. She managed to keep a level head while coping with a difficult situation. So, given her admirable qualities, why had no one given her a gift? What of her parents, her sister, her brother? That was an enigma.

Chapter 19

Monday December 29, 2008 — Sunday January 4, 2009

The sky was hazy, the traffic heavy, the diesel fumes palpable as they rolled slowly along the boulevard like a line of worker ants headed for the Financial District. Elliot was playing the Gottschalk piano pieces that Curtis had given him for Christmas.

"I've never heard the pianist before; he's fabulous," Elliot enthused.

The conversation came in fits and starts and took odd tangents, for as they listened to the music their thoughts took them in different directions. "How was Sammy's Christmas?"

"Great, I got him a bike with training wheels. He drove off the sidewalk and scraped one knee, but other than that he enjoyed himself." They made one light and were stopped at the next. "Are you having a New Year's Eve party this year?"

"We're passing on that. Samuelson is visiting his mother in South Carolina, and the Gleasons are away. Didn't seem worth it. I'll be happy to start the New Year without a hangover."

As they accelerated away from the light, Curtis said, "I was watching the news. Maybe you can enlighten me, seeing as you're Jewish."

"It's doubtful. What about?"

"Why anyone would fight for thousands of years over a godforsaken piece of desert? If your ancestors were the chosen people, they should have ended up in France, or Bali, or just about anywhere but the Mideast."

Elliot chuckled mirthlessly. "We did try to go elsewhere, but the goddamned Christians turned on us."

"If god had given that property to *my* ancestors, I'd feel short-changed."

"Maybe he's one of the lesser gods," Elliot quipped irreverently, and a minute later asked, "What happened with Goody Two-Shoes?"

"Who?"

"The strawberry blonde."

"Oh. I think that bird has flown."

"Good, I didn't trust her. Vicky's cousin is on the market again."

"No thanks, I'm lying low for awhile. I don't need the drama. Anyway, if I want female company, I know a girl who's easy to hang out with and not my type." As he said it, he remembered what Irene had said and he thought, *she doesn't have Linda's classical beauty, but she's so much better in other ways.* It seemed he'd been willing to settle for much less with Gretchen and Rhiannon. And despite her precarious pecuniary situation, Stephanie was generous and warm-hearted. He didn't quite know what was holding him back from pursuing her.

"Do I know her?"

"You met her once at the art store. She's my watercolor teacher. Her daughter likes to play with Sammy. Her name's Stephanie. And Irene's good for a conversation, too."

"Who's Irene?"

"My neighbor."

"Is *she* your type?"

"She's a very nice lady, but she's old enough to be my mother."

After another few minutes of listening to Alan Marks play Gottschalk, Elliot asked, "Did you read the liner notes?"

"Nope."

"Well, just to keep on point, Gottschalk was *half* Jewish and *he* had women troubles. He toured Europe until irate husbands chased him to Brazil."

Another minute passed in the midst of Gottschalk's prancing arpeggios, before Curtis asked, "Do you think Samuelson would lend me his truck?"

"Would you really want to drive it? The brakes are shot."

"I need a truck."

Returning to the apartment on Tuesday, Curtis shucked off his suit and tie, and got into a comfortable pair of jeans and a flannel shirt. He took the laundry down to the deserted laundry room in the basement, shoved his quarters in, and returned to the apartment. Then he put on a compilation of French *musettes* and *chansons*, and sat down with his laptop to do a little research and strategizing. He wanted to take advantage of the flow of institutional money, insofar as it could be ascertained.

At ten past seven his cell phone rang. Caller ID couldn't identify the caller. He didn't give his cell phone number to many people outside of his small circle of friends and family, so he picked up.

"Curtis, this is Edgar Smith. I'm here with Jim Dayton. He's eager for us to meet; can we come over?"

"I'm not at the office."

"I know; we called Erickson. As it turns out, we were having dinner at Emile's, so we're just around the corner anyway."

Curtis hated this intrusion of his professional life into his private life. Even when he chose to bring work home, it was on his own terms. He was in a different frame of mind at home. On the other hand, Erickson had given them his address and phone number; he was sure to ask how the meeting had gone, and Curtis couldn't very well say he'd told them to bugger off. He really had no choice. "Give me fifteen minutes," he said.

There was just time for him to clean up the dishes, put the wine into the refrigerator and change back into something less comfortable — at least he now had some presentable clothes.

The pair that stood at the door might have been father and son. Dayton was wearing an open-collared blue dress shirt, a cashmere sport coat and jeans. The jeans were just jeans, but the shoes and jacket were expensive, if casual. It was the kind of look that said, 'I have the money to dress any way I please.' Smith was in his late fifties or early sixties, fit and polished and a natty, if eccentric dresser. He wore a full set of tweeds, including vest, tie and cap, and affected a walking stick. He could have come straight out of an English movie set, circa 1940.

Introductions were made as Curtis ushered them into the small apartment. He was aware that it didn't look like the home of a successful money manager. "I'm afraid this is my humble abode; I'm in the midst of a divorce," he said by way of explanation. As they preceded him into the room Curtis was chagrined to realize he'd neglected to turn off the music. A *musette* accordion was squeezing out a particularly jaunty piece that gave the apartment a circus atmosphere. "Sorry, I'll turn off the music."

"No, no, I like it," Smith said. "Reminds me of Paris."

He might have looked like an Englishman, but he spoke with an accent that Curtis thought was probably Ohio tempered by an Ivy League education.

"Can I get you a drink?"

"You don't happen to have a single malt?"

"Macallan."

"18-year?"

"No, just the 12."

"That'll do."

"Jim?" Curtis asked.

"Orange juice with ice."

As Curtis fixed the drinks, Smith wandered around the apartment looking at the paintings, "Jim tells me you've kept him solvent," Smith said facetiously.

"We've had a good month. Do you take water?"

"A tablespoon. What makes you think stocks are the best investment?"

It seemed an innocent enough question, and there was no sense of belligerence to his tone, but Curtis didn't want to be put on the defensive right away. Instead, he asked a question in return. "What do you have your money in now, if not in stocks?"

"I didn't say I don't invest in the stock market. I do. But it's just one small facet. I believe in diversification — real estate, Forex. Hell, my best return over the past two years has been in wine. It's recession-proof. So why should I invest in stocks? And why now?"

"Historically, it's one of the best performing investment vehicles," Curtis said, handing out the drinks. Edith Piaf was singing *La Vie en Rose*.

"Tell me about the last six months."

"Yes, well that's been difficult. I don't know who's handling your stock portfolio, but it's been a challenging environment ever since Bear Stearns went under last March."

"Tell me about it; I lost a bundle."

"It's volatile, but there are a lot of opportunities because of it," Curtis said, retrieving his Chardonnay from the refrigerator. "We try to identify stocks that are oversold and undervalued, stocks in rising sectors, sectors that institutional investors are moving into, not out of."

"So, you've done well over the past six months?"

"We haven't been perfect, but we have a good track record," Curtis said, careful to couch his answer in terms of the plural corporate "we," and not in the singular personal "I." He didn't want to give the impression of infallibility; it would be too hard to live up to expectations, and frankly, his personal performance had been pretty miserable. "Stocks are still the most liquid investment vehicle outside of currencies..."

"And wine."

"...and we also handle currencies. It's not my area of expertise, but we do have experts in the Forex market."

"So, if you're trying to sell me on stocks, why do you invest in art?"

"Me? I don't..."

"Why did you buy these pieces? I like this one," he said, standing in front of Sammy's blue dinosaur. He gestured toward the lighthouse / white tower, shook his head, and frowned.

"What's wrong with that one?" Curtis inquired, in proprietary defense of his tower.

"It's crudely drawn and overtly allegorical. But this dinosaur — this is cute — it captures the essence of childhood. But you didn't answer my question – why do *you* invest in art?"

"Oh, well, I don't really invest...I wouldn't sell...it has sentimental value."

"Ah," Smith said, nodding his head, "you'd sell if the price was right. Even sentimental value has its limits." He was peering closely at the corner of the painting. "Who is the artist?"

"Nobody you'd know."

"This has potential," Smith said, raising his index finger from the rim of his tumbler to point at Sammy's scene of Del Mar beach.

Si la Photo Est Bonne, played sweetly on the stereo.

Dayton came up to have a look. "What kind of art do you like?" he asked of Smith.

"That's irrelevant. The question is, which artist will give you the most return on your money? You know that actor from *Four Weddings and a*

Funeral? Hugh Grant? He went on a blind drunk binge, woke up to find he'd bought an Andy Warhol for two million at some auction. Couldn't remember a thing. Swore off drink. Five years later he sold the same painting for twenty million! Best investment he ever made."

"I was never much of a Warhol fan," Dayton said.

"Doesn't matter, he was great at marketing. Campbell's soup can, for Christ's sake!" Smith stepped sideways to look at the collage that Curtis had made from pieces of Sammy's paintings. "The crap Picasso painted was worthless in the beginning. Galleries couldn't sell it. People wouldn't buy it. Forty years later some collectors made a mint." He put his nose up close to examine the painting. "Marvelous texture," he said, pointing at the edge of the canvas where the previous tenant had troweled alternating swatches of thick oil paint, "and all those tiny fine strokes," he added, pointing to where the paper had flipped over in the grass. "I'd never have the patience." Straightening up, Smith caught sight of the easel in the corner with Curtis's half-finished Madison Street Bridge. "You paint?" he asked, surprised.

"I dabble."

"These aren't *yours*?" Smith said with an air of something like alarm in his voice.

"I painted that one, the white tower."

"Ha! You should stick to finance. You're no artist. Just look at the difference."

Curtis felt like kicking the prick, thinking '*You wouldn't know a Picasso from a Sammy Cooke.* "I take it you like art," Curtis said dryly.

"I do like *some* art. But I try not to let that cloud my judgment. It doesn't matter if I like it or dislike it. I invest in it. You don't have to like it to know something about the art *business*. I don't like black-and-white photography, but I bought Ansel Adams' prints when he was an old man. I knew when he croaked his work would appreciate. I was never so happy to see someone go!" he chuckled gleefully. "Tripled my investment in less than three years! I wish my stocks did that well." They moved on to the original pencil drawing of Make Love Grow. Curtis had tacked it to the room divider next to the collage. "So really, who is the artist?" Smith asked, still looking for a signature and finding none.

"Just a friend," Curtis dissembled. If he embarrassed Smith by revealing that the artist was a six-year-old first-grader, he might lose the man's business.

"Does he have a name?"

"He's not a professional."

Smith turned around, and seeing Stephanie's Make Love Grow on the opposite wall, he did a double-take, then looked slowly back and forth from one to the other. "Collector's love studies. Your painting is worth a lot more, because you have the original study to go with it. You should have that framed." He stepped over to Stephanie's Make Love Grow, looking closely at the skillful transition of colors. It was expertly rendered, Curtis observed over Smith's shoulder, but it *was* just a reinterpretation of Sammy's original line drawing. "Interesting mix of themes. And this flower painting, these nasturtiums, it's not the same artist, is it?"

"Yes, it is. Done years apart, but the same artist." In that, at least, Curtis didn't lie or obfuscate.

"Years apart — then you've had your money tied up for a while." Smith looked again at the lower corners of the paintings. "Why no signature?"

Curtis looked, himself. He was surprised Stephanie hadn't signed them. He didn't feel good enough about his own doodles to put a signature to them, and Sammy probably didn't even know that artists customarily sign their work. But he would have expected Stephanie to put a signature to hers. "I never asked her."

"Ah, hah! Now we're getting somewhere. Earlier you said, '*He's* not a professional.' You just slipped. You said, 'I never asked *her.*' At least we now know the artist's true gender. Does she have a name?"

"I'd rather not say," Curtis said. He wasn't thinking fast enough. He should have said Margaret White or some other fictitious name. He wasn't trying to be evasive, but he didn't want to reveal Stephanie's name. What if Smith were to look her up? In the course of conversation, it might come out that Sammy had painted several of the paintings that he had most admired. Making the client to feel a fool was not good for business.

"How much do want for them?"

"What?" Curtis exclaimed, caught off guard.

"How much? Every man has his price."

"They're really not for sale."

Smith chuckled. "Okay, I understand. You're waiting for the artist to make a name for herself. Fair enough. That's smart. But I can ease the process along. Apparently, you've been collecting these for some time, and you're not seeing any return on your money. I know people who can get an artist recognized. It doesn't take much, if you know the right people. I don't know what you paid, but it shouldn't be too hard to..."

"I'm not interested in selling."

"Have it your way." Smith finished his drink and abruptly changed topic. "So, tell me something more about Bass Erickson. I'll give you ten minutes."

New Year's Eve the stock market closed early. This last trading day of the year, the DOW finished at 8776, down 3,685 points year over year, just shy of a 30% loss, but still up 1,327 points, or 18%, since its low on November 21st. Allison Essman rang Curtis in his office. "Jon wants to see you," she said, smacking her gum in his earphone.

Erickson was sitting at his desk, looking weary. "Your six weeks are up. Symington wants a report. What's the news?"

They went over Symington's portfolio, which was up since their meeting, though not substantially. "What about Edgar Smith? Did they stop by? Do you think he's coming on board?"

"I don't know. He listened. I couldn't tell if he was just humoring Dayton, or if he's really interested. He..."

"I want you to work that angle hard," Erickson interrupted. "We need that kind of client. People with money know other people with money. If we get him on board, he might bring others with him."

"I'll do my best."

"Do better than that," Erickson grumbled.

After the short trading day, it was a fast commute; the Financial District was already deserted. At the apartment he shed his coat and tie and swapped his work shoes for sneakers. He picked up Sammy and was back at the apartment by 3:30.

Curtis made up a light snack of macaroni and cheese for Sammy. Then they lay on Sammy's sofa bed and watched a DVD of *The Rocketeer* until they fell asleep. The last of twilight was just illuminating the window when

Curtis stirred. It was 5:42. He got up and made some coffee. He needed to fortify himself to stay up until past midnight; he'd sleep-in tomorrow.

They dressed in matching outfits of khaki pants, white dress shirts and blue sweater vests. Curtis topped it off with a camel hair sport coat.

On the way, they stopped at a liquor store for a bottle of Roederer Estate sparkling wine and a King Estate Pinot Blanc. Curtis vowed to himself to have no more than four glasses spaced out over the course of the night. Even then, he thought he might need more caffeine to balance the alcohol.

The front door was open, as was the door to Mrs. Bossert's ground floor apartment where a crowd had already gathered. The front room, which doubled as sitting room and formal dining room, was as big as Stephanie's parlor and kitchen combined, and let onto a kitchen at the rear. There was a bay window with a window seat that looked out onto the street. The floor was carpeted. The antique furnishings had carved wooden legs. Several small paintings hung on the walls of flocked red wallpaper (Curtis thought he could detect Stephanie's hand). A chandelier hung from the center of the high ceiling, and lamps of stained glass stood in the corners and on the end tables, lending a warm glow and splash of color to the scene, in sharp contrast to stark fluorescents that bathed the kitchen in a sterile light.

Gwyn ran up when they entered. "Come and meet Mrs. Bossert," she said, determined to act an adult. She led them to a pleasant, shapeless lady in her middle sixties. "This is Mrs. Bossert. She takes care of me when Mom's at work."

"Oh, don't listen to her. She's the one who takes care of *me*. She's a great help."

Curtis introduced himself and Sammy, tucking a bottle under his arm to shake hands.

"She makes the most amazing raisin custard tarts," Gwyn said.

"And sour cream pastries," Mrs. Bossert reminded her, "but this year is my turn to do the hors d'oeuvres. Not my specialty, but I hope you enjoy them. There's savory meat pies, potato blinis, prawns with a couple of sauces, and stuffed mushrooms."

Stephanie came across the room. She wore a silver-grey wrap draped over her shoulders, a long black dress with décolletage that showed off a bit of cleavage as well as a hematite pendant, and the silver bracelet Curtis had given her. From her smile and the gleam in her eyes, Curtis could see she was genuinely happy they'd come. "You can put the champagne in my fridge; the door's open. There's a corkscrew on the counter for the other one." She and Gwyn took Sammy off to admire Mrs. Bossert's Christmas tree.

Curtis went upstairs to deposit the sparking wine in the refrigerator and pop the cork on the Pinot Blanc. On the way out he paused to examine the bookcases. They were crammed with art books and textbooks on art, psychology and business, literary novels, romances and mysteries, cookbooks and biographies, travel guides and children's books, books on history and books on philosophy. Stuck in amongst them were old magazines, a half-shelf of National Geographics, and a few photo albums.

Curtis picked up one of the albums. The first photo was a posed portrait of the family when Stephanie was about twelve. Her father was short and bald, with large sad dark eyes. Her mother looked to be a cheerful woman with wide hips and large breasts. Her older sister was skinny as a rail, projecting the disdain of a teenager. Her younger brother, about nine in the photo, had a bad haircut and a cheesy smile. Stephanie was a cute pre-teen, with dimpled cheeks, a pleased-as-Punch smile, and long tresses. The photos seemed to follow a chronological progression. By the sixth page they included a handsome young man that Curtis surmised was Gwyn's father. Then there were baby pictures of Gwyn. He recognized Mrs. Bossert in one photo, holding the hand of a four or five-year-old Gwyn. He flipped through the pages, noting that photos of her parents and siblings ceased with the birth of Gwyn.

Curtis heard a rustle and turned guiltily to see Stephanie. "Sorry," he said, ducking his head. "I'm a terrible snoop."

Stephanie smiled and came up to see what he was talking about. She leaned against him and looked at the open album. "Oh-h-h, she was so cute! She was just three there. That was taken...(where was it?) at a cabin of an old boyfriend. God, I'd forgotten all about that," she said dreamily, lost in recollection. "He was a loser, but his parents had a nice place up by Yorkville on the lake. Oh, there's that silly doll. Lord, she carried that thing around until its clothes fell off."

Curtis turned back to the first photo. "Your family?"

"Yeah," she said in a flat tone, and added "happier times," with a sarcastic edge. "I gotta put this in the fridge."

She hefted a bottle of Mumm champagne. Curtis heard the door of the refrigerator open, when she said, "First they wanted me to get an abortion. Then they wanted me to give her up for adoption." The refrigerator door closed. She came back into the parlor. "They've never seen her: Their loss."

"And your brother and sister?"

"I haven't seen my sister since I left home. My brother helps out sometimes. He's all right. He has his hands full with his girlfriend, or significant other, or whatever you call her. It's funny how my parents don't mind him living with his girlfriend, but I was the whore of Babylon for getting involved with Tommy."

"I can't imagine grandparents not wanting to see their grandchild."

"It's complicated. My parents didn't approve of Tommy, so when I graduated from high school I moved out amidst a lot of screaming, and when he was killed and they found out I was pregnant, they were sure the responsibility was going to fall on their shoulders. My dad is the kind of man who sees the world in simple terms; there's his way, and the wrong way. When I refused to give her up he said, 'You made your own bed, now sleep in it.' And I have, and I'm glad I did. Gwyn is everything to me."

She 'made her own bed' all right, Curtis thought. It was an awfully crowded bed.

"My brother comes by sometimes. You might meet him tonight. He's invited, anyway."

Curtis looked at her with added respect. She was brave — much braver than he thought he would be under the circumstances. He picked up the bottle of Pinot Blanc and offered her his arm. "Shall we?"

To the couple of newcomers looking up from the entry, the couple descending the stairs must have appeared like royalty arriving at the ball. Stephanie reached the bottom step and greeted them. "Curtis, this is Mary Anne Stevenson. I work at her gallery Tuesdays and Thursdays. Is Gerry coming?"

Ms. Stevenson stood tall in five-inch heels. She was slender, in her early forties, with long brown hair and bangs cut straight across her forehead.

"He didn't say. I got the impression he wanted to, but you know how he is; it's hard to get a definite commitment. We can only stay a little while. Arnie needs his sleep. We never stay up past ten." Arnie (her partner or husband?) was dressed in a tuxedo with a red cumberbund. He was a good deal older, with a fringe of white hair beneath a bald pate, and seemed content to let her do the talking.

Stephanie escorted them all into Mrs. Bossert's crowded apartment and led them to the table of hors d'oeuvres. Curtis sampled a potato blini. Sammy came up and said he was hungry. Curtis handed him a plate with a blini and stuffed mushroom. Sammy took a bite of the mushroom. His jaws worked up and down, slowed, and stopped. His face turned sour and he spat the wad onto his plate. "Yuk!"

"Sammy!"

"I don't want it."

"That's not polite."

Sammy put the plate on the table and turned away. Curtis put a napkin over the plate to hide the disgusting blob from sight.

"That's how it starts," said a man at his elbow.

"Huh?"

"Boys are the worst," the man said in reply, almost as though he was speaking to himself. "Who are you with?"

"Stephanie invited us."

"A nice girl. I'm Ken Burkowicz, across the hall. You're?"

"Curtis Cooke."

Burkowicz offered Curtis a hand and Curtis automatically shook it. He would have shaken Hitler's hand, had it been offered, the reflex was so thoroughly ingrained.

"I should have taught my son manners. They think being polite is weak. Being polite is a social responsibility. You have to teach them young, or they never get it."

Curtis had run into this type before. They made enigmatic statements or offered unfinished pronouncements in the hope of being drawn out. If you asked for clarification, the dam would burst. They would unburden themselves, as though you'd asked for it. Curtis didn't want to be a dumping ground. He looked for Stephanie to rescue him.

Of the eighteen people in the room, more than half were guests. Curtis recognized Roy, the young man from Bolton's who'd sold him the adhesive spray. His partner was a good looking, neatly groomed young man with closely cropped hair and a pencil-thin mustache. Roy was telling Stephanie, "We're just stopping by for a minute, dear. We have to make the rounds and be at the Crocadero by 11:30. Lovely party."

Curtis fled from Burkowicz and was soon in conversation with a UPS driver, who had a remarkably fine grasp of macroeconomics. They were joined by another, who wanted to turn the focus toward the intersection of political and economic boundaries.

Someone clapped loudly and announced that the party was moving across the hall to the Burkowicz's for soup. The crowd shuffled across the hall, followed by two young men who carried a cooler of wine, beer, soda and water from Mrs. Bossert's kitchen to the Burkowiczs' kitchen. The Eagles were playing from wall-mounted speakers.

While Mrs. Bossert's antique furnishings were, if from an even earlier era than the house, the Burkowiczs' Danish modern furniture, chrome lamps and track lighting were in opposition to the high ceilings, the narrow windows, the Victorian moldings and the carved wood mantelpiece. It was a small apartment, mirroring Stephanie's above, except for the bay window and the extra bedroom that Stephanie had alluded to, somewhere in the back. A small but exquisitely shaped Christmas tree filled the bay window, glowing with tiny white lights that illuminated colorful glass-blown ornaments in the shape of animals.

A tall, middle-aged woman with sandy hair (once red but now fading) stepped up on a chair to make an announcement. Clad in tan pants and white turtleneck, she held her hands clasped reverentially at her bosom. "The soup is a vichyssoise. It's meant to be served chilled, but if you'd like to warm it up, the bowls are microwave safe. I tried it out, and recommend 1 minute 20 seconds with a stir at the end. There are chives on the side, if you'd like a garnish. And if anybody is on Weight Watchers...well, forget it." General chuckling at this last remark. The soup was rich and creamy. Curtis had two small bowls, and Sammy even deigned to try a spoonful.

Curtis was hoping for some time with Stephanie, but she had followed Amy Burkowicz into the kitchen. At one point, Curtis found himself standing next to a young man in a dark blue suit with a blood-red muffler wrapped around his neck. He judged him to be about twenty-three or twenty-four — it was hard to tell, because he'd gone prematurely bald up top, and had shaved the rest of his head, leaving a faint five-o'clock-shadow on the sides. His tight scalp gleamed like a cue ball.

"Hello, Gerald," Curtis said.

The young man looked startled. "Do I know you?" Curtis flicked a finger toward the name tag that Gerald Richards still wore clipped to his breast pocket. "Oh, I forgot."

"Where do you work?"

"The Stevenson Gallery," Gerald said. When he spoke, his furtive eyes rested on Curtis's shoulder, cheek, mouth and forehead, but he never met Curtis's eyes.

"So, you work with Stephanie. What do you think of her?"

"She's a beautiful artist...I mean *wonderful*...she's very talented."

"Have you known her a long time?"

"Two years," Gerald said, staring at something on the wall above Curtis's left shoulder and gulping.

Though Curtis couldn't be sure, he thought Gerald was exhibiting symptoms of unrequited love. "She's in the kitchen."

"I know," Gerald said in a tone that encompassed both longing and trepidation.

Gerald fell into that category of people that Curtis viewed with pity and a grateful heart that he wasn't among their number. Their debilitating shyness left them impotent to act on their most ardent desires. Curtis had passed through a shy phase in high school, enough so that he could identify with current sufferers.

Gerald kept glancing toward the kitchen and seemed to be teetering on the brink of taking that first step, when two girls came up, one dressed as a 1920s flapper, the other as a Goth vamp — a black dress, shiny black vinyl boots, heavy mascara, dyed black hair cut like a helmet, and bright red lipstick accentuating abnormally pale skin. Curtis wondered what she looked like under the makeup. "Are you guys single?" the flapper asked. She'd addressed them plurally, but she was looking straight at Curtis. Gerald nodded silently, his eyes darting at the floor, the table, the mantle.

Curtis wiggled his ringless left finger. The Goth vamp eyed Gerald like a cat sizing up a mouse. "I was beginning to wonder. Everyone seemed paired up, or old. Are you a friend of Amy's?"

"Amy?" Curtis asked. "Amy who?"

"Amy Burkowicz? Your host, in whose apartment we're standing? You're not party crashers, are you?"

"No, I was invited. Not by Amy. I take it you're a friend of the Burkowiczs."

"Not exactly; we work together at the hospital."

"And what do you do?"

"X-ray tech. What about yourself?"

"Financial management," Curtis said, and noticing her plastic wine glass, he asked where she'd found it. She directed him to the kitchen. "Gerald, would you like a glass of wine?"

"Sure," Gerald said, sounding unsure and a little miserable.

As he passed out of earshot in search of a glass, Curtis heard the vamp ask Gerald, "What're you into?"

Gwyn and Sammy sat on the floor by the tree with a Siamese cat. Curtis passed into the kitchen where Stephanie was talking to Amy Burkowicz. The plastic glasses were lined up on a glass and chrome table. He poured two glasses. He caught Stephanie's eye on the way out and winked. She smiled back and it gladdened his heart.

The flapper's silver dress hugged her hips like she'd been poured into it and he wondered if she had any tattoos. Snakes came to mind. He shook his head, trying to repress his carnal impulses. Her left hand held her right elbow tight against her stomach, which left the glass in her right hand perched just at lip level. She bobbed her head slightly to take a sip. The vamp had Gerald against the fireplace. Curtis placed Gerald's glass on the mantle.

"Where were we?" the flapper asked Curtis.

"I don't think we got started."

"I'm Gloria DeVoto." She touched her plastic glass to his. "Ding," she said.

"Please to meet you. Curtis Cooke."

"Why are you here, Curtis Cooke? I *had* to come, Amy's my boss."

"I was invited."

"By?"

"Stephanie Walzer. She lives upstairs."

"Are you an item?"

The truth was that they weren't an "item," but he wasn't sure where their relationship was headed. Since he'd given her the bracelet she seemed to look at him differently, but he was hesitant to act, for if he misinterpreted her feelings, it could ruin a very nice friendship. "She's my teacher; she teaches watercolors."

"You're a painter?"

"Just beginning."

"Are you any good?"

"Depends."

"On?"

"What I'm painting."

"Have you tried a nude?"

"Not yet."

She smiled conspiratorially. "Well, I've put in my appearance. Would you like to split? I'd like to see how well you paint."

"I can't," he said. "I'm here with my son."

"Oh! Well, I wouldn't want to interrupt your babysitting. Grace, we should go; Glen's having a party."

Grace, who had her face pushed close to Gerald's, said, "I'm not going anywhere without this kitten."

Gerald smiled weakly but hopefully at Grace. "You want to go somewhere with me?" he fairly squeaked.

"I like you; you're cute."

"Okay. Okay, l-l-lead on. I'm game," Gerald said, his voice cracking with an effort at control, while the banana in his pocket did nothing to hide his enthusiasm.

The trio departed. Curtis finished his glass of wine, feeling rather old. It would certainly be easier to start afresh without the added responsibility and expectations of fatherhood. But while he might have wished for more freedom, he wouldn't wish for a world without Sammy, and as he couldn't have one without the other, he had to be content with his situation, and approach future opportunities with a sense of reality. Besides, a woman like Gloria DeVoto was not ready for motherhood.

He sat down in the window seat next to the Christmas tree and watched Sammy and Gwyn dragging a piece of yarn to get the cat to pounce. A very pregnant young woman stepped into the open doorway and announced loudly that the party was moving upstairs. Curtis corralled Sammy, and was enlisted to help carry the cooler upstairs to the Valsecchis'. Roy and his partner said their adieus.

The Valsecchis' bookcases were filled with DVDs and CDs. Their tree (if they'd had one) was already gone. The furniture, a mishmash of styles and age, had been scrounged from garage sales. An exercise bike stood in front of the window. The Hot Club of Paris played from hidden speakers, which, together with the general shabbiness of the apartment, combined to give this segment of the party a Bohemian atmosphere.

A folding table had been put up for the serving platters heaped with breads, deli meats, cheese and condiments.

Sammy condescended to eat a ham sandwich. Then he and Gwyn took turns on the stationary bike.

Stephanie came over to stand with Curtis. "Didn't I see you talking with Gerald earlier?"

"Yeah, he left with a girl."

"A girl? Really? Gerald? Good for him. He wasn't angry?"

"About what?"

"I don't know. He didn't even say hello. I thought he might be angry with me."

"You two aren't...?"

"Dating? No, I haven't been on a date in I don't know how long. Not too many men are interested in becoming instant fathers."

"It's the same on the flip side of the coin. Thanks for inviting us, by the way."

"I know Gwyn likes the company. She's usually stuck with adults."

"Your neighbors seem nice enough," he said, then allowed that, "Burkowicz is a little strange."

"Kenny? He's been a little off, ever since their son was arrested for selling dope. Kenny Jr. is in prison."

There was a thought that Curtis couldn't quite wrap his mind around. How did little boys grow up to be felons? He didn't know, but they did, all too often. He couldn't imagine what it would be like to see your son off to prison, instead of off to college. Parenthood was no cakewalk.

"When do you go back to school?"

"One week. I have a morning class, and then we have the last Beginning Watercolors class. Are you going on to Intermediate Watercolors?"

"I wouldn't miss it," he said, thinking about what Smith had said about his white tower, and thinking that he was a much better painter now than when he'd painted that scene.

Julie Valsecchi joined them and the talk turned to petty financial concerns, the expense of the party so soon after Christmas, and food stamps. Curtis took this cue to fade to the sidelines. He sat on a wicker chair against the wall, watching Sammy and Gwyn take turns on the bike before crawling under the folding table, where the long white tablecloth hid them from view.

A man about his own age sat down next to him, sipping a tall glass of what looked like gin and tonic. Where he'd got either, Curtis didn't know, as there didn't seem to be any hard liquor available in the cooler. The stranger hunched over, leaning his forearms on his knees, and surveyed the party. He had the deadpan stare of someone who was very drunk and making a valiant effort to appear sober. "They got us by the balls."

Curtis could feel another rant coming on, but he was in a more sanguine mood than earlier in the evening, so murmured a non-committal, "Hmmm?"

"You know — all these feminists. It's equal this and equal that? They think we're pigs 'cause we objectify them, but they wanna tease you at the same time. You know? 'Cause they say they don't want you to look at their tits, and then they wear dresses cut down to here, like that one." He squinted one eye and extended a finger from his glass, pointing toward Stephanie, who was in conversation with Julie and Piero Valsecchi. Reassessing her assets, Curtis had to admit that she did look much sexier in that particular dress. "Like, what's that about? They show cleavage, but don't think o' lookin', let alone touchin'; they'll sue for sexual harassment. It's like I say, they got us by the balls."

"Would you rather they wore sweatshirts?" Curtis said. He was thinking burkas, but said sweatshirts in an effort to calm the waters.

"No, but wouldn't the world be a happier place if you could just go up and give a friendly squeeze? You know? You walk into a party, she shakes your hand, you give her tits a friendly squeeze, no acting offended, just a nice smile and a how'd you do."

"Well, that'd be different."

"You bet it would. That would be heaven."

Curtis thought the poor man had lost sight of the target, but kept his comments to himself.

The party moved over to Stephanie's at 10:45. The crowd had thinned a bit. Mrs. Bossert had stayed behind to clean up when the party moved to the Burkowiczs. The Burkowiczs had slipped out sometime after 9:30. Mary Anne Stevenson and Arnie had said their goodbyes when the party moved to the Valsecchis, and Julie Valsecchi, who was pregnant, stayed behind when the party moved to Stephanie's.

Gwyn and Sammy went into the bedroom to play Quarto. Curtis poured himself a half glass of Beaujolais Nouveau.

Shortly after 11:00 pm two men arrived with instrument cases, dripping wet. A cold rain had been pelting down for the last hour. The cellist was a thin young man in his early 20's, with wet black hair plastered to his head. The violinist was taller and perhaps in his late 30's, with blue eyes, a wide grin, and a dopey looking hat that had kept his thin, blond hair perfectly dry. Stephanie went to them, glowing with pleasure. "Steven, Ed! I thought you two had a gig tonight."

"We did," the older musician said. "It was a private party at the Hyatt Regency, a bunch of old fogies who couldn't stay up past 10:30! I tried to get Iris and Diane to come, but they had other plans."

"I'm so glad you came," Stephanie said appreciatively, and turned her attention to the younger one. "Steven, you need a towel; you're soaking. There are kitchen towels in the drawer next to the refrigerator." Noticing Curtis close by, she made the introductions. "Ed, Steven, this is Curtis, another of my students. Ed and Steven took my class last year."

By a quarter past eleven the duo began to play a chamber piece, as best they could without the second violin and viola. After the first piece, they coaxed Stephanie to join in on flute. She claimed to know only three pieces, and those not well, but she sounded pretty good to Curtis. When she'd exhausted her repertoire, Piero Valsecchi returned to his apartment and brought back a guitar. They switched to playing jazz tunes, with the cello played as an upright bass.

This wasn't so unlike the New Year's Eve parties they'd had on Westlake Drive, Curtis thought (all such parties tend to follow the same progression), but the music was better. It was a lively party and Curtis was glad he'd come. And it was an instance in which the presence of Linda was not missed, for she had never stayed up late on New Year's Eve. In their ten years together, he'd always seen in the New Year with friends.

Remembering that the kids might like to listen to live music, Curtis opened the bedroom door and found them both sprawled on the bed asleep, the Quarto board between them. He quietly closed the door and went back to the kitchen.

He had a piece of sponge cake with vanilla ice cream, while tapping his foot to the rhythm of the music. At five minutes to midnight the instruments fell silent. The crowd gathered around a small television to watch the ball fall in Times Square. Champagne corks were popped in anticipation. Sparkling wine was poured into plastic champagne flutes. Stephanie poured a real glass for herself and one for Curtis, saying, "Because I know you appreciate the difference."

At the stroke of midnight, the noisemakers went off, firecrackers popped in a back alley, Roman candles whistled somewhere in the street, and the party crowd raised a jubilant shout. A young couple kissed passionately behind the Christmas tree. Others kissed casually or hugged. Curtis rocked on his heels. Stephanie kissed Ed and Steven on their cheeks as they bowed Auld Lang Syne on violin and cello. She gave Piero a hug. Then she came to Curtis beaming, clinked his champagne flute, and pecked him on the lips. It was a chaste kiss, but it was sensual. She had soft, generous lips. He thought he'd like to experience that a second time, but she was on to other guests. He wondered at the distinction between those she pecked on the cheek, and those she favored with a kiss on the lips.

The music started up again. Steven and Ed, being professional musicians, played to Piero's strengths, providing the structure and the key, and though it was outside their usual repertoire, they played flawlessly. As a talented amateur, Piero was less proficient, but what he lacked in technique, he made up for with enthusiasm and a determination to soldier on through his mistakes.

Curtis listened for ten minutes while he finished his champagne. Then he gathered up Sammy, who flopped against his shoulder like a sack of potatoes. He wished Stephanie a happy New Year, and seeing her lips purse, brightened at the prospect of another kiss, but she bypassed him and planted a kiss on Sammy's cheek. "Sweet dreams," she whispered in Sammy's ear. Then Curtis carefully negotiated the stairs, and carried his son into the night. He'd neglected to bring an umbrella. Sammy awoke with a start at the splash of rain on his face. It was half a block to the car. They fell into bed just after 1:00 am.

THURSDAY, NEW YEAR'S Day, the rain turned to sleet. It blew in ragged gusts down the length of the street and deposited a rim of slush on the windowsill. Curtis and Sammy ate breakfast and watched The Rose Parade roll slowly down the sun-drenched streets of Pasadena. When it was over, the bowl games began. Sammy rode his bike around and around the apartment. Curtis jumped up at every commercial and at half time to take ornaments off the tree, all the while keeping an eye on the weather — he had to drive Sammy home, because Friday, January 2nd was still a workday.

Snow snarled the commute, and Elliot insisted on running the Volvo's heater cranked up all the way. In tribute to the weather, Elliot had the Winter section of Vivaldi's Four Seasons playing on the stereo.

"You do anything for New Year's?" he asked.

"Went to a nice party."

"With Sammy?"

"Yeah, we went over to his little friend's house."

"What friend?"

"Gwyneth Walzer, my watercolor teacher's daughter."

"Sophie will be jealous."

"She gets to play with him all week."

"She misses him on the weekends. Vicky says you should come over and spend Sunday with us. We can play some chess."

Curtis was sweating by the time they pulled into the lot, forty-two minutes late. Barbara had his charts up on multiple screens and hot coffee waiting for him when he sat down to start his day.

After the gut-wrenching plunges of October and November, the Market had seen a steady progression upwards, following the typical wave pattern. It seemed to Curtis that the worst was over, the panic had subsided, December had been a good month and January was starting off with a bang. So he was in a buoyant mood when the call came from Allison Essman to report to Erickson's office. He didn't anticipate a problem. More likely, his boss would have a request.

"What's up?" he asked expectantly.

"Sit down," Erickson said tonelessly. Curtis took a seat in front of the desk. "I just got off the phone with Gene Symington." Erickson's voice was grave. "He's not going to sue."

"That's a relief."

"But he's closing his account. His account isn't worth that much, but he's taking some of our other clients with him, Wiggins, Desmond and Hallit, and their combined accounts do make a difference. This is the kind of thing that can snowball out of control. If it wasn't for Dayton, I'd can you on the spot. Somehow you managed to turn him a nice profit."

"Good timing."

"If you're finished being glib, I want you to listen, because I'm giving you one chance and one chance only."

The storm was petering out as they left the building, a few flakes still falling to add to the four to six inches of accumulation. Curtis and Elliot crunched through the snow, blowing steamy breaths, sat in the car with their legs dangling out, banged their shoes together in unison to loosen excess snow, swung their legs in and closed their doors with a thud-thud. Elliot started the engine and waited until he had a warm stream of air to clear the windshield before sliding around the lot and out into the alley, where he nearly crumpled his fender against a dumpster, passing close enough to snap the rearview mirror back on its hinges. Once on the boulevard, the roadway was clear and the commute slow but steady.

"You seem preoccupied," Elliot said after driving two blocks in silence.

"Erickson gave me an ultimatum. It's very simple. I bring Edgar Smith to the table, or I can kiss my job goodbye."

"Is there a deadline?"

"I don't know. I only know I have to get it done or I'm in big trouble. I don't have a lot of money put aside for a rainy day."

That troubling announcement set Elliot to wondering about his own situation. "Let me know if I can help," he said, and put some Mozart into the CD player. For Elliot, music was the cure for all ills.

Curtis took his time at the apartment, turning on the heat, changing into casual clothes, checking his emails and eating an apple before leaving to pick up Sammy. By the time he slid up to the curb behind Roger's idling Mercedes, Linda was standing on the sidewalk, looking put out. She opened the door of the Mercedes and Sammy jumped out with his book bag. She ruffled his hair and looked crossly at Curtis. Sammy got into the Honda. The Mercedes was gone by the time Curtis had Sammy in his seat belt. *So much for pleasant conversation*, Curtis thought.

Saturday morning Curtis put away the last of the Christmas ornaments and Christmas lights. It was a day like any other day, and would only dimly be recalled as memorable for other reasons, though in hindsight it might be seen as a point in time when their futures took another trajectory. It was a hazy, cold day, with patches of ice on the sidewalk that precluded riding a bike, so Sammy spent the morning watching cartoons, then doodling with his watercolor pens. Curtis dragged the dry tree to the service elevator and down to the large yellow dumpster in the alley, leaving a trail of needles that took twenty minutes to sweep up. When he finally put away the broom and dustpan, he looked over Sammy's shoulder and saw a landscape drawing of five dark blue circles, upon which Sammy was drawing "Smiley Faces." So much for brilliant art, Curtis thought, but he looked approvingly at the uniformity of the circles. Sammy had traced the circles around a tuna can — now that was using his head.

Curtis put the two boxes of ornaments and lights into the bottom of his closet. He poured out the water from the tree stand, and dried it with paper towels. Sammy had pushed his Smiley Faces to the side and was busy with a watercolor. Curtis sat down and looked at the doodle. To the second of five Smiley Faces, Sammy had added a nose and eyebrows and hair. "Can I doodle on your doodle?" Curtis asked.

"Uh huh." Sammy was too involved in his painting to care one way or the other.

Curtis took up a brown watercolor pen and began aging the Smiley Faces, each a progression from left to right. The first Smiley Face he left alone — that was the baby. To the others he added ears, and a crescent resting on the dot of the eye for an upper eyelid. To the third, the young man, he added hair. On the fourth, middle-aged man, he reduced the hair to a patch on top and at the sides, and added a double chin and mustache. The fifth, an old man, was bald, and with a black pen Curtis added crows' feet at the eyes, lines from the nose to the mouth, bags under the eyes, and three lines of wrinkles across the forehead. Now *this* was high art, he smiled to himself. *Tres amusante.*

They read aloud from *Frog and Toad Are Friends*. Curtis read "Spring," and Sammy read "A Lost Button," with very few promptings from his father (his reading was improving each week).

In the afternoon Sammy worked on his painting of the park, while Curtis watched the NFL playoff game between the Cardinals and the Falcons. During a commercial break, a local announcer told them to stay tuned for the latest news after the game, and in a perky voice advised watchers to "find out where to put your money in 2009." *In your mattress*, Curtis thought sourly. Who were these idiots, to advise people where to put their money? What did they know? At half time the same announcer changed his demeanor, somberly reporting the headlines, "Israel invades Gaza, a vigil for baby Jessica, and snow sparks a hundred car pile up on the Pennsylvania turnpike; stay tuned after the game!" Why did they think it necessary for him to be apprised of these particular tragedies? He wondered what it must have been like before TV and radio, when most people worked on their farms, insulated from so-called "news." Their concerns were personal and local. They were in touch with the people who affected their lives. Today you couldn't know the people who most affected your life. The complex interaction of global bankers could bring the financial industry to a standstill, could affect your mortgage rates, the value of your home, your savings, your investments, and your income. Which made the choice of headlines all the more puzzling. They ignored events that might be relevant, and gave us instead a picture of impotent people holding candles for a toddler who fell down a well; a tangle of jackknifed trucks and crushed cars; and tanks rolling over rubble in a dispute that had been going on for a thousand years. Did he really need to know any of it? Could they really be that stupid?

He got up and poured himself a generous glass of Dry Creek Fumé Blanc. Sammy had moved to his easel by the window and was adding buildings and edges in oil pastel. From across the room, Curtis was struck by the unusual perspective. Like the beach scene, in which the waves and the beach converged at cliffs in the middle, the buildings to the left and right of the park converged at an intersection in the center of the painting. His own, rather uninspired attempt to paint the park had been a straight on view across the grass to a line of buildings that spread horizontally parallel to the top edge of the paper. Sammy was better. Sammy had a gift.

Three plays into the second half, the Cardinals recovered a fumble and ran it into the end zone. Curtis was watching the replay when Sammy came up to him and said, "I got blood." Curtis snapped instantly into emergency mode, the game forgotten, as he focused on his son. There were drops of blood on his shirt, his chin and a finger.

"What happened?"

"Just started bleedin'," Sammy said with a shrug and a sigh.

Curtis could see blood in his mouth. He wiped the blood off his chin and pushed up Sammy's upper lip. Then he relaxed into a grin of overwhelming relief. "You have a loose tooth! You're about to lose one of your baby teeth!"

"Will it hurt?"

"No. Just leave it alone; it'll fall out in the next couple of days. When it falls out, put it under your pillow and the Tooth Fairy will leave you some money."

Sammy's worried face turned suddenly brighter at the prospect of making some money for nothing. He didn't know the Tooth Fairy, but if he (or she) was anything like Santa Claus, he was looking forward to losing more teeth.

On Sunday Curtis piled Sammy's bike into the back seat of the Honda (a tight fit, but doable), and they drove home to Westlake Drive. It was an unseasonably balmy day, barely under forty degrees Fahrenheit, and Sammy was excited to show his mom his new bike riding skills. She, however, was showing a house for sale. So he showed off for Sophie instead, riding back and forth on the sidewalk, basking in her envy and admiration. Curtis played chess with Elliot, and watched the Baltimore Ravens demolish the Miami Dolphins.

"Now this feels more like home," Vicky said at half time, as Elliot put the *coup de gras* on Curtis's cornered king. "It hasn't been the same around here without you."

"I miss it, myself."

"I'd like to see your apartment. I have this picture in my head when Elliot talks about it."

"It's not much. A little apartment, but it's..." Here Curtis brought to mind his apartment, the empty feel of the place when he'd first moved in, the way it looked now with its plants and paintings and a little history. "...it's home."

"You should have us over for dinner. I could cook," Vicky volunteered.

"Fine with me. Let's make it a Friday or Saturday."

Chapter 20
Monday January 5, 2009

Monday and Tuesday constituted a lull in the Market, so Curtis was in a calm mood that evening, contentedly reading *Time* magazine when the intercom to his apartment unexpectedly buzzed at 7:32 p.m.

"Curtis, this is Edgar Smith. I have a friend. Can we come up?"

This guy was getting tiresome; he didn't seem to recognize the boundary between private and professional life. For a moment Curtis considered turning Smith away, and yet this was an opportunity he mustn't miss, if he wanted to keep his job. He buzzed them up.

They bustled in full of energy. Smith was in tweeds again, and wore a camel hair overcoat, a muffler in earth tones, and a brown fedora. He introduced his companion as Lee Bernier, a tall, big-boned, wide-faced man of German stock in his forties, with blue eyes and a shock of pale blond hair topped with a black beret. Under a black overcoat he wore a dark, three-piece suit, and a blue shirt with white collar and French cuffs. Barely acknowledging Curtis, they took off their hats and overcoats, threw them over the easy chair, and continued their conversation as though Curtis was merely the doorman in his own apartment. They moved over to the room divider.

"Now I want you to abandon all of your preconceived notions," Smith was saying. "Just imagine you're at a show, or better yet, a small gallery. You've been looking at the same old, same old, and you come to this." With a flourish of his hand he presented Sammy's blue dinosaur.

Bernier's lip twitched on one side, seeming to vacillate between amusement and incredulity. Then he grinned and burst out with a loud, "Ha!" followed by a giggle. He tried to repress a smile but simply couldn't. "Well," he said, cocking his head to one side, "I see what you mean. I mean, it could almost be a joke, but it does have *some*thing. It captures the essence of childhood, but with the grace and sophistication of an artist who lets his painting speak to us without getting in the way with artifice. Who is the artist?"

"A female. I don't know her name." Looking pointedly at Curtis, he said reproachfully, "*He* won't tell me."

Bernier snapped out a pair of thin reading glasses and peered at the corner of the painting for a signature. Finding none, he said, "Oh come now," with a faint gay lilt, "what's the mystery?" and looking over the top of his glasses, turned his gaze on Curtis.

"It's..." Curtis had to think of something fast, and nothing was coming to him. "She...she wishes to remain anonymous."

"No artist 'wishes to remain anonymous,'" Bernier said slowly, his voice taking on a deeper resonance. "What's the catch?"

"There's no catch."

Bernier hurrumphed and glanced at Smith with a look of annoyance. "Well, show me more." He stepped over to the white tower. "This isn't the same artist!" he declared accusingly.

"No," Smith replied with disdain, "that's *his*," and jerked a thumb at Curtis.

"Quite," Bernier said, and turned a sneer at Curtis. "You should stick to whatever you do."

"Finance."

"Of course." They moved on to the scene of Del Mar beach. "This is a refreshing perspective." Bernier took a few steps back to get another angle. "Very nice." Curtis stepped back to give them some privacy as they quietly discussed the art, but he still heard Bernier say, "Unique...eh-h-h, y-y-yes, I...I suppose you could say individually unique, but not as a cohesive unit."

"You're looking for a particular vision, or angle," Smith suggested.

"Precisely."

"Well, then look at this."

They spoke quietly, examining the paintings as Curtis popped a cork on a German Riesling. Bernier turned around and gazed at Stephanie's Make Love Grow. "Oh my! That is precious! Oh!" He looked back and forth from the study to the painting. "You would hardly know it's the same artist. What a transformation. It's...it's so simple...."

"That's what I thought. It's so childlike that it makes me want to smile."

"Child*like*, yes, but not child*ish*. And the smirk on that Smiley Face sun is just priceless."

"Smirk?" Smith asked, astonished.

Curtis looked up with more attention. He didn't see any smirk.

"You can't see it?" Bernier said, shocked at his friend's lack of perception. "It's what makes the painting."

"I just liked its childlike air."

"Well, yes, I suppose you could take it like that. Oh, but the rainbow, and the smarmy message is just so cynical in the presence of that smirk. Oh god, I love it, I just love it! I know just who would want to buy this. He'd just di-i-ie!" Bernier put a hand to his heart and looked appreciatively heavenward. "You know, it's as Picasso said: 'Every child is an artist. The problem is how to remain an artist once we grow up.' This artist has captured the spontaneity of the child's vision, with an adult subtext."

"And what do you think of the nasturtiums?"

"*Very* nice," Bernier said, without quite as much enthusiasm as he'd lavished on the love flowers. "Lovely composition. Really accomplished watercolor technique. But that's not the same artist."

"Yes, it is," Curtis blurted out. He had meant to stand in the background, stay out of the discussion, and let it play itself out, but his subconscious couldn't let the factual error pass without comment. "It's definitely the same artist," he muttered.

"They were painted several years apart," Smith explained.

"Which ones are the most recent?"

Curtis pointed them out in order.

Bernier shook his head and muttered, "Where's the cohesion?"

After discussing the remainder of the paintings, Smith asked, "So what do you think? Of the whole, I mean."

Bernier furrowed his brow and looked at the ceiling, gathering his thoughts. "Pleasant, pleasant, mmmm... professional, but maybe not so commercially viable. I mean, the subject matter — the subject matter is all over the board. The pieces are well done, but when you buy an artist you want the piece to be identifiably of that artist. The dinosaur, the heart-shaped flowers, that one with the kid flying the kite, and these aging

Smiley Faces (when it's made into a painting) — these have cohesion; they're of a piece. This park here, the beach, that wonderful one of the buildings (the one that looks unfinished?) — those are of a piece. The nasturtiums, and the girl looking out on the lake are of a piece. The collage and the still life of the peach are in their own categories. The work is good enough, but I don't see this artist as marketable." He hooked his thumbs in his vest pockets and nodded, as though agreeing with his own pronouncements. Curtis felt a flood of relief. Now if they would only go away. "And, of course, you'd have to get the artist to sign them."

"You don't think they're marketable?"

"No, not as an investment. Oh, you might be able to sell them to the hoi polloi, but not, I think, to a serious collector. The subjects and styles are too broad."

Smith looked affronted. "I disagree. It's all a matter of marketing. What you'd have to do is put on a show of all the artist's works in chronological order. That way you show the growth of the artist, and the way she displays two different sides of her personality, the adult and the child. She must be a fascinating person."

"You can disagree all you want, but you asked for my opinion, and that's it."

"What do you mean by 'commercially viable'?"

"I mean worth an investment."

"How much of a return justifies an investment, in your opinion?"

"I don't know...I'd want to make at least thirty percent on a quick sale. If I were investing for the long term, I'd want to make at least seventy-five percent. A real collector is looking for two or three hundred percent, or more."

"It's all a matter of degree, isn't it? If you buy a painting for $100 and sell it for 200, it's the same percentage Return On Investment as if you bought it for 100,000 and sold for 200,000. I'll bet I could make 200% profit, over and above cost, on any of them."

"You're fooling yourself."

"Would you like to make a bet on it?"

"I don't have your resources, Edgar. Betting would be foolish."

"We'll make it a bet you can afford. Just a minute." Smith turned and asked Curtis, "How much did you pay?"

"I didn't pay anything; they were presents."

Smith rolled his eyes. "Okay, how much would you sell them for?"

"They're not for sale."

"We've been down this road before. How much?"

"They're not..."

"I'll give you $1,000 for the lot."

"...for sale."

"2,000."

"Not for sale."

"Listen, Cooke. I believe in a diversified portfolio, and art is part of my allocation. Now, you'll sell me these paintings for $2,000, or Bass Erickson can kiss my ass. If you want my business, you'll play ball."

The situation was getting seriously out of hand, but Smith had him in a corner and he couldn't see a way out. If he confessed now, he'd never get Smith's business, Erickson would be upset, and he could very well lose his job. If he lost his job, he had just enough saved to stave off the creditors for three months. After that, he wouldn't have enough to pay the mortgage, his rent, and his car payment. He was skating on thin ice.

Smith plowed ahead. "We only have eight paintings here. That's not enough for a show. Do you know if she has more?"

The impulse to answer a poised question, and answer honestly, was so ingrained that Curtis didn't hesitate to answer truthfully. "Lots," he said, the memory of stacked canvases beside Stephanie's bed coming to mind. He could have kicked himself a moment later, but by then it was too late.

"All right," Smith drawled, turning back to Bernier, and pausing to organize his thoughts. He held his chin a minute, staring at the floor. Then he straightened up, everything clear in his mind. "I'll make this a win-win proposition for you. Here's what we'll do. You'll organize the show. I'll pay you ten percent for your time."

"Of what? Profits, or gross proceeds?"

"Profits."

Bernier turned to Curtis. "How many paintings do you think she has?"

"I don't think she wants to do this," Curtis said, seeing a way out.

"She'll do it," Smith said.

"I don't think so."

"Trust me."

"She's very private."

"Let's not be naïve here. Money talks."

"How many?" Bernier insisted.

"I don't know," Curtis said, flummoxed by the speed of the conversation. "Maybe thirty?"

Bernier made a mental calculation. "Twenty percent of the gross profit and you have a deal."

"Done."

"But wait," Bernier said. "You got me all turned around. I won't agree to anything unless we set a minimum price per painting. If the price is too low, it won't be worth my time."

"Let's make this really interesting," Smith told Bernier. "We'll set the price on half of the pieces, and we'll put the rest up for silent auction and let the market dictate the price. What do you think is a fair minimum price?"

"Unknown artist, first show — maybe 350, $400."

"Too cheap, you can't create buzz if it's too cheap. Let's say we set the minimum price at $600. I'll bet I could buy all thirty for 200 apiece, so I'd make my 200% profit right off the bat."

"If they sell."

"If they sell, yes. So hypothetically, let's say she has 20, plus these 8. That's 30 times 600, equals 18,000, less the cost of the paintings — say 6,000 — that's 12,000 gross profit. So, at a minimum your payment for organizing would be 24 hundred. Is that fair?"

"Sure, that's fair for the price of organizing the thing. What's the bet?"

"What did I say? I bet I could make 200% on my investment?"

"What if she wants more than 200 apiece?"

"I don't think she'll sell," Curtis said, knowing full well that she would probably be thrilled to sell, and knowing that if they succeeded in selling Sammy's paintings under Stephanie's name, it would constitute fraud.

Smith and Bernier looked at him as if they'd forgotten he was in the room.

"She'll sell," Smith said with conviction. "I may have to pay more, but she'll sell." Turning back to Bernier, he said, "So I'll guarantee you 24 hundred dollars for organization, or 20% of the net profits, whichever is more."

"Right. So-o-o where's the bet? What do I lose if you win? What am I putting up?"

"If I succeed, you agree to write a glowing review of the show in the Sunday section of the paper, with color photos. And post it on the Internet. If I lose, you can write whatever you like."

"That's it?" Bernier asked, a bit flabbergasted. "That's all?"

"I don't need your money, but your reputation is worth something. Any paintings that haven't sold will be worth more if you give the show a good review."

"You're right, I hadn't thought of my reputation. I can't do it; I can't review a show I've organized; it would be a conflict of interest."

Curtis sighed with relief.

"Alright, here," Smith said, sounding peeved. He pulled out a wallet and fanned out a sheaf of bills. "Here's your 24 hundred, plus 600 extra to find someone else to front for you. Just make sure the right people come to the show. And keep me in the loop; I want to know all the details."

Bernier shrugged and took the money.

"I don't think she'll sell," Curtis repeated, wondering how he was going to keep Stephanie out of it without alienating Smith. His job depended on it.

Smith handed him two one-thousand-dollar bills. "I've never met an unknown artist who could turn down $4,000. Now, what's her name?"

PART FOUR

BULLSEYE

Chapter 21

Wednesday January 7 — Sunday January 11, 2009

Wednesday Curtis couldn't help thinking about the predicament he'd gotten himself into, as both Bernier and Smith had separately called to cajole him into revealing the artist's name. "I can't tell you until I talk to her. I'm not at all sure she'll go for it."

"Have her call me."

While worrying about Smith and his antics, the stock market was taking a serious dive, finishing the day down 245 points. If that weren't bad enough, Curtis went online to see if his rent had been automatically paid, and found his joint checking account seriously depleted. He called Linda. "What's up with the checking account? Where's the money gone?"

"Don't take that tone of voice with me."

"What tone would you like? Just answer the question."

"It's really none of your business. I've had some expenses."

"Alright, but you just keep this in mind: If I lose my job, which isn't outside the bounds of possibility, I'll be moving back in, because I won't be able to pay the rent *and* the mortgage."

There was a long silence as she digested this piece of news. "Then you better not lose your job."

He hung up the phone. "Fuck."

He arrived at Bolton's in a foul mood with ten minutes to spare. How was he going to explain to Stephanie that he'd unwittingly gotten her involved in a ridiculous wager between two idiots who couldn't tell the difference between her paintings and the paintings of a six-year-old? Actually, taken in that light it might seem humorous, had his job not been on the line. He had to work up his courage and the right approach. Conflicted about how to broach the subject, he took a seat in the back row

271

and avoided looking at Stephanie. He might as well have hung a sign on his back.

She was on him before he'd finished setting out his brushes and palette. "Are you alright? You don't look well."

Never able to hide his emotions, Curtis looked up with a pained expression. "We have to talk."

She imagined the worst. "Has something happened to Sammy?"

"He's fine."

"What's the matter, then?"

"It's a long story. Can we talk after class?"

"If it doesn't take too much time; I have to catch a bus. There's not a lot of leeway."

"You take a bus?"

"How else do you think I get home?"

"God, here I've been driving every week and I've never even asked. I'm sorry, I'm such a pathetic friend."

"If you'll drive me home..."

"Yeah, of course, that would be good." He gave a strained smile and looked at her with worried eyes.

"We'll talk after class," she said, worried in her own right. What could possibly be going on to cause him such distress?

He didn't get much out of the class, so preoccupied was he with how she would react. Though the more he thought about it, the better he felt. All she had to do was refuse. If she refused to do the show, he couldn't be accused of stonewalling. Erickson couldn't be upset with him, he would still have a chance of attracting Smith's business, and all would be as it should.

At the break, Stephanie approached him in the hallway. "Can you explain now?"

"No, I think I better wait."

"You've got me worried."

"It's nothing to be concerned about really. I just have a favor to ask, but I'd rather wait until I can explain the background in full, if you don't mind."

At the end of class, Stephanie announced that Intermediate Watercolors would begin the following Wednesday, for anyone who was interested. When everyone had said their goodbyes and left, Stephanie looked at Curtis, who stood by the door with his watercolor kit in hand. "Now, what's the problem?" she asked.

"Would you like a drink?"

"No, I'd like to know what's bothering you."

"Let me drive you home first."

They drove half the way in silence. Stephanie wondered where this was leading. Was there something ominous behind his strange behavior? Was he about to go psychotic on her? "Tell me what's on your mind. It can't be that bad. Just tell me."

"I'm afraid I got you involved in something," he said, "nothing to be worried about, nothing illegal or anything," and then giving vent to some of his own worries, added "yet."

Back at her apartment building, Stephanie collected Gwyn from Mrs. Bossert's and they went upstairs. To Gwyn she said, "You go in the bedroom, honey; Mr. Cooke and I have to talk."

She poured them both a glass of cheap Chardonnay and pulled a chair from the kitchen table into the parlor for Curtis. She sat in the wingback chair. "Now, what's this all about?"

Curtis explained how the mix-up had happened. "I didn't mean to mislead him. I just didn't want to insult him."

"So, he thinks Sammy is me, or I'm Sammy? I'm confused."

"He was saying nice things about Sammy's pieces, and what was I going to say? If I told him, he'd've looked foolish. So then he looked at Sammy's Make Love Grow, and he looked at your Make Love Grow, and he concluded Sammy's was the 'study' for yours. And then he asked if the same artist had done the nasturtiums, and of course, I said yes. So, he assumed they were all by the same artist."

"Unbelievable."

"Believe it."

"And you can't tell him — why?"

"We could lose his business."

"Is he a good client?"

"He's not a client at all, not yet, but if I don't get him to sign on with Bass Erickson, I'll lose my job."

Stephanie took a sip of wine. "So, I'm still confused. And what has this got to do with me, exactly?"

"I'm getting to that. So, later he comes back with this other guy and they start talking, and somehow it got around to how much money could be made if they did a show, you know, 'return on investment,' and this guy says the paintings are good, but there's no...what was the word? — cohesion. There's no cohesion of subject matter and style. But Smith disagreed, and the long and the short of it is they made a wager. And that's where you come in."

"Step back a minute. Who is this other guy?"

Curtis fished in his pocket for the business card. "Lee Bernier."

Stephanie's eyes went wide and her glass tipped into her lap. "Shit!" she yelled, jumping up. "Lee Bernier was looking at my paintings?" She started shaking and plopped back down in her chair. "You're sure?"

Curtis peered at the card. "It just says Lee Bernier, The Tribune."

"Oh my god."

"I take it you know him?"

"He's just the most important art critic in the city, maybe the state. Go on — what about a show?"

"That's the point. They're pestering me for your name. By the way, none of the paintings are signed — what's that about?"

"Huh?" Stephanie was staring at him, stunned. It was a moment before the question registered. "Oh, they're signed on the back. I did them for class, years ago; our teacher didn't want to be influenced by knowing who'd painted what, so she had us sign on the back."

"You didn't sign Make Love Grow, either."

"I didn't want to take credit for Sammy's idea, and then there was the one you started, which was as much yours as mine."

She got up and went into the kitchen to dab the wine from her jeans and pour herself another glass. She came back to the wingback chair. "You said there was a wager."

"Yes, see, Smith said he could make a 200% return, and the other guy..."

"Bernier."

"Yes, Bernier, he said he couldn't, and Smith said if he could, then Bernier had to give the show a good review. But the point is, we can't let it get that far."

"Why not?"

"Because then your paintings and Sammy's paintings will be all mixed up."

"What have *your* paintings got to do with *my* show?"

"Well, see actually, he sort of forced me to sell him all of the paintings you gave me," Curtis said sheepishly. "Sorry. He wanted them for the show."

She leaned forward, forearms on her knees and eagerly inquired, "You sold them? For how much?"

"My hands were tied," Curtis apologized. "I said I wouldn't sell, and then he said he wouldn't give his business to Bass Erickson, so I didn't know what else to do. He bought them all for a flat $2,000, which reminds me...." Curtis pulled the bills from his pocket and handed them to Stephanie, "This really belongs to you."

She stared at the money with incomprehension. "For me? For how many paintings?"

Curtis winced at the thought of giving up his son's paintings, not to mention Stephanie's gifts, to satisfy a stupid bet. He mentally counted them and silently ticked them off on his fingers. "Seven or eight. Eight I think."

"And the problem is?"

"They'll put Sammy's paintings in the show as if you painted them. It would be fraud. But if there's no show, there's no problem, and they can't do a show with just eight paintings. Anyway, he wants to know who the artist is, and if I keep prevaricating, he'll be pissed. So if I give him your name, all you have to do is refuse to sell your paintings. Then he can't do the show, he can't blame me, we won't be committing fraud, and everything will be okay."

"Wait a minute; what do you mean, refuse to sell my paintings? You mean he wants to buy more?"

"For the show."

"How many does he want?"

"That doesn't matter."

"How many?"

"I suggested you might have thirty."

"Thirty!"

"I told him you wouldn't sell."

"How much is he willing to pay?"

"Less than they're worth, I'm sure, but that's not the point."

"How much?"

"He thinks he can buy them for $200 apiece and sell them for $600. But that's not important. What's important is you have to tell him you won't sell your paintings."

"But that's..." She did the math in her head. "$6,000!"

"Don't even think about it."

"Why not?"

"Do you want to go to jail? Fraud is a felony."

"But $6,000 is a lot of money."

"It's nothing to Smith; he carries that much in his wallet."

"Do you think I could get more?"

"Don't be thinking like that. We can't do it."

"I need the money. Besides, I won't go to jail — I didn't tell him I painted Sammy's paintings. He wants thirty of my paintings!" Her brow suddenly furrowed as doubt crept in. "Jesus, do I have thirty? I better check." She put down her glass, jumped up and began counting the paintings on the walls. Then she crossed quickly to her bedroom and did a quick accounting.

Curtis followed her. "You're not really considering...?"

"I wonder if he'd take more."

"Stephanie! Didn't you hear anything I said?"

"All I need to hear," she said, looking under the bed.

"You're letting greed cloud your judgment."

"What's going on?" Gwyn asked, peering over the edge of the bed at her mother.

"I've got over forty paintings here. They're not all framed, but that's easy to fix. And I have some at Mrs. Bossert's. And Mary Anne keeps a few at the gallery to put up when there's empty space."

"Did I not make myself clear? Hello! Fraud?"

"Oh, shush." She waved a dismissive hand at him as they left the bedroom. "How many of Sammy's paintings are we talking about?"

"Three, four."

"So, four out of thirty or forty. Who's to know? I'm certainly not gonna tell'im. You're not gonna tell. This is so exciting!" She ran up, pressed her palms to his cheeks and gave him a rather long peck. There were no tongues involved, but it was nonetheless an astonishingly sensual kiss that left him speechless. "Thank you! Thank you, thank you, thank you! Woo-who-oo!"

"I don't suppose there's any dissuading you?"

"I've never had a real show before. Mary Anne will be kicking herself she didn't do it first. No, wait! Maybe we can hold it at The Stevenson Gallery. That would be very good for my job." A frown clouded her face. "You didn't sell Make Love Grow, did you? It was a present to Sammy."

"He didn't give me much choice."

"No matter, you can buy it back at the show. There's so much to think about." She flopped into the wingback chair, smiled to herself, and took a long sip.

Bernier called mid-morning. "Have you asked her?"

Curtis almost answered that he'd talked with her and she wasn't interested, but she'd been so excited he didn't have the heart to squash her dream, despite his misgivings.

"Yup."

"And?"

"She's interested."

"Of course she is. I could have told you; she'd be a fool not to be."

Curtis gave him the number to The Stevenson Gallery, where she worked Tuesdays and Thursdays.

After the Market closed Erickson called him in for his weekly report. They went over the current positions in his portfolios, then Erickson asked, "Have you been in touch with Edgar Smith?"

"He's been by a couple of times. I'm doing him a little favor, and I think that'll go a long way toward reeling him in."

"Is this favor something I should know about?"

"It's nothing to do with the firm. He has a diversified portfolio, some real estate, art, wine, vintage cars, you-name-it. Somehow I got involved in a private bet."

"Is it legal?"

"Mostly."

"Okay, I don't need to know. Just don't let him get away."

"I'm on it."

That evening he was reading *Hornblower and the Atropos*. It was the kind of historical fiction that could immerse him in another world, and it was with a shock that his mind stepped off the deck of the Atropos to answer his phone. It was Stephanie.

"Hi, Curtis? I just wanted to thank you for giving Lee Bernier the gallery number. You should've seen Mary Anne's face when he asked for *me*. She about jumped out of her pants. She's all, 'You know Lee Bernier?' And I'm just as nonchalant as could be, because I knew what he was calling about. So then we're talking and he asks if I know anyone who could organize a show, and of course I recommended Mary Anne, which gives me a few Brownie points with my boss. So he's coming over Saturday to look at the paintings. It's really weird how differently she treats me now. It's annoying, to tell you the truth. I've worked there part-time for four years, and after all this time I suddenly have her respect. I like it, in one way, but it's disturbing at the same time. I mean — I'm no different today than I was yesterday."

"Oh yes you are. Yesterday you were a Nobody, like the rest of us. Now you're a Somebody."

"I haven't even had the show yet. It might flop."

"With *your* talent? Not a chance."

"I'm still worried."

Curtis was about to reflexively reassure her, when he remembered Sammy's paintings. He was worried too. What was it Stephanie had said last night? — He would have to buy back Make Love Grow; it was her present to Sammy, and he shouldn't have allowed it to be sold. Then the light went on: He could buy them all back, all of Sammy's paintings. If he bought them, no one need be the wiser, and no one would be defrauded. "I can buy them back."

"What?"

"Nothing. You have nothing to worry about."

"Would you like to come over when they come on Saturday?"

"I can't; I'm having company. And anyway, Sammy'll be with me, and he might inadvertently spill the beans."

"Spill the beans? Where do you get these expressions?"

"Just something my father used to say."

There was dead air as they had exhausted this line of conversation.

"Well, I just called to thank you for pointing Bernier to the gallery. I'll never forget the look on Mary Anne's face."

"Glad to have been of service."

"*Au revoir.*"

"After 'while, crocodile." He could hear her sniggering as he hung up.

He opened his book and stepped back onto the cold, damp deck of the Atropos. It was night and the ship was anchored in the Downs, enveloped in a thick, impenetrable fog. The tide was running at two knots, and a drifting oar had just thumped against the hull...

Linda turned an uncharacteristic smile on him when she opened the door Friday night. "He'll be down in just a minute." She called up the stairs, "Sammy, your father's here!" Sammy bounded down the stairs, his bookbag flopping on his back. To Curtis, Linda said, "He has something to show you."

Sammy bared his teeth, revealing a gap where his tooth had been. "And the other one is loose, too." He demonstrated by wiggling it with the end of his tongue.

"Did the Tooth Fairy leave you anything?"

"Five dollars!"

"Five dollars!" Curtis looked at Linda. "The Tooth Fairy must be crazy; I only got a buck in my day."

"Inflation," Linda reminded him.

Curtis led the way down the sidewalk to the Samuelson's house, where he arranged to borrow Chris Samuelson's Ford F150 pickup for the weekend. He left Samuelson the keys to the Honda in exchange.

The truck cab was appallingly dirty. The floor and the seat were littered with beer cans and crumpled fast-food bags, unopened mail, a scattering of coins, a peach pit and a blackened banana peel. A pair of sunglasses and a baseball cap adorned the dash, beneath a deodorizing Christmas tree that dangled from the rearview mirror, its usefulness long since spent, as evidenced by the musty smell of the interior. He fished under the seat on the passenger's side for the missing passenger seatbelt, coming up with a spoon, a wad of used Kleenex, a sticky breath mint, a few pennies and a plastic straw. When he'd installed Sammy's booster seat, he drove the truck down the street and backed into his driveway. Elliot had been right about the brakes.

He loaded his bike into the back of the truck, along with a box of books and photo albums, and drove slowly back to the apartment keeping plenty of distance from the car ahead, in case of sudden stops.

"Can I ride my bike?" Sammy asked after Saturday morning cartoons. Curtis was at the window staring into a chill grey day. Bare branches quivered in the wind that swept down Washington Street, and patches of snow still clung like white moss in the shadows. "It's too cold," Curtis observed, and as he said it he pictured their two bikes locked into the bike rack in the basement parking garage. The garage was heated to a relatively comfortable fifty degrees Fahrenheit. "Unless you'd like to ride in the garage," he added.

They rode in a large oval, down one aisle and up the other, Curtis trailing Sammy to assess his progress, as well as to get in a little exercise himself. The low ceilings, fluorescent lights, and vague smells of motor oil and rubber gave Curtis a claustrophobic uneasiness, but Sammy was in his own world, a squirrel in a cage, running for the joy of it. After twenty minutes Curtis loosened the wing nuts and adjusted the training wheels up three inches, allowing Sammy to lean a little into the corners, and to find that point on the straightaways where he could balance without relying on the training wheels.

Curtis begged fatigue at the close of an hour and locked up the bikes. Then they took a quick trip to CostCo to pick up a folding chair and salmon for dinner. The Fines arrived at 3:20.

"It's not easy finding parking around here," Elliot complained. All of the buildings have white zones." He carried Nathan in the crook of his right arm and a wooden case under his left.

"They never patrol this street," Curtis replied confidently. The construction trucks and cars seemed to be exempt from parking rules, so the meter maids steered clear. "You can just throw everything on the bed in there," Curtis said to Vicky, who was struggling to take off her coat while holding Nathan's baby bag and blanket.

"I brought my chess set," Elliot said, laying the carved wood case next to the fish tank. He noted the tank, the paintings and the plants. "You've done a lot since I was here last."

"Elliot *said* you'd taken up painting," Vicky remarked, returning from the bedroom. "You didn't paint *those*?" It was as much a statement as a question.

"No, those were done by my watercolor teacher. This one is mine — well, most of it; she added Sammy with a kite, and her daughter with the ducks."

Vicky moved closer for a better look. "Ah-h-h," Vicky crooned, the teacher's gender having not escaped notice. "Is she pretty?"

"She looks a lot like you," Elliot piped in.

"Oh?" There was more than a simple interrogative in her inflection, accompanied by raised eyebrows and a repressed smile. Speaking to Curtis she said, "Not your type, hmmm?"

Now that put Curtis in an awkward position. If he were to answer in the negative, it might imply that he didn't find Vicky attractive, and he did, to a degree. Like Stephanie, Vicky wasn't classically proportioned; she didn't have Linda's elegance, nor Rhiannon's limpid eyes, but she was pretty enough in her own way. Her looks depended to some measure on her personality, which animated her features and gave life to eyes and lips that might otherwise have been unremarkable. He avoided the question by replying, "She's just a friend."

"Did she give you a deal?"

"They were gifts."

"Oh, just a *friend*," she mocked in disbelief. "A very *generous* friend."

"She has a lot of paintings."

Sammy and Sophie had followed. He pointed to Make Love Grow. "She painted that one, but it was my idea. Those are love flowers."

Sophie clapped her hands.

"Oh, my god, you've lost a tooth!" Vicky cried.

"An' the other one is loose — see?" He wiggled it with his tongue.

"Akk! Don't wiggle it, it's creepy!" At this, Sammy wiggled it all the more.

"Sammy painted these," Curtis pointed out, turning toward the blue dinosaur on the teak screen.

"It's very nice," she told Sammy. "Stop wiggling that!"

"And I do pastels, too. See!" Sammy dragged her to his beach scene.

Vicky looked genuinely startled. "Really? You did this? How very amazing. You should give Sophie lessons."

"She doesn't like to paint."

"She might, if she painted as well as you."

While Sammy and Sophie shot Nerf darts at the window, Curtis poured Remy Pannier rosé d'Anjou and set about putting the salmon in the oven, cooking a saffron rice, and cutting up zucchini and red bell peppers. The conversation, never difficult with the Fines, drifted from the year-round availability of fruits and vegetables, to cooking, Nerf toys, toy guns, boy toys and girl toys, and nurture versus nature. "You can say what you like," Curtis said, "but Sammy was a boy from the start. We tried giving him a doll. His doll liked to jump off of high places and tumble down the stairs. Linda wouldn't have any toy weapons around. Then one Saturday morning (this was when Sammy was about three) he woke me up at 6:30 and said he wanted to play with Sophie. I said, 'not now, it's too early' and he hit me with a sharp stick! After that, I got him a nice, dull, plastic sword."

"I hope you gave him a good spanking," Elliot said.

"Spanking is counter-productive," Vicky said to Elliot, showing how much they were on the same page. To Curtis she said, "I don't know about swords, but I don't like guns. There are too many guns in this country, too many kids killing other kids."

"If you deny them toy guns, they just point their fingers." Curtis illustrated by pointing his index finger and dropping his thumb.

"A sword is nothing," Elliot said. "Have you seen some of the video games these days? They're incredibly violent."

"It's still all about Good triumphing over Evil," Curtis opined. "Kids just have to be taught the difference between make-believe (which is just wish-fulfillment), and reality (with its attendant consequences)."

By this time Sammy was demonstrating his prowess at navigating the remote-controlled car, much to the delight of Sophie, until he began chasing her with it and rammed her ankles. She burst into tears. Vicky comforted her, while Curtis made Sammy put the car away and take out Leggos. The conversation then turned to Christmas presents, schools, school budgets, taxes and the economy.

The salmon, poached in diced tomatoes with basil, was about ready to come out of the oven, when Ode to Joy began chirping from Curtis's phone. Caller ID read Stephanie Walzer. He picked up.

"Mr. Cooke? Hi, this is Lee Bernier. We want to bring over some paintings, get everything together in one spot and stage the show from there. I just wanted to make sure you were home."

"You can't come over now; I have dinner guests."

"We won't be a minute. We just have to drop them off."

"Not tonight; I have guests. Let me talk to Stephanie."

Instead, Smith came on the line. "Cooke, we're coming over. We have some paintings to drop off."

Curtis could see the scene unfold before him: Smith and Bernier would bluster in, Vicky or Elliot would ask what it was about, and one way or another it would become obvious that Sammy's paintings were somehow being included in a show. Smith would lose face. He'd lose Smith's business. He'd lose his job. Stephanie would be disgraced. He put his foot down. "Not tonight. As I told Bernier, I have dinner guests."

"But you have the perfect place for it; you have a blank wall where we can hang them up, see what they look like side by side and such."

Curtis looked at the large trapezoidal wall behind the television, devoid of ornament. "It's perfect, but not tonight. If you insist on coming over, I won't buzz you in. If some other fool lets you in the lobby, I won't answer my door."

"Ha! Haw!" Smith let forth a blast of mirth. "Very good! Ha!!" He was apparently not used to being denied and found it most amusing.

"Put Stephanie on the line," Curtis demanded. In a moment she greeted him tentatively. "Steph, why don't I drive over there tomorrow and pick..."

"I work at Bolton's until 3:00. We really need to talk. Alone."

Something was going on, but he had no way of knowing what. "I could come over after I drop off Sammy. I'll take him home a little early."

"That would be great," she said, some relief creeping into her voice. "Why don't you come for dinner? Around 6:30. We can pack up the paintings after."

"Okay. Sounds like a plan."

After he'd hung up, Vicky had to ask, "What was that all about? Was that your *friend*?"

"Yeah, she needs my help with moving some things."

"We could take Sammy," Vicky offered helpfully, "if Linda's busy."

"Not necessary," Curtis said, fully aware of Vicky's intentions.

After the meal, which Vicky pronounced a success, the chessboard was set up and the NFL Playoff game came on the TV. Curtis played Elliot to a stalemate, as neither of them could keep his mind on chess. The Fines said their farewells when the football game ended, shortly after 8:30.

Sunday had a hectic feel to it. In the morning he took Sammy to the movies. In the afternoon he watched the first half of the playoff between the San Diego Chargers and the Pittsburg Steelers. He wasn't a rabid football fan, but the Chargers were his hometown team and he wanted to watch. At half time he drove Sammy home, and having no way to record the game in the apartment, he listened to the third quarter on the radio until he arrived at Stephanie's. It was with a sense of frustration that he turned off the engine and knocked on her door.

"I took Sammy to see *Bedtime Stories*, this morning," Curtis said. "He liked it."

"I'm not a big Adam Sandler fan," Stephanie said; "he has a potty mouth."

"Yeah, but his movies have heart. Kind of like Stephen King — he's great if you can overlook his pathological obsession with shit."

"*Christine!*" Stephanie exclaimed in affirmation. "Oh, my god, someone should count the number of times he uses 'shit' in that book. I almost thought he had a bet with his agent to see how many times he could use it in one book without being censored. It was so over-the-top it was funny."

"Exactly."

"We're just having chicken and potatoes; I hope you weren't expecting a gourmet dinner."

"No, anything's fine. You sounded worried yesterday. What's up?"

"Oh, where to begin? First of all, Smith and Bernier — they're nut cases. They're so totally self-absorbed, and so totally hyper, I couldn't get a word in edgewise. I suppose I should start at the beginning. First, Mary Anne came over and we were looking through what I have, and what they might want. We had about fifteen all picked out, when *they* arrived. They had a whole different idea of what I was about. They said they wanted 'flow' — something to show a progression, and they wanted the dates when I'd painted them all. I mean, I've been painting for ten years, and to tell the truth, I really don't remember. So what do you think? Which ones in this room do you think they picked?"

Curtis scanned the walls. There were watercolors, a few in acrylics, some oils, some pastels. The subject matter was varied, but it was mostly representational; there was nothing in the Abstract Impressionist vein, nothing surreal, nothing as stylized as cubism. If there was a theme, it was that the juxtaposition of mundane objects imbued them with a significance they otherwise lacked. Like the nasturtiums, the objects in the paintings were not special; it was the composition that created an emotional response in the viewer. "If it had been me, I'd have picked..." and here Curtis pointed out his favorites of the almost thirty on the walls.

She then led him to the bedroom, rapped her knuckles on the door and opened it. Gwyn was lying on the bed doing homework. Behind the headboard were a dozen more paintings, smaller than those in the parlor. "And these?" she asked. Curtis gave his opinion. "Well, I'll tell you," she said, "they liked only three, but the one they went gaga over was that one." She pointed a finger at Sammy's *Balloon Boat*. "They said that had to be in the show, because it fit in with The Blue Dinosaur, and Make Love Grow, and something they called the *Smiley Faces* (I don't even know what they were talking about), and they wanted more of *those*! Bernier kept going on about 'a return to innocence,' and 'the simplification of line.' I could have barfed!" She looked aghast at her own outburst. "Excuse me, that wasn't very lady-like. Don't you use that language," she admonished Gwyn, who only smiled. "I was so angry...no, not angry — flabbergasted, perplexed, confused. I don't know what they want! Do you know what they're talking about? What *Smiley Faces*?"

"Oh lord," Curtis moaned. "Sammy made some smiley faces, and I just drew wrinkles on them. They thought it was a 'study.'"

Stephanie's lips twisted up in a crooked smile and a twinkle shone in her eyes. "Well, if that's what they want, that's what I'll give them. I can paint Smiley Faces all day long."

"How many of your paintings did they take?"

"Twenty-three."

"Can I ask how much?"

"The smallest ones I sold for $200. The biggest for $325."

"That's a pretty good haul."

"And he paid in cash."

Stephanie delayed dinner by a few minutes, so Curtis could catch the end of the game (the Chargers lost). She turned out to be a pretty good cook. It was nothing fancy, just a lemon-herb chicken, roasted new potatoes basted with olive oil and balsamic vinegar, and frozen peas steamed just enough so they popped when pressed against the roof of the mouth. Comfort food, he thought. Like the cook, it wasn't elegant or fussy; it was just satisfying. Curtis reflected on what Elliot had said about Stephanie looking like Vicky. It wasn't strictly true; though they shared stature, dark curly hair and brown eyes, Stephanie had more refined features. But she was like Vicky in another way — she wasn't 'high maintenance.' Curtis had always envied the ease of the Fines' marriage. Not that his own marriage had been tumultuous; they'd rarely had harsh words for one another, but Linda was hard to please, exacting in the way she wanted everything done, and most of the time he'd accepted her direction in order to keep the peace. But it was like walking on eggshells — one misstep and she'd find fault.

After dinner, he helped Stephanie with the dishes. It was a bit of a shock to find she had no dishwasher or garbage disposal. He'd never lived in a house or an apartment without both. "It's really not a problem," she said. "It's only me and Gwyn."

When the last plate was put away, they began taking down the paintings that were going in the show and wrapping them in bubble wrap that Mary Anne Stevenson had left for that purpose. "I took five of them to Bolton's to be framed. They're happy for the extra business." Stephanie dusted the frames as they came off the wall. Curtis cut bubble wrap with scissors. Stephanie wrapped it around each painting and held it in place, while Curtis taped it shut. When it came to Sammy's balloon boat, she picked it up and looked at it thoughtfully. "I can't take this; this was a present for Gwyn." So was the present she'd given to Sammy, Curtis thought, but to his discredit, he'd allowed it to be sold. He wondered how much it was going to cost him to buy it back. She set the balloon boat aside. "I'm going to paint another one just like it; I doubt they'll notice the difference," she went on, and after a moment added, "It's really a bit depressing. Maybe I'll just improve on it a little."

It took them three trips to get all of the bubble-wrapped paintings into the trunk and back seat of the Honda. Stephanie told Gwyn to call on Mrs. Bossert if she had any problems. "Or call me; I'll have my phone on." They drove back to Washington Street in silence. Curtis wondered how it was that some silences were awkward and uncomfortable, while others were natural and unforced.

They carried the paintings from the garage to the apartment, unwrapped them, and leaned them against the walls. By far his favorite was an oil painting of a bicycle from an unusual perspective. It was a dog's view of the world, low to the sidewalk. The vantage point was so close to the back tire that only a portion of the tire was visible, along with a left calf and tennis shoe pushing down on the peddle. The bike was off-center to the right side of the sidewalk, while the viewer looked straight down the center of the sidewalk, past the peddling foot to an approaching skateboarder crouched with arms spread wide for balance.

"Show me the smiley faces." Curtis pointed her to the easel. She sighed. "I think 'you've caught the essence of childhood,'" she quoted ironically, and yet she couldn't suppress a smile; it was a silly doodle. "It kind of makes me wonder: What was the point of all those art classes I took?" Then she looked at the half-finished painting of the park clipped above it. "Is this yours?"

"No, Sammy's."

"I should have guessed. I'd like to see it when it's done."

Chapter 22

Monday January 12 — Sunday January 18, 2009

Monday the sell-off continued, which triggered automatic sell signals with 10% losses for several of his stocks.

He'd switched off his cell phone at work and didn't turn it on again until he reached the apartment Monday evening. His mother's laconic voicemail — "Call home" — was uttered with such distress that he was worried that something might have happened to his father who, at 60, was getting to that age where health became an issue. He may have had a heart attack, or who-knows-what? When she answered, he asked, "Is it Dad?"

"Is what Dad? What are you talking about?"-

"Why you called."

"No, it's your brother."

Again, the distress in her voice was apparent, and the range of disasters that could befall a young man raced through his head. "Has he been in an accident?"

"No, he's left Denise! Oh, everything is coming apart. You've got to call him."

"I don't think he wants my advice. He'd call if he..."

"It was all just fine until you moved out of your house."

"I didn't move out; I was kicked out. There's a difference."

"Patrick wouldn't have had the idea, if you'd kept your marriage together. You have to call him. Oh, I thought everything was so perfect; I'd gotten the three of you married off and out of the house, and now this."

"He hasn't moved back home?"

"No, he's moved in with that woman — Kim Somebody-or-other."

"Then he's still on his own; he's not in your house. Just leave him be; he's an adult; it's his own business. "

"But he's moved in with another woman. It's disgraceful. And now Denise is calling, and crying, and what am I to say. I'm so ashamed of him.... What am I to do? Denise is like a daughter to me."

Somehow Curtis couldn't imagine his mother thinking of a daughter-in-law as her own daughter. She'd never treated Linda that way, and he told her as much now.

"Well, you lived so far away, I really never got to know her. And she didn't encourage communication; you know that. But Denise and I are very close, and I just want to know how am I supposed to deal with this? Patrick has broken up a perfectly happy home. Denise and I used to go shopping together, especially in the summers..."

"It couldn't have been a very happy home, or he wouldn't have left," Curtis interrupted.

"He's not thinking straight; he's thinking with his...well, you know. Men are all the same that way. They can't control themselves, and it just makes me sick. Denise is one of my best friends. We can't very well go on as if nothing has changed. If he knew the misery he's causing us all.... Maybe you can talk sense to him."

"I already spoke to him about it at Thanksgiving."

"You knew about it at Thanksgiving?"

"He mentioned it."

"And you didn't tell *me*? Oh!" Curtis could hear her calling, "William, talk to your son."

He could hear his father in the background saying, "About what?" He came on the line. "Hi, son, how are you doing?"

"Ok. I told her, I already talked to Patrick. I don't really have anything more to tell him."

"I know — just humor her. Call him."

Curtis first changed into jeans, a flannel shirt and slippers, and had half a glass of mediocre Chardonnay. The convenient thing about cell phones was they followed the owner wherever they happened to be. Patrick answered on the third ring, "Hey, big bro!"

"Hey yourself. You sound awfully happy."

"I *am* happy. I feel on top of the world!"

"Good, I'm happy for you. Our mother's not so happy."

"I know; she doesn't want to see it my way. But you wouldn't believe how much better I feel, having followed my heart. It's a great weight off my shoulders. Like they say, 'The heart can't be denied.'"

Curtis could hear Kim Somebody-or-other giggling in the background as his brother spouted endorphin-fueled clichés, and his mind echoed with Linda's words — *When you moved out it was like a great weight lifting off my shoulders.* "Uh hmmm. Yeah, well, I'm glad you're so relieved, and I'm not trying to talk you out of it, but as your big brother, I have a few words of caution. First, Mom's blaming me for *your* breakup — you might..."

"Real rational."

"...disabuse her of that notion."

"You'd think I'd left *her.*"

"What did you expect? These things affect a lot of people. Incidentally, I also know how Denise is feeling because I've been through that myself, and it's no picnic, so be kind to her, as much as you can. And *of course* Mom's unhappy, 'cause apparently she and Denise were chummy (you'd know more about that than I would). Anyway, I assume this is the girl you were talking about at Thanksgiving."

"Kim, yeah."

"Does she have a last name?"

"Cantrell. It has a musical ring to it, don't you think?"

"Totally melodious."

"Do you want to talk to her?"

"No, I think not. Ask me again in about six months." *If they're together in six months,* he thought.

When he'd hung up, he microwaved a burrito for dinner and sat down in front of the TV to eat it. The news wasn't appetizing. Nearly 900 Palestinians had been killed in the seventeen days of fighting in Gaza. Israel admitted to accidentally bombing a UN School. A U.S. Government Report pegged jobs lost in December at more than 500,000, bringing the official unemployment rate to 7.2 percent, while economists estimated the actual unemployment rate at 13.5 percent. It was a typical day. It was enough to turn his stomach.

"Some years are different than others," Erickson said, once again addressing the managers. "Some years it's all about return. But the essence of asset management is not return; it's managing risk. We all know that these are risky times, difficult times, the most difficult since The Great Depression, and our clients won't be judging us on how much their portfolios grow, but on how little they shrink. If we can keep them from shrinking more than expected, we'll have done our job, and we'll retain our client base. If we can grow their portfolios in this challenging environment, we'll provide a catalyst for explosive growth in the future — but the first order of business is managing risk."

It seemed to Curtis that Erickson's job description, as President of Bass Erickson, must include 'Rally the Troops,' as he seemed to spend an inordinate amount of time doing just that. On the whole, it wasn't a bad speech, and Curtis supposed it wasn't a bad idea to remind everyone of the risks. He made a mental note to do the same with his Associates. Life was all about risk management, every bit of it.

After the usual exchange of pleasantries regarding the weather as they exited the building in the twilight, Elliot said, "Have you had any luck bringing in...? Who was it you were supposed to bring in?"

"Edgar Smith. It's moving in a positive direction."

Ode to Joy chirped electronically in Curtis's pocket. It was Stephanie, asking if she could come by at 6:30 with Mary Anne Stevenson.

The first thing he did, after switching on the lights, was to take his White Tower down and turn it to the wall (he didn't need any more abuse). He had better paintings and made a note to have a couple framed. He'd changed out of his suit and had eaten a Lean Cuisine Chicken Cacciatore by the time they arrived at 6:43. Stephanie carried an armload of newly framed paintings, Mary Anne a roll of wire and a bag with eye-bolts, stud finder, wire cutter and pliers.

Curtis poured them all a glass of Australian rosé.

Stephanie showed Mary Anne the paintings already hung on the wall and room divider without comment. Mary Anne gave a non-committal nod or tilt of the head at each one, only uttering a barely audible and dismissive "tss" at Sammy's blue dinosaur and Make Love Grow. Stephanie noticed the gap where the white tower had hung and, looking sidelong at Curtis, fought to suppress a smile. Mary Anne cleared her throat and said, "I can't *believe* they want more of *this*," shaking her head for emphasis. "And honestly, Stephanie, I don't know that you're ready for a show, even without all this nonsense. These two are so simple, so artless. What do you think, Mr. Cooke?"

"What do *I* know? I think they're charming."

"In what way?"

"Well, I think Bernier got it right when he said they were childlike, without being childish. I don't know anything about the technical aspects, the things that make art critics salivate; I just know how they make me feel. It's kind of like Asti Spumante, if I can draw an analogy. It's not the most complex wine. In fact, it's nothing serious, but it's impossible not to like it."

"Hmmm." Mary Anne stared at the floor, considering. "That would be the way to present them. Would you like to write the brochure?"

"I'm no writer."

"We'll need a good writer, if we're to convince collectors to take these seriously. I have no doubt we'll sell some of them. But this new work — you might as well illustrate children's books. I just don't understand the appeal, Stephanie. After all of your training and hard work, why would you choose to...to...devolve like this?"

"I'll draw stick figures, if I can sell them," Stephanie said.

"Who would take you seriously?"

"I haven't been taken seriously *before*; why should I expect to be now? I don't much care, as long as someone's willing to pay me to paint. I have a daughter to support."

"Think about your future. Will they really continue to buy these kind of...silly scribbles?"

"It doesn't matter, as long as they're willing to buy them now. It's like my instructor at community college says — 'If somebody has to invent the Pet Rock, it might as well be me.' I'll skip all the way to the bank. That would be a change. So far, I've only felt guilty for painting, guilty for spending money on paint and paper and canvas, guilty for all of the time I've spent. It's been an expensive hobby."

"And when they grow tired of you?"

"Then I'll go on to something else; I'm not going to paint the same thing, or the same way, my whole life."

Mary Anne sighed. "I have my doubts about the direction of this show." She stood silently in front of Make Love Grow, hands on hips, for a full minute. "What the hell, if they're willing to pay, who are we to tell them they're wrong?"

For the next two hours, they set eye-bolts in the walls and stretched two rows of wire across each facing wall, just below and above eye level. Then they hung all thirty-two paintings in chronological order, as best Stephanie could remember, from the still life of the peach to Make Love Grow. "Well," Mary Anne declared, standing back to take in the whole, "no one can say you're lazy."

Most of those attending the Intermediate Class were graduates of Beginning Watercolors. A few had either taken instruction elsewhere, or had taken Stephanie's beginner's class at an earlier time. Two were young women, obviously friends, obviously unmarried, obviously available. Unlike so many female duos, these two were of equal beauty, though they gained far more from the liveliness of their personalities than from mere appearance alone. While Stephanie set up easels at the front of the room the pair turned to talk with a burly young man in his mid-twenties who pulled up a chair just behind them. He wore blue jeans and a black T-shirt. His blonde hair was pulled back in a ponytail, an earring stud gleamed discretely from his left ear, and when he looked around to survey the rest of the class Curtis noticed a silver loop piercing his eyebrow. It was now so commonplace that he could almost look upon these accessories without grimacing in empathetic pain. The young man leaned forward and said something the girls, who listened and giggled as he chatted *sotto voce*. As the class commenced the young man, who answered to Nicholas when the roll was called, showed himself to be the kind of easygoing, gregarious student who focused on the teacher as though this were a one-on-one tutoring session and his classmates were extraneous. Throughout the evening he asked questions and joked with Stephanie, who seemed to respond with a kind of animation and glow that made it obvious he was flirting with her and she was enjoying it. Curtis had never been terribly reserved, but he'd never been so uninhibited either. The comparison left him feeling old and staid.

After class Nicholas swaggered out with the two blondes, pausing at the door long enough to catch Stephanie's attention. He pointed his finger at her and winked. She smiled back.

Curtis lingered to drive her home. She washed her brushes and took out the trash. On their way out she shut off the lights and locked the door to the basement room where the class took place.

Curtis smiled and offered her the crook of his arm. She took it with a small smile of acknowledgment, but it was obvious that she was troubled. "What's on your mind?"

"I think I've bit off more than I can chew — school, working here and at the gallery, trying to get ready for the show. I'm not Superwoman."

"Can I help with anything?"

"No, but thanks for the offer. It's just too much. I've been brainstorming with Gwyn, trying to come up with a marketing project for my class, and even if I come up with a project, I don't have the time to do that and get ready for the show at the same time."

"What kind of project?"

"I think I told you about it — it's the next phase of our Marketing course, where we take a product from conception to production? I really wanted to take the course, but when I signed up I didn't know I'd have a show. I paid good money for tuition and I don't want to lose it."

"What are the parameters?"

"The whole idea is to look for a product that satisfies a need of the end-user, advertise it, and sell it."

They fell silent, each trying to think of a solution to her problem as they turned onto the boulevard. A few minutes later, as he turned off the boulevard, Curtis said, "You remember that painting I said would make a good T-shirt design? T-shirts with logos are a form of advertising. Why not sell a T-shirt that advertises the show?"

Stephanie was about to dismiss the idea until the logic became plain. "I don't know if it's advertising for the show, or the show is advertising for the shirt, but it's perfect — it has an element of advertising, it's timely, it plays to my strengths, it has a strong visual component for instant recognition, it's marketable, and it has a built-in clientele (all of the people who come to the show). Lord, that's a load off my mind! Thank you so much!"

She reached over and squeezed his arm, and when she unbuckled at the apartment, she kissed him on the cheek. He watched her go with a light heart and the satisfaction of doing a good deed.

"He's lost another tooth," Linda told him as he arrived to pick up Sammy Friday night. I might be working late on Sunday, so don't bring him home early."

Sammy flashed him a toothless grin.

"What are you going to do with all that money?" Curtis asked.

Sammy just shrugged.

When the phone rang on their way home, Curtis clicked on his Bluetooth headset. It was Stephanie, calling for sympathy. "Mary Anne is driving me crazy. We have to send out invitations. We have to prepare the space, and find places for the other paintings. There has to be enough room so people don't feel crowded. The lighting has to be just right. The *flow* has to be just right. We have to decide what kind of music to play, and whether or not we want live music or just a CD. We have to have someone cater hors d'oeuvres and serve champagne." Her tone turned conspiratorial as she confided the next tidbit. "She says they're more likely to buy if they've had something to drink. I think that's kind of dishonest, but it's really out of my hands. She's really unhappy with me."

"Why?"

"Because I already sold the paintings to Mr. Smith. She says it's never done. It makes the show more like a private sale or auction. But hey, at least it helps promote my career. I don't know what she's complaining about anyway; she still gets her cut. And if we can attract buyers at the show, I'll have ready buyers for new work and they'll pay more. She seems to think I could have done better if we'd done it all ourselves."

"If she thought so much of your work, she should have organized a show earlier. You've been working for her long enough."

"That's what *I* thought. She could have done it; I would have been happy to do it. But hey, I'm not complaining; I have six thousand dollars in my checking account that I didn't have last month."

"That's something to cheer about."

Saturday afternoon Sammy was taking a nap when Stephanie called after 4:00. "This is totally crazy," she said without preamble. "They want to do the show in three and a half weeks! Smith is going out of town or something. We need lists of people to invite. Can you get me your list A.S.A.P.? Like yesterday. Friends, family, colleagues. Anyone you'd like to invite. We need their addresses and their email addresses, if you have them."

He sat down with a pad and pencil. Who could he invite? His erstwhile neighbors weren't collectors of fine art. They typically had a few posters on the wall, and perhaps a few prints. Any original work of art was likely to have been found at a flea market. They just weren't in the same league as art collectors. His clients, on the other hand, might have the resources and inclination to invest in art. He began to make a list, and in the end he added John Erickson, who could get chummy with his old college roommate and chat up Edgar Smith.

Then he called Stephanie back. "It occurred to me that the people who are likely to come to the show aren't the kind of people who wear T-shirts, but if they might not buy one for themselves, they might buy one for their kids. You ought to have some made up in kid sizes."

"I hadn't thought of that. That's such a good idea. I swear — there are so many details!"

Sunday found Curtis happily surrounded by friends and old neighbors at the Fines', watching the NFC championship game. Elliot and Vicky, Doug Veeder, Chris Samuelson, Paul and Anita Poblador, and Henry Jancee were gathered around the Fines' big-screen TV. Loyalties were split and bets made, but there were no ardent supporters of either team.

Sammy and Sophie and Paul Samuelson spent most of the afternoon under the dining room table, eating cookies and nuts.

Curtis was feeling the soporific effects of beer and bean dip when his phone began playing Ode to Joy. He got up to take the call in the kitchen. Stephanie's name was lit up on the display.

"I take it you're not watching the playoffs?"

"For what?"

"Football."

"Is that today? I don't watch football. I was wondering if I could come over. I have a couple of new paintings."

"Now?"

"If it's ok."

"Actually, I'm not at home. You can come tomorrow."

"It'll have to be after work then; we don't get Martin Luther King Day off. You wouldn't, by any chance, be able to pick me up? I'll be at Bolton's 'til 4:00."

They made arrangements and Curtis went back to the game, mulling over the division of people who enjoyed watching a contest, and those who did not. Like Stephanie, Linda was one of the latter. It wasn't just indifference, it was an aversion — Linda found sports unpleasantly tense and confrontational and viewed the outcome from the perspective of the vanquished rather than the victor.

At the half time report headlines streamed along the bottom of the screen: *Trade Deficit Widens; Congressman caught in sting operation; Israel withdraws from Gaza. Estimated 1,300 Palestinians and 13 Israelis killed in two-week action.*

"Jesus," Samuelson said, "it would be a lot cheaper and lot less bloody if they'd just play a game of chess and give Gaza to the victor. Hell, they could sell tickets."

Curtis wondered if world leaders thought of war as an elaborate game. *Pity the poor pawns*, he thought.

Chapter 23

Monday January 19 — Sunday January 25, 2009

The Markets were closed on Martin Luther King Day and Curtis stayed home with Sammy. The month had thus far been the coldest on record, but this day the temperature soared to 47 degrees. They bundled up and for the first time rode their bikes around the block, feeling warmth on their cheeks in the patches of sun, and bracing cold in the shadows. Sammy, with smaller wheels, peddled furiously, while Curtis followed lazily behind. Like an old-fashioned train, they trailed steamy breaths on a circuit of their neighborhood. They peddled down the sidewalk on Washington Street, squinting into the bright sun, then turned on Jackson Street, passing apartments and duplexes, a laundromat, a sushi bar, a tiny Mexican grocery with a green awning, and a dog-grooming parlor. On Franklin, with the sun on their backs, they passed an old brick Episcopal Church, a used bookstore, and a bicycle shop (of which Curtis made a mental note). From Colfax back to Washington they peddled in the shadow of tall buildings, under leafless trees, beside a black, wrought iron fence topped with imposing downward curling spikes that spanned the entire length of the block. Automobile and bus traffic was heavy on Colfax, and the scent of diesel fumes hung in the air. Then they were back to the friendly confines of Washington Street.

In the afternoon Sammy painted as Curtis read aloud from *The Hobbit*.

They picked up Stephanie at Bolton's, arriving a few minutes early so they could stock up on more tubes of paint, and ended up buying a new set of oil pastels with a wider color palette.

Stephanie came down the stairs from the loft, carrying two paintings wrapped in brown paper. Curtis took them from her as a matter of course — it was what men did.

"And what have you been up to?" Stephanie asked Sammy without preamble.

Sammy proudly announced, "We rided our bikes around the block!"

"My goodness! Open your mouth. When did this happen?" she said, holding his chin and peering at the gap where his upper front teeth had been.

"They fell out."

"I see that. Did the Tooth Fairy reward you?"

"Ten dollars!"

"My word, what are you going to do with all that money?"

"We buyed pastels."

"*Bought* pastels."

"Yep."

"I think your dad chipped in." She turned an amused glance on Curtis. "Shall we?" she said, and led the way out the door.

"Where's Gwyn?" Curtis inquired.

"Mrs. Bossert's. It's a dull way to spend a holiday. I would have traded days with someone, but I had to come in to get these paintings framed anyway. I'm finding it really hard to work and go to school and get ready for this show."

At the apartment she unwrapped a long, narrow package, revealing her version of his aging Smiley Faces that gave Curtis a chuckle. "That's marvelous."

"I'm glad you like it."

"It's really amazing; I don't know how you got those expressions!"

"I had fun with it."

"It shows."

She had added a sixth face. The baby and child faces were bright and happy and innocent. The adolescent face looked hopeful. The young man exuded an air of confidence. The mature man was obviously proud. A middle-aged man wore a harried expression. And the old man, wrinkled and haggard, looked grumpy. They were drawn in pastels, in colors ranging from pink to shades of brown and rust, while the eyes were blue, and the hair turned from light brown, to grey, to white. Like Make Love Grow, it was a very simple idea, almost too simple, yet expertly rendered.

She hung the aging Smiley Faces on the wire at the end of the line. The next picture she carefully unwrapped and held up to Sammy. "I hope you don't mind. I wanted to do a painting like the one you gave to Gwyn." It was another balloon boat, but different from Sammy's. The boat floated against a light blue sky with puffy white clouds and a chevron of ducks. Below the boat in the distance were snow-capped mountains. A green pennant streamed out from the top of the balloon. The passengers were a smiling hippo, an elephant's ass, and a bear dressed in a red Drum Major's uniform. She handed the painting to Curtis and said, "I'll need two or three more in this vein."

Curtis hung the balloon boat and they stood back to take in the whole wall. Stephanie whispered in his ear, "He doesn't know about the show, does he?"

Curtis shook his head. "It's probably best if he doesn't. How about a glass of wine before I take you home?"

"That would be lovely."

He poured two glasses of Pinot Blanc and a glass of apple juice for Sammy. When he handed her a glass, he noticed her brow pinched with worry. "Something bothering you?"

She took a sip, and timidly said, "I have a favor to ask, and I'll understand if you say no, but we have such a short time to get ready, and I was wondering if Mary Anne and I could come over while you're at work."

He opened a kitchen drawer, pulled out an extra key, and dropped it into her hand. "Just remember to lock up when you leave." It was nice to have as friends, people you could trust — people like Irene, and Elliot and Stephanie. It made the sting of Linda's betrayal easier to bear. "Why don't we go pick up Gwyn and take the kids out to eat? Then I have to drop off Sammy; tomorrow is a workday."

"That's a lovely idea," she said brightly, laying her hand on his arm. Then, as if realizing for the first time, she said in wonder, "I won't have to worry about the money."

Curtis felt a momentary thrill at her touch, not so much aroused, as warmed by the developing intimacy of their friendship. "You better take your name tag off."

"Arrgh, I forgot," she said, pursing her lips in a self-deprecatory smile that Curtis found endearing.

Tuesday was inauguration day and as much as Curtis would have liked to watch the proceedings, it was also a workday. It was an historic and surprising day. Who could have predicted that America, xenophobic America, in the midst of two wars, fearing Muslim terrorists almost as much as change, would have elected an intellectual black man with the most astoundingly un-American name of Barack Obama. For all its faults, and they were legion, America never failed to surprise. The stock market, for its part, didn't fail to surprise investors that day either, falling 332 points to welcome in the new president.

All the way home Curtis worried about the direction of the Market and second-guessed his decisions. He let himself into the apartment and was taken aback at the site of Mary Anne and Stephanie gazing at the wall.

Stephanie hurried over. She reached out and squeezed his hand. "Don't let us keep you from anything. Just pretend we're not here. We won't be much longer."

He changed into casual clothes and slippers and went into the kitchen to start dinner. He poured himself a glass of Pinot Blanc, started to put it back in the fridge, and remembered his manners. He poured two more glasses and threw the empty bottle into the recycling bin under the counter.

"Steph?" She looked over at him and he pointed to the glasses on the counter.

He turned on the oven to preheat. He poured a bag of fingerling potatoes into a glass casserole dish, tossed them in olive oil and balsamic vinegar, put the dish in the microwave and pushed the button for 10 minutes. He set a pot to boiling on the stove, and dumped in a package of frozen peas. Then he emptied a box of frozen fish sticks onto a baking sheet, slid it into the oven, and set the timer for fifteen minutes. If they didn't want to join him, he'd have leftovers for tomorrow night.

He carried his glass over to the easy chair and switched on the TV to catch highlights of the inauguration on the news. Stephanie and Mary Anne moved paintings around and stood back to see the effect, wandering into his line of view more often than he'd've liked. Mary Anne made notations on a clipboard. After a few minutes the timer chimed. Curtis got up and took the fish sticks out of the oven. He made up three plates, cut lemon wedges, prepared a small bowl of tartar sauce and carried it all to the table, along with the two glasses of wine they hadn't yet touched. He still had one tall pillar candle left over from Christmas, and this he lit and placed in the middle of the table. He opened a bottle of Kenwood Sauvignon Blanc and poured himself a second glass, then rapped the side of it with a fork, producing a bell-like ring, and called, "Ladies?"

They had a quick meal. He basked in his guests' appreciation and listened to them pour over the minutiae necessary to prepare an art exhibition. Mary Anne had hired Fly on the Wall Public Relations to help spread the word. She complained that the frames were all different and not of the quality she would have liked. "I know you did the best you could, given your means, but we could do so much better, and it's such a mish-mash of styles." But Smith wouldn't authorize the expense of changing frames, so they were stuck with what they had. This, in part, dictated the placement of the paintings. They were ostensibly to be in chronological order, but that was easily fudged, particularly with the older paintings. They were attempting to pace the flow of the show by size, color and style.

After dinner, Curtis insisted on cleaning up while the ladies went back to moving pictures around and discussing the merits of one placement over another. On the way out, Mary Anne shook his hand and thanked him for his hospitality. She passed into the hall. Stephanie said, "Thanks, Curtis," and made to peck him on the cheek. He swiveled around to kiss her lips instead. They were as soft as he remembered. She blushed.

"Good luck," he said, gladdened by the smile on her face as she closed the door.

The rest of this short workweek was hectic and played against expectations, for as soon as he'd adjusted his sights in one direction, the Market whipped in the opposite.

After they'd cleaned up from Wednesday's Intermediate Watercolors class, Stephanie said, "My professor is excited about my project. He suggests we do a poster, too. I've decided to use Make Love Grow. I think it'll appeal especially to kids. The only thing is — I'll need to borrow it for a few days, to scan it. And I need your signature on a release."

"Why my signature?"

"The painting was Sammy's idea, and...."

"You changed it; you made it your own."

"Well, it was his idea originally, and of course the 'Make Love Grow' rainbow is yours."

"By that logic, Gwyn should have a share; she made the Happy Faces. It's a collaboration."

"Whatever. Just humor me and sign the release. It's required for my class project. We'll get the image copyrighted, and the school has an arrangement with the private sector, so we can get it trademarked for next to nothing, and the T-shirts we get at just a little over cost."

"How many are you going have made up?"

"I don't know. I wouldn't think more than fifty or so. I'll have to ask Mary Anne who's on the invitation list. There's your list, my list, the gallery's mailing list. Lee Bernier will have some people on his list, and Mr. Smith. Once we know who's coming to the opening, then we can decide how many to make up. What do you think? How many people would buy a T-shirt? One in ten? I'd rather run out than be stuck with a lot of unsold shirts. They may be cheap, but they're not free."

Thursday night he'd no sooner kicked off his shoes than Mary Anne showed up at his door with a writer. They pretended that Curtis wasn't there and Mary Anne discussed the paintings, while the writer made notes and took photos.

Friday Bernier called at work. He wanted to see how the show was shaping up. "I'd like to bring a couple of people by this evening, if that's not a problem."

"Actually, I have a previous commitment," Curtis demurred (he wanted to take Sammy to the movies).

Not long after he'd hung up on Bernier, Stephanie called and asked if she could come over Saturday evening. "I'm stymied. I don't really know what Smith wants. I need some inspiration from Sammy."

She showed up on Saturday with Gwyn, sketchpads, and an apple pie. They all sat around a table and had some pie. When they were finished Stephanie insisted on washing the dishes. In his easy chair, Curtis bent over his laptop, pouring over stock charts, checking option spreads, and trying to make projections. Gwyn set out her homework on the table.

"You wanna play?" Sammy asked.

"I can't; I have homework."

Sammy marched sullenly around the screen, plopped down on the couch and picked up his Gameboy. A few minutes later Stephanie sat down beside him with a sketchpad.

"Would you like to draw with me?" she asked.

"I'm playin' my Gameboy," he said, not looking up.

"I could use your help. I don't know what to draw next."

Sammy studiously ignored her, his fingers rapidly pressing the buttons as he stared at the tiny screen.

"I really like your ideas. What have you been working on?" Sammy remained silent. "You're not mad at me, are you?" Silence. "Would you like to show me?"

If he hadn't been so frustrated in his work, Curtis might have acted with more discretion. Instead he prodded with annoyance, "Don't be rude, Sammy; answer the friggin' question."

Stephanie raised her eyebrows and held an upturned palm at Curtis to tell him to back off, then said soothingly to Sammy, "What's the last thing you painted?"

After another interval of silence, Curtis piped up again. "Come on, Sammy, don't be a little jerk. You want to lose that Gameboy?"

Stephanie got up, leaned over Curtis's chair and put her face in his. She enunciated slowly and softly, "You're not helping."

"He's being rude."

"He's being a child. Let it go. You can't force cooperation."

Stephanie had obviously never met Linda, Curtis thought.

She sat back down and started drawing a charcoal pencil picture of Sammy bent over his Gameboy. She tore it off and dropped it on the coffee table. "You want me to draw anything? Something for you?"

"Lots o' love flowers," he said, but still he didn't look up from his game.

She sketched an entire field of love flowers, all hearts without the Smiley Faces. "Here you go."

Sammy put the Gameboy aside, plucked the pencil from Stephanie's lap and slid onto his knees in front of the coffee table. There he laid the picture flat and filled in five hearts with the red pencil before losing interest. "This is for you," he said, handing it back to Stephanie. He gave her a hug and went back to his Gameboy.

Another source of inspiration presented itself when she went to the kitchen for a glass of water. A jack-o-lantern Sammy had drawn for school was stuck to the refrigerator with a magnet. It was a non-traditional jack-o-lantern, and it set her to thinking of the possibilities.

Linda opened the door before they were halfway up the walk. Sammy ran ahead to give her a hug. Curtis started to turn back to the car, when he remembered her reproaching him about his lack of communication. "Actually, I would like to talk to you about something. Are you....could you take Sammy on the seventh? It's a Saturday. Just during the day. I can pick him up in the evening."

"The seventh? I'll have to see. What's going on, on the seventh?"

"I'm helping with an art show. One of my clients is an art collector."

"No kidding? That's a change."

"It should be over by...I don't know, five or six, I expect."

"I'll have to see what houses we're showing. But I can always get someone to cover for me. See? This is what was lacking before — you never asked ahead of time. But I can always be accommodating if I have enough time to make arrangements." He turned back toward the car. "Would you like to come in?" she called after him.

The answer came to him in a millisecond, more a feeling than a reasoned argument. There was no point. They might have a few moments of civil conversation, but it wouldn't mean anything. They weren't getting back together; he realized that now. Even if she were to suddenly welcome him back with open arms, he'd never be sure she wouldn't reject him the following week. There was no going back, no pretending everything was the same. She was a loose stepping-stone, a house on a weak foundation. He raised a hand in farewell and turned away.

Chapter 24
The last week of January 2009

M onday the Market offered no definitive direction, but hinted at a possible recovery. Mid-morning Elliot peeked around the door. "You hear what happened Friday after we left?" Curtis looked up and shook his head. "There was a big blow-up. They fired Davidson and one of his Associates. King, I think. The kid lost a ton in Forex and Davidson was in the dark."

"Fuck," Curtis muttered, stunned at the news. It was bad news for the firm, and would put more pressure on the rest of them to perform, and to keep closer tabs on subordinates. As soon as Elliot left, Curtis called a meeting with his own cubicle rats. He needed to monitor their trades more closely.

Stephanie and Gwyn showed up without notice a few minutes before 8 o'clock on Monday night. "I forgot — I have to sign all of the paintings."

Gwyn sat at the kitchen counter, puzzling over math problems. Curtis tried to concentrate on stock charts, until he was so confused that he put his laptop aside and picked up his Hornblower book. Stephanie took down one painting after another and carefully signed her name in the corner, a time-consuming process. Curtis lost himself in the pages of the novel, and at one point he became aware of music. Stephanie had put on a CD of J.S. Bach. It seemed to fit the prose. His imagination took him away and he found himself in a world that was, if not less precarious, at least bounded by a sure sense of order and allegiance. In time he noticed that Stephanie was no longer taking paintings down from the wall, and in fact, had hung them all up. She sat on the end of the couch, staring up at her work.

"You're looking awfully pensive," he said; "anything wrong?"

"No, nothing wrong. I was just thinking." In another moment she contradicted herself. "That's not true. I can't put my signature to Sammy's paintings. The blue dinosaur and the beach scene are all his, and the 'studies'; I didn't add a thing. I wasn't worried about it before, because I never said those were mine. They never asked. But if I sign them, it really would be fraud. I'm not comfortable with that."

"Why not just 'forget' to sign those two. I doubt anyone will notice in the midst of the whole show, and I'm going to buy them back anyway, so it's not going to be fraud."

"That makes me feel better."

She looked so forlorn that Curtis laid down his laptop, sat next to her and hugged her shoulder. "Don't worry; it'll all work out."

She smiled appreciatively. "I've always dreamed of having a show, and now that I'm going to have one, it doesn't feel like I thought it would feel. You have this vision of how it should be, but the reality is different."

"Is it better or worse?"

"It's just different. Reality is so much more complicated. There are all these details that have to be worked out, the logistics, the placement, all the business end of it that I never contemplated in my dreams. I've daydreamed about this since high school, but it was always so easy — you know the dream, it's common enough — you're discovered and appreciated, and that validation allows you to keep on doing what you love to do and give up your day job. I suppose I'm getting ahead of myself though, because having a show doesn't mean it'll be successful."

"Well, you've sold a lot of paintings, and that's a big accomplishment, even if you never did anything else. It's more than a lot of artists can say."

"But I just don't *feel* the way I *thought* I'd feel. I thought I'd feel liberated, exhilarated. I know it's stupid; I should be happy, but I'm so worried about the details all I feel is dread."

"Well, there's one consolation: One way or the other, it will all be behind you in a couple of weeks. Anyway, there's no point in speculating on how it will go — things usually have a way of turning out differently than we expect."

"That's not reassuring."

"It's like the old song says — *Que sera sera*, 'whatever will be will be.' Just hold on tight and hope for a good ride."

"How 'bout you pour me a glass of wine."

As he poured her glass he understood, for the first time, that this was a special woman, a woman with big dreams. She wasn't just a clerk in a store; she was an artist, whereas he was exactly who he seemed to be, nothing more, nothing less. If he could be defined by his dreams, he was an unimaginative creature, for he had never aspired to greatness. Being a realist instead of a dreamer, he simply wanted to find a role and accept his responsibilities as a cog in the great wheel of society, to strive to be competent and respected, to buy a home and provide for his family. Anything more was just icing on the cake. It was, in many respects, the American Dream that informed so many politicians' speeches. In Stephanie he saw something more — she had that spark of creativity coupled with talent, that he so sorely lacked. Even his recent attempts at painting had been paltry and prosaic. He'd tried. He'd learned a few techniques, had become somewhat competent by virtue of diligent application, but he was uninspired. He was, he realized, relegated to the role of critic, rather than artist, one who appreciates rather than creates. He admired her all the more for the humility with which she pursued her vision. Linda, despite her outward beauty, was nothing in comparison. Like him, Linda was a mere bystander.

In bringing them both to mind in the same context, Linda came off the poorer for it. For all her regal bearing and haughty good looks, she'd never really seemed comfortable in her own skin; she seemed always to be on the defensive. Whereas Stephanie was effortlessly comfortable with who she was, and was so humble that she didn't even realize how special she truly was. It was a revelation to him that character could trump physical beauty, that character could infuse a person with a transcendent beauty that far surpassed the physical.

As the week progressed the Market eked out small gains and seemed poised to regain lost ground. Curtis remained cautiously optimistic.

Wednesday night Stephanie taught her class in Intermediate Watercolors. "Last week we worked on shading. Did everyone do their homework?" Curtis cringed at the back of the room. Their assignment had been to paint an apple with appropriate shading to give a three-dimensional look. He'd put it off so long that he'd put it entirely out of his mind. "This week I want to start with a simple technique for delineating background layers with masking tape. Then we'll work on texture. One of the hardest things for the novice to learn is to use the white of the paper (or canvas) like a pigment. You'll learn how to lay down a wash to show shadow, then use a dry brush like a sponge to take away color and create a dappled look, like sunlight coming through trees." The time sped by for Curtis as he followed her lead. He could mimic her directions well enough; the hard part was remembering which of the many techniques to use when he approached a painting on his own.

At the conclusion of the class she announced that she'd be having a one-woman show at The Stevenson Gallery on the weekend of February seventh and eighth, and invited the class to attend.

When the last student had left, Stephanie turned a beaming face on Curtis. "I have a surprise for you," she said, spreading a T-shirt out on the front table. "This is the prototype. What do you think?" Stephanie's painting of Make Love Grow had been stenciled on the chest.

"Sammy will love this." Curtis held it up to get a better look. Small print in the bottom corner showed both a copyright 2009 symbol, and a trademark symbol next to Love Flowers Inc. "You're a corporation now?"

"No, actually, *we're* a corporation now, if you'll just sign this form." She placed a paper and a pen on the table.

"What's this about?"

"It's part of my class. We had to decide how to structure our businesses. Our instructor says incorporation is the safest way to own a business, and there are some tax benefits too, I think. I'm not sure."

"Why me? Why not just incorporate yourself?"

"It's just for the class. The love flower thing was Sammy's idea, so I thought you ought to be part of it, in case it made any money, which it won't — I mean, we're only making a hundred shirts. I wouldn't've made up *that* many, but it's the smallest run they'll do. I figure, if we can sell 25 for $10 apiece, I'll break even."

Curtis signed the paper and looked at the shirt again. "You trademarked it?"

"Not really, not yet; we're working on it. My teacher matched me up with a business mentor, a retired executive, and we're working with a lawyer who's volunteered to help students through the process free of charge (except for the government fee)."

"That's magnanimous."

"It's also good business. Any work he does for us after the class is over is billable. Who's going to bother looking for another lawyer?"

"Love Flowers Inc. Sammy will get a kick out of that."

She handed him a long cardboard tube. "The poster."

He took it out and unrolled it on the table. In blood-red letters under the flowers and sun, were the words:

STEPHANIE WALZER

An artist's evolution

Paintings 1997 - 2008

THE STEVENSON GALLERY

"Can you have it mounted on foam core for me?"

"It'll cost about $40."

"That's fine."

"I'm sure Mr. Bolton will be happy for the business."

"Let's get you home."

"I'm getting so nervous."

Sometimes the ducks and rabbits don't even look like ducks and rabbits.

In the hours before giving his report to Erickson, Curtis sat mesmerized by streaming charts. On four flat panel monitors he watched various stocks and indices as prices plummeted, found support at previous levels of demand, rose, fell back to test support, and fell with breathtaking speed, as though a trap door had been sprung. Each chart was a blueprint of trader psychology, a map of supply and demand, and they tended to follow repeating patterns. As a window into the past, they were easy to interpret. As a crystal ball to the future, they only provided hints, for on any given day the release of data, news, or rumor could move the stocks up or down. Retrospective analysis made it seem easy. It was anything but.

Erickson paced his office like a cat in a cage, hands in pockets, stopping to gaze out the window, crossing back to his desk, looking at the floor and glancing up now and then at Curtis, who stood by the door. "What's going on? How is Dayton's portfolio holding up? We've got to keep him happy; he's the key to Smith."

Curtis explained his strategy and his take on the direction the Market was moving.

"And Smith's art show? How is it coming along? Is everything in place? Do you know anything about it?"

Curtis had ceased to think of the show as Smith's. Despite the show's inception, it was Stephanie's show; whether Smith won or lost his silly bet seemed of secondary importance. "You got my invitation?" Curtis asked, wondering if it had been lost in Erickson's spam filter. Email wasn't always reliable.

"I got it. I'll be there. I *have* to be there. It'll be our best opportunity to reel him in. Who else have you invited?"

"They're all CCed in the email."

"McMillan?"

"And Brewster, Newman, the guys at Wallenby, all of the locals."

"Has Smith given any indication...?"

Erickson left the question unasked, but the implication was plain enough, and Curtis answered, "Not yet."

"Is he toying with us?"

Curtis gave his reply with a shrug.

Dawn on Saturday, the last day of January, revealed high mare's tails and a cold wind shaking naked branches as it swept down Washington Street. At least he presumed it was cold, though standing at the window, with warm air from the floor vent blowing up his robe and a hot mug of coffee cupped in his hands, he might have been in the tropics. The clouds, (wisps of ice crystals, he remembered reading) were exceedingly high, as evidenced by a lower contrail streaming out behind a tiny passenger jet. Since jets generally cruised at about 32,000 feet, he reasoned that the clouds were seven or eight miles high.

His phone, charging on the kitchen counter, began playing its electronic aberration of Beethoven's Ode to Joy. Curtis crossed the room, glancing at Sammy who lay undisturbed on the sofa bed.

"Good morning," Stephanie said cheerily. "Is it all right if I come over this morning? I have the last of the paintings to bring over."

"Do you need a ride?"

"Mary Anne's driving. We can be over around 10:00."

"I thought you were at Bolton's on Saturdays."

"I had to ask for time off. I couldn't get ready for the show and do my school work, and.... It was all too much. Some things you just can't delegate."

Curtis and Sammy were dressed and the sofa bed turned back into a sofa, when Stephanie and Mary Anne arrived, as advertised, at precisely 10:00, bearing between them three paintings swathed in bubble wrap.

"I think this is what Smith and Bernier were after," Stephanie said. "I hope it is. It seems ridiculous I can produce these so quickly and get paid for it. Still, you know — whatever pays the bills," she sighed. "But I'm starting to see what they like in them. Sammy, give me your opinion. Which do you like best?"

All three were landscapes, about 3 X 4 feet, plus matting and frames. Their large size and the quality of the frames imbued them with added significance. The first was a watercolor of a whole field of love flowers as Sammy had first drawn them without the Smiley Faces. Above the field a cursive scrawl in brown paint spelled out "Cultivate it." The next was another field of love flowers, drawn in charcoal, with the exception of one (offset a few inches from the center) in color that seemed to glow in the midst of the gloom. The last was a mixed media (watercolor and pastel) of a field of seven jack-o-lanterns. Their exteriors were muted in a kind of twilight murkiness, while their interiors glowed with candlelight. Three in the foreground partially obscured the other four, whose visages only hinted at their expressions. Of the three in the foreground, the round one on the left was the most traditional, grinning happily with triangular eyes and nose. The middle one, slightly misshapen, leered with arched eyebrow and a cruel mouth. The last, tall and squeezed about the middle, was reminiscent of Edvard Munch's The Scream, evincing utter terror.

"I like that one," Sammy said, poking his finger at the jack-o-lanterns. "It's scary."

They hung the new paintings and stood back to view both walls, turning first one way, then the other, trying to get a sense of how patrons of the show might react. It was an impressive display of work.

"Oh, this transition just doesn't work," Mary Anne said with exasperation. "Just look!"

Curtis could plainly see her objection. The transition of subject matter was abrupt. The early work was rather conventional and competent, growing by degree in confidence and gaining an intuitive sense of design. Her later work added a human element. Gwyn in the gazebo, for example, was an accomplished and beautifully rendered subject, in which the human element (Gwyn's expression of languorous boredom) transformed one's appreciation of the whole. This transitioned somewhat jarringly to Curtis's more primitive depiction of the gazebo and pond, with elements that she'd added. Next was Sammy's beach scene, followed by Curtis's rather dark painting of apartment buildings that she'd finished in her own way, meticulously adding some elements, while purposefully leaving some of the buildings unfinished (a change of mood and style). Then, as though she'd turned into a forgotten alley, came Sammy's blue dinosaur, Make Love Grow, Aging Smiley Faces, Stephanie's balloon boat, the fields of love flowers and the jack-o-lanterns. On the surface, these latter paintings presented a charming lack of sophistication, a child's joyous view of the world. Yet there was an adult cynicism beneath the Aging Smiley Faces, a bleakness about the field of charcoal love flowers (with its one colored flower standing in brave contrast to the rest), and sheer terror in the visage of that one jack-o-lantern, hinting at dark undercurrents in otherwise innocent paintings. On the other hand, Make Love Grow, Cultivate It, and The Balloon Boat were all expressions of joyful imagination. And The Blue Dinosaur, Curtis noted with pride and astonishment, stood up well in this context.

"All the major food groups are represented," Roddy Flynn pointed out: "Beer, wine, vegetables, protein and starch." The coffee table in front of the Flynn's couch was covered with a plethora of food — platters of sushi, cut vegetables with a ranch dressing dip, Maui chips, tortilla chips, salsa, a cheese plate, deep-fried chicken tenders, stuffed olives, jalapeño poppers and Vienna sausages.

"I had no idea how much food prices had gone up," Roddy said. "Jesus, this stuff is expensive."

"It's the cost of transportation," Elliot said. "Every time gas goes up, so goes the cost of food."

The entire neighborhood, plus friends from Roddy's work, had gathered at the Flynn's house to watch Superbowl XLIII between the Steelers and the Cardinals. The children were scattered around the house, and in the empty garage where Gary and Charlene Flynn had their playhouse.

Curtis was ensconced on the couch between Vicky and Paul Poblador. Three minutes into the first quarter he was on his second glass of cheap Pinot Grigio and he was feeling a tingling of the scalp and a softness of the shoulders. Inebriation could be a pleasant thing, if not taken to extremes. The problem was: he was tempted to keep doing what had brought him to this state in the first place, and in so doing push himself into a sluggish torpor. The problem with all such addictions, from chocolate to cocaine, was that they invited excess.

The neighbors chatted amiably, drank, and grazed the snack table and commented on the Doritos and Budweiser commercials, giving half an eye to the game, only to erupt in boisterous shouts and hooting whenever a particularly exciting play was made. Curtis found football far more satisfying on television than in person. TV had the advantage of multiple slow-motion replays to fill in the time between plays and show what everyone had missed seeing in real-time, and during the commercials you could eat or go to the bathroom, or (it had been known to happen) watch the commercials, which were occasionally entertaining.

"Why didn't you bring your artist friend?" Vicky asked. "What's her name?"

"Stephanie. She doesn't like football. And anyway, I'm not sure if it's that kind of relationship."

"What kind of relationship is it?"

Curtis took a moment to answer. It wasn't really a question he'd tried to put into words; it was more a feeling. "It's comfortable," he said.

"Comfortable?"

"She's just a friend."

"Can't you invite a friend to a party?"

"She's a girl."

"I'm a girl. What difference does that make?"

She smiled, enjoying teasing him, but her question opened up a whole line of reasoning. Could a man and a woman ever really be just friends? The answer, he thought, was yes, but with qualifications. Vicky was his friend, as were the wives of his other male friends, but they were all married. They were "off-limits." Nonetheless, there was a level of his consciousness that continually assessed women, all women, on a physical level (without a shred of guilt — he was sure this was a deeply ingrained reproductive strategy). He gravitated toward those who were the most healthy, vibrant and full of life (some might say sexy). It was only natural. He didn't spend his time in prurient daydreams (it would be too frustrating), but on a subconscious level, he was always dividing women into two broad categories — desirable and undesirable. There were any number of reasons why a woman could fall into the undesirable category: too young, too old, unattractive, unhealthy, untrustworthy, needy, dangerous or creepy, those who were related, those who would complicate other valued relationships. Stephanie did not fall into any of these categories. She didn't have Linda's classical beauty, but she was real and full of life and, remembering the softness of her lips when he'd stolen a kiss, she definitely fell into the kissable category. But did he want to go that direction?

"It might complicate things," he said. The fact was that between unmarried adults of the opposite sex there were expectations and unspoken possibilities. There was no point in encouraging those expectations if there was no possibility of developing physical intimacy. Inviting her to meet his friends, to take part in his broader life, might infer he wanted a more intimate relationship, and he wasn't sure he wanted that extra complication. After his floundering attempts with Gretchen and Rhiannon, he'd sworn off his pursuit of women and for now he was happy to just 'hang out' with her. She was easy to be with and he didn't want to lose her friendship. He sipped his wine, wondering if he'd be happier sitting here next to Stephanie, rather than Vicky.

"You got that right," Paul Poblador interjected with a wave of his beer bottle. He'd been eavesdropping and gave his advice. "You can't be a buddy to a skirt. Sooner or later you're going to want to get under it."

Curtis turned back to Vicky. "Besides, she's too busy; she's got her first art show next weekend, and too much to do."

The Flynns' Bichon jumped into Curtis's lap and curled up contentedly. Curtis massaged the dog's shoulders. It was like having a soft blanket in his lap.

Roethlisberger connected with Santonio Holmes for a 36-yard gain and Steeler supporters crowed lustily. "In your face, Cardinals!" shouted the usually decorous Annette Jancee.

It was a close contest with the Steelers edging the Cardinals by four points. When it was over and the victors were spraying each other with cheap sparkling wine, the neighbors began to disperse. Curtis followed Doug Veeder to Elliot's to play a couple games of chess and have a cup of coffee. Then he drove home and mentally prepared for another uncertain week at Bass Erickson.

Chapter 25

Monday February 2 — Saturday February 7, 2009

T he week leading up to the show, Curtis was nervous. He wanted to get Smith to commit. He'd been roped into this business against his will (well, to be honest, he'd been weak enough to allow himself to be manipulated). He'd done his part and now he wanted Smith to come through on his end. On Monday morning he called several times without success. Feeling Caller ID was working against him, he called Mary Anne Stevenson and asked her to forward the message to have Smith call him. A few minutes later he received a terse email from Mary Anne: "Done." Still Smith did not call.

Stephanie called at noon to inform him that they'd be taking the paintings to the studio. "I didn't want you to get home and think you'd been robbed," she said. Curtis imagined that scene and appreciated her forethought, and yet he'd forgotten all about it by the time he got back to the apartment. He flicked on the lights and stopped short in alarm, and it was a long moment before he remembered the call and exhaled with relief.

The walls and the room-dividing screen were barren of all paintings but his white tower, the collage, his Madison Street Bridge, snowy field, and Sammy's buildings on the edge of the park (which had never been finished). In the weeks her paintings had hung there, he hadn't really realized how much color and life they'd added to his little apartment. Each frame had been like a window to another world. Now their absence sucked the warmth out of the room. In their place strands of taut wire stretched across the bare white walls, calling attention to what was missing. His sense of home was diminished.

He put a Chris Botti album on the stereo, ate some pasta with jarred marinara, and made a pot of tea. Then he set up his paints and paper on the gate-leg table, and for the rest of the evening he finished his homework for Intermediate Watercolors. The idea was to practice techniques learned the previous week, and to try to get the students to think in terms of layers. The assignment had been to paint a wooded snow scene, as seen through a window. It had taken four washes to accomplish, allowing the paper to dry out between each wash.

He was adding the finishing touches to the window frame (he'd chosen a mullioned window), when Botti's mellow trumpet blended with the wail of a siren as an ambulance passed down Colfax. Curtis remembered that Linda always cringed at the sound of sirens. She imagined mangled, bloody bodies writhing in agony, while he imagined people rushing to rescue someone in distress. Life was all about perspective and expectations. It comforted him to know that there were institutions in society that would help in the event of catastrophe. Had he heard the same sound at work, he may have had a different reaction, but painting, like exercise, calmed his mind. Painting was therapeutic.

Meanwhile that week, traders seemed to lack the commitment to push the Market in either direction. It left Curtis emotionally wrung out with nothing to show for it.

When he'd settled into his seat in the basement of Bolton's on Wednesday, Stephanie asked everyone to hand their paintings to the front of the room. While they were being gathered, she announced that this was the last class for Intermediate Watercolors, and asked who was going on to Advanced Watercolors.

Curtis was among the four who raised their hands. He didn't fool himself about his lack of talent, and that was okay. He'd come to realize that as he became more proficient, what he lacked in imagination he made up for with technique. The subject matter might still be prosaic, but his efforts were rendered more artistic. Then, too, he didn't want to disappoint Stephanie. She and Irene Niece were his only friends outside of the old neighborhood, and he did not want to lose their support.

"The Advanced class starts the first week of March," she went on. "We'll be learning more about texturing and shadow, and there'll be one Saturday field trip, depending on the weather."

Stephanie stood the homework along the tray at the bottom of the chalkboard, and discussed them one by one. Curtis could see his was a clumsy effort, but far from the worst.

At the end of class, she thanked her students for their participation, and reminded them of the show at The Stevenson Gallery the following Saturday and Sunday. As she locked the door Curtis asked if they had hung the paintings in the gallery yet.

"We've put up three or four at a time, just to see how they'll look. We can't disrupt the day-to-day running of the gallery. We're doing the entire installation tomorrow and Friday. I'm so nervous thinking about it. There are so many things that can go wrong. Incidentally, your mounted poster is upstairs. I had a few more mounted on foam core, and one framed, so we can sell them at the show."

"It'll be good to have something to hang on my walls. They look awfully naked. Do you know how many people are coming?"

"Not everyone has RSVPed, but we expect forty or so. Mary Anne's hoping for more, but I have my doubts."

"Is there anything I can do? I feel kind of responsible, since I got you into this mess."

"Gerald's out of town — You can help us set up Saturday morning. We're opening the doors at 11:30 and the invitations are for 2:00 to 5:00, when the silent auction is being held. We'll be there by 9:00 to set up."

"I could pick you up."

"Could you? That would be wonderful; I can use the extra sleep."

"You had your hair cut, didn't you?"

"You're the first to notice. They didn't take off much."

"It looks good," he honestly observed. It was subtly layered and made her look both younger and slimmer. He patted himself on the back for noticing.

"Is everything on for tomorrow?" Erickson asked. "No last-minute glitches?"

"Everything is on schedule."

"And Dayton's portfolio? Can I tell him everything is hunky dory?"

"Well, it was better last week. We took a hit this week."

"What the hell!" Erickson declared with disappointment. "The DOW was up 277 points this week! So tell me: Why is he getting screwed?"

"He's not getting screwed. He's ahead since the beginning of the year, just down for the week."

"He's up since we talked with him last?"

"Yup, I think."

"All right then. You keep a close eye on that; he's the key to Smith. What's the timing of this event?"

"It kicks off at 2 PM."

"Two. Okay. Any idea when Smith will show up?"

"None."

"Well shit, I don't want to waste my whole day. I'll show up around 2:30. Are these paintings expensive?"

"No, they're dirt cheap."

"Are they worth anything?"

There were so many ways to answer that question. "Well, they're good, but she's not a well-known artist."

"And what's this bet about? Fill me in."

Curtis gave him the background.

"So let me get this straight," Erickson said. "Is getting his business predicated on his winning the bet?"

"I wouldn't say that. He said if we wanted his business I had to play along and sell him my paintings, and the inference was that I also had to get the artist to agree to a show. All of which I've done. But whether that's enough to lure him in, I couldn't say."

"He'll obviously be happier if he wins his bet. And what is that again?"

"He has to make 200% profit, over and above his cost."

"What's that mean exactly? Three hundred back for every hundred invested?"

"That's how I'd interpret it."

"Good return. How much are these things going for?"

"I don't know for sure. He bought most of them for 200 apiece. The plan was to peg the minimum price at 600, but I'm sure some will go for more. And half the pieces are being put on silent auction — so who knows what they'll go for?"

"Silent auction? That solves everything. All we have to do is bid the price up! He'll win his bet and we'll get his business. We'll hang them around the office and write them off as a business expense. They may even be a good investment. Sweet, sweet, sweet. Okay then, I'll see you tomorrow." Erickson looked like the kid who had just won all the marbles.

After enduring two and a half hours of her mother's restless turning, Gwyn sat up, sighed with exasperation and said, "You should get up. Have a glass of alcohol, or take some sleeping pills. I'm sorry, but you're driving me crazy. I can't sleep with you turning over every two minutes." Stephanie dutifully got out of bed and went to the kitchen, where she poured herself a generous glass of cheap Chardonnay. She couldn't stop thinking about how the next day would unfold. Her entire future as an artist might hinge on the next 48 hours.

She'd daydreamed about this day since she was thirteen. She'd worked toward it through art lessons, classes at community college and incessant practice. She painted until it became an obsession. She painted not because she was compensated for her work, but because she felt compelled to make sense of her world by recording her impressions in the only way she knew — painting had become as elemental to her as breathing. She'd spent years of her time and thousands of dollars on painting supplies. She'd been working for money on the periphery of the art business clerking at Bolton's, teaching what she knew, and using what she knew to help at The Stevenson Gallery. She'd gained in expertise month by month by year. The payoff was about to come in.

She could be forgiven if she let her hopes and dreams take wing, for they had long been repressed. In one moment she dreamed of all that might be, of validation, admiration, even significance, and in the next she tempered her exhilaration with a dose of sober reality, reminding herself that this was, after all, an insignificant show that would be viewed by a few dozen art collectors at best. Her work might be dismissed as unoriginal, second rate, even sophomoric. Yet who could fault her for wishing? If everything went as well as she hoped, she would no longer be one of those on the periphery looking in; she'd be in the center looking out. Her work would be seriously considered. She'd find her paintings appearing in museums alongside her idols. Oh, she knew these were only fanciful daydreams, of course she did. She knew this was only a minor debut, not something that would likely cause much of a stir, except.... Except for the fact that Bernier and Smith were both intimately involved, and they were people who knew people; they were people with connections. A small word of encouragement from them could have a profound effect on her future. Certainly, she knew that even if the show went well, she might still have years of struggle ahead of her. At the same time, she knew that if she was lucky enough to attract just a small following, she really might be able to quit her day jobs and devote herself entirely to her art (and to Gwyn, of course).

Yet one thing still bothered her. Sure, Bernier had praised her work (albeit with reservations), and Smith had bought her paintings (for an undoubted bargain). But the truth was they were as impressed by six-year-old Sammy's concepts. And even that missed the point. Sammy was, if not a prodigy, at least a very gifted little boy who should be encouraged, and whose best work, as exemplified in his Del Mar beach scene, was worthy of praise. But what most impressed the Critic and the Collector were Sammy's simple doodles, his 'love flowers.'

She really didn't know what her critics were looking for, nor did she know if she was comfortable taking the direction they seemed to want her to take. She'd never before painted for an audience, had never painted to please a critic. Could she be content to paint like a six-year-old, if that's what the critics wanted? At what point did the tail wag the dog? Smith's patronage had padded her savings account, but his goodwill could dry up in a minute. This show might be her only chance to make her mark, to earn the notice of other collectors. And that notice was what made the difference between the thousands of artists whose work filled galleries around the country, and the select few whose work was discussed, hung in museums and added to collections.

She wasn't foolish enough to think success in her field would bring fame, nor did she aspire to those heights. She simply wanted to be taken seriously, that she might pursue her craft (her art) full-time, and be able to pay the bills. It would be enough if she could command a couple thousand dollars per painting. Particularly if she was painting such nonsense as Make Love Grow, which she could turn out in days instead of weeks. They were, she knew, inconsequential paintings, but they were rather fun to do, or more accurately, they were fun to conceive — the ideas were more important than the execution, and they did strike a chord in some people (Smith, for instance). To be honest, Sammy's original had struck her that way, which was why she'd felt compelled to imitate him. "Imitation is the sincerest form of flattery," as the saying goes. And why fight it? She could paint in more than one style. She could be one of those painters who made a living selling calendars of their work. Someone like Linda Nelson Stocks, whose original paintings sold for upwards of $15,000, while her limited edition Giclée prints of the same sold for $350, and her calendars sold in the tens of thousands for $15 apiece. That was the way to market yourself. But it still took a show or a patron to get the art buying public to take notice in the first place. And that was what she was trying to achieve this coming weekend.

Having come to terms with her imagined future, with a better sense of how she could market herself, she put down her glass of wine and went back to bed with a calmer mind.

She awoke with a start a few minutes after six, suddenly aware that she didn't know what to wear. How should she present herself? What would potential buyers expect an artist to look like? On one level it seemed ridiculous, but it was a subtle and complex issue. Everyone, regardless of their protestations, was informed by subconscious prejudices. Working at the gallery she'd met many semi-successful artists, and she knew by experience that she had different expectations and made different judgments depending on her immediate impression of the artist, rather than the art. There was one young artist, much impressed with herself, who dressed all in black with strategically scissored cuts and spikey hair. Stephanie actually liked some of her work, but the artist was so pretentious that it was hard to take her work seriously. Another rather frumpy woman was nearly eighty, and had been painting farm landscapes for more than forty years. While she was a competent painter, her lack of energy and enthusiasm was mirrored by her stultified paintings, which had a following but had not increased in value in a decade.

Gwyn woke to the click and screech of hangers being slid along the bar as her mother looked for something to wear. Should she wear pants, a skirt or dress? Should she dress flamboyantly or conservatively? Should she dress in subdued colors, or bright colors? She tried on the dress she'd worn for Christmas and decided it was too formal. She tried on a skirt and blouse combo and thought it made her look too much like a clerk. Unable to sleep through the commotion, Gwyn sighed and raised herself up on her elbow.

"What do you think?" Stephanie said, holding up a bright paisley blouse and a navy blue dress with white polka-dots.

"What does it matter?"

"It's important how potential buyers see me. I want to look like an artist."

"You can't *not* look like an artist; you *are* an artist. So anything you wear is what an artist wears."

"Granted. But what would a *successful* artist wear?"

"Well, you don't want to look too fancy or weird."

In the end she opted for a calf-length brown skirt; knee length boots with inch-high heels; a white, long-sleeved, scoop-necked blouse, bright red dangling earrings; and a beige corduroy jacket. She thought it made her look comfortable and mature. Some artists had a reputation for being eccentric, but she wouldn't be one of them. Still, looking at herself in the mirror over the dresser, she did think she was a bit boring, and on the way out the door she grabbed a crushable gold velvet hat that she'd bought at a street fair.

Unable to find a parking spot, Curtis double-parked and called Stephanie's cell phone. He was preoccupied with possible scenarios for engaging Smith in conversation and coaxing him to commit a portion of his investment portfolio to Bass Erickson. So he was surprised to see Gwyn follow her mother down the steps, and he was equally as surprised at how pretty Stephanie looked. He wondered if she'd lost weight or something — there was a glow about her. She got in the front seat. Gwyn got in the back.

"Love the hat," he said.

She smiled knowingly as she buckled her seatbelt.

He noticed she had applied subtle make-up, a bit of blush and a touch of lip gloss.

Pointing with his thumb to the back seat, he mouthed *Does she know?* Meaning did she know about the subterfuge surrounding Sammy's paintings.

"Oh, I told her. She understands."

"I don't approve, but I understand," Gwyn spoke up from the backseat.

"Gwyneth," Stephanie said sternly.

"I know, 'do as I say, not as I do.'"

"Oh god, spare me the lecture."

"I'm zipping my lips."

Stephanie smiled at the amused glance Curtis turned her way. As they accelerated down the street toward their individual and collective destinies (those anticipated ducks and rabbits about to cross their paths), Stephanie let the nervous thoughts of the coming day slip away.

They drove on, lost in their own thoughts. It was only when they were sitting at the second light that Curtis noticed the silence. It was possible to sit in comfortable silence with this woman. With Linda, silence was a dire warning of the coming storm; there was always a subtext to any conversation or silence. With Stephanie there was no subtext; what you saw was what you got. It was a relief.

Stephanie was thinking about Curtis. It had been such a generous gesture to offer to drive her to the gallery this morning. Every time they passed a bus, she was glad she wasn't aboard. She was used to public transportation, but she didn't like it; the buses in the city were crowded and smelly and the windows and backs of the seats were scratched with graffiti. They were also filled with enough unpleasant characters to make each journey an adventure, and not in the best sense of the term. Curtis made her feel safe, and she wondered if there might be more than friendship in the offing. He wasn't the most exciting man she'd ever known, but he was smart and reliable, and he seemed genuinely nice in a world that was so full of selfish, egotistical jerks.

Her last real relationship was almost two years in the past. He'd been a Scotsman with a strong brogue and a knack for saying the wrong thing at the wrong time. She could pinpoint the exact moment he'd fallen out of her favor: As they were making love he'd said, "Lord, lass, I'm as happy as a pig in a wallow," as he pushed deeper into her. She couldn't get it out of her mind that she was the wallow, and she came to view him as the pig. It had never been the same after that.

The Stevenson Gallery, on 2nd between Hilgert and Kinsman, occupied the bottom floor of a three-story building, with office space on the upper two floors. It was in a block of galleries, high-end clothing and shoe stores, a deli, a theatre, and a Vietnamese restaurant. They parked in the parking garage in the next block and walked back, arriving shortly after 9:00.

It was the first time Curtis had ever seen the inside of the gallery, though he'd passed it many times. The door was offset to the right side of the storefront, next to a large picture window that let in light and allowed passers by to view the merchandise. In the center of the window there now hung the framed poster of Make Love Grow. Stephanie rummaged in her purse for the keys and unlatched the door. An old-fashioned bell on a spring tinkled above the door as they went inside. It was a long rectangle of a room, deeper than wide. This weekend the left and right walls were dedicated to the gallery's other artists: Annette Etcheverry, Scott Dewar, Michael Powers and Ellen Olney, among others. The middle portion of the long room was made up of a series of seven freestanding walls placed parallel to the storefront like dominos on their sides. Stephanie's paintings hung on both sides of each wall, beginning with her earliest work and ending at the back of the gallery with her latest work.

Curtis gained a fresh appreciation for her talent as he strolled through the exhibition, getting a feel for how others would see her art for the first time. He saw that the work of other artists hanging nearby served to define her style as separate and distinct. It was odd to see these paintings, with which he was so familiar, in another context. It reminded him of visiting his father at work for the first time. He'd only known his father as the man at the center of their lives at home. He'd never understood, until he saw him sitting behind a desk in the midst of strangers, that his father had a broader life. It was like that with these paintings. Just as a frame lent significance to each painting, the gallery lent significance to the exhibition. Properly hung and lit to set off each to best effect, they looked worthy of any collector's consideration. There remained, however, the transition to the new work, though its very abruptness reinforced the motto on the poster in the window — Evolution of an Artist. Here Mary Anne Stevenson had employed her bag of psychological tricks. On the last set of freestanding walls, the Aging Smiley Faces (with its 'study') and The Balloon Boat faced Make Love Grow, together with its 'study,' which acted as a set-up for the finale. Coming around the last freestanding wall one faced the back wall of the gallery, devoid of all but two paintings that hung side-by-side above eye level — the grey field with one colored love flower (now entitled Light the Way, according to the small legend beside the painting), and the jack-o-lanterns (entitled The Horror). Facing these two, on the backside of the last freestanding wall, hung Cultivate It. These last three, together with Make Love Grow, provided the greatest departure from her previous work. Their size and placement added to the impact. In addition, Mary Anne had transitioned her other artists, on the left and right walls, to show a progression from more representational works toward the front of the gallery, to more abstract art toward the back.

"I didn't know they had titles," Curtis said.

"They didn't; I had to come up with a name for each of them. That was the most fun I had getting ready for the show. I'd never named them. Some were obvious — I mean, what else would you call 'Nasturtiums'? — But some were hard. The one of the buildings I finished for you? — That one I called 'Under the Surface,' but I thought about calling it 'Unfinished Business,' and then 'Fragile Foundations.'"

"What about the prices? Who decided...?"

"Mostly Mary Anne, but Mr. Smith had his say. Nothing under $600." She screwed her mouth up in a gesture that meant *It wouldn't have been my choice; I hope he's right.* "It's his funeral if he's priced them too high; I already got *my* money."

Mary Anne arrived twenty minutes later, full of bustle and resolve. She set them to work checking the prices of those with a fixed price. Then she directed them to hang a small clipboard beneath the paintings that would be auctioned.

"Who decided which ones are being auctioned?" Curtis asked her.

"Edgar Smith for the ones he owns. And we're auctioning all of the newest ones, the ones that Stephanie owns outright."

"How does that work?"

"It's a silent auction. You write a bid on the clipboard, and if someone wants to outbid you, they write their bid under yours. The bidding starts at 2:00 and ends at 4:30."

Curtis quickly ascertained the status of those he intended to buy back, namely his and Sammy's paintings, and Make Love Grow (which had been Sammy's gift and not his to sell in the first place). The Blue Dinosaur, his own interpretation of the gazebo (now entitled 'In the Park'), and 'Under the Surface' were offered at the minimum $600. Sammy's view of Del Mar Beach carried a price tag of $700. Only Make Love Grow was to be auctioned. He began to regret giving Stephanie the $2,000 Smith had forced him to accept for the paintings. He'd now have to come up with $2,500 out of pocket, plus whatever the auction set him back. He decided to lowball his first bid, and thus depress the price. Accordingly, he wrote $300 and his name on the first line on the clipboard.

Mary Anne directed Gwyn to setting up the posters and T-shirts for sale at a counter in the back corner where the caterers would be serving hors d'oeuvres. Stephanie busied herself with the sound system, programming the music and sound level. When he'd finished putting in his bid Curtis approached Mary Anne.

"I'd like to buy four of the paintings," he said, and in anticipation of any objection quickly added, "I know the gallery doesn't open until 11:30, but I'm going to buy them anyway, so you might as well put a sold sign on them now." She assented, and he paid by credit card with a sense of relief. There could now be no taint of fraud, at least from a monetary perspective. However, she stopped him when he lifted one from the wall.

"You can't do that! You'd ruin the flow of the show! No one can remove anything until five o'clock tomorrow."

He sheepishly put it back on the wall. Mary Anne added a "Sold" ribbon across the bottom right corner.

Stephanie had selected five CDs and solicited Mary Anne's and Curtis's opinions. It was a small detail, but an important one as background music could set the mood, or destroy it. The clientele was likely to be over forty, so they'd presumably not appreciate current pop or hip-hop tunes.

The Mozart seemed to Curtis a bit pretentious, as well as too staid. Curtis liked the harp music, but Mary Anne thought it was too tranquil to inspire bidding. "Besides," she pointed out, "there's something about harp music that makes people want to talk softly, like they're in a museum. We want some energy in the room." To that end Stephanie keyed up a Ramsey Lewis Trio CD, which along with a compilation of Ella Fitzgerald and Sarah Vaughn standards, and a medley of Swing era tunes, seemed to fit the bill of being both safe and energetic. They were adjusting the speaker volume when Edgar Smith rapped on the door. It was 10:37.

Mary Anne opened the door and ushered him in. He clapped his gloved hands together and fairly shouted, "All right, troops, how is it coming? Is everything under control? Are there any last-minute problems? Show me, show me." He was obviously not one to stand passively in the background and hope for the best. He walked a serpentine pattern around the walls, taking in the lighting and the juxtaposition of the paintings, nodding, frowning, raising an eyebrow in consternation, smiling with satisfaction. The others followed him, watching his reactions.

"What the hell's this?" he said, coming to 'In the Park.' "How can it be sold? The show hasn't opened."

"I bought it," Curtis supplied. "I bought back a few."

Smith turned an amused grin on Curtis, which was as much to say *Sucker.* "You're quite the businessman. You sell low and buy high. Is that the kind of man I want handling my money?"

"They had sentimental value."

"Sentiment and business don't mix. Business has its own rules, and one rule...well, never mind," he said, turning dismissively away and continuing his examination of the exhibition.

At Make Love Grow, Smith paused and picked up the dangling clipboard. "*Three hundred dollars*? Look here; let me teach you something about perceived value. If someone else came through and saw *three hundred dollars*, they would think this is a painting with very little value, not one that another collector would covet. So, here's what you do...." He picked up the pencil and added a 1 in front of the 300. "There, now that's more like it."

"But I can't afford thirteen hundred dollars!"

"It's no matter; you're not going to get it for thirteen hundred." At this statement, Smith wrote $1,500 under Curtis's bid and signed his name with a flourish.

"But you're bidding against yourself," Curtis said; "you own the painting."

"Yes, but no one else knows that. When they see I'm bidding, they'll want to get in on the action. My reputation will drive the price up, making all of them worth more." He looked Curtis squarely in the eyes and said succinctly, "Take note."

Curtis deferentially lowered his gaze. He was getting a lesson in working with Edgar Smith. It was a valuable lesson in its own way: Smith would micro-manage even the smallest investment.

Coming around the last wall Smith stopped. "*Very* nice. Why haven't I seen *these* before?"

"They're new," Stephanie explained, hoping he wouldn't object or insist on buying them for $200 apiece, which was far less than she hoped to get for them. As far as she was concerned, these were hers alone. She had put them on silent auction, to see what the market would bear. How else could she know? "I just painted them this past month."

"They're marvelous. Yeah, I like'm. Terrific. I might bid on them myself. In fact, I will." He walked back and forth in front of the paintings, turning to Cultivate It, turning back to Light the Way and The Horror. He wrote $975 on the clipboard under 'Cultivate It,' and signed it John Willits. Under that fictitious name he wrote $1,200 and signed his own name. Likewise, under Light the Way he wrote $750 by Janice Morgan, and upped the bid to $975 under his own name. John Willits bid $1,200 for The Horror and Smith followed by raising the bid to $1,500. "That'll do nicely," he concluded.

Stephanie was beaming. He'd already bid more than she'd expected to get.

"Okay, now," he continued, "who picked out this awful music? Here, put this on." He handed a plastic jewel case to Mary Anne. As they would find over the course of the afternoon, it was a strange, eclectic medley beginning with Bartoc and Satie, progressing inexplicably to Dixieland jazz and Thelonious Monk, and ending with a few Beatles tunes interspersed with Nora Jones and Josh Groban. It wasn't what they would have picked, but Smith wasn't to be denied.

At 11:30 Mary Anne unlocked the front door and flipped over the open/closed sign. Smith announced, "I'm going to lunch. I'll be back at 2:00."

Curtis felt an opportunity slipping away. He almost called after him, but Smith hadn't extended an invitation and Curtis didn't want to impose. In this respect, he ruefully acknowledged, he was not a born salesman. He worried what Erickson would say if he knew how poorly he'd handled his morning's encounter with Smith.

The caterers were showing up at 1:15 for a two-o'clock start to the party. Those few customers, presumably uninvited to the event, who wandered in before hand got a surprise preview of the show. One interested middle-aged man engaged Stephanie in conversation about her work and took one of Mary Anne's business cards.

At 12:15 Curtis asked if they would like him to go out for sandwiches.

Mary Anne said she'd wait for the caterers.

"I'm too nervous to eat," Stephanie said.

"Well, I'm too nervous to stand around here waiting. I'm going to the Subway. Would you like to come along for the walk?"

"Gwyn?" Stephanie inquired.

"I'm hungry."

Stephanie looked to Mary Anne, who said, "Go ahead, if you want to. I'll hold down the fort."

"Do you want me to bring anything back? An iced tea? Anything?"

"No, I'll wait."

It was cold outside. Curtis stuck his hands into his overcoat. Stephanie pulled on her knit gloves, and somewhere between the gallery and the Subway sandwich shop Curtis became aware of a slight pressure in the crook of his arm, where she'd so naturally placed her hand.

"You've already turned a profit," Curtis said, "with Smith bidding up your new pictures. I'm afraid I can't afford to buy back your painting, your gift. I'm sorry."

"I'll paint Sammy another one."

"I'd be eternally grateful." She was silent, staring at her feet. "You really *are* nervous," he observed.

"I could use a stiff drink."

"I don't think they'll let Gwyn in a bar."

"It was only a figure of speech."

"It might help."

"I think I'd be sick. But I will have a glass of wine when the caterers come. It wouldn't do to be too nervous in front of the guests."

Gwyn ordered a turkey sandwich. Curtis ordered teriyaki chicken. "You're sure you don't want one? We could split it."

"No thanks," she said. But when their sandwiches came and they'd sat down at a tiny table she did ask Gwyn for a bite. "Oh my god, what's in this?" She grabbed for Gwyn's iced tea and took a long pull through the straw.

"Jalapeños."

"I don't know how you can taste anything after that."

Her eyes were watering. Curtis handed her a napkin to dab her eyes. Then Ode to Joy chimed from his pocket. It was Linda.

"I have an emergency. Jane Colbert got sick while she was showing a house. She's got the stomach flu. She needs me to fill in. Is there any way you can take Sammy?"

"I really can't. Not at this event. Why don't you take him with you?"

"Oh-h-h-h," she moaned, "that never works. He'll break something, or interrupt right in the middle of things. Besides, it looks unprofessional."

"Exactly right, and I'm entertaining clients, so I can't take him."

"Why should *your* clients be more important than *mine*?"

"I'm not getting into this. You agreed to take him. It's your problem."

"I know, I know. All right. I'll think of something," she concluded grumpily and hung up.

"Sammy's mother," Curtis explained, slipping the phone into his pocket. It was just like her to act peevish when he couldn't accommodate her whims.

They were back at the gallery by the time Smith came back. The caterers did a quick job of setting up in the back corner. There were California Chardonnay and Cabernet Sauvignon, Prosecco, beer, soft drinks and

Pellegrino water; buckwheat blinnies with *Crème Fraîche* and caviar; new potatoes stuffed with garlic aioli and bacon bits; crab stuffed wontons; sea scallop crostini gratinée; shrimp satay; chicken satay; medallions of sesame and coriander crusted ahi tuna with wasabi cream, fried wontons and pickled ginger; *pollo relleno*; and lemon-honey sorbet — in short, enough to keep the guests hanging around at the back of the gallery to create a buzz of conversation, which might turn to Stephanie's art.

Invited guests started showing up a few minutes before 2:00 pm. Mary Anne greeted her best clients and handed out brochures. Curtis greeted some of his clients, talked a little shop, and walked them through the exhibition. He hardly recognized some of them out of their business suits.

"I was surprised to receive your invitation," Gerald Boyd said. "I didn't know Bass Erickson was into art."

"Well, we're looking into alternative avenues of investing. It's unconventional for a firm like ours, but it appeals to a certain level of client who wants greater diversification, like Edgar Smith there."

"Smith's here?"

"He collects Miss Walzer's work."

"Ah-h-h-h-h-h!"

Lee Bernier swept in with an entourage about 2:45. He effused about his favorites, while his photographer took photos of the paintings and of Bernier contemplating them.

Curtis kept sidling over to Smith in the hopes of engaging his attention and talking business, but Smith was busy talking art and wine and seemed to be making an effort to ignore him.

Erickson arrived forty minutes later than he'd promised, dressed in a business suit, and got to work with a quick perusal of the exhibition. He upped the bids on all of the paintings that were on auction, having calculated exactly what was needed to bring the total up to a 200% profit level. "I can't believe people pay this kind of money for a painting. I swear, my twelve-year-old could have painted a few of these. Have you talked with Smith yet?"

"I've been trying; he hasn't given me the chance."

Erickson got a wine glass full of sparkling water (more as a prop than to slake his thirst) and approached Smith, interrupting an ongoing conversation by thrusting out his hand and saying loudly, "Mr. Smith, I'm John Erickson of Bass Erickson. You know my employee, Curtis Cooke." He'd completely ignored the elderly man Smith was talking with. Smith looked perturbed, ignored the hand and went on to say, "It really doesn't matter what the First Growths cost, because the Chinese are buying them. If you've got anything from the '90s (I'm referring to the 1990's, not point scores), you ought to talk to Sotheby's."

"I have several vintages of Latour back to '86. I'll give it a go."

Then, and only then, did Smith turn to Erickson. "Yes, Curtis has been instrumental in bringing this show to the public. You know Marcel Duchamps, of course?"

The white-haired gentleman he'd been speaking with gave Erickson a slight bow over his wine glass.

Smith went on to address Duchamps. "What do you think of the show, Marcel?"

"Oh, well, I'm not particularly astute in such matters. I have old-fashioned tastes. I rather like the earlier than the later work, but I did put in a couple of bids on the heart-shaped flowers. I like that one that's all in charcoal, except for the one flower in color. That makes a statement. Yes, you're like that one flower, you know — you make the rest of us seem drab."

"Not at all."

"It's true; you are a true connoisseur."

"I'm just a businessman."

"That's like saying Michelangelo was just a painter. There are degrees of competence, my friend. But I'll be giving you a swelled head." Duchamps turned to Erickson then and said, "You know, I was at a dinner party where some bore was expounding on the history of an obscure wine that was being served, and Edgar here took him to task. It was beautiful to see."

"That was nothing," Smith said. "The idiot didn't know what he was talking about, and I happened to know something about it."

"He'd been there," Duchamps told Erickson. "Where was it?" he asked Smith.

"Errazuriz, a lovely property in the Aconcagua Valley in Chile, owned by the Chadwick family. And it's not all that obscure."

"Well, none of the rest of us knew of it."

"There's plenty I don't know. How much did you bid for the flower, Marcel? I think I'll have to up the ante." With that Smith moved off to raise the bid.

Erickson trailed after him like a sycophantic dog.

Jim Dayton appeared, accompanied by an attractive blonde. As more people arrived, Curtis noticed that very few left. Perhaps they wanted to keep track of their bids in the silent auction, which would end at 4:30, or perhaps they were looking for networking opportunities (the roster of guests was impressive for this city). Some wandered perpetually through the exhibition, though most congregated around the caterer's station at the back table Clustered into small knots of conversation, colleagues and competitors having in common a love of art and an eye for investment. Curtis kept busy circulating among his own clients and trying to keep out of Erickson's way.

He gravitated toward Gwyn. She was doing a brisk business in posters and T-shirts at her table beside the caterer. "How's it going?" he asked.

"We're almost out of the kids' shirts."

"That was a good idea your mom had."

A thin young man leaned over the table. "I'll take one," he said, and pulled a wallet out of his back pocket. He paid Gwyn, then asked, "Are you in charge of the merchandise?"

Gwyn looked to Curtis, who replied, "It's her mother's show."

The man handed Gwyn a business card and left with his purchase. Gwyn gave the card to Curtis, who glanced at it before pocketing it. The man's name was Michael Jusko, and the company was Your Logo, a competing printer, Curtis surmised.

Towards four o'clock the general murmur of the crowd was punctuated at intervals by raised voices from somewhere within the exhibit, presumably in heated conversation, though the words were unclear to those at the back of the room.

Soon Tom Birmingham, one of Erickson's cronies, came storming around the last freestanding wall with a stern and angry countenance. He crooked his finger at Stephanie and said with the air of a school principal about to dole out punishment, "Come with me, young lady."

Stephanie followed Birmingham back into the exhibit. Curtis excused himself from his conversation and followed. Rounding the corner, he gasped and his heart gave a lurch as he came face-to-face with Elliot and Sophie, then saw Vicky with baby Nathan, and behind her Sammy peeking out at Birmingham with trepidation.

Birmingham stood pointing at the 'study' of Make Love Grow. "Did this boy paint this picture?"

Momentarily flustered, Stephanie regained her composure before Curtis and answered truthfully. "Yes, he did. Sammy's drawing was the inspiration for my painting."

Birmingham fumed. "Why doesn't it say, 'study by...by...Sammy?'"

"Did we forget to note that?" she asked, peering at the legend between the study and the painting. "Well, that can be rectified. In any case, the 'study' isn't being sold separately; it comes with the painting. They're a pair."

"Come this way," Birmingham demanded, and led the now growing entourage around the wall. Pointing at Curtis's park scene he shouted, "Did this boy's father paint *this*?"

"Well...this actually is my work," she said without much hesitation, and with little dissembling. It was, after all, partly her work. She'd painted the little girl with the ducks, the boy with the kite, and some of the cattails, and she'd guided Curtis as he painted it. It was as much her work as Curtis's. "As you can see, I painted it at the same time as this more elaborate interpretation," she added, gesturing toward the painting of Gwyn in the gazebo.

Curtis noticed Mary Anne standing ashen faced in the background, with Smith and Erickson among the interested bystanders.

"And that?" Birmingham demanded, pointing at Sammy's Blue Dinosaur. "This man," (here Birmingham pointed at Elliot) "says this boy painted it." Stephanie fought her urge to tell the truth. "And that?" Birmingham pointed at the Del Mar Beach scene.

"I...." Stephanie began, suddenly losing her composure and looking as though she was about to be sick. "You can see, I didn't sign these. They're...they're not mine."

"Yet they're in this catalogue! They're in *your* show!" What are you trying to pull? Who's responsible for this despicable hoax? I'll sue for fraud! You should be ashamed of yourself. Who owns this gallery?"

"I-I-I-I do," Mary Anne whispered. "Stephanie?"

"They were part of Mr. Smith's collection," Stephanie explained in a quavering voice. She was shaking all over. "I...."

"It was my fault," Curtis said, stepping forward. "I suppose I might have let Mr. Smith believe they were from the same artist. But," he continued, speaking to Birmingham, "as you can see, they're all sold — I bought them back."

"You knew?" Mary Anne asked Stephanie, already knowing the answer.

"He wanted them in the show." It was a lame excuse and she knew it.

"Oh, Stephanie, how could you?"

"I didn't know what to say."

"Who are we to believe? Do you know how damaging this is? We'll have to call off the auction and nullify all sales. I assure you all, I knew nothing of this. The paintings were presented to me as the work of a single artist. They came with the highest recommendations from recognized authorities. My gallery cannot be held responsible for this...this...this outlandish deception."

Birmingham turned his attention to Mary Anne. "You can disregard my bids, and you can rest assured I'll spread the word to anyone I know to avoid your gallery. This is outrageous, totally unacceptable."

Curtis felt a small hand take hold of his and looked down to see a sad and scared little boy.

Feeling betrayed, Mary Anne focused her ire on Stephanie. "You've disgraced my reputation. Do you realize you could ruin this gallery?"

Stephanie's hands flew up to hide her face and she ran sobbing from the gallery.

"Aren't you going after her?" Vicky asked quietly.

"She'll be back."

"Are you certain?"

"She left Gwyn here."

"Erickson," Birmingham continued, "I assume you knew nothing of this when you invited me here?"

"I had no idea," Erickson said, stricken to the core. To Smith he added, "I apologize for my employee, Mr. Smith; this is not the way we do business." And to Curtis he struck the parting blow. "I'm flabbergasted. I'm speechless. Cooke, you're fired."

Curtis had anticipated Erickson by thirty seconds, so the blow was deflected. *Of course*, he thought, when the words were finally out of his employer's mouth.

"Come on, Sammy, let's get Gwyn."

They walked quickly to the back of the room where there were still many patrons too involved in their own conversations to have noticed the commotion deeper in the gallery.

Gwyn was a bright child and the grave look on Curtis's face, together with a disconsolate Sammy, told her all she needed to know before Curtis had time to explain. "Uh oh," she exclaimed. "Where's Mom?"

"She's run out. We'll go find her."

The Fines were waiting at the door. Elliot was obviously upset. "I'm sorry, Curtis. If I'd known.... Linda mentioned the show and I just thought it would be a fun outing, and then when we saw Sammy's paintings, and he was so proud, and.... Well, I wouldn't have talked to that man, if I'd known. I still don't know exactly what happened here."

"I'll explain it all later. We have to find Stephanie."

"Oh!" Gwyn exclaimed. "Wait!" She ran into the gallery and came back with her mother's coat and purse.

They found her leaning against the car with red eyes and nose. She laughed, half hysterically, "I need a Kleenex. I'm cold as hell."

Stephanie put on her coat and got into the back seat with Gwyn; she didn't want Curtis looking at her. They drove in silence, until she said in a shaky voice, "My mother always used to say, 'Oh what tangled webs we weave, when first we practice to deceive.'" Then she burst into tears again.

When they arrived at Bailey Place, Curtis asked if she wanted them to come up and was glad when she declined, as he had no idea how he could possibly help, and it was just possible the sight of him might be unpleasant to her at the moment. What had he gotten her into?

Driving on to the apartment, Curtis glanced at Sammy sitting solemnly beside him. "I guess I owe you an explanation," he said.

Chapter 26
Saturday February 7 – Sunday February 15, 2009

When he'd put Sammy in the bathtub with his toys, he closed the bathroom and bedroom doors, plopped into his easy chair and called Linda. "Thanks so much," he said when she picked up, and refrained from adding *you bitch!* though his sarcastic tone conveyed the message very nicely.

"How was I supposed to know the Fines would take him to you?"

This statement told him that she already knew he had Sammy, that she'd talked to the Fines and knew the outcome of Sammy's visit.

"Didn't I say I was with clients? Didn't I say that I couldn't take Sammy? What part didn't you understand?"

"Don't try to hang this on *me*; I didn't take him to the gallery; I left him with the Fines. They're *your* friends."

"How did they know where to go?"

"I might have mentioned you were at an art show, but I didn't tell them to take Sammy there."

Nor, obviously, did she tell them *not* to take Sammy there. Curtis could feel the rage boil up inside him, his emotions racing too quickly to express in articulate sentences. *She's ruined me; she might as well have put a bullet through me head*, he thought, perhaps losing perspective. *Mean-spirited, vindictive bitch!* And what had he done to deserve such treatment? "Fuck you!" he screamed into the mouthpiece and hung up, not particularly pleased with himself for losing it.

He was furious with Linda, but he was no less angry with himself, for with a sick sense of guilt, he knew he was responsible for Stephanie losing her job — a part-time job, it was true, but a job nonetheless. Even worse, he may have derailed her career, or the career she aspired to. Who in the art business would talk to her now? Who would take her seriously? Maybe worst of all (he realized selfishly), this would destroy their friendship. *At least*, he thought with some consolation, *she made a good deal of money from this debacle.*

His own situation was no better. He paced the room, worrying about how he would find another job; people were being laid off all over the country. No one was hiring. He poured himself a tall glass of King Estate Pinot Blanc and went to check on Sammy. His son was happily playing with a plastic boat and a rubber duck. *How am I going to pay child support? How am I going to pay rent? What could she have been thinking?* The wine had a silky texture. *Like a tongue massage,* he thought. *Screw it. Linda can go to the devil. This is a nice wine,* he thought, slipping from negative thoughts of Linda into a distracted appreciation of the here-and-now.

He went back to his easy chair and stared across the room at his reflection in the dark window. His mind turned back to the events of the day, fragments of scenes and dialogue racing through his mind. Everything had been going so well, and had turned so horribly wrong. Maybe Erickson would have him back if he explained things.

He felt sick about Stephanie. He dialed her, but the phone went to voicemail. "Just wondering how you were holding up," he said.

He tried again later that night and the next morning but left no message. Sunday afternoon he tried a fourth time with the same result. A few minutes later his phone rang. It was Gwyn. "Mom says she'll call in a day or two."

"How's she doing?"

"She's been crying. A lot."

"I'm not surprised." He didn't know what else to say, so he just told Gwyn to take care of her mother.

"I always do," she said, sounding much older than her years.

"And tell her I'm so sorry."

"I will. Bye."

He couldn't stop thinking about what he could have and should have done differently. The same conversations kept replaying themselves in a continuous loop through his mind.

He didn't walk Sammy to the door when he dropped him off. He had no wish to talk with Linda, or with Elliot for that matter. He knew it wasn't Elliot's fault, but he didn't want to talk about it. When he was feeling bad about something, talk only made him concentrate on the very thing he was trying to forget. Talk only made things worse.

He spent most of Sunday evening in a state of semi-inebriation, which at first served to disconnect his mind from his troubles, and eventually left him sleepy and depressed. Smith and Bernier, Erickson and Linda, Stephanie and Mary Anne all danced round and round his thoughts. Snatches of conversations played through his sleep, both actual conversations and conversations that might have been if he'd had the presence of mind to say what he might have said, to say what he would say even now if only he could go back in time and say it all again for the first time. At two a.m. he gave up and took a sleeping pill. At least he could sleep in; he didn't have a job to go to.

Nonetheless, his internal clock woke him, still fuzzy from the pill, at 7:00. It was hard to break with established routine. He took a shower and had breakfast at the usual time. Then he stood in the kitchen nursing a cup of strong black coffee, as he watched the Market open on his laptop.

Maybe Erickson had spoken in anger; maybe he had fired him because Smith and Birmingham had expected it. It may have been a matter of form, a matter of an obligation of the moment. In the light of reflection, Erickson might feel he had over-reacted. Curtis might get off with a reprimand and retain his position. The thought sustained him as he dressed in his suit and headed for the office, intent on pleading his case before Erickson. It was a vain hope, however, as the guard stopped him in the lobby. A call upstairs only brought Barbara down with a box of his personal effects. She gave him a hug of commiseration.

"Nobody's explainin' anything. What happened?"

"I made a mistake, lost an account. Erickson was pissed."

"Uh huh. Well, I'm gonna miss you."

"Who's taking my spot?"

"Susan Nicholson."

It wasn't a bad choice; she was the most competent (or at least the luckiest) of his cubicle crew. "Tell Elliot to give me a call at home."

"I will, Mr. Cooke, Curtis; you take care now."

He smiled and carried his box out of the building without looking back, and that was the last he ever saw of Barbara Browne, or any of the other people he'd worked with, save Elliot. He would think about that from time to time. It was strange to work intimately with people on a daily basis for years on end, and then to one day simply walk out of their lives. Losing a job was like graduating from school; old associations were severed in one quick stroke. These partings always closed the book before the story was complete. Years later he would wonder what had become of all the people he'd worked with: He would wonder who had married whom; who had divorced; who had risen in the company; who had quit; who had seen unusual success; who had failed miserably; who had died; whose dreams had come true. He would wonder about it years later, from the perspective awarded by time and age, but on that first day he merely felt excluded.

Before driving home, he drove to the Unemployment Agency at Fifth and Grant, and filled out the paperwork necessary to receive his unemployment benefits. It was close enough to the gallery that his mind turned in that direction. He didn't relish the confrontation he knew he'd provoke just by showing up there, but he steeled himself for the task he had to perform. In the front window of the gallery, the poster from the show had been replaced by an oil painting of a lop-eared rabbit in a garden, by Annette Etcheverry. The bell over the door tinkled as he stepped inside. Gerald appeared from behind the first freestanding wall, where Curtis was surprised to see Stephanie's paintings still hanging.

"I know you," Gerald said. "You were at the New Year's Eve party."

"That's right."

"If you're looking for Stephanie, I'm afraid she doesn't work here anymore."

"I know; I was at the show. That's why I'm here; I bought some of the paintings. I came to pick them up." He was hopeful Mary Anne was gone and not just lurking in the back.

"Did you want your money back?"

"No, I just want the paintings." He was surprised to see that the show was largely intact, with the exception of a blank spot here and there. It looked like some of them had sold, despite the disaster.

"Did Make Love Grow sell?"

"Which?"

Curtis felt a sudden hope that perhaps he could still buy back Sammy's gift, but when he came around the last corner but one, it was gone. He peeked around the last wall and saw the back wall was also empty. He wondered if Stephanie had picked them up, or if they'd sold, and asked for an explanation.

"You didn't stay 'till the end then?"

"No, what happened?"

"Well, I wasn't here, but Mary Anne said after Stephanie left, Smith and a couple of other collectors bought all of the new work."

Mary Anne's acerbic voice spoke up from behind them. "Tell her not to expect a dime. What we got won't even come close to paying for the cost of the show, let alone my loss of reputation."

"I'm sorry, Mary Anne; it really was all my fault."

"Save your excuses. Just pick up your paintings and go."

She turned and disappeared behind a wall, and in a moment they heard the front doorbell jingle as she exited the gallery.

Gerald helped him take down The Blue Dinosaur, In the Park, Under the Surface, and Del Mar Beach, and carry them to the front of the store.

Being fired was a shock, but coming on top of his divorce, it was just another bump in an already difficult road. If nothing else, he'd learned to roll with the punches in the past six months.

Those first few days of unemployment required a mental adjustment. He had never been unemployed since Abernathy & Associates had recruited him out of college. More than a decade had passed since those carefree school days when he'd dreamed of the life he'd build.

Stephanie called Tuesday morning. "Hi, it's me."

"How are you holding up?"

"I could be better. I haven't got much sleep."

"I feel terrible. Is there anything I can do?"

"If you hear of someone who wants to hire a disgraced painter...."

"I'm afraid my contacts would be useless."

"Gerald came by with the unsold T-shirts and posters. He says my newest paintings sold, but Mary Anne's not paying me."

"She told me."

"Can she do that? I feel bad for her, but I need the money."

"You might get it back; I'd say it depends on your contract."

"I didn't have a contract. I didn't think I'd need one. I'm worried. I need the money. I really need it now — I only have my three-days-a-week job at Bolton's, and that doesn't pay the rent. I was counting on making something more from the show."

"I don't think you can afford to take it to court."

Curtis waited for a reply, but heard only whimpering on the other end. He wished he could reach through the phone line and give her a hug. "Hey, I'm sending a hug through the line," he said. She laughed, then began crying in earnest and the line went dead.

In the afternoon Curtis opened his laptop to check the Market. It was a bad day, the DOW down more than 350 points. He made a call to Susan Nicholson to caution her about Dayton's account.

She was not pleased to hear from him. "I've got a handle on it, Curtis; they're *my* clients now." The way she said it didn't leave any room for comment. "I'm busy; I'm *working*." Her emphasis on the last word was like a dig in the ribs.

He told her to call him if she had any questions.

It was hard to let go.

Wednesday he registered his name online with various job search websites, kept track of the stock market and checked his portfolios, or rather his clients' portfolios, or rather his *erstwhile* clients' portfolios — he had to keep reminding himself that these things were no longer under his control.

After the market closed, he took a brisk walk to the park. Around the perimeter of the baseball diamond and playground, forlorn, leafless trees stood bleakly waiting for spring. A thin, pure layer of snow still lay on the ground, marred by a serpentine line of dark tracks where boots had broken through to the mud below. A still, low vapor hung over the duck pond, where frosty rime edged the brown cattails. With hands stuck deep in his Mackinaw pockets, puffing steam with each exhalation he strode the sidewalk for a full circle of the park and headed back, almost stopping at Starbuck's for a coffee, until he balked at the price — he would have to be more frugal until he could find another job. Back at the apartment he thought of passing the rest of the afternoon at the movies and again denied himself for monetary considerations. He was beginning to realize it was as frustrating to have time and no money, as it was to have money and no time. In the end, he spent the afternoon and early evening painting, and went to bed early.

Thursday morning he called Stephanie to gab. "I hope you're doing better."

"I've been busy looking for a job," she said. "I asked Bolton's for more days, but they're not hiring. None of the galleries will have me — Mary Anne's been busy (I don't blame her). It'll be easier when I'm finished with school, when I can work a regular five-day week. As it is, I can only get part-time work, but nobody's hiring."

"I know; I haven't had any luck online. I'm thinking of registering with a headhunter agency next week. In the meantime, do you want to go to lunch?"

"What? Why are you going to a headhunter?"

"To find a job."

"You lost your job?"

From the incredulity of her tone, he realized she didn't know. "I forgot; you ran out before I was fired."

"Oh god, I feel terrible. Here I was feeling sorry for myself, and I didn't even think about...I didn't even consider.... Oh, I'm so sorry."

"It's not your fault."

"I didn't think...."

"It's my own fault." Stung by the thought that his actions had resulted in the fiasco that had cost her not only her part-time job, but the one shot she'd had to break into the ranks of paid artists, he said, "I really screwed things up. If I'd been honest to begin with...."

"No, it was my call. You didn't want me to do the show, remember? I should have listened."

"It shouldn't have gone that far in the first place."

"I guess we both stepped in front of that train together. I mean, we teach our children right from wrong, don't we? We just didn't live up to our words."

"You want to go out to lunch?"

"Can't afford it; I have to watch my pennies until I get another job."

"We could split a Subway sandwich; it's cheaper than eating at home."

The shop was halfway between Washington Street and Bailey Place. She was waiting out front when he arrived. He wrapped her in a hug of commiseration and was surprised to feel himself start to inflate. He stepped away, knowing that was more likely to frighten her away than comfort her. He stood close to the counter, pretending to study the menu until his ardor deflated.

They discussed job prospects, the advisability of changing careers, and what to put in and leave out of a résumé. There was something comforting about having a common trouble; each understood the other's concerns, and each was the other's best cheerleader.

Certainly, they now had more in common. Their orderly lives had been turned upside down by recent events, and they were now actively, alertly searching for that next opportunity, the key to their futures. Sometimes, however, we don't recognize the rabbits hopping across our paths. Sometimes we hit the mark and fail to see the target fall. Sometimes we hit the bulls-eye and don't realize it until much later.

Ode to Joy chimed as Curtis stuck a rinsed plate into the dishwasher. He dried his hands and reached for the phone on the kitchen counter. "Happy Friday the 13th," said the voice on the other end. It was Bruce Niederer, his lawyer. "Are you feeling lucky or unlucky?"

"Unlucky," Curtis replied without hesitation. It had not been a particularly good week.

"I suppose that's appropriate, given the date. Anyway, I just called to say your divorce papers have come through. You have to sign in front of a notary. I could send them to you, or..."

Curtis drove across town and over Madison Street Bridge to his lawyer's office.

"We should have the property settlement papers ready by next week or the week after. The house goes to your wife and the stock goes to you. We set the valuation on December 15th. I don't think you got the best end of the deal."

"Doesn't matter, as long as it's quick and clean. Where do I sign?"

Niederer slid a document and pen across his desk. Curtis glanced cursorily over it, and with his signature put an official end to his marriage.

He usually picked up Sammy at six o'clock. It was after 3:00, Sammy would be home from school, and having no job Curtis had no reason to delay. So he took the long route to Westlake Drive following Jefferson Boulevard along the curve of the river through Jackson Park. He drove in a daze, filled with resignation and sorrow for his failures.

Sammy was joyous at his father's early arrival. He ran up to his room to get his things.

"You're early," Linda said.

"I was at my lawyer's. Did you get your papers?"

"Yesterday."

Sammy came bounding down the stairs in his love flower T-shirt and a backpack bursting with Valentines. He thrust one into his father's hand. "Happy Valentine's Day!"

"Valentine's Day? I forgot. No, the 14th is tomorrow."

"They celebrated today at school," Linda explained. "He's been busy; he made thirty-two Valentine's for his classmates."

It seemed an inordinately high number; he didn't see his son as a Casanova. "Isn't that excessive? How big is his class?"

"Thirty-two. They have to be politically correct these days."

Of course, Curtis thought, shaking his head, *they wanted to make sure no one would feel left out.* In his day the boys gave Valentines to their favorite female classmates and vice versa. It was a gauge of one's popularity. The misfits didn't receive false hopes, and everyone looked up to the boy and girl who took home the most Valentines (even as they were teased about it).

"I made one for Mommy, and one for you, and one for Sophie."

"Thanks, kiddo," Curtis said, looking at the hand-drawn love flower. "I'm afraid I forgot Valentine's Day this year." He glanced ruefully at Linda who looked nervously away. "I'll bet you were the only kid at school with a Valentine's T-shirt."

"My teacher wanted one."

"I'm sure Stephanie would be happy to sell her one," Curtis said. "We better be going." He wanted to get out of Linda's presence. He had nothing more to say to her and there was more potential for unpleasantness if he were to stay. "Oh," Curtis said, turning back, "I almost forgot: Monday's Presidents' Day. Is it okay if Sammy stays with me?"

"Sure; I don't have anything planned. Is that okay with you, Sammy?"

Sammy assented.

As they headed for the car, Curtis racked his brains about what they could do to fill the time without spending money. Money, it was said, didn't buy happiness. But it did buy experience, and to the extent that one derived happiness from that experience, money did buy happiness. Of all the things he could think to amuse himself in the city — dining out, movies, museums, concerts, theme parks, skating rinks in the winter, boat rentals in the summer, even the smallest treat — all cost money. Driving cost money. So did public transportation. Painting supplies cost money. Toys cost money. If he did nothing but sit in his apartment, there were the static bills to pay: food, rent, utilities, furniture rental, cable hook up for his TV and Internet, medical insurance, automobile insurance, life insurance (he made a mental note to make Sammy his beneficiary), trash disposal, the loan on the car, his wireless phone. Of all the things money could buy, peace of mind from the incessant bills was the most valuable.

Curtis buckled Sammy into his seat. Then he looked closely at his Love Flower valentine. He leaned over and kissed the top of his son's head. "Thanks, Sammy. I have an idea this could make someone else very happy."

They pulled to the curb on Bailey Place shortly after four. He pushed the button next to S. Walzer, but the request went unanswered. "She's not home," Curtis told Sammy. He pushed the button next to Mrs. Bossert's name. Her voice came through the intercom, asking who it was, and in a few moments, Gwyn was opening the door.

"Mom's still at school. She doesn't get back until 7:00."

It took them an hour to go to the market and return. At 6:45 Curtis lit candles around the apartment and at the kitchen table. He looked in at the roasted chicken and new potatoes, and turned the oven to warm. Then he sautéed mushrooms and steamed peas. He was cutting up the chicken when Stephanie came in the door. She looked momentarily bewildered before a wide grin brightened her face. Curtis stepped forward and handed her the valentine. He said nothing. He didn't have to. The look in her eyes said it all.

At the door, as they left that night, Stephanie thanked them both, then stood on her tiptoes and gave Curtis a light kiss on the lips. Only this time the tip of her tongue darted out and caressed his upper lip. He doubted the children noticed, but *he* sure did.

That Sunday they all drove across the river to Griffin Park, the only park in the city with a decent hill for sledding. The snow was thin, but sufficient for sliding down the hill on a plastic dish. Sammy and Gwyn trudged up the hill and slid down for the better part of two hours. They stopped for lunch at a Burger King on the way back, and parted company with wistful gazes.

The rest of the weekend Curtis and Sammy spent watching television, DVDs, playing with toys, and painting (they had plenty of paint and paper and brushes, and by the time they required replenishing he might have a job).

It wasn't until the Presidents' Day holiday that Curtis bothered to check where the Market had ended on Friday. The DOW had lost 410 points the previous week and he was surprised to find that he really didn't care. The minute-by-minute fluctuation that had set his adrenalin to racing in the office was no longer relevant. Even daily fluctuations were of no concern to him. As long as his own portfolio managed to outpace the Market from month to month, he would be a happy camper.

Chapter 27
More Ducks and Rabbits

It wasn't long before Curtis fell into a new routine, rising a bit later, searching for job opportunities on the Internet during the morning hours, and beginning an exercise regimen that included Yoga to stretch his muscles and tendons, as a decade spent behind a desk had robbed him of his limberness. He'd never enjoyed exercise for its own sake and had spent most of his life avoiding it, but now he found the discipline of the routine and the physical exertion helped relieve stress, and he was beginning to see a difference in the mirror, as the pounds slipped off to be replaced by firm muscle. Every second day in the afternoon, weather permitting, he either ran three miles, or biked seven.

One warm Saturday he and Sammy went to the park wearing their Make Love Grow T-shirts. A young mother pushing a stroller said, "Cool shirts; where did you buy them," which gave Curtis an idea.

The next time he had lunch with Stephanie, he said, "I have to tell you; I think I may have found someone who'd like to license our T-shirt design. We have a meeting on Friday."

"How...?"

"A guy at the show gave me a business card. I gave him a call. He said he thought he could license the image to a T-shirt company. So, there's your silver lining."

"How much would we get?"

"Well," Curtis chuckled, "we're not going to get rich. We'll only get about 20 cents for every one they sell, but it's better than nothing, isn't it?"

"Every little bit helps," she answered, and smiled — they were full of clichés today, but it was pleasant to have someone to talk to for an hour before getting back to the business of life. More than that, she thought it was sweet of Curtis to be thinking of her welfare. The T-shirt deal was inconsequential, but the thought behind it was significant and appreciated.

Curtis registered with two headhunter firms to find a new job, but the hard fact was that thousands of people in the financial industry were being laid off and no new jobs were being added. Until the situation stabilized, he would be unlikely to find employment, and with all of the layoffs there would be intense competition for any openings. He nonetheless faced each day with equanimity, trying his best to maintain an optimistic attitude, and comforted by the fact that he was now unencumbered by the mortgage payment on the Westlake house, and his unemployment checks were adequate to pay his rent and grocery bills. In his best moments, he thought of his enforced idleness as a kind of vacation.

He still kept tabs on the Market, checking his laptop each evening, and watched as the DOW continued its slide. From the first of the year to the middle of March the DOW lost 26% of its value and pundits warned of a new Depression to rival that of the 1930s.

One Saturday in March he received a call from Stephanie, inviting him and Sammy to dinner. There she presented Sammy with a new and larger painting of Make Love Grow to replace the one now owned by Edgar Smith. Sammy was overjoyed. Curtis was appropriately appreciative.

"I have to admit I wasn't happy when you let Mr. Smith buy the original, but my one consolation is that he didn't make me take back all my paintings and ask for his money back. That money is keeping us afloat at the moment."

"It was sweet of you to paint another," Curtis said, feeling guilty for having let Smith coerce him into selling the original for a measly $200. "You've got to let me pay you for it; after all, I'm the one who let the first one get away."

She was on the point of demurring, but changed her mind. They knew each other well enough by now that she felt she could be totally honest with him. "If you really want to help, I would appreciate it if you'd pay for the materials. It's not much, but I'm trying to stretch every penny these days."

Her lips twisted into a crooked, regretful smile. "Maybe this was a wake-up call. Time to face the music, stop wasting my time and get a real job." Curtis followed her eyes as they strayed to the wall where more than a dozen paintings still hung. "It was nice to dream, though."

"Hey," he said, laying a hand gently on her arm, "don't give up on yourself. You have talent. You can get another show."

"Not in *this* town. Those doors are closed and bolted."

"I think you're selling yourself short," he said, trying to be reassuring and knowing in his heart that she was probably right. "If anyone can do it, you can. It just takes a bit of marketing."

She pursed her mouth in thought, but didn't reply. Once in a great while the forces seemed to come into alignment, the Fates opened the door to opportunities that could be seized for the asking. But when the door shut, no amount of hoping would pry it open again. Once squandered, those opportunities were lost forever.

So the days passed into weeks and winter turned toward spring. The last light dusting of snow arrived on March 18th, followed by two weeks of warm weather that brought out new green leaves on the trees and melted the snow to reveal dark green grass that turned luxurious in the lengthening afternoons.

Of all the things he might have considered about losing his job, loneliness wasn't one of them. But of all the adjustments he had to make, learning to be at peace with himself in a quiet room was the biggest of all. In the morning he imagined the hundreds of thousands of people around the city getting up with a purpose and heading off to work like worker bees streaming from the hive, leaving him behind to wait alone in his quiet apartment. He felt irrelevant and excluded and alone. The loneliness struck him as particularly ridiculous given that he had barely interacted with anyone at work, so intently had he immersed himself in his work. Yet the conversations with Elliot during commute, and the few words he exchanged with Barbara during the day, provided at least a semblance of human contact, not to mention all of the people bustling about the office making terse comments as they passed in the hall or filled their cups at the coffee machine.

To fill the void, Curtis began having lunch with Irene on Wednesdays and with Stephanie on Tuesdays and Thursdays (the only days she wasn't either going to school or working at Bolton's). He recognized the therapeutic value of talk. They were his sounding board, his relief valve, and his spiritual advisors all rolled into one. Beyond the conversation and companionship, their stories served to remind him (when he felt inclined to count his losses) that everyone lost something along the way, and each of them was in the process of rebuilding lives that had been disrupted by death or desertion. He also knew that his own situation was so much better in comparison with Stephanie, who had no unemployment insurance to fall back upon, and he took strength from her positive attitude, for despite bleak prospects she approached each day with optimism and determination.

Linda had always been his intellectual equal, but there had also been a careful reserve there, only allowing him a peek at her inner thoughts. Stephanie had no such reserve. "You're fearless," he observed over lunch one day, as she laid out her plans.

"No I'm not; I have plenty of fear. I fear not being able to pay the rent. I fear one of us getting sick, because I can't afford doctor bills. But I can't let that stop me from moving forward. I can't afford to sit still and hope things will get better; I have to make it happen. I'm going to target Public Relations firms. I know a bit about marketing now, and with my art background I can sketch out concepts and storyboards."

"I wish I had your confidence; I'm feeling a little overwhelmed by the prospect of looking for a new job."

She smiled. "I'm feeling whelmed."

"What?"

"Whelmed. You know, if you can be *over*whelmed and *under*whelmed, can't you be whelmed? Every day that you take action is a whelming day."

He laughed. "That reminds me of another word like that. You hear of ruthless people, but you never hear of ruthful people."

"I'm ruthful. At least I try to be."

He had his own fears, and he wasn't so confident that any action on his part would yield him the results he was looking for. You could put your name in with a headhunter agency, but what could you do if there were no jobs? It frightened him into inaction. But with Stephanie's prodding, he began looking to other avenues to meet his goal. He made calls to old clients, making it known that he was looking for a job. "After all," she said, "even if they can't offer you a job, they might know someone who can. It's all about getting your name out there, so when an opportunity comes up your name will come to mind."

The subject came up again when he was having lunch with Irene. He said he had taken Stephanie's suggestions to heart. "She's always trying to help. I just wish there was something I could do for her, particularly as I've done so much harm."

"You seem to like this girl," Irene said.

"I do; she's growing on me," he admitted. "I'd like to help her. I feel responsible for her troubles."

"Could it be you're romantically attracted?"

"I've been asking myself that same question for the last month. I do enjoy her company."

Irene went on. "My father used to say that you know you're in love, when you put someone else's welfare ahead of your own. Could it be that you love this girl?"

If it was love, it was unlike the physical infatuation he'd felt in high school and college, that peculiar mix of lust and giddy joy that made talking uncomfortable. This was easy and comfortable, and infinitely more intimate. He looked forward to their lunches, and he realized how she made him light up with pleasure whenever they were together. Was it was the same for her?

It was almost a month before he called home to admit his latest failure. His mother answered the phone and with little preamble he told her (without going into detail or explaining his errors in judgment) of losing his job.

"I'm so sorry to hear that, Curtis. Are you doing all right financially? Do you need help? Because we have a little set aside, though I should tell you, your father's company has cut him back to four days a week, so everything's a bit topsy-turvy around here. I wish you'd talk to him; he's treating it like early retirement; he spends his Fridays golfing. And your brother was laid off and rehired all in a week. The company he's working for was going to move out of state, but then they reversed the decision. Your sister is looking like a balloon about to burst."

Beyond his lunches, his only other social outlet was Stephanie's Advanced Watercolors class. It was smaller than her previous classes; only five students, and he was the least accomplished of the bunch. One of the students was a woman about his age, unmarried if you could judge by her ringless finger. She engaged him in friendly conversation on the first day of class and took the seat next to his. He enjoyed the interaction, but had no interest in asking her out. He wondered what woman in her right mind would want to get involved with a divorced, unemployed father with no status and limited prospects? Besides, what he needed was amply supplied by his lunches with Stephanie.

At the end of the second meeting, he gathered up his painting kit and block of paper and waited at the back of the room for Stephanie. But she caught his eye and said, "You don't have to stay Curtis; Nicholas is driving me home. I'll see you Thursday."

Nicholas gave him a small nod of the head and smiled apologetically. Curtis went out to his car feeling the unexpected sting of jealousy. What if Stephanie and Nicholas became romantically involved? Where would that leave *him*? Curtis was certain they could remain cordial, but it wouldn't be the same. The intimacy they now shared would be diluted. If Nicholas stepped in to fill his place, she would no longer need him to tell her troubles to, or share her dreams, or strategize about the future, or even engage in meaningless banter. He didn't think he could bear losing that close connection.

He called her as soon as he got home. "Are you busy?"

"No, I just got in. I'm catching the end of *Glee* with Gwyn."

She wasn't with Nicholas then. Good.

"I just wondered if you'd like to come to my place for lunch tomorrow."

That first home lunch set the tone for those that followed. He made soup and salad, and poured two glasses of wine. Though the conversation veered from the practical to the philosophical to the political, Curtis was aware that there was a growing warmth about the way she gazed into his eyes across the table. He wasn't sure if the wine was perhaps altering his perception. They took their plates to the sink and their conversation to the sofa. It was over the second glass of wine that she said, "We could do this every Tuesday and Thursday, until one of us gets a job."

"That would be nice."

"Gwyn and Sammy are in school."

"It's nice getting together without the kids. We could do anything." He reached out and took her hand.

"We're all alone."

He picked up the tenor of the argument. "We're adults."

"Um-hmm."

She put her glass on the coffee table. As he bent toward her, she curled a hand behind his neck and kissed him. Nothing chaste about it this time. It was a long, deep, satisfying kiss.

"Oh, I could get used to that," he groaned happily.

"Practice makes perfect."

Linda called the second week of April. "Hi," she said with a heavy sigh. "I was wondering if you could advance me your child support for next month."

"Why? What's up?"

"Things have been slow at work. Houses aren't moving as fast as they used to. Actually, they're not moving at all. I'm behind on the last couple of mortgage payments. But I'm sure things will pick up. I just need a little breathing room."

"How much?"

"I think a couple thousand would do, or fifteen hundred. I wouldn't ask, but I don't want to run up the credit card; the rates are so high."

"Can you borrow it from Roger? In case you've forgotten, I'm unemployed." There was a sharp edge to his voice as he remembered the role, deliberate or not, that she'd played in his losing his job.

"I'm not seeing Roger anymore."

"Whoever your current boyfriend is then," he jabbed.

"Don't be that way, Curtis. I know this hasn't been easy for you..."

He reluctantly agreed to send her a check. Upon hanging up he opened his laptop to take a look at her financial situation. Linda had kept their old Wells Fargo checking account and he was right in assuming she hadn't changed the password (she was technologically challenged). The mortgage payments (all her responsibility now) were automatically deducted every month and the last one had depleted her account to less than a thousand dollars. He checked her credit card balance and found she owed $882.62. He had mixed feelings about her predicament. On the one hand, he took spiteful pleasure in her groveling for money. On the other, he felt anger at seeing his hard work and thrift of the past five years crumble under her management. She had never known the meaning of 'frugal.' And there was Sammy to think about.

No sooner had he closed his laptop than his phone began mocking Beethoven once again. Seeing Stephanie's name come up on caller ID he answered, "Hey Steph, what's..."

"Turn on your TV to channel 2!" she interrupted. "Now!" By the time he found the remote and turned the television on she said, "No, now it's gone. Wait a minute. Try...try channel four. Okay, now wait a minute, here, look at this. I think this is the same footage."

"What am I looking for?"

"You'll see; just wait."

The local news anchor somberly provided commentary to Associated Press footage of a peace march in Jerusalem, notable for its participants — both Palestinian and Israeli mothers banding together to protest the recent invasion of Gaza. The women stood with locked arms confronting helmeted riot police armed with shields and batons. They held two banners strategically written in English (obviously meant for the coverage they were now receiving in the Western press) that read, "No More War," and "Choose Peace."

"Do you see it?" Stephanie yelled excitedly into the phone.

"See what?"

"Just a minute; there'll be a close-up." Then, for a brief moment the camera focused on two women in the front row wearing Make Love Grow T-shirts. "There! Do you believe it?"

"Ha, ha! There's your '15 seconds of fame," he laughed, alluding to Andy Warhol's prediction that one day we would all find 15 seconds of fame. Then he quickly corrected himself. "Or maybe not — that close-up was only about one and a half seconds. Though it might count as 15 seconds if you add up all the channels that carried it."

"It's a small world," she said.

"It's amazing, really."

"If you hadn't suggested I make a T-shirt for my project, that would never have happened."

"How many do you think they've sold?"

"Oh, I don't know. They make an accounting every quarter. Not many, I imagine. But no matter how many it is, we get 20 cents apiece. That's $20 a hundred. Who knows? — it might pay for a few lunches."

The segment segued into other news as he said his goodbyes. Another suicide bomber had killed worshipers at a Shiite mosque in Bagdad. As he hung up, a news commentator standing in front of a house with a For Sale sign mounted on the front lawn said, "Here on the homefront, a Standard & Poor's study reveals an average 19 percent decline in home prices across the nation's 20 largest metropolitan areas, hampering an economic recovery that depends largely on the housing market."

Curtis pointed the remote at the TV and switched it off, contemplating the strange fact that his son's artwork (as reinterpreted by his art teacher) was being worn by women in the Middle East. He had always viewed the news as random, remote events having little to do with his own reality — until now. Now, suddenly, he had a connection, however tenuous, to international politics. Life was beginning to take a strange turn, but he could not envision how strange it was about to become.

Curtis and Irene walked three blocks to a Chinese restaurant. "Are you having any luck finding a job?"

"No, not a nibble. No one is hiring."

"Yet you seem in a good mood."

"I can't complain."

Irene could read it in his face, the look of a satisfied man. "You're seeing that young lady, the artist, aren't you?"

Curtis smiled beatifically, nodding. "We've been seeing a lot of each other. It's going well, very well."

"I so glad. Am I going to have a new neighbor?"

"If it comes to that, we'll need a bigger apartment. By the way, you won't believe what happened the other day," Curtis said, and told her all about the T-shirt at the peace rally.

The camera bounced a little as the cameraman moved into position. A group of women stood arm in arm across the width of a street, at least two-thirds of those in the front row now wearing Make Love Grow T-shirts. They were singing a song, though Curtis couldn't make out the words, or even what language it was. Behind them he could see a street packed for blocks with women and children and banners held high: No More War; 300 Children Dead; Children Are Not Pawns; Killing is Not the Answer. A tense barricade of black helmeted riot police huddled behind shields, barring the marchers' way to Israeli government offices. Curtis thought the police outfits weirdly reminiscent of Darth Vader and wondered if it was a matter of life imitating art or the other way around.

It wasn't clear from the video record what, if anything, first provoked the firing of a tear gas canister into the crowd, but it was clearly the match that ignited the conflagration that was to follow. The canister came arcing back into the police line followed by a couple of bottles. Then gunfire erupted. The police would later claim they'd been fired upon, though not a single policeman had been hit and the only victims were among the marchers. Six women and one child were shot dead. Nine more died in the stampede of panicked marchers that turned en masse and pushed back up the street.

His phone rang. It was Stephanie. She was sobbing. He didn't have to ask why.

The following Thursday Curtis went down to the lobby to collect his mail. As he rode the elevator back up to the eighth floor he shuffled through the bills, solicitations, catalogs and magazines. His stomach clenched and his breath caught in his throat as his gaze fell upon the cover of *Time* magazine. On the cover a dark-haired girl of about three or four years of age lay on a sidewalk like an abandoned marionette, her lifeless limbs bent in unnatural angles. Blood spattered across the Smiley Faces of the love flowers on her T-shirt, which bore the ironic inscription, "Make Love Grow." Extending from the upper left corner of the page to just above the child's head, an adult's dead hand lay limp, palm upward, with partially curled fingers. The elevator doors slid open, paused for twenty seconds to allow egress, and closed. It was at least a minute before Curtis could stir himself from his stupor and with shaking finger push the button to open the doors again.

In defending his use of such a horrific cover photo, the editor wrote:

"They're called 'collateral damage,' an antiseptic way of saying civilian casualties. It's bad enough that soldiers die, for even soldiers have mothers who grieve their loss. But it's unconscionable that innocent bystanders should also pay the ultimate price for their country's inability to settle conflicts peaceably. We know this, but we ignore it, hiding behind patriotic slogans and national anthems. 'Our side is better than yours,' we say. We settle disputes the way we settled them on the playground — with a mighty fist — and we call ourselves civilized.

"I did not choose this week's cover to be controversial, though I know it will be. I chose it because it says all we need to be reminded of when we hear people beating the drums of war. We read the statistics without ever knowing who the victims really are. In the end, the victims are just numbers. It's not until you put a name and a face to the numbers that the reality of war can be felt in a visceral way. War is not a marching band and a well-tailored uniform. War is not a slogan. War is not a game. War is mass death plain and simple. The next time you hear 'patriotic' politicians clamoring for war, perhaps you should demand they be the first to send their sons and daughters to the front lines. I wonder how many wars would be fought if politicians were forced to sacrifice their own.

"In Jerusalem this week, Palestinian and Israeli mothers marched together, pleading an end to the constant conflict. The fifteen women and a little girl who died in that Peace Protest gone horribly wrong were 'collateral damage,' just peripheral victims of a long-standing conflict. You may not have seen it on TV, but they were handing out fliers with the names of the 300 children who died in the latest skirmish in Gaza. To those names can be added Raya Anwar Baalousha, daughter of Lina Al-Sersawi, who lost her life dreaming of a more peaceful world. She is the face of 'collateral damage.'"

It was a hard photo to look at and even harder to look away. Raya's face relaxed in eternal sleep, juxtaposed with the blood-spattered Smiley Faces was riveting — powerful enough to win the Pulitzer Prize for a hard news photo later that year.

Galvanized by the outpouring of sympathy around the globe, Palestinian and Israeli mothers marched again the next week. This time many more thousands joined the march, at least a third of them wearing

Make Love Grow T-shirts. They carried a large banner with the Time photo printed on it over a caption that read "How Many More?" and "Blood is on Your Hands," and "Make Love Grow."

During the following week, the image sparked the imagination of political cartoonists around the globe who came out with their own take on Raya's death. One sick bastard drew a rendition of the *Time* cover with the caption, 'EVERY GIRL WANTS TO BE A COVERGIRL." Another, who had either been to Stephanie's show, or had talked with someone who had attended, drew a version of her field of Love Flowers with "CULTIVATE IT" as the caption. Latching onto the idea, other cartoonists provided their own captions to the Love Flower motif: COMMIT TO IT; BELIEVE IN IT; DON'T NEGLECT IT.

Each of these spawned T-shirts of their own.

Within a month, peace protesters around the world were wearing T-shirts based on the Make Love Grow theme. Hardly a day went by that Curtis didn't see the shirt showing up in one guise or another on network TV with images from Britain, Germany, France, Italy, Egypt and Nigeria.

A New York Times editorial addressed the viral explosion of the symbol:

"What one might dismiss as facile and trite, takes on a new meaning when imbued with purpose. Sometimes a movement produces a symbol. During the '60's it was the Peace Symbol. Today's Peace Symbol is a heart-shaped flower with a Smiley Face. It might have been easy to dismiss its childish message, until you saw the picture of Raya. Now it's about her, and all of the children like her. On both sides of the conflict reasonable people do exist. They stand shoulder to shoulder wearing their Love Flower T-shirts. It's not about taking sides. It's about taking a stand for peace. Our children deserve that much. We should demand no less."

Next came the Love Flower pins and refrigerator magnets.

"This is getting ridiculous," he observed one Tuesday over lunch with Stephanie. "I saw a guy in the park with a T-shirt. It's unbelievable."

"I know; I see them everywhere. I saw two people with pins yesterday. Hallmark is picking it up for a Valentine's day card."

They were having lunch on Thursday the 21st of May at her place, when Curtis interrupted Stephanie's recitation of Gwyn's latest school project. She was unusually animated.

"What's going on?" he asked. "Something is up; I can tell."

She looked embarrassed, thought about delaying her announcement for a moment, then gave in. "Okay. I wanted to work up to this gradually, but here goes." She handed him an envelope.

He opened the envelope, glanced inside and saw a check. "What's this?"

"It's your half of the royalties."

"For what?"

"Love Flowers Inc. For the T-shirts and pins, magnets and cards. Even lunch boxes and purses, and blouses and…. Anything, anything you can think of."

"Great. Thanks." He placed the envelope beside his plate.

Stephanie arched one eyebrow and looked down at her plate. "Wow. I didn't expect that."

"What?"

"Such a cavalier attitude towards money."

"I said thanks." His mother had always told him it was impolite to make too much of money.

She studied his face. "Wait. You didn't even look at it, did you?"

Curtis frowned and opened up the envelope again. This time he really looked at the check, almost closed the envelope, and snapped it open again. Then he grinned with the joke. "Yeah, right," he chuckled sarcastically. Practical jokes had their limits, but she'd gone a bit over the top on this one.

She reached across the table, snatched the check from the envelope and held it up in front of his face. "Listen closely. This is your half of the royalties from last quarter. I'm not kidding."

He looked at the check again, making sure the decimal point was where it seemed to be. It was more than he'd ever made in a year. He cleared his throat. "This is real?" he said, part question, part statement.

"It's real."

His face transformed in a few seconds from sarcastic smirk, to dumb incredulity, to wide-eyed excitement. "Holy shit!" he exclaimed.

"Yeah."

"Oh my god," he murmured quietly, as the possibilities flooded in.

"Uh huh."

"We should do something to celebrate!"

"I'm making plans. I thought about this all last night. I feel guilty profiting from someone else's misfortune, but I have Gwyn to look out for. So, I think the first thing (and I was hoping you could help me with this) would be to take 10% to set up a trust fund for Raya's family. It's the least we can do. Then I'd like you to invest the rest in something safe, something that will give us an income and maybe grow with time, hopefully."

"I can do that," Curtis said, mulling over what she'd just said. He remembered what he'd always dreamed of doing if he won the lottery, and this was almost like winning the lottery. It was no 150-million-dollar jackpot, but it was a nice start. If he set up a charitable trust, paid himself a reasonable portion of the proceeds to administer the trust, say 10% of the annual profit, and held 30% back to build up the principal, he might turn this into a nice retirement income with time.

Sometimes you don't find opportunity; sometimes opportunity finds you.

Chapter 28

Bullseye

One early afternoon Curtis was awakened by his phone chiming Ode to Joy. He looked at the clock, saw it was already 2:00 p.m. and looked at Caller I.D. "Private Name, Private Number" it read.

"Hello?"

"Hey Curtis, this is Edgar Smith," came the bright, energetic voice on the other end. "Is this a good time? You're not busy, are you?"

"Actually, I was just napping."

"Who is it?" came a sleepy voice at his back. Curtis rolled over and mouthed, "Edgar Smith."

Stephanie sat up in bed, suddenly awake, and propped a pillow behind her back as Curtis listened. "What!" Curtis had heard him clearly enough, but it didn't make sense. Then he turned to Stephanie and whispered, "He just sold Make Love Grow for six figures!"

"That's Return On Investment for you! Ha!" Smith crowed so loudly that Curtis had to hold the phone away from his ear.

Smith continued. Curtis listened intently for another minute.

"What's he saying?" Stephanie asked impatiently.

Curtis held up his index finger to quiet her. "Absolutely," he said. "I'd be happy to. What? Uh huh. I'm sure it would be no trouble. Okay. Okay. Right. I'll call your secretary."

When he hung up, he looked at her in stunned silence.

"What?" she prodded.

"He's offered me a job as his assistant — at 10% more than I was making at Bass Erickson. And he wants me to organize another show of your paintings."

"He got six figures?"

"All the publicity made the original worth a fortune to somebody. I expect your other paintings will be worth a lot more now."

"That would be nice. Where should we live?"

"I have an idea," he said, all the pieces falling neatly into place in his mind.

Midday on summer solstice they pulled to the curb behind a U-haul truck on Westlake Dr. It wasn't a large truck, but it was crammed with boxes and suitcases. Sammy sat on the tailgate dangling his legs. Gazing through the windshield at his son, Curtis mused on the way small events sent out ripples that had enormous and unforeseen ramifications. If an artist hadn't left behind a few brushes and tubes of paint, Sammy would never have painted on the wall, Curtis would never have stopped at Bolton's, they'd never have met Stephanie, Sammy would never have drawn Make Love Grow, and the world would be a little more divided, a little colder, a little darker, a little less hopeful.

Linda came out of the house carrying another box. She looked hot and grumpy as hell.

Curtis got out and surveyed the truck. "Can you handle this?"

"I got it here, didn't I?" she replied testily.

"You won't have room for all of that," he observed.

"Don't tell me what I can and can't do." She stormed back up the walk to the open door.

Gwyn looked the house over. "It has a big yard."

"The backyard is bigger," Curtis said.

Gwyn looked to her mother. "Can we get a dog, Mom?"

Sammy jumped off the tailgate of the truck. "I want a dog," he reminded them.

"I don't know, Gwyn," Stephanie said, looking to Curtis for his opinion. "A dog is a big responsibility."

"I'll take care of it!" Sammy and Gwyn both cried at the same time.

Curtis nodded his head. "I think if you share..."

"We will!" they screamed.

"Not too big a dog," Stephanie said.

"But not too small," Curtis countered.

Sammy bounced with enthusiasm at the prospect.

Vicky crossed the street and introduced herself to Stephanie and Gwyn.

As Linda slid the last box into the back of the truck, Sammy hugged his father's legs. Linda pulled down the door with a loud clattering and locked it.

"You show your mother where everything is, okay? Are you ready for a truck ride?"

Sammy nodded his head eagerly. "When can we get a dog?"

"Soon," Curtis said, lifting him into the passenger seat. It was a big adventure sitting so high.

Curtis handed Linda the keys to the apartment. She reached in her purse and handed him her set of house keys, careful to avoid looking at Stephanie or Gwyn. She was upset and didn't want to show it in front of strangers. She had to remind herself that it was all for the best. She'd sold the house herself, so she had received a commission check (Curtis had generously allowed her a full 6%), and she now had more than enough to stave off the creditors. Most importantly, this arrangement would be less disruptive to Sammy.

"I'll drop Sammy off and pick up my car tomorrow around five," she said.

"That'll be great. See you then," Curtis said cheerfully (he might have been more subdued to spare her feelings, but his joy could not be bound).

The U-haul started up with a puff of black diesel smoke. "Drive carefully!" he shouted above the roar as Linda gunned the engine and the truck lurched forward.

Elliot crossed the street grinning broadly. He stood by Curtis as they watched the little truck move slowly down the street until it disappeared around the corner. Then he turned and extended a warm hand. "Welcome home, neighbor!"

<<<<>>>>

Don't miss out!

Visit the website below and you can sign up to receive emails whenever S.W. Clemens publishes a new book. There's no charge and no obligation.

https://books2read.com/r/B-A-WHAK-PBNFB

BOOKS 2 READ

Connecting independent readers to independent writers.

www.ingramcontent.com/pod-product-compliance
Lightning Source LLC
Chambersburg PA
CBHW020516260626
47156CB00006B/2020